Praise

A charming tale of c ............ sparkly summer at the beach, *Counting Chickens* takes you deep into the real Martha's Vineyard. You'll finish loving the characters, longing for the scenery ... An infinitely fun read for anyone who wants to escape to the New England summer island. I was on vacation from beginning to end.

— Brooke Lea Foster
bestselling author of *Summer Darlings*

Bell paints a lovely, vivid picture of the vibrant, year-round island community ... Remy is compelling ... beautiful inside and out ... a stunning protagonist...

— *Kirkus Reviews*

A cast of quirky and endearing characters, chickens, and a rescued dog all in search of security, purpose, and love during a tumultuous Martha's Vineyard summer make *Counting Chickens* a captivating beach read.

— Alice Early
author of the award-winning *Moon Always Rises*

To read *Counting Chickens* is to be directly transported to the island on a beautiful summer day... I immediately fell in love with her compelling cast of characters, and as I followed their various mishaps, I found myself laughing out loud, gasping in surprise, and often tearing up with emotion....

—Julia Spiro
bestselling author of *Someone Else's Secret*

Reading *Counting Chickens* is like peeking through the pages of *Vineyard Life* magazine ... An entertaining romp around the island as pleasurable as a summer's day at the beach.

— Emily Cavanaugh
author of *Her Guilty Secret*

# Counting Chickens

## A MARTHA'S VINEYARD NOVEL

♡ Bunch of Grapes!    T. ELIZABETH BELL

T. Elizabeth Bell

PABODIE PRESS

Counting Chickens is a work of fiction. Names, characters, places, and incidents are the product of the author's imagination or are used fictitiously. Any resemblance to actual events, locales, or persons, living or dead, is entirely coincidental.

Copyright © 2021 by T. Elizabeth Bell.

Pabodie Press books may be purchased for educational, sales, or business promotional use.

Printed in the United States of America.
First Pabodie Press edition 2021

ISBN: 978-1-7330851-1-3
eISBN: 978-1-7330851-2-0

Library of Congress Cataloguing-in-Publication data not available at this time.

Cover design by Tilden Bissell
Poems printed permission of D.B.M.

10 9 8 7 6 5 4 3 2 1

*For Duncan, Jak, and Jessie*

*The neighborhood of close-knit houses*
*The ladies are all friends*
*Roosting on their porches*
*Clucking over whos and whats and whens*
*The rooster is a scoundrel*
*But so it is with men*
*Should a plumed gallant appear*
*We'll see what happens then*
　　　　　　　　—D.B.M.

# CHAPTER 1

*Oh dear. Not again, Teddy.* Dear, sweet, tripping Teddy.

Remy sighed as she looked out the window at the naked man strolling down the middle of State Road. A few of the cars backed up behind him began to beep politely as Remy quickly cleaned her paintbrush and covered the palette with a piece of plastic wrap. With a last glance at her unfinished oil painting of a curious hen, Remy slipped on her flip-flops and headed out the door.

"Teddy, what are you doing—and where are your clothes?" Remy asked when she caught up.

Teddy's blue eyes were dark pools above a scruffy black beard. "Milk," he replied, giving her a beatific smile as he pointed toward Alley's General Store.

"You're shrooming again, aren't you?" Remy tugged at Teddy's elbow and guided him to the side of the road. "I've got milk at my house. How about we stop there? Then I'll take you home. Besides," she said with a smile, "It looks like you forgot your wallet."

Teddy looked down where his pockets would be. "Oh."

Remy's generous mouth broke into a grin. "Can I take your hand?"

"Would you like a foot too?" he asked, lifting his red sneaker off the ground.

"No, thank you," Remy laughed. "Let's keep your feet on the ground for now."

"OK." Teddy swung their clasped hands overhead. "Feet on the ground, hands in the air." He looked at her again with that glorious smile.

"Oh, Teddy."

As best she could, Remy ignored the stares of the pedestrians and the people in their cars. A few were snapping pictures with their cell phones, adding "the naked guy" to their vacation photos. It was a short walk to Remy's clapboard-and-shingle cottage but Teddy wouldn't be hurried, slowing whenever a leaf or flower caught his eye. At last, she opened the gate of the white picket fence and ushered her friend into the front yard. "Wait here. I'll be right back."

When Remy returned with the milk and a beach towel, she found Teddy lying stretched out on the grass staring up at the sky.

"Milk clouds," he whispered.

Remy looked up at the fluffy white clouds. "Whatever you say, Teddy." She held up a canvas tote bag. "I've got your milk—and a towel for you to wear."

Teddy stood and stretched out his arms, waiting for her to wrap the terry cloth around his slightly chubby waist. "Blue stripes," he said, looking down. "I like blue stripes."

"So do I." Remy sighed. She tied her dirty-blond hair into a messy bun and picked up the paper supermarket bag with her milk. Teddy was a dear, but he was going to owe her for this; and more than a free bag of shiitakes. "Ready to head home?"

"Okey-doke."

Somewhat less conspicuous now, Teddy gave Remy his hand again. They strolled past the white-steepled church, the town hall, and the gingerbread-trimmed Grange Hall which, along with Alley's General Store and the library, made up the tiny village of West Tisbury.

Teddy stopped to gaze happily at the pale green filigree of lichen on the branch of an oak tree. "Lichen is pretty, but mushrooms are magical."

Remy tugged at his hand. "Maybe you should stick to growing the regular kind?"

"Nope. Magical is magic. And I'm having such a lovely trip."

After pausing to examine a pink tea rose, peeling white paint on a picket fence, and an evergreen's new soft growth, Teddy let Remy steer him down the dirt road that led to the Maddens' driveway.

The front door of Teddy's modest gray-shingled saltbox stood wide open.

"C'mon Teddy. You're home," Remy said, pulling him up the front steps. "And look: here are your clothes." She set down her bag and picked up a T-shirt and shorts from the floor and handed them to him. "You still want milk?"

"Yes, please," he replied.

Remy took a glass from the cupboard, filled it with milk, and handed it to Teddy.

"Ooh, lovely," he crooned. Teddy stared deep into the glass, beaming. "It's so white, like...like...wow."

"Oh boy," Remy muttered to herself. She sat down at the table and typed *how long is a magic mushroom trip?* into her phone. *Four to six hours* was the reply. Remy groaned.

After popping the bubbles around the edge of the glass, Teddy slowly tested the surface tension with his fingertip. Suddenly, he plunged his index finger into the glass up to the knuckle. "Whoa," he whispered. He pulled his dripping finger from the milk, mesmerized by the drop forming on his fingertip.

"Why do you do shrooms, Teddy?"

"All-natural goodness," he replied, plunging his finger back into the milk.

Four to six hours. Remy looked at her watch. If Teddy wasn't coming down in an hour, then she'd go get her laptop and do some work. She left Teddy to his milk project and went up the half-flight of stairs to the living room. The Maddens had left the original 1960s house unaltered but for painting the wide cedar boards white and installing solar panels on the roof. Huge windows framed views of the pond and the neighbors' fields, and the spacious deck was awesome for both sunbathing and stargazing. Furnished in beach-house shabby, the midcentury-modern teak furniture was so old it was back in style. Despite its modest size, the Madden place was light and airy; more sailboat than house.

Remy glanced through the open door of the master bedroom at an unmade bed. "Teddy, have you moved bedrooms?"

"Nope," he replied.

Remy flopped down into a squishy gray sofa festooned with cat hair. To kill time, she picked up a copy of the *MV Times*. The Steamship Authority ferry had broken down once again, stranding cars over in Woods Hole. Remy put the paper down. Hardly news, that.

A series of soft "whoas" came from below. Remy sat up sideways on the couch and peered over the railing. Teddy was now dripping milk into a circular pattern on the tabletop. "What are you doing there?"

He looked up. "Making milk rings," he replied. "For my brother. He likes philosophy."

"OK. Whatever." Remy shook her head, stretched back out with the paper, and turned to the local column for West Tisbury. The library was starting Tai Chi, the church would hold the strawberry festival on July 3, and the list of birthdays and visitors took up a whole column.

"Oof," Remy said as four paws landed on her stomach and started kneading, tiny sharp claws piercing her shirt. "Turk. There you are." She put the paper down. "I should have remembered to bring you your smoked bluefish skins."

The big black cat arched his back in pleasure as Remy ran her fingers down his spine, then walked over the paper to butt Remy with his furry square head. She scratched his chin, and he started to purr, deep, satisfying vibrations. "You're going to drool on me, aren't you?" she said as the cat lay down on her chest. Remy closed her eyes as she stroked Turk's plush fur. Catnap with a sweet cat…. There were worse ways to spend an afternoon.

A car door slammed. Startled, Remy sat up, dislodging the cat who sashayed off with his tail in the air. Her blue work shirt, now coated with short, black cat fur, also sported a dark, wet circle of cat drool.

Down in the kitchen, Teddy was naked again. He had a dish towel and was dabbing his cheek. Looking up at Remy with blue, still very stoned, eyes, Teddy said, "Milk bath. Very good for the complexion."

"Cripes." Remy laughed. "Please put your clothes on. Somebody's here."

"After my bath," he replied.

Remy got up from the sofa and went downstairs. If she was lucky, it would be Willow or one of Teddy's other friends; she'd be more than happy to hand over her babysitting duties. Teddy was now washing his arm with milk and about to start on his armpit.

"That's gross, Teddy," she said, taking the milk away. "You need a shower."

The screen door opened. Remy's eyes widened in surprise. There stood Jake, Teddy's stuffy, some-kind-of-professor big brother, her teenage crush. The Madden boys were what Remy's grandmother called "black Irish." They had wavy black hair, startlingly blue eyes under straight, thick eyebrows, and fair skin that tanned only in August when their freckles merged. It was as if Teddy had been cloned, shaved, and sent to the gym.

Jake took in the scene—naked brother, girl—and turned around to leave. "Sorry, Teddy. I didn't know you had company."

"Don't go. It's not what you think," Remy blurted as a blush rose to her cheeks. "Teddy's tripping. He ate some shrooms. I was keeping an eye on him." She shook her head in exasperation. "He keeps taking his clothes off."

Recognition lit Jake's face. "Remy?"

"It's been a while," she said, wishing she were not in a drool-stained, paint-smeared shirt with her unwashed hair pulled up in a scrunchie. "I found Teddy wandering through town naked. Down the middle of the road, actually. He was going to Alley's for milk, he said," her lips forming a fond, wry smile.

"Uh-huh," Teddy said, picking up his T-shirt and examining each of the openings.

Looking exasperated, Jake shook his head at his brother. "Thank you for bringing him home," he said to Remy.

The years had, if anything, improved Jake's looks. His hair was a little long, the way she liked it, and his skinny torso had filled out nicely. Quite nicely, in fact. "No problem," she replied as her stomach did a little flip-flop.

"Remy had milk," Teddy said, inserting his face halfway through a sleeve and using it like a periscope to peer around the room. "Lovely milk."

"Wrong hole, Ted," said Jake.

Remy laughed as Teddy turned his sleeve-periscope on her.

"Teddy didn't tell me you were visiting."

"I just arrived Saturday. More than a visit." Jake looked around the house. "Spur-of-moment idea, really. I'm on sabbatical."

Remy tried discreetly to brush the cat hairs off her shirt. "Oh," she said.

"It's not entirely vacation. I'll be working on several articles. For academic journals," Jake explained. "I'm looking forward to having the whole summer to write." Turk jumped onto the table, and Jake stroked his furry black back. "And I have some other projects." He looked pointedly at his brother and turned back to Remy. "I thought you had moved away?"

Remy grew self-conscious under his scrutiny. "I had. School, then I lived in Austin for a while. But I moved back about a year and a half ago."

"Lots of cows in Texas," said Teddy, focusing his sleeve-periscope up at the ceiling.

"Here, Teddy, let me help you. Let's try this over again." Remy started to pull Teddy's T-shirt off his head. "I moved to the Island a year ago January. I run my own concierge business here," she added, hoping to sound professional. "And I paint landscapes. That sort of thing," she added to explain her messy shirt.

"Remy paints cows too," Teddy said. He held his hands up as a megaphone. "Moooo," he lowed, sounding convincingly like a cow. "Moooo…" Teddy's eyes brightened. "Is there any more milk?"

Remy automatically moved toward the refrigerator. Jake reached out to stop her. "It's OK. I've got this."

His hand on her arm set off a disconcerting jolt of electricity, and Remy felt her entire face flush red. "Oh. Right. Sure. I'll be going then."

Jake kept his hand on her arm. "I'm glad Teddy has friends to watch out for him," he said, looking into her wide gray eyes. "I mean it."

"No big deal," she replied, breaking away from Jake's gaze to glance at her dear friend. "We've always been good buddies, me and Teddy."

"He's a lucky guy," Jake replied, his blue eyes smiling.

# CHAPTER 2

"Chook-chook-chook-chook," Remy called, shaking her can of dried corn. "Come on, Ada. Off your nest." Remy rocked back on her heels, staring at the chicken in frustration. "Give me your egg," Remy cajoled. She gave the corn another shake.

With a tilt of her silly feathered head puff, the big hen turned and glared at Remy with one round black eye. Fluffing out her gray-and-cream banded wings, Ada flattened in the nesting box. The message was clear: My egg. Not yours!

"You're not going broody on me, are you?" Remy tried to slip her fingers under the hen, but Ada was having none of it. In a flash, she delivered a sharp peck to the back of Remy's hand.

"Ow," Remy yelped. She licked the spot of blood and considered her options. The chicken emitted a gravelly growl and continued to glare. Yep, broody. Usually, Ada was the sweetest of chickens, the one who'd strut over and sit on Remy's lap—like a feathered dog. But a broody hen would stop laying and rarely leave the box in a futile attempt to hatch her infertile eggs. Not good for the chicken and not good for Remy's egg basket.

"Ada Queetie, I promise I'll get you a totally hot rooster this fall, and you can hatch a pile of baby chicks. But I need those eggs."

Remy got the bag of dried mealworms and selected two particularly big ones—disgusting things—and distracting Ada with the treat, slid her hand back under the soft warm feathers. Success. But the hen still sat, her internal timer set for three weeks whether she had eggs under her or not.

"I'm putting an ice pack under you tomorrow if you're still sitting there," she threatened. Ada glared back, sputtered, and fluffed, still lovely in her feathered temper. Remy wagged a finger at the chicken. "Consider yourself warned."

Remy's flock of "designer" chickens—Crested Cream Legbars, to be precise—had come to her by chance. Thoughtlessly left to "free-range" themselves at a fancy Chilmark farm over the winter by one of her caretaker uncle's clients, the hens needed to be fed, and Remy had been more than happy to care for the beautiful, silly creatures. When the Chilmark clients sold their property the following spring, the flock was hers to keep.

Remy set the eggs on the back porch. It was her favorite spot to work and read, the best kind of outdoor living room, with its comfortably old wicker furniture and ceiling painted the pretty shade of pale blue-green known as "haint blue" in the South. She went inside to get her coffee, which she would have to drink black because she'd given Teddy her milk.

Remy put down her mug and flopped onto the armchair with its faded cabbage rose cushions. So after all these years, Jake was back. She hadn't thought about him, or her stupid teenage crush, in years. It couldn't have been more awkward, Jake finding her with his naked brother and assuming the worst.

But poor Teddy. Professor Jake Madden was here for the summer, and it looked to be a long one. The brothers never had much in common, and they'd have even less now. Not that Jake ever had anything in common with her either.

Enough of that, Remy reprimanded herself. She sighed and took a sip of coffee, inhaling the fresh green scent of June. Like a curtain of gauze, the early morning fog had paled and softened the edges of trees and bushes; sweet quiet mornings like this were to be savored; the summer craziness would soon set in.

After she'd moved into the cottage, Remy tackled the neglected yard with the passion of a thwarted gardener, replanting the cutting garden by the picket fence with zinnias and cosmos and the vegetable bed with herbs and five kinds of tomatoes she'd started from seeds. Along the back, gnarled apple trees shaded a lichen-covered stone wall, and a trellis arch, barely visible through a tangle of grapevines, marked the path to the chicken coop. In the fall, Remy would pick apples and grapes and put up jars of concord grape jelly and apple butter. And, if she was lucky, the beach plum bush in the front yard would yield its tart fruit to be transformed by sugar into the very best jelly of all.

A breeze rustled the leaves, and her flock clucked contentedly in the distance. A little quarter-acre of paradise, all hers. For now. Remy knew she was very, very lucky to be living in Luce Cottage, her uncle's rental property. She'd left Austin (and her now ex-husband) and fallen into a dark January in Massachusetts, taking her uncle up on his offer to visit anytime, for as long as she liked. After three weeks of sobbing on the phone to her mom, binging on Netflix, and hiding under the warm quilt in the guest room bed, Remy was still a mess. Then her uncle broke his ankle falling from a ladder. Unlucky for him, but it got Remy to her feet: Uncle Danny needed help with his caretaking duties, and Remy needed work.

The job, driving around the Island in the cold sunshine and fresh air, checking on people's summer homes, kept her busy. She'd learned how to turn the water on for the season and do minor repairs: caulking leaks and installing handrails for grandma, fixing pet-damaged screen doors, and replacing shingles torn off by the winter winds. Useful work—and her uncle's taciturn, gentle presence—brought Remy out of her funk. Then, in the fall, Uncle Danny offered her a deal: free rent for his rental property, a small Greek Revival house in the heart of West Tisbury. In exchange, Remy would paint the house, inside and out, after Mike, the carpenter, and his crew finished repairing the dry rot and installing new windows. It was the best deal on the Island, and Remy hoped Mike's repairs would take a long, long time.

When Remy moved back, she felt as if she were seeing the Island for the first time. Growing up, she'd taken for granted the gentle beauty of its landscape, stone walls, windswept beaches, ponds, and rolling farmland. Not anymore. Remy leaned back in her chair. She loved her house, loved her backyard, loved hearing the clucking of the hens in their pen. Remy would have to work her tail feathers off this summer, but she was right to have come home, leaving the dust of Texas behind.

All was quiet as Remy started down the path to the Tiasquam River at the head of Tisbury Great Pond. The trail, an "ancient way," was one of the old carriage roads and footpaths that still cobwebbed the Island. The dew soaked her sneakers as she walked along a misty field planted with early corn. Entering a tunnel of gnarled oaks, Remy, overwhelmed by a sense of déjà vu, shivered in her flannel shirt. Eerie, but kind of cool, to walk in the footsteps of the old Island families who'd made their way from farms to town along the same tracks for hundreds of years.

She reached the dirt road to the small floating dock where the Maddens and their neighbors kept their boats and—thanks to Teddy—Remy, her kayak. The Maddens' boat was in. The previous week, she'd helped Teddy flip over the small aluminum skiff, drag it down to the water, and attach the heavy 8-horsepower outboard motor: a fair quid pro quo for rides to the beach. A sailboat Remy hadn't seen before was tied up in the last slip. It was a gaff-rigged catboat with the classic wide beam and shallow hull, a true pond boat—not just a pretty play toy for some summer person.

Remy put her kayak in the water, slid inside, and pushed off into lifting fog. The morning paddle on the pond fell into the last of her three priorities for the summer: work, first; friends and family, second; time for herself, third. There was no room in that list for anything else until she was able to get her concierge business, Nest, off the ground.

Unexpectedly, she felt a wave of anxiety. Starting Nest, Remy had put all her eggs in one basket. She took a deep breath and exhaled a cleansing breath to chase away the worries. So far, her clients had been happy. Being a concierge—shopping and arranging flowers and making reservations—wasn't rocket science. Remy just had to keep track of all the details and never ever drop the ball. She could do it. She *would* do it.

The serenity of gliding on still water past the marsh, so quietly that the great blue heron barely glanced at her, calmed Remy as the adrenaline drained from her body. She liked it best when the pond's mirror surface floated clouds in the water, but misty, magical mornings like this came a close second. Muffled by the fog, the bleating of goats drifted over from Nate and Sky's place, reminding Remy that she needed to nail down the details of Sky's private goat yoga classes for the Hartwells—and visit cute little baby Gaia and the new goats. She added that to the list.

Remy headed from the cove into the broad waters of Tisbury Great Pond, still dancing with shreds of mist. By the time she reached Tiah's Cove, the fog had lifted to reveal a clear blue sky. Remy stopped paddling and let the kayak swing around in a lazy circle. To the east, sheep, lit by golden light, grazed in the field at Flat Point Farm. Remy took a mental snapshot: that was a landscape to paint. To the south, a line of dunes, still a mile and a half away, marked the barrier between Tisbury Great Pond and the sea. On the western shore, the morning sun flashed off the window of a gray-shingled vacation house tucked discreetly among the trees. And to the north was Town Cove—and home.

# CHAPTER 3

Jake watched Remy paddle up the cove with strong, effortless strokes. Still a pond girl after all these years. The orange kayak cut through the still water, rippling the reflection of sky and clouds into blue and white pleats. He remembered her as a teenager— Teddy's summer buddy: gawky, somewhat chubby, bad skin. Something about her being an au pair in France. It was always Teddy, Remy, and the other girl, the skinny one—Willow— hanging out at the house, messing around. Of course, Teddy was still goofing around. Some things never change.

"Hi," Remy said as she neared the dock. "I was wondering whose sailboat that was."

Jake put down his scrub brush. Remy, kind Remy, retriever of mushroom-tripping little brothers. Her hair, dampened by the fog, had set into waves and curls, now backlit by the morning sun into a nimbus of light. The breeze picked up a strand and she became, for a moment, against the calm blue water, a goddess. There was a painting, somewhere….

"Catboats are so pretty." Remy ran her eyes over the graceful almond shape of the blue-painted hull with its low transom and broad beam, ideal for tonging oysters in days gone by. "The shallow draft is great for the pond," she said, breaking his reverie.

"Yes. This is *Utopia*," Jake said, still searching his memory. The Uffizi Gallery, Florence. Botticelli, *The Birth of Venus*—Venus on the half shell, the famous painting of the nude goddess rising from the sea, only somewhat modestly draped in her long blond hair. Remy had the same wide eyes under arched brows, long neck, and shapely arms. He imagined Venus's perfect hemispheres lay under her T-shirt.

"Nice," Remy said.

Jake realized he was staring. And not at her eyes. Apparently amused and not at all offended, Remy raised her eyebrows and grinned, and the spell was broken. He ran a hand across the gunwale, forcing his mind back to his new sailboat. "Thanks."

"Where did you get her? On the Island?"

"Boston. A friend had inherited her from his grandfather, but she was just sitting under a tarp in his backyard. I asked if he'd be interested in selling, and here we are," Jake said, blue eyes gleaming with pride. "I've got a lot of work to do to get her back in shape," he said, pointing with the scrub brush to the teak, weathered gray with neglect. "But I like doing this kind of thing. Clears my head."

Remy slid up to the edge of the floating dock. "Kayaking does that for me. It is so beautiful this morning. I get out as often as I can."

"I agree with you there," Jake said. "Can I give you a hand?" Jake stepped lightly from his boat to the dock and crouched down to steady the kayak. The breeze lifted Remy's hair and blew it into his face. "Hold on a second," he said. The silky lock smelled wonderfully of fresh air and citrus. Reluctantly, Jake cleared the hair from his lips and braced the kayak again. "OK. Ready," he said.

Remy placed her paddle on the dock, then lifted her wet bottom up and onto the boards. "Ooof," she puffed. "My shoulders are tired."

"I'll help you up." Jake put out his hand. Remy gripped it, and he pulled her to her feet. An electric jolt shot from his palm, like something in a sappy romance novel. Only it was real.

The girl, the pond, the morning sun. Up close, Remy was even taller than he remembered. Her hand was strong and almost as large as a man's. But much softer. Remy smiled into his eyes.

"You can let go now," Remy said. "I'm not going to fall off the dock."

Jake looked down at his fingers still gripping hers and let go. "Sorry," he said, not sorry at all. When was the last time he'd held a woman's hand? Not in a handshake and long enough for the warmth to join them together. A year? Two? Liz had never liked holding hands. Said it made her feel like a child.

Remy bent over and pulled the kayak up and onto the dock. "I hope you don't mind me launching from here. Teddy said it was OK."

"Of course not."

"Nice to see a sailboat docked here again," Remy said, picking up her paddle. "I remember your old Sunfish with the wooden tiller that always popped out."

Jake chuckled. "It's still under the deck up at the house."

"You should pull it out and we can have races again. Bet I can still beat you," she teased.

Jake supposed the promise was always there, but somehow everything had come into balance: Remy's large, amused gray eyes needed the prominent nose and generous mouth, quick to smile. And she was easy to talk to, with a fresh, confident air, as natural as the Island. He had a sense that he'd known her forever. Which, of course, in a way, he had.

"I'd forgotten about the Sunday races. You did beat me once for the Demarara cup, didn't you? But you cheated."

"I absolutely did not cheat. You just didn't know where the starting line was. You were over."

"That's not how I remember it. George McIsaac wanted to give you a head start."

"He did not." Remy pressed her lips together, dimpling her cheek. "Well, maybe he did. But that was because you always won." She eyed the catboat. "Have you taken her out sailing yet?"

"Not yet."

Jake looked up the mast. He could easily sail the catboat by himself—it was one of the reasons he didn't get anything bigger—

but he had a better idea. "I'll be looking for a crew on my maiden voyage. Interested?"

Remy's eyes lit up. "You bet. Just tell me when." Remy tipped the kayak over to dump the water out, then tugged to unstick her shorts from her bottom. "Were you up early enough to see the fog?"

"Yup, I was up with the chickens. Got my coffee and watched the sunrise from the deck." The morning had reminded him how much he'd missed the Island: the way the fog dropped layers of scrim across the trees, the rising sun diffusing the misty landscape with a pink-gold glow. Jake struggled to put into words how he'd felt. "It was…magical."

Remy's smile deepened. "It was," she agreed. "Do you get much fog in…where *do* you live?"

"Chicago," Jake said. "But it's usually dank and nasty. Not like here. I've been looking forward to this summer. All I'm going to do is write and sail. Eat lobster rolls whenever I want. And go to the beach, of course."

Remy laughed. "Lucky you. I'll be working."

"Aw, you must get some time off."

"Not much. July will be bad. And August—I don't even want to think about it." Remy made a face. "How's Teddy?"

"Took him another hour to come down. Of course, that wasn't until after he'd decided he needed a 'milk bath.'" Jake rolled his eyes. "Poured the rest of the bottle over his head and made a huge mess. It got down between the cracks in the floorboards. Now the house smells like sour milk."

"Oh no. That's awful," Remy said. "Teddy," she added, shaking her head.

"Teddy," he agreed with a grin. "Thanks again for bringing him home."

"You're welcome." She cocked her head. "You could try mixing fresh coffee grounds with baking soda and putting that into the cracks. Let it sit for a day, then vacuum. That might help."

"I'll try anything. The smell is vile."

Remy ran appreciative eyes over Jake's sailboat. "So, you named her after the beer?" she asked, leaning against her paddle. "I had some clients special order it last summer. Two hundred bucks for a beer? I couldn't believe it. I didn't get to taste it, of course, but I loved the bottle—it looks like it belongs in *Game of Thrones* or something."

"There's a beer called Utopia?" Jake laughed.

"Sam Adams Brewing." Remy frowned. "I guess not, huh?"

"A beer." Jake chuckled again. "That's a good one. She's named after the other utopia. The island." Remy looked blank. "Sir Thomas More?" Jake prompted her. "Surely you know him?"

She sucked on her upper lip, thinking. "The only 'sir' I know with an island is Richard Branson—but I don't know that other guy," she said.

Jake burst out laughing. "Sorry. No, not Richard Branson." He composed himself and began to explain. "Sir Thomas More was a Renaissance humanist, lawyer, philosopher, statesman, and even the Lord High Chancellor of England under Henry VIII. Have you read *Wolf Hall*?"

Remy's cheeks were dotted with two pink circles. "No, I haven't."

Jake continued, "Well, Sir Thomas More also wrote a book in 1516 about a fictional island community—Utopia—that operated under egalitarian principles, with everything designed for the happiness of its occupants. That's where the concept—and the word—utopia came from."

"Right. Of course."

"Didn't you go to UMass? I would have thought a party school like that would have offered a major in utopia," Jake chuckled.

"Nope." Remy eyes drifted across the cove.

"Sorry. Bad joke. It's what I did my dissertation on—utopian philosophy and the communities that lived under utopian principles. Like the Oneida Community in the 1800s," he added. He'd seen that look on his students' faces before: he was losing her. Jake reached for the one fact that always perked up their ears. "They had some unique ideas on what would make a 'perfect society.' Complex marriage, for one. Open or plural marriage, we'd call it."

"Oh."

Jake warmed to his subject. "Everyone thinks free love was a '60s thing. But here was this whole community of religious swingers hanging out in upstate New York in the mid-1800s. They went on to become a silverware company, of all things."

"Really," said Remy.

Wisely, Jake decided not to go into some of the more titillating aspects of the community's life, including coitus reservatus to maximize the sexual pleasure of women, as taught (with the active encouragement of the community) by the matriarchs to teenage boys. He might be a nerd, but he didn't want her to think he was a pervert. "And they had very progressive views on the role of women," he said instead. "But what's most fascinating? At one end of the spectrum you have the Oneida Community and free love, and on the other end, the Shakers. The Shakers banned sex— as everyone knows—to cement communal solidarity. So both groups, in their pursuit of a perfect society and the elevation of the community over the self, chose a path that contributed to their eventual downfall."

Remy gave Jake a tight smile. "Huh. Well, I didn't know that." She picked up the handle at the end of her kayak. "I should go. I've got a ton of things to do. Oh, and tell Teddy it's soup night at Willow's and to bring something."

She turned and started dragging the boat off the dock. "Remy," Jake said. He'd made a mistake, rattling on about his thesis topic. What made him think she'd be interested?

Remy stopped and looked back at him. "Yes?"

"Um, want to join me for a beer sometime? Can't promise it'll be *utopia*, mind you," he winked, "but Bad Martha is brewing a good saison. And I'll let you know when the sailboat's ready for her maiden voyage."

Remy's warm gray eyes had turned to stone. Gone was the open, laughing girl with the wet bottom who wanted to race him across the pond. "On second thought. I don't know. Like I said, I'm going to be super busy with work. But say hi to Teddy for me and remind him about tonight."

# CHAPTER 4

*No, Professor Madden, I don't want to have a beer with you and listen to another boring lecture on utopian philosophy.* Remy yanked the kayak over a bump in the path. Utopia, the beer. That was a dumb thing to say. Why did she think he'd have named his sailboat after a beer, even a really expensive one? But she had. She'd expected him to grin and say, "I can't believe you guessed that." And then, making it worse, to bring up Sir Richard Branson when Jake was talking about Sir Thomas More. She had a vague idea of Sir Thomas More in a dusty Masterpiece Theater kind of way, but that was it. And then that crack about her going to a party school offering a major in utopia. Like that was supposed to be funny.

She flipped the boat over next to a paddleboard with a yank. Remy knew what utopia meant, of course, an imaginary place where everything was perfect. But she didn't know it was an island, too, in a book some old dead white guy wrote in 1516. *"Surely* you know who Sir Thomas More is?" Remy told her kayak in a snide tone. Ha, surely you know you sound like a pompous ass, Professor Jake Madden.

She glanced up at Jake's house, sitting on a rise overlooking the pond. Remy had been surprised to find him working on the pretty little catboat. There she'd been, thinking how cute he looked in his blue T-shirt and that maybe having Jake around this summer wouldn't be a bad thing. Not at all. Remy noticed the way he looked at her, that zing when he helped her out of the kayak and wouldn't let go. Her imagination had taken them sailing on the wide, empty pond, just the two of them, tacking back and forth and talking as they sipped beers and ate the sandwiches she'd pack, in no rush to get anywhere. Then Jake would lean over, like she'd imagined for so long, look into her eyes and say, "You know, I've dreamed about doing this for years." And she'd say, "Doing what?" And then, with the wind filling the sail as they flew across the water, he would kiss her.

But he had *laughed* at her, capsizing her sweet little daydream in the cold waters of reality. Remy felt the heat rise to her face again. The last time she had felt so dumb was when she'd asked Adam and his partner to explain coding to her, and they'd ended up laughing and rolling their eyes at her questions and calling her Fortran, which Remy didn't find funny at all. It didn't matter that she'd quit college because of money, not grades. Whether he knew it or not, Jake had found the crack in her confidence and poked it.

Remy tried to shake off the wave of insecurity that had smacked her upside the head. Jake was, what? Condescending? Yes, but there was another word. Remy kicked a stone in the road. Patronizing, that was it. Lifting her head, she glanced up at the Madden house again. Jake was *patronizing*. Did he think that she was going to be impressed or something? Or to remind her, the college dropout, who he was, a big important *professor*? Then to bring the beer thing up again, like that was some kind of little joke.

Remy turned onto the path to home, her morning ruined by Jake Madden. Jealousy added itself to the mix. Like Remy would be able to take a summer off, ever, for the rest of her life. Instead, she'd be working seven days a week for four solid months, like all the other locals. Snooty Professor Madden would be just another typical summer person. He'd lie on the beach all day reading serious books that he'd read about in the *New York Times Book Review* and go to cocktail parties in Chilmark and Edgartown at night and discuss Sir Thomas More and utopian principles over gin and tonics with other egghead people who knew what he was talking about.

Well, good for him.

Buckets of fresh flowers, boxes of wine and liquor, and shipping boxes full of impossible-to-buy-on-the-Island luxuries crowded Remy's small kitchen. She'd get the Soulanskis out of the way first. Their special order of craft Brooklyn-distilled gin had arrived. Peering at the yellow liquid, Remy wondered why anyone would drink something named after a toxic Brooklyn canal that looked like—well, what it looked like…. And at nearly $50 a bottle to boot. Clients. Go figure.

Where they lived gave Remy clues. Edgartown, with its tidy white clapboard houses and picket fences, called for neat nosegays of roses, smoked bluefish pâté, and Hendrick's gin for G&Ts, while Oak Bluffs went in for mixed bouquets in vivid hues and signature cocktails full of fruit and fun. West Tisbury was casual cosmos in Ball jars and microbrewery beers, and Chilmark exercised restraint with pastel dahlias in antique pitchers and cases of fine Bordeaux wine.

Her clients were demanding, but predictably so. And she predicted that the Soulanskis were going to need a case of Fever-Tree tonic to go with their gin and a whole bag of limes, plus jumbo stuffed olives for martinis. Remy opened her eggshell-blue binder emblazoned with her logo and "Nest, a Bespoke Concierge Service" and jotted a note.

Turning a tab, she reviewed the checklist she had put together for the Hartwells: dinner reservations (tick), arrival platter of cheeses and charcuterie (tick), flower arrangements (to-do), wine and beer (tick). She'd stop by Cronig's for their groceries on her way over. The dear-heart Hartwells, her first clients, had encouraged her to become a concierge. The summer before, Remy had been fixing their leaky sink when she overheard Mrs. Hartwell go into a panic: she'd just learned that the party planner had the wrong date for her nephew's engagement party, and 30 guests would be arriving in less than 24 hours. Remy stepped in to help.

She stayed up all night making hors d'oeuvres, did the flowers, set up the bar, and even managed to find a last-minute replacement for the jazz trio, creating success out of disaster and giving her the most loyal clients ever. Three weeks later (on the Hartwells' recommendation), the Bottimores hired her to replace their concierge who had been "dropping balls" all summer, and by the end of the summer, she'd landed the Soulanskis too.

Nest had two more new clients this summer. The first was Mathew Cinch, an uber-rich guy on the board of this and trustee of that, and his trophy second wife, Enid, a renowned horsewoman. One teenager, which meant parties, mess, and broken things. Their spectacular Chilmark property was a plus: a dozen acres with a sprawling, modern house on Squibnocket Pond across from Jackie O's Red Gate Farm. (Which proved, indisputably, that Martha's Vineyard was far superior to Nantucket: Jackie, with her exquisite taste and money, could have vacationed anywhere in the world, but she chose the Vineyard.)

Her second new client was Eli Wolff. She knew nothing about him except that he'd recently bought a gorgeous property on the north shore and needed a concierge.

Remy then flipped to the Bottimores' list, which grew longer and longer with every email and text. No wonder their old concierge had been dropping balls. Mrs. Bottimore kept tossing more and more of them with every message: rental bikes with child seats to be delivered to the house, a private tennis lesson, and instructions to stock the outdoor showers with Aveda Sap Moss shampoo (whatever that was) and that lovely soap from France— you remember the one. Remy sighed. All this on top of the arrangements she'd already made: a tee time for four at Farm Neck (with hopes of sneaking a peek at a golfing Barack), fishing charter, catered clam bake on their private beach—and, of course, reservations at the Island's best restaurants.

Soap. Remy did not remember the soap. Maybe lemon verbena? Almond? Honey? Remy sucked her lip, thinking. This was the kind of detail she needed to get right.

Gravel crunched in the drive and a truck door slammed. "Remy?" called a male voice.

"Back porch, Mike," she yelled.

"Hey, Remy. This a bad time?" An old friend from high school, Mike was one of the best carpenters on the Island, where you had a choice among good, fast, and cheap—but you could pick only one. Maybe it was his only-on-the-Vineyard Wampanoag-Black-Portuguese boatwright heritage, or maybe just Mike, but when he finished the house, it would be perfect.

"Nope. Can I get you some coffee? There's more in the pot. And hello to you, you bad dog," Remy said as Mike's big chocolate Lab bounded up and nose-lasered into her shorts. "Ha! I've got a shield this time," she said, fending off the friendly crotch-sniffing canine with her binder.

"Sit, Buddy," Mike ordered. "What're you working on?"

Remy leaned forward to rub the dog's ears. "I'm trying to get organized for the big weekend. All my clients are coming for the Fourth. And I've got an interview coming up, so I've been practicing my sales pitch." Her hand slid to scratch under Buddy's collar. "This lady mostly wants me to do her shopping—her idea of a 'perfect summer vacation' is when she doesn't have to set foot once," she said with a mock shudder of horror, "in the *Stop & Shop*." Remy knew she shouldn't count her chickens before they hatched, but a sixth client on retainer would solve her cash flow worries.

Mike laughed. "Actually, she's kind of right about the supermarket," he said. "I'm sure you'll get hired. Can't let them run out of milk and sunscreen."

"Oh, shoot, thanks for reminding me. I almost forgot to order the La Roche-Posay Anthelios 60 Melt-In Sunscreen Milk for Mrs. Bottimore." Remy wrote another note.

"What?" said Mike.

"Exactly," replied Remy with a snort. "You working on the house today?"

"Just need to take a bunch of measurements. No saws."

The dog flopped on his side, eyes beseeching Remy to rub his stomach. "Oh, you know I love dogs, don't you, boy." She bent to administer a belly rub. Buddy's face melted in bliss.

"He's a good dog—but for the sniffing—great hunting dog too, really soft mouth. Come on Buddy, let's get to work."

Mike's work boots clumped up the creaky stairs followed by the patter of dog paws. Remy turned back to her binder. Nest's success depended on her setting the perfect stage for her clients' Instagrammable, Facebookable vacations, so all they had to do is put on their costumes (designer casual, deceptively expensive) and play their parts. Money didn't buy happiness, but it bought some really nice, big houses and the best of everything the Vineyard could offer, including (she hoped) the services of the Island's top concierge.

Per the Bottimores' instructions, Remy had already stocked their house with high-thread-count sheets and fluffy towels (their last concierge used the Island linen service, which was *not* acceptable), bug dope for ticks, guest toiletries (in case someone forgot a toothbrush), toilet paper and tissues, and on it went. Remy ticked through her 164-item spreadsheet, double-checking that she hadn't missed anything. What was left were the soaps, food and other perishables, cut flowers, and the who-knows-what-else-they-might-want last-minute requests.

But back to soaps. She closed her eyes and tried to imagine herself inside the Bottimores' outdoor shower. Ah, there it was: she could see the blue dish with the pale greenish soap sitting half-melted into a viscous goo. Verbena, for sure. And she'd replace the soap dish with a wooden one that drained.

Remy sighed. Another item for the list.

Remy inhaled the delicious garden aroma of flowers and herbs as she opened the box of French Marseille soaps. Three rose-colored bars (so pretty with the crushed petals), three almond bars, and two of the olive oil cubes went into the Hartwells' crate. Scent-memory then conjured up Madame Julie in her dressing gown the year Remy was an au pair on the outskirts of Paris.

It had been the best year of Remy's life. Madame had taken a gawky sugary-cereal-and-pizza-loving American under her wing as if she were her own Eliza Doolittle and transformed her into, if not quite a Parisian, an attractive, polished and (mostly) confident young woman with a passion for croissants, champagne, and foie gras.

Madame Julie had relished her Pygmalion role, providing firm and opinionated instruction in all the important subjects: food, fashion, grooming, flowers, cooking, art, wine, chocolate—and sex. Madame was amused by Remy's gaucheness, her unfamiliarity with the most basic pleasures of life: a soft, perfectly ripened Camembert cheese (Madame was horrified by the abomination that was "the American Cheese"), farm-fresh roasted Bresse chicken, and, most important, good bread and better wine. Madame broke Remy of her American habit of eating too much, too fast, anywhere and anytime. Remy learned the art of shopping for the best ingredients to be simply prepared and served at a table set with silverware, a wine glass, and flowers. She learned to taste her food: small bites, small portions, enjoy three bites then wait. Drink, chat, take your time, then three more, until you are not full, but *satisfaite*. All of Madame's rules came in threes. Remy didn't know if that was French or just Madame. But if she could have a quarter of Madame's confidence and beauty at 40, she vowed to follow them to a tee.

Remy would sit on the bed in the house in St. Germain en Laye as Madame executed her toilette, combining Remy's instructions for the day with a strict lesson on grooming. Madame showed her the trick of spraying just a touch of Nuxe dry oil on her brush before running it through wet hair. *It is not just the volume,* she would say. *Americans think that. What is important is the shine, the health. When you touch it, will it bend? That is the test. Why have hair that is bad to touch?* Remy still had the round boar-bristle brush she'd been given after Madame tossed the plastic and nylon Goody—*c'est du junk that will ruin the hair*—in the trash. Lesson two had been on the mandatory application of face cream. *Start young, do not give the wrinkles an opening to start and you will have skin like mine. Le maquillage,* her makeup. *Seulement s'améliorer,* Remy was told: enhance, do not change. And to make a statement of power, Dior rouge lipstick.

Remy learned to appreciate her large Roman nose, far smaller than Madame's high-bridged beak. She had labeled Remy's nose *aristocratique. Small noses, pheuf,* pronounced Madame, *they are for peasants. Good hair, good height, good eyes—you will not be a beautiful woman but you are très très séduisante,* very, very attractive, was Madame's final judgment at the end of the year.

But the most important lesson Madame Julie taught was *le pouvoir sexuel de la femme.* "French women have it, but so do you. You have freshness, charm. Stand up straight, be confident and not ashamed of your breasts. Men will look. Let them. You look at *them* too. Whatever part catches your eye. Eyes firm and steady." Remy pulled her shoulders back, stuck out her boobs, and tried to look Madame straight in the eye. "And you must learn to flirt properly. That is how to have control. No more shy little schoolgirl." She got a devilish glint in her eye. "I have a test for you. If you win, I will get you that blue blouse you want but decided cost too much. Yes, I saw you looking. I win, and you will get that blouse, and pay me back in babysitting gratis."

There was, as always, no way out. Madame Julie identified the victim to Remy the next morning at the café where they stopped after walking Danielle, Nicole, Gabrielle, and little Juji to their schools. "There he is, behind the counter, a bit older than you, but see how he is looking at you. Go up and ask for a new napkin. See if you can make him fold," Madame said, the last phrase in English. (Madame had an inexplicable weakness for televised Las Vegas poker and had decided "make him fold" was a very good English expression indeed.) Remy sighed. Either way, there was a new top in it for her from Madame's favorite boutique.

"Monsieur," she had said, trying her hardest to keep her accent pure but failing even to her own ears. "Do you have a napkin? I have soiled mine," Remy added, suddenly fearful she'd just told the handsome young man she'd pooped her diaper. Still, unwilling to babysit for free, she did her best to ignore her possible faux pas and looked him in the eye, thinking to herself that she appeared *très forte.*

"Oui, Mademoiselle," he replied to her breasts. She let her eyes slide down in an equivalent appraisal—broad shoulders for a Frenchman, not tall but more muscular than was usual—then back up to large dark eyes framed by the longest eyelashes she'd ever seen on a man. The waiter bent to pull the napkin out from under the counter and smiled when he caught Remy's equivalent appraisal. He then met Remy's eyes, and as Madame had predicted, he looked away.

"Merci," Remy replied and emboldened, added a flirtatious half smile. "You have a crumb," she said, brushing a speck from his sleeve. He looked down at his arm, then back up at Remy.

"Je m'appelle Jean-Paul," he said, showing excellent white teeth in an open smile.

She smiled back. "Je suis Remy."

"Ah, but I saw the end too," Madame said with a glint in her eye. "I did not tell you to press your advantage but for you, it was *très naturel.* He is still looking at you," she added peering over Remy's shoulder. "You will see, at our next visit, we will get a sweet *gratis.*" As Madame had predicted, the next day Jean-Paul brought to her table a Paris-Brest, the delicate circle of choux pastry filled with praline *crème au beurre* that had become Remy's most favorite food in the world. That was the first of many gifts, and she wore the soft pale-blue-silk blouse and Dior rouge on her lips on their first date. Jean-Paul turned out to be the best kind of first lover: patient, sensitive, and expert in both instruction and execution. Dear Madame had chosen well.

Remy left Paris at the end of the year with a suitcase full of excellent, classic French clothes (hand-me-downs from Madame); an appreciation of fine food, wine, and art; and an eye for the elegant and beautiful. None of which were any use at all in the cafeteria-fed, frat-party-fueled cinder-block environs of UMass. But at least Remy took advantage of her improved French for her classes and, when she chose, her *pouvoir sexuel* in the XL-twin dorm beds.

# CHAPTER 5

"Yoo-hoo, Remy, are you home?" Willow let herself in without knocking, as always.

"In the kitchen, doing flowers," Remy called.

Willow pushed open the screen door, radiating enthusiasm and excitement. As usual, she was in one of her own creations, a patchwork batik sundress paired with Remy's "borrowed" cowboy boots. "Big news!" Willow bounced on her toes. "I got a commission! Some lady in Edgartown has a trunk full of fabrics she's collected and wants a king-size quilt, two-sided. And shams."

"Awesome!"

"I quoted her a totally outrageous price—she had these big honking diamond studs and a handbag so ugly it had to cost a fortune—but she didn't blink an eye. 'A wonderful memento of my travels,' she said." Willow spun around in a swirl of color. "What I make on my tote bags and other stuff is chicken feed compared to this!"

"Great news, Wills." Remy put down the bunch of daisies she was snipping and hugged her.

"And then maybe all her friends will want custom quilts too." Willow's creative eye started imagining the possibilities. "If I use those indigo-and-white yukata prints, it would look awesome in their stuffy white houses…. Oh, before I forget, here. These are from my sister," she said holding out a plastic container. "Her plants went crazy this year."

"Ooh, strawberries?" Remy asked, prying off the lid. "Oh wow—tell Rosemary thanks. They're beautiful." The small, skinny red berries shone beneath their fresh leafy caps, so different from the obese supermarket kind. Remy stuck her nose in and sniffed. "Mmm, they smell so good."

"They taste even better." Willow reached over and grabbed a berry. "Oh, and I got more news." Willow's eyes went wide. "Remember Jake, your old teenage crush? He's here for the whole summer."

Remy popped off a green cap and ate a strawberry. She'd managed, mostly successfully, not to think about him. "I know. I've already run into him. Twice." Remy gave Willow a look. "He's not my crush."

Willow ate another berry. "But he was," she said. "Big time."

"We were teenagers, Wills," Remy said. "You had a crush on Ethan, remember?"

"That was only the one year," Willow replied. "Yours was like three summers long. He was all you would talk about. Oooo, *Jake*." She gave Remy a devilish look. "Remember all those blondies we used to bake for him? And when you pretended the motor broke down so he'd sail out to rescue you from the middle of the pond?" Willow was getting on a roll. "Oh, and best, that time at the Ag Fair…"

"Yes, I remember," Remy interrupted. Willow's memories, although accurate, were mortifying. Remy's crush had been world-class. She'd planned her days in hopes of running into him, planned every outfit to catch his eye. He'd been the topic of every entry in her diary and every conversation with Willow. Remy was convinced it was true love, and he'd fall in love with her too. Once he noticed her.

"Oh, and you'd flirt like mad when he'd drive us to the dock dances! So what do you think?"

"About what?"

"About Jake."

"I don't think anything about Jake," Remy lied.

"Right," Willow laughed. "Like you didn't even notice how incredibly hot he is. I ran into him at Alley's, picking up milk. It made me wonder what our Teddy would look like if we cleaned him up. Anyway, I invited him to Mike's party on Friday."

"You didn't."

"Sure, I did. Come on. He's hot. He's here. You like smart guys. Of course, I invited him."

Mike's boots clumped back down the stairs. He pushed open the screen door. "Who'd you invite?"

"Teddy's older brother," Remy said, rolling her eyes. "Jake. I don't know if you know him. He hasn't been around in years."

"He's like a way cuter and less spacy version of Teddy," Willow volunteered. "Remy used to have the biggest crush on him."

Remy ignored Willow. "He's here, taking the summer off to 'write and sail.'" Remy rolled her eyes. "He thinks he's a big deal because he's a college professor."

"A professor?" Mike whistled.

"Yup," Remy said. "Philosophy. University of Chicago."

Willow gave Remy a sly look "You two can talk philosophy. What came first, the chicken or the egg."

"Ha," Remy said.

"Speaking of chickens, I'm going to go visit my girls," Willow teased. "See if you missed any eggs. Can I bring Ada out for a visit?"

"I wouldn't," Remy said. "She's acting broody. Even pecked me. Grab Tweedle or Beauty Linna if you want." She turned to Mike. "Speaking of the party, what can I bring? Booze? Food? You name it."

Mike thought for a second. "How about tequila?"

Willow's eyes opened wide. "Margaritas?"

"Shots. Della's request." Mike smiled his crooked grin.

"Of course. Maybe I'll even upgrade us from Cuervo," Remy laughed.

Remy jotted "Friday—Mike/tequila" on a sticky note and put it on the front of her binder.

"I'll make my *pao de queijo* to sop up the alcohol. You know, those little Brazilian cheese breads?"

"They're addictive. A double batch, please," Mike said and turned to Remy. "Any chance you could come early with your giant cooler?"

"No problem. I can bring ice too."

Mike clipped his tape measure onto his belt and whistled for Buddy. "And don't forget your dancing shoes. I'm putting together a new playlist."

Willow stood up and wiggled her hips. Mike took her hand and, with deceptive grace, executed a smooth series of salsa steps.

Remy laughed. "Save a dance for me too, Mike."

Hours later, tired, sweaty, and thoroughly cross, Remy turned down a rutted one-lane dirt road that she hoped led to her new client's house. "Ugh," Remy groaned as her ancient 4Runner bottomed out, sloshing her coffee-filled bladder like a water balloon and rattling the cases of beer and wine in the back of the truck.

Remy's day had gone downhill. When she arrived at the Bottimores' place to deliver the groceries, Remy discovered that the cleaning crew, probably mixing up her instructions (or did she screw up?), had neglected both to scrub the deck furniture and to make up the beds. Which made her the pinch-hitting housemaid.

Branches added more "Island pinstripes" to the sides of the gray SUV as Remy swerved around a particularly deep rut. Confidence in her "great idea" (or so everyone said) to launch her own concierge company had been worn away by hours scrubbing scunge and making the Bottimores' nine beds. Then there was the condescending tone of a new message from Enid Cinch attaching a three-page single-spaced set of instructions to be "discussed, in person, as soon as possible."

But maybe Eli Wolff would be different.

Or he'd be a nightmare, expecting her to read his mind and getting pissed off when things weren't done "just right." Remy hadn't even talked to him on the phone. All she had was a terse email sent late Monday night: "Remy, got your note. Make sure the house is ready. Six guests, Saturday to Monday. We'll cook at home one night and eat out the other. Do whatever you like. Eli."

Remy knew the property from her winter beach walks along the Island's north shore with Willow and Teddy. It was a beautiful place, an old sailing captain's house set on a point. But who was her new client? Remy hadn't a clue. She considered her Google searches business research, not stalking (at least not much). Professional websites listed interests, prominent people did interviews, Facebook pages disclosed favorite vacation spots, and the *New York Times* wedding announcement invariably produced useful information. The Bottimores were skiers, so they got jigsaw puzzles of the Swiss Alps and the Aspen trail map in their rainy-day cabinet. For the tropical-beach-loving Hartwells, she'd stocked palm tree–print beach towels and the makings for her (soon to be) famous rum punch. And Mr. and Mrs. Soulanski were very pleased to find a Yale cooler in their hall closet. Remy found no wedding announcement for the new client—or anything else. No LinkedIn, no photos, no magazine articles, nada. Only a couple of articles in the business press on the sale of the "data mining" company he'd founded (whatever that was). Why would someone be so invisible? Remy guessed, reclusive techie weirdo with personal hygiene issues. Willow, deep into her spy novel, voted for European arms dealer or cyber-criminal.

Eli Wolff, enigma man. He'd been too busy to talk or to fill out Remy's online new-client questionnaire that she'd worked so hard to develop. Remy had sighed in frustration; at least she knew what her picky clients wanted. After starting to prepare a list to ready the house for anything from teetotaling vegans to bourbon-pounding paleos, Remy changed her mind. She'd take the client at his word and do the prep with what she liked as if the lovely home were hers.

Remy glanced at her phone. As expected, no cell service. No service meant no map, not that Google Maps reliably showed the Island's private roads in any event. She'd followed the directions: drive 2.3 miles from the intersection, take a left then a right at the birdhouse, go 0.9 miles and turn left, then 1.8 miles to the house. But doubts were inevitable after 20 minutes of bone-jarring potholes down an unmarked dirt road through thick woods. Remy sighed and pushed on. If this wasn't the right way, at least there'd be something worthwhile to see at the end of the road. On Martha's Vineyard, there always was.

Resting a bunch of lavender on the porch table, Remy flopped onto one of the big wicker chairs, the old-fashioned kind with blue striped ticking and horsehair cushions, and popped open a beer. Her irritation had disappeared as soon as she'd pulled through the gate. The property was simply stunning. The gray-shingled house and barn stood handsomely on the headland, surrounded by a private beach and not one, but two, freshwater ponds. The gardens took Remy's breath away. Bounded by ancient stone walls, blooming perennials mixed with native plants in a lush, loose, natural style, edged with a hedge of fragrant, purple lavender. Then she discovered the guest house, a tiny one-bedroom whitewashed shack with a miniature front porch tucked into a dune by the beach. A pang of pure envy shot through her body. Whoever Eli Wolff was, he had good taste.

Remy had peeked into every cabinet and closet as she did her inventory, relieved to find the house in good shape and nearly fully stocked. Cotton flat-weave rugs (perfect for bare feet) warmed the original wide wood floorboards, squashy slipcovered sofas asked to be napped on, and fabulous oil paintings of whaling ships honored the house's history. The dusty attic held a treasure trove of bric-a-brac, including a box of antique bowls and pitchers, perfect for her flower arrangements. Fortunately, the cleaning crew had done an excellent job opening the house: no smelly fridge, no mouse-dropping-filled drawers, no unmade beds. With some new beach towels and the usual stocking up of liquor, food, and flowers, the house would be ready for guests.

The IPA was cold and flavorful, and a pleasantly warm buzz spread from Remy's core. The late-day sun had warmed the porch and worked on her tired body like a cat's, melting her into the chair. An immaculate lawn rolled down to a pond edged with granite boulders, like nature's most perfect swimming pool.

Beyond that, the beach and the calm blue waters of Vineyard Sound beckoned.

Maybe it wasn't such a bad idea, her business. Remy closed her eyes, the sun on her eyelids and soft sea sounds in her ears. At least not when she had afternoons like this one.

Remy woke with a start. Looking like he'd just stepped out of a Ralph Lauren ad, a blond man sat in the wicker chair across from her, lips turned up in an amused smile. Remy stared befuddled at the stranger. Realization hit. Oh, shit. This must be the new client. This was his porch, after all. And he'd found her, like Goldilocks, sleeping in his chair.

This was not the plan. In fact, it was about as far from it as you could get. The plan had her arriving Thursday, precisely on time, in her meet-the-new-client outfit—a crisp white shirt, Hermès scarf (*au revoir* gift from Madame Julie), tailored skirt, and sensible flats, her hair smoothed into a neat chignon. She'd make friendly small talk and pull out her blue binder emblazoned with the Nest logo to confirm Eli Wolff's instructions, leaving him confident he'd hired the most fabulously competent concierge on the Island. Ha.

And here he'd found her sound asleep with her mouth open and legs splayed apart in a most unladylike manner. Instead of her tidy outfit, Remy was in a dirty *I don't give a cluck* purple cartoon rooster T-shirt, cutoff shorts, and flip-flops. Oh, and to boot, she wore the hippy-dippy feather earrings Willow had made. This wasn't just a poor first impression, this was a mortifyingly bad first impression.

Remy felt a flush rise from her collarbones to the top of her head. She resisted the impulse to stammer something—any excuse—and run away. Instead, she took a deep breath to clear the panic from her eyes and forced her lips into a smile. "I'm Remy Litchfield, your…" she started, standing up to extend her hand. The empty beer dropped from her lap to the porch with a clunk and started to roll. Eli Wolff muffled a laugh behind her as she ran after the bottle.

She put the bottle on the table and started again. "You must be Mr. Wolff. I'm Remy Litchfield from Nest Concierge Services. I apologize for this. I was doing my opening inventory, and I didn't expect anyone to be here until Thursday." She was relieved to hear her voice present a professional tone, even if nothing else did.

"I flew up early. Sorry if I surprised you," Eli said with a hint of a British accent. He held onto her hand just a beat too long, his smile deepening. "Nice to meet you, Remy. Can I offer you another beer? I assume they're in my fridge."

"No. I mean yes," Remy sputtered, losing the tenuous hold she had on her professionalism. "They're in the fridge. No thank you, I'm fine."

"Back in a flash," he said standing up.

Remy collapsed onto the chair and put her face in her hands, listening to Eli Wolff opening the refrigerator door. Surely this would be the shortest job ever held. "Shit," she muttered.

The screen door banged shut, and Remy looked up. Her new client, still wearing that amused look, sat down in his chair and took a long slug from the bottle. "Good ale." He examined the label. "Local?"

"There's a new brewpub on the Island. They fill growlers too if you're a beer fan. I'm happy to pick one up for you." She hesitated, pressing her lips together. "I really do want to apologize for falling asleep on your porch."

He waved his hand. "I'll be taking a lot of naps here myself. That's why I bought the place. To relax. You were just testing the chair for me." He raised one eyebrow. "I assume it was satisfactory?"

Remy stared into green eyes. Not just looks and money and that accent. Charisma. Eli Wolff just oozed charisma—and ego. "Oh. Yes. Very," Remy said, pulling herself together. "But I can get you some throw pillows for the sofa there. That might be even better for napping," she added, confidence returning. "Do you have a few minutes to go over things? I'd like to make sure I've set up the house properly for your weekend guests."

Eli lifted the bottle to his lips, drank, then stretched out his legs. "No need. As I said, whatever you like is fine with me. I like beer. I don't like eggplant. Or Brussels sprouts. If you remember that, I'll be happy."

"Do your guests have any other dietary restrictions or preferences? Gluten-free, paleo, or anything else?"

"Honestly, I don't know." His eyes drifted out across the water.

"I thought dinner Saturday night at the Beach Plum Inn? They're doing an amazing pop-up thing with all local ingredients."

"I'm quite sincere, Remy. Whatever you think best." Eli raised one eyebrow and fixed her with a look. "Now, how about a swim? I'm going in."

Standing up, Eli stretched his arms over his head, exposing a sliver of his flat torso. "I shouldn't—couldn't. Work to do," Remy stammered as she pulled her eyes away. Argh. What? He's a client. "No bathing suit," she added.

"That's no problem," he grinned. "We're very private here, in case you hadn't noticed. By the way, I'll be here most of the summer. I'm converting a corner of the barn to an office. So, it'll be me during the week plus guests on weekends. No need to call. Just drop by anytime."

Remy stood up and collected the empty bottles. "Thank you. I'll finish up and be on my way. You have my phone number and email if you think of anything."

"Stay as long as you like. You're not a guest; you're my concierge," he winked.

Remy carried the empties inside. Was she just invited by a bombshell-gorgeous client to go skinny dipping? Really? She shook her head in disbelief and looked around the kitchen, Time to make up for that horrible first impression. She'd already unpacked the cases of beer and wine. But food. Eli Wolff had no food. Deciding against another trip to the supermarket, she grabbed her own purchases from Mermaid Farm from the car. The cheese, lamb, and pea shoots would be enough for a simple dinner if he wanted to stay in. She'd supplement the mango lassi for breakfast with early shop-and-drop first thing in the morning.

Setting the shopping bag on the kitchen table, Remy glanced back out the window. Eli Wolff was standing on the beach at the water's edge. He had pulled off his shirt and appeared to be unbuttoning his shorts. Remy stared—the groceries could wait another minute. "Oh my," she muttered as his shorts dropped, then his boxers. The late afternoon sun lit Eli's body like a bright bronze statue. He waded out thigh-deep in the water, then turned to the house and waved before diving in. Remy's face reddened as he swam out with strong strokes. He couldn't have known she was looking. But she was.

Remy pulled out the chops and King's Highway cheese, still seeing Eli in that gorgeous light: personal-trainer-chiseled torso, the contrast between the pale, sculpted buttocks and tanned legs. Not exactly her type but very nice to look at. Too bad Eli hadn't been the model instead of that skinny bearded guy with the saggy, pimpled tush in her life painting class at the Featherstone Gallery. Remy chuckled. No wonder her painting had turned out so awful.

Eli Wolff was now a speck, swimming parallel to the beach toward the point. Remy sat down to write a note, regretting that her pale blue paper and the fountain pen she used for her "nesting notes" were at home: a steno pad and ballpoint would have to do. She chewed on the end of the pen, trying to decide whether to start with "Dear Eli" or "Dear Mr. Wolff." Well, she'd just seemed him naked—the second naked man in a week—so Eli it was.

*Dear Eli*, she wrote in her tidy hand, *it was a pleasure to finally meet you* (that was true) *and I look forward to being your Island concierge* (also very true)*; I am at your service 24-7. I'll swing by tomorrow morning to drop off the coffee and some other groceries and to go over the schedule and shopping for the weekend.* Remy then jotted down a simple recipe for the lamb using herbs from the kitchen garden together with butter and garlic to make a quick, rich version of a *persillade* to be served over wilted pea shoots. She snipped a handful of parsley, added a few stalks of rosemary and thyme, and put them alongside the note, then unwrapped the cheese on a cutting board. Nearly done. A bunch of daisies joined the lavender in a pewter pitcher, and Remy chose a Santenay Burgundy to complement the lamb. Having admired her composition, Remy then turned back for one last look out the window. Eli floated on his back a few yards from shore.

Remy smiled. Client as eye candy, and a gorgeous property to boot.

Ready to tackle her endlessly growing shopping lists, Remy grabbed some canvas shopping bags and headed by foot to the West Tisbury farmer's market. The old Grange Hall set a quaint backdrop for the rows of stalls offering the best of the Vineyard's farms and kitchens. This was one of the little pleasures of her job, buying what she wanted—with her clients' money.

Today, Remy was shopping for her fresh-and-local welcome baskets. She waved at Teddy, wearing a too-snug T-shirt printed with a psychedelic mushroom, set up in his usual spot between the flower vendor with the technicolor zinnias and the smoked-fish guy. He claimed to be the laziest farmer on the Island. All he did was water, wait, and bag his crops.

"Hi Teddy," Remy called. "What's up?"

"A fine crop of sprouts and a lovely bloom of shroomies," Teddy said, waving her over and handing her two baggies. "Broccoli sprouts and enokis. On the house. A thank you for escorting a very buzzed and naked self safely home."

"Happy to do it," Remy smiled, shaking her head. "You were high as a kite."

He beamed at her. "And a very fine flight it was! I guess it was a little too public display of my pubes, but I needed to test my crop." He stroked his scruffy beard. "I think that old oak log had some special magic. Happy to share, if you want a little trip."

"I'll take a pass!" she laughed. "Not my thing. But the shiitakes look nice. Can I have four bags?"

"Uno, dos, tres, cuatro," he counted as he dropped them into her shopping bag. "How about coming over for dinner tonight? I'm making your mushroomy pasta."

"The recipe I taught you last winter?" Remy asked. Teddy had been delighted to learn how to make her favorite mushroom sauce, a simple béchamel with lots of mushrooms, a splash of heavy cream, and a sprinkle of thyme.

"The very same. No messing with perfection." He looked pensive. "Perhaps I should rename it mushroomy-Remy pasta, in your honor. And Jake likes it too. He's going to make a strawberry-rhubarb cobbler for dessert." Then a rare shrewd look showed in Teddy's eye as he gauged her reaction. "So, what do you think?"

"Sorry, Teddy. Busy tonight." Remy wanted to avoid Jake, not eat dinner with him, even though she did love anything strawberry-rhubarb with a passion. "What do I owe?"

"Twenty-eight, my dear. A hug, of course, is free." Along with sprouts and mushrooms, per his hand-lettered sign, Teddy dispensed "free Teddy-bear hugs, no purchase necessary" at his booth. Kids would get a lift-and-spin, and the old ladies would emerge from Teddy's arms beaming and feeling ten years younger.

Remy handed Teddy her credit card and came around for a hug. Willow, with her aura thing, said Teddy was pink, a loving, giving, healing color. There was a more scientific explanation, that hugs released oxytocin, the love hormone. No matter, Remy felt better after a moment spent in Teddy's arms, inhaling his clean-earth smell and feeling the tickle of his beard on the top of her head.

"I should go," Remy said, stepping back. "You've got a customer." A familiar mahogany-skinned woman in a big hat and sunglasses ran a finger over a furry clump of lion's mane mushrooms. "Those are great, the shiitakes too—and the hugs," Remy advised, smiling as she tried to place the woman. One of the Hartwells' friends, perhaps? Remy turned to Teddy. "Thanks for the mushrooms."

"My pleasure."

Feeling a lovely pink glow, Remy moved quickly from booth to booth, chatting with the vendors and neighbors and friends. Soon her bags were filled with bright green heads of loose-leaf lettuce, tender green beans, the early cherry tomatoes, fresh herbs, Island-made chocolates, local jams (West Tisbury Traffic Jam for herself and beach plum for her clients) and pretty bottles of flavored olive oil.

Remy had just added a dozen cheeses from the Grey Barn to her bag and was about to head home when she spotted Jake walking through the market. "Damn," she muttered to herself. Remy quickly stepped beside a vegetable truck to avoid being seen. She watched Jake made a beeline to Teddy's booth. Brothers, so alike yet so different.

The smile fell from Teddy's face at something Jake said. Then Jake turned, face tight, and looked straight at her. Remy chose two bunches of parsley and rooted around in her purse for her wallet, hoping he wouldn't come over. She glanced up. No such luck.

"Hey Remy, looks like you've been doing some shopping," Jake said, looking at her stuffed-to-the-gills bags.

"For my clients," Remy said, forcing a polite smile. She shifted a bag from her hand to her shoulder, feeling the canvas straps dig into her flesh. "Sorry I can't come over for dinner tonight."

Jake looked blank. "What dinner?"

"Um, Teddy invited me for pasta? And cobbler?"

"Oh, he did," Jake replied, then looked back at Teddy in his booth. "Not the only thing he's forgotten to tell me today."

"Teddy's a bit flakey sometimes," Remy replied in his defense. "But we love him anyway."

"Maybe that's the problem," Jake replied. "No one around here expects anything of him."

Remy's hackles rose as she bit back her retort. Jake, away for years and years, doing his own thing, not paying the least attention to his brother. What gave him the right to show up and start criticizing Teddy—and her? Teddy was a bit of a flake, true, but so what?

Remy pulled out her wallet and handed the farmer a bill. "I took two bunches of the parsley."

"Thank you, dear," the gray-haired woman in the gingham kerchief replied. "Anything else today?" Ignoring Jake, Remy checked over the truck bed laden with lovely early-summer vegetables and herbs. The tiny haricots verts looked particularly appealing, but Remy could barely carry what she had.

"No, I think I'm good," Remy replied.

"Well, enjoy. I'll have some more of that sorrel you like next week."

With an effort, Remy hoisted the other shopping bag up and onto her shoulder. Jake took a step closer and laid his hand on Remy's arm. "Sorry. I'm just annoyed at Teddy. I shouldn't take it out on you. Can I help carry your bags?"

At his touch, Remy felt herself redden as she cursed the gods who so often paired masculine beauty with arrogance. Jake was just another guy who thought he could do anything, say anything, and get away with anything. Like criticizing her dear friend Teddy. Plus, the Sir Thomas More lecture still smarted. Remy's instinct to avoid Jake was right. She could use help, but she wouldn't take any from him.

"Really, I'm not doing anything right now."

Remy picked up the third bag in her hand. "No, thanks. I've got it."

# CHAPTER 6

Remy had eyes only for the horse as her new client took the big bay through his dressage routine: piaffe, the horse "dancing" in place; passage, the bay appearing to lift and float in midair as horse and rider trotted around the ring; and, to finish, a 720-degree pirouette. Remy chewed on her thumbnail. Bad habit but the run-in with Jake had left her irritated, mostly at herself.

"Mother's very good," said a voice from behind. Remy turned around. "World-class, in fact," the teenage girl added with a twitch of her lips.

This must be the daughter. A spray of pimples spaghetti-sauced her chin, and where the mother was elegant and lithe, the daughter was chunky in her oversize gray sweatshirt. But for the narrow noses, Remy would never have guessed that the two were related.

Remy put out her hand. "I'm Remy Litchfield of Nest Concierge Services. You must be Morgan."

"Right, you're Mother's new errand girl," Morgan said with an unappealing sneer. "Lucky you, landing that shit work job," she added and went back to watching her mother in the ring.

Remy held her tongue. The client's daughter. Be nice. "Well, it's called concierge services but, yes," she paused and caught the girl's eye. "It is mostly shit work. Still, I'm happy to have it. Beautiful place, beautiful horses. You must love it here."

"Oh, yes," Morgan said, clearly meaning quite the opposite. "I just love it."

Remy chose to ignore the sarcasm. "Will you be here for the whole summer?"

"Got no choice," she replied.

"I'm happy to put together a list of fun activities for you. Have you jumped off Jaws bridge? Or visited the alpaca farm? The alpacas are supercute, and there are three new babies this summer."

"No," said Morgan.

"We'll have to fix that," Remy said. "I can pull some strings, even get you and your friends a private after-hours visit."

Morgan sighed in reply. They watched Mrs. Cinch make another circuit, this time executing a flying change of leg. The horse and rider spun in another pirouette. "Mother judges people by how well they ride," Morgan said. She ran a dismissive eye over Remy. "And whether they ride. I don't imagine you do."

"I used to, a little—back when I was a teenager," Remy replied with a polite smile. "Not anymore. And not like that," she added with a glance at Mrs. Cinch. "But I still love horses. That's a magnificent bay your mother is on."

"He is. Mother doesn't accept anything less than perfection. Consider yourself warned," Morgan added with a wicked look.

Mrs. Cinch loosened the reins, allowing the horse to relax and stretch, then approached the rail. She sat ramrod straight in the saddle, lips pinched sour-lemon tight. "You must be Remy. I see you've met my lovely daughter, Morgan," she said, not bothering to hide her disappointment.

Morgan rolled her eyes. "Yes, Mother named me after a horse."

"You know that we did not. You're named after my side of the family."

"The Morgans of J.P. Morgan, Remy," the teen said with another impressive eye roll. "We've been having a nice chat. Remy rides. Did you know that?"

"Oh, not for ages," Remy demurred. "But I did have my horse-crazy phase when I was a bit younger than Morgan. I mucked out stalls at Arrowhead Farm in exchange for lessons for a couple of years."

The bay horse fixed its big dark eyes on Remy and took a step toward her. She leaned over the fence and stroked the length of his handsome face, inhaling the familiar, warm scent of horse. "He's beautiful. I loved watching you ride." Remy held up her blue binder. "Whenever you're ready, I'm happy to go over the instructions you sent."

"Yes, of course. I must have lost track of time." Mrs. Cinch looked Remy up and down. "How much do you weigh?"

"About 135," Remy replied. "Maybe a bit more." Her weight, ten pounds over where she wanted to be, seemed irrelevant to the execution of concierge duties.

"Same as me, Mother," Morgan said. "I'm going inside. To eat more."

Morgan's mother ignored her. "Your shoe has a heel. Let's see how you do." She turned to the stable. "McGraw," she shouted to a tiny groom working over a large gray horse's hoof with a pick. "Saddle Rajah."

Morgan turned around to stare at her mother.

"As I said, I haven't been on a horse in years," said Remy. She was about to be subjected to Mrs. Cinch's test of quality. Which she would fail.

"Either you sit properly, or you don't." Enid narrowed her eyes. "You have good posture. And Frederik walked right up to you, which he doesn't always do."

The stable door opened. Remy's breath caught as the groom led out what was easily the most beautiful horse she'd ever seen. "That's a Marwari, isn't it?" The glossy dark chestnut horse had a white blaze and adorably curved ears that met at the tips—the distinctive trait of the rare Indian breed. Exquisitely proportioned with an elegant, deep chest, long body, and powerful, graceful legs: this was a special horse. "He's gorgeous, Mrs. Cinch," Remy exclaimed.

"Enid. Yes, he is. I got him for Morgan. She doesn't appreciate all the trouble and expense I went to. There are very few breeders—luckily there is one on Chappaquiddick—and they do not like to sell."

The groom threw the blanket and saddle over the horse's back, adjusted it, and started cinching the girth. "Really, Mrs. Cinch…Enid." This made no sense. Remy glanced at Morgan's retreating back. Was the woman punishing her daughter by putting Remy on the horse?

The door slammed and Enid glanced at the house, then turned her attention back to Remy. "Let's see how you do." Remy considered chickening out, but she climbed over the fence, heart pounding with trepidation. "Go on, I don't have all day."

Remy inserted her foot into the stirrup and swung into the saddle. So far, so good. The horse took two steps backward when he sensed her hands on the reins. "Calm down, now," Remy said to both of them and reached down to pat his neck. She hadn't ridden since she'd left Austin. And that was on a chewy old trail horse with a beat-up western saddle. Nothing like this magnificent animal.

"Take him through his paces," Enid commanded, backing her horse to the center of the ring.

Rajah began to walk the instant Remy let up on the reins. A mere touch of her heel and the horse moved unexpectedly into a smooth four-beat ambling gait instead of a trot. It was like the lope of a wolf, a fast, steady pace to carry horse and rider for miles and miles.

"Now canter," Mrs. Cinch ordered. Muscle memory kicked in as Remy kept her shoulders relaxed, hands low, and shifted her weight slightly back, giving the horse the slightest squeeze with her outside leg. Almost before her thigh muscles tensed, Rajah started cantering elegantly around the ring, as if he sensed the electrical impulses before the pressure. She made two circuits then Enid called out, "That's enough."

Remy wanted to keep riding, to open the gate, and take that amazing horse out of the ring and gallop away. Reluctantly, she dismounted and handed the reins to the groom. Her eyes gleamed with exhilaration as she stroked Rajah's white blaze, feeling the unfamiliar tug of muscles in her inner thighs. "Thank you," she said to Enid. "He's a fantastic horse. Your daughter is a lucky girl."

Enid again narrowed her eyes as she appeared to weigh a decision. "Your balance is adequate. I want Rajah to get used to weight in the saddle—McGraw is too light," she said. "That fat girl," Enid added under her breath. "Remy, you may exercise him. On the clock, of course."

"I'd be happy to do that." Remy's heart rose. She didn't want to get in the middle of whatever battle mother and daughter were having over the horse, but no way would she turn down the opportunity to ride Rajah—and get paid to do so.

"I'll be using the ring," Mrs. Cinch said, "So take him out on the trails. And on the beach. He's used to that on Chappy. Morgan will lend you her extra jodhpurs. I assume you don't have your own." She turned her horse toward the barn. "I'll meet you in the kitchen. Please wait for me there. I'd like a glass of Pellegrino. Cold, no ice."

Remy stared at the whiteboard calendar marked with her clients' comings and goings, lost in thought of where to find Aleppo pepper flakes and sumac before the weekend. "Hey, girl. What's up?" Willow said as she opened the back door. "You're still working? It's after 6:00."

"Hey Wills, I didn't hear you pull up," Remy said. "Yeah, I'm still doing my lists," she said, holding up a notebook.

Willow flopped onto a kitchen chair and gave her best friend a stern look. "Ah, Rem, you're too uptight. So are your clients. The world's not going to end if somebody runs out of limes." She twisted her mahogany hair into a bun and reached over to take a banana from the bowl.

Remy pursed her lips. "Willow Silva, that's what they're paying me for. To make sure they don't run out of limes."

"Remy, ever the perfectionist."

"No, I'm not. Look at this mess," she said, sweeping her arm around the kitchen. "My laundry has been sitting there for three days."

"Messy perfectionist then." Willow peeled her banana and added the skin to the compost bin. "Are we going to get to do

Project XXX again this summer? That's more fun than picking up limes."

"No idea." Remy chuckled. "I'll have to ask the Soulanskis if they're renting to the same people. I hope so."

The Soulanskis' renters had asked Remy to stock not only the fridge and bar with food and drink but also the guestrooms with lingerie-garbed sex dolls. Gleefully, Willow had helped Remy inflate the rubbery blonds, donning a pair of crotchless red-and-black panties from a Frederick's of Hollywood package as a hat and groaning "oh harder, faster, give me more, more" when it was her turn to man the unfortunately phallic-shaped bike pump from Remy's Schwinn (the air pump at Up-Island Automotive being out of the question). It was a challenge to slide panties over Tatiana's unbending legs and position bras sized for human bodies rather than Ivanka's watermelon-size balloons. And when Remy returned with sandwiches, she found Willow incapacitated with giggles and the vinyl tarts in a girl-on-girl orgy in the master bedroom. Remy returned at the end of the rental to find the threesome gone and a nice, fat $250 tip for Remy's "discretion."

"Let's see what these clients want." Willow took a page and started to read. "Boring. Toilet paper: Charmin Ultra Soft Super Mega roll, hung over (never under), minimum of four spares per bathroom." She looked up. "Anal retentive for sure. I bet they keep poop logs too."

"What?" Remy's nose wrinkled in distaste.

Willow broke off half the banana and offered it to Remy. "Yup. It's a thing." She held up her phone. "Apps. My weird cousin told me about it. You can input the details, make a photo gallery..."

"Gross, Willow," Remy interrupted. "I am officially changing the topic. I met the new client, Eli Wolff. I told you he bought the old captain's house on the point?"

"Are these his instructions?"

"No, different client." Remy leaned back in her chair and set her notebook in her lap. "I had this really hard day, and I was over there doing the inventory—he wasn't supposed to be around. Then he caught me sleeping on his porch. And drinking his beer. I thought I was going to be fired." Willow's eyebrows shot up. "I'm not. But you're not going to believe it. He's like 35, 40, British accent, and totally hot. Then he went skinny dipping so I saw *everything*."

"Blimey!" Willow exclaimed in a broad Cockney accent. "Even the old twig and berries?" She winked at Remy. "Bet he's got buckets of quid, eh luv?"

"Ha. I forgot you could do that accent." Remy stretched her arms overhead and yawned. "But oh yeah. I bet he paid five, maybe even ten million for the place."

Willow's eyes flashed with a devilish glint. "Is he single? You should invite him to Mike's party."

Remy snorted. Tequila shots in Mike's backyard were unlikely to be Eli Wolff's scene. "For you? I don't think he's your type."

"No, no, no. Not for me. Or you. For Della, luv. She could sell him ah-art." Della, as the old saying went, could sell a snowball to an Eskimo. And she'd jump on any opportunity to make a sale for her Soho gallery.

"Ha," said Remy. "Maybe I should invite the rest of my clients too." She cracked a grin at the idea of the Cinches and Bottimores mixing with her gang. The Soulanskis on the other hand, well, hell, they'd probably have a fine time.

"Oh, yeah. All those tighty-white-pants people. They'd fit right in." Willow giggled. "OK. I also wanted to ask if you had a beach key I could borrow for the weekend?"

"Sorry, no." The last thing Remy needed was Willow losing the key to a client's private beach. "Ask Teddy. Maybe he found their Quansoo key."

"I hope so. Then we can get Teddy—and that cute Jake—to join us."

"Teddy, yes; Jake, no."

Willow narrowed her eyes "You're attracted to Jake. Your aura got a little brighter there. Sorry, Remy, you've got a tell. Fess up, what's going on?"

Remy tilted her head back, closed her eyes, and sighed. Like a dog with a bone, Willow would keep digging. "OK. Remember I took Teddy home that day he took off all his clothes tripping on shrooms?"

"What's with you and naked men?" Willow asked. "Never mind. Continue."

"Jake showed up, which was awkward, Then, the next day, I saw him on the dock. He's got a new catboat. We talked about sailing." Remy took a sip of iced tea. "Oh hey, did you hear the Donovan's boat floated away? Teddy spotted it beached all the way down on Big Sandy."

Willow was not to be put off the scent. "You talked about sailing—and?"

Remy frowned. "And nothing."

"Liar. But…" Willow looked at Remy hard. "Something else happened. Not so good."

"Maybe," Remy admitted. "I said something dumb. Jake laughed at me. And gave me a lecture on Sir Thomas More and utopian philosophy." Remy rolled her eyes as if she didn't care.

Willow poked Remy in the arm. "You're not dumb. You're the smartest person I know."

"Ha."

"You're awesome, inside and out. Smart and pretty and talented," continued her fiercely loyal best friend.

"Stop it, Willow." But Remy did feel better. "And then at the farmer's market, he said something mean about Teddy being flakey and irresponsible. And it sounded like he blamed us—Teddy's friends."

Willow tilted her head. "Well, Teddy is flaky and irresponsible, but that's not our fault." She reached out and patted Remy's hand. "I get it. Just don't let Jake get under your skin."

"My plan is to avoid him."

Willow stood up. "You coming to the Tank for a beer tonight? Katya's playing, and a bunch of people are going."

"Uh uh." Remy shook her head. "Too much to do."

"Come on. All work and no play makes Remy a dull girl." Remy sighed in surrender. "We'll be there at 8:00; don't be late!" Willow chirped as she headed out the door.

# CHAPTER 7

Texas plates on a white Toyota RAV4. A Texas Longhorns bumper sticker. Her ex-husband's car. Not *his* car, of course. The SUV was moving slowly, the driver looking for a parking spot at the Granite Stores. Ex-husband. It still felt strange to call Adam that, a year later.

Remy avoided thinking about her failed marriage. It still hurt to know how little Adam cared that she'd left and how quickly he'd started hooking up with the cute software designer in the apartment next door. She'd finally realized Adam was a taker, not a giver. He couldn't even remember her birthday. That should have told her something.

But mostly Remy kicked herself for not realizing sooner that her marriage—while never the heady careening bliss of early love—had settled into a dull gray. Gray as the ashes Willow had insisted they scatter at Quansoo when the divorce became final. The ceremony at the beach had helped, especially when the wind took inspiration from *The Big Lebowski* and blew bits of the burned wedding photo back at her and Willow, leaving them laughing and spitting out ashes.

Remy had met Adam when she was working in Boston after the painfully awful withdrawal from UMass. He, with his goofy grin, cornstalk hair, and Texas drawl: the most unlikely MIT computer nerd imaginable. They'd met at the Magnolia Smokehouse in Harvard Square where she'd been tending bar. Remy poured him a Jack Daniel's, neat, and he'd flashed her a smile as wide as the Rio Grande. "Why not," she'd said when he'd asked her, after six months of dating, if she'd "be willing, darlin', to come home with me to the Lone Star State."

Remy had fallen in love with Adam—and, for a time—with Austin too. They'd meet friends and play board games in the two-hour-plus line for the most awesome barbeque in Texas, stay out late listening to music at the bars on 6th Street, then wander slightly hungover the next morning down to their favorite food truck for *migas tacos* and watermelon *agua fresca* to recover and rehydrate. She'd had no problem finding work in a city famous for its bars, and Adam's job at a hot startup made their bank account happy. Funky, quirky, and lively, Austin had everything. Remy found the perfect Ariat cowboy boots at Allens, shopped at thrift stores, and loved to swing in Adam's arms to the dance hall music down the highway at Gruene Hall. Growing Austin offered job opportunities too, and Remy soon found steady, well-paying (and dull) work as an administrative assistant at Dell. And so, they danced the two-step, swam under the hot summer sun at Barton Springs, and slung back cold beers to some of the best music in the country. Maybe there were no great ponds, but Austin had wide, cool lakes.

A year later, she and Adam had married under a wide Texas sky, Remy wearing her boots and a lacy white dress she'd found thrifting, and Adam, his wide-brimmed cowboy hat. She slowly set roots in the dry Texas soil. It was great. Until it wasn't.

"We're building the app from scratch, Remy. I have to work hard," Adam would say of his 16-hour days. "It has nothing to do with you." It was worse than moonlighting: Adam's passion became an obsession. He started working seven days a week, home only to shower, sleep, and (on occasion) watch his beloved Longhorns. Adam was too exhausted to go out, too busy to remember her birthday, their anniversary. Too tired even for sex.

Remy tried to be understanding. He was doing this for them, after all, for their future. "Zoing is a great idea," Adam assured her, they'd get bugs out soon and find that angel investor. He'd quit his day job, he'd have more free time. "But you promised you'd take a day off this weekend," Remy would plead. "Just one day." But Adam would break his promise, leaving Remy solo or a third or fifth or seventh wheel to what their friends were doing.

There would be glimmers of the old Adam, enough to give her hope. But as the months passed, Remy resented Adam's choice. She felt abandoned and angry. And most of all, lonely. She wanted her husband back; they needed to talk; she couldn't go on living this way. Remy started picking fights just to get his attention. But Adam would stare right through her, mind on whatever piece of code that wasn't working. "Yeah, right. The dishwasher. I'll get it next time."

Then there was that night when he'd promised to come home and eat a real dinner with her at dinner time, at the table, the two of them, and they'd talk. About what was happening to them, to him, to her. He'd remember, this time. Remy had made Adam's favorite jambalaya, the one with 14 ingredients, from the cookbook they'd bought in New Orleans, back when they still took vacations. The table was set with candles, wine glasses, and the nice linen napkins they'd received as a wedding gift. Remy showered and changed into the short red dress Adam liked and switched the music to his favorite playlist. Tonight, they'd eat, talk, make love, and get their marriage back on track.

She checked her watch, 7:00, stirred the pot, opened the wine. Remy distracted herself for 15 minutes, unloading a too-hot dishwasher, rinsing the cutting boards, and wiping the splatters from the stove. Then she texted and sat staring at her phone. He was Adam, he was never good at keeping track of time. Getting mad wouldn't do any good. *Soon, finishing something up* came the reply. Remy checked that the stove was on the lowest temp and poured herself a glass of wine. She sat down on their sofa to wait, scrolling through pictures of her friends' happy, busy, Instagrammable lives. Minutes turned to an hour, then two. Remy refused to text again.

When Adam came home, he found her sitting in the dark with a dirty plate and an empty wine bottle. "Sorry," he said, flicking on the light. "I thought I'd finally found that glitch in the code, the one that's been causing all the problems. And Alex ordered pizza so I had a couple of slices—sorry, should have told you. You weren't waiting for me, were you?"

Remy looked at him, this familiar stranger. "Yes," she said. "I was."

Adam took a beer from the fridge. "Why were you sitting in the dark?"

"I've been thinking. This isn't working. Not for me."

Adam came into the living room and stood in front of her, exhaustion reflected in his sagging eyes. "Don't start this, Remy. I'm tired."

"I'm not starting anything, Adam."

"Oh, for God's sake, can't we talk about this some other time? I was late, I said I was sorry I missed dinner. What else do you want from me?"

"I want you, Adam. I want you back."

He sighed and pressed his lips together, looking at her. His cell phone buzzed. Adam pulled it out of his pocket. "Shit. Got to deal with this."

Remy ran her fingers over the nubby weave of the sofa. Adam's voice came from behind the closed bedroom door. Nothing would change. Either she was OK with this life, or not. Had Remy's anger found fuel, she and Adam could have fought. And then, at least, there would have been makeup sex. Finding only indifference, the flame turned against itself, picking up bits of Remy's ego to consume instead. For months her brain had been running in a negative loop: if she'd been more interesting, sexier, smarter; if she knew about computers and coding, about angel investors and beta testing, things would be different.

"I've decided to go to the Vineyard for a while," she said when Adam came out. As soon as the words came out, Remy knew it was the right thing to do.

"In February?" he asked. "Suit yourself."

And so, Remy left the shell of a near-sexless marriage, a dead-end job, and the feeling that she was living the wrong life. Adam hadn't even seemed to care when she didn't come back, which was probably what hurt most.

Abuse by neglect, Willow had called it.

But try as she might, Remy called it failure.

# CHAPTER 8

Struggling with the bags from Granite, Remy yanked open the backdoor of her house. In the kitchen, she sniffed the familiar and enticing scent of the sea. "Crab!" she exclaimed, spotting a cardboard box on the table. There, in a line, claws up and still warm, were seven large red steamed crabs. Remy picked up the note. *Hey Remy, happy to show you the cove where I found these big boys hiding. Give me a ring—Jake.*

Jake. Remy might not like him, but she wasn't about to turn down a mess of crabs. She took the note, crumpled it up, and tossed it into the trash next to a rotten onion. Picking up the biggest crab, Remy's mouth watered at the thought of crab hors d'oeuvres on Bremer wafers, crab salad on avocado, crab cakes with lemon-caper sauce, crab claw lollipops with cocktail sauce.... Sweet, white, firm—there was nothing better than crab, although freshly caught Katama bay scallops came in a close second.

"Oh, Grandma would have approved of you," Remy told the crustaceans, dumping them into the sink.

First, the prep: twist off the claws, prise off the apron shell (the Washington Monument on the males and the Great Pyramid on the females), pull off the big back shell. These Remy saved to be crushed and fed to the happy chickens for calcium. Next, a rinse under the faucet to remove the white worm-like guts and the yellowish mustard, always nasty. Next, she tore off the spongy lungs and cracked each crab in half. Newspapers, bowls, mallets to crack the claws, fresh coffee, WMVY on the radio: she was ready to go.

Everyone in the Litchfield family followed Grandma's rules. Your catch had to include at least six good-size jimmies (never the females) to be deemed worth the bother. And they should never, never ever, be cooked and eaten Chesapeake Bay-style for dinner. Grandma would set the table for picking only after the crabs had submitted to an angry, snapping, boiling death in the white-speckled black lobster pot and one night in the fridge. The morning light guaranteed that not a bit of crabmeat was overlooked, and the unsavory combination of coffee and shellfish ensured none was eaten en route to the bowl.

Remy fell into the Zen of picking. Unwillingly, her mind wandered back to Jake. Were the crabs some sort of apology? Willow was right. She was attracted to him. And she had let him get under her skin. It wasn't as if they had anything in common. He was a snooty professor, and she was a college dropout. Suddenly, Remy was back in her dorm room in Amherst, tears filling her eyes and blurring the computer screen before splashing onto the keyboard as she clicked "withdraw," "withdraw," "withdraw."

Remy drew in a deep breath and blew it out. It would've been a waste of time and money to have gone into debt to finish her degree. She did what any sensible person would have done. But with Jake, she felt like a dumb cluck.

Annoyed with herself for going down the Jake rabbit hole, Remy took it out on the claws, banging them hard with her mallet. The grainier, brown-speckled claw meat filled the paper towel-lined bowl to the top. Sucking on a tiny cut on her index finger, Remy sat back to admire the heap of crab. It was tempting, just this once, to keep it all for herself. But she knew that she'd just feel guilty; there was more than enough to share.

But who was deserving of crab? Her elderly neighbor, Betsy, would be ecstatic. Willow, for sure. None for Mike: he was allergic to shellfish. Maybe her little brother, Solly, if she could be sure his shipmates wouldn't get into it first.

Brushing the specks of shell from her shirt, Remy stretched and took out the water crackers and a lemon and mayo from the fridge. In her book, crab reached the pinnacle of perfection with the barest touch of lemony dressing and a few grinds of pepper. She mixed the dressing with the crabmeat and, eyes aglow, spooned the first glob onto a cracker and took a bite.

Perfect. Just perfect.

The alarm, set for 6:30, woke Remy from a dream: She had been searching for beach stones. Each stone she picked turned out to be an egg. As heavy as a rock but as fragile as an eggshell. She'd made a sling of her shirt to hold them, fearful that they'd fall and break. Then the path at the end of the beach grew farther and farther away (as it always does in dreams) as she trudged, arms tiring, with her delicate, heavy load. Willow would probably tell her that the dream was about her own eggs—no man, no marriage, the prospect of kids still far in the distance. But there was an easier interpretation: each precious egg-stone was an item on her client to-do list. But today, Remy vowed, she would tackle them all and then dance the night away at Mike's.

Ice packs had done the trick. Ada Queetie, no longer broody, followed Remy around the pen like a feathered lap dog, clucking for attention. "I'm glad you don't lay beach stones, beautiful girl," Remy told her, lifting the chubby chicken and stroking her soft feathers. Ada fluffed out her neck feathers and trilled. Remy put her down and tossed the shells from Jake's crabs. "Special treat, chooks!" Instantly, the hens perked up and dashed over to peck at the delicacy. "Thanks for the eggs, ladies," Remy called as she fastened the gate behind her.

The day sped by, and at last, Remy was at her final stop, Eli Wolff's. For better or worse, he'd been out when she'd returned to stock his kitchen after their disastrous first meeting. Remy parked, opened the 4Runner's back gate, and started to unload the shopping bags.

"Hey. Exactly who I was hoping to see," Eli Wolff called from across the field. "Beer delivery girl." He strode up to her, wearing a faded Yale T-shirt and carrying a pair of hedge loppers. "More of that IPA in there, I hope. I finished what you brought the other day."

"Yup, brought a case," Remy said. She'd forgotten to turn the dryer on, so today she was in the most unflattering of her preppy thrift-store concierge outfits, a pale lime green seersucker dress that zipped up the back and hung like a sack.

"The littleneck clams too? And the Veuve Clicquot?"

"Everything you said your friends wanted," Remy replied.

"Excellent. I like having a concierge." Eli put the loppers down on the stone wall. "Here, let me take that," he said and reached for the cooler.

"I've got it." She grabbed the handles, ignoring an annoying twinge under her shoulder blade. "It's my job. I'll be out of your way in a minute."

"No rush."

Remy had gone all out for Eli Wolff's weekend guests: a gorgeous arrival platter of local cheeses, prosciutto, grapes, nuts, and olives, all artfully arranged like a still life; no supermarket platters with cubes of orange cheese and sliced salami for Nest's clientele. Remy was stocking extra drinks in the pantry cabinet when Eli returned in a striped robe and swim trunks.

"Hard work," he said, pulling an IPA from the fridge. "I've been trying to reopen the path back to the other pond."

"I can hire someone to do that for you. No trouble at all."

"Ah, but it's what I do to relax. And now I'm ready for a beer and a swim." He popped off the cap and took a deep swig. "It's after 5:00. Care to join me?"

"Thanks, but I shouldn't," she replied.

"I think you should," Eli said. "I've asked you before, I might not ask again," he teased. "Your choice, freshwater pond or ocean." Eli leaned back against the counter, smiled, and crossed his arms, looking supremely confident of her answer. "Or both. It's lovely washing the salt off in the pond. I'd like the company," Eli added in a serious tone. "I've been here all week by myself."

Remy looked out the window. The blue water was sparkling invitingly, and she did have a swimsuit in the car. But swimming with the client? No question, most unprofessional. "I've still got a bunch of things to do here."

"Well, I'm going in. By the way, the new beach towels go in the changing room at the end of the barn."

"I'll take care of it," Remy said.

At last, she'd finished putting the groceries away, filling the fruit bowl, stocking the bar, and sorting the trash. Remy carried the new towels to the barn and, before stacking them onto the shelves, refolded them so the little lobsters all marched in the same direction. The stubborn, painful pinch beneath her shoulder blade was getting worse. A pinch of regret, too, that she'd never live a life of opulent leisure, in which her only worry would be whether her guests would prefer their littlenecks on the half shell or steamed with butter to go with their fancy champagne.

But Remy knew her place in the pecking order: she had her work to do, and work she would. The trash had been a mess. Eli Wolff hadn't thought to rinse out the containers before throwing them into the recycling bin, leaving it to her to scrub out yucky dried bits of food.

"Hand me one of those towels, would you?"

Remy spun around. That bare chest with all those muscles, only a few feet away. "Just one?" she asked, trying not to stare. "How was your swim?"

"Lovely," he replied. Remy winced as she reached for the towel at the top of the pile. "Is something wrong?"

"No, it's nothing. Just a knot in my back."

"Told you I would have carried that cooler in. Let me see if I can work it out." Remy backed into the towels as Eli took a step forward. "For God's sake, Remy. It hurts and it's not going away by itself. I don't bite." Remy took a deep breath and turned around. "Where?"

"Below my right shoulder blade," she said.

Eli's fingertips probed her back until they hit the spot. Remy winced again. "Found it. Why don't you go lie down on the chaise? I'll have you fixed in a minute."

"I'll be fine. I'll just take a hot shower and an Advil at home."

Eli raised his eyebrows in mock reprimand. "I can't have a concierge who can't carry my groceries," he said. "Come on. I insist."

Remy paused. Her back hurt, and if pleasing the client meant he'd get the knot out, it was a win-win. "Thanks," she said.

Remy followed Eli to a pair of cushioned chaises positioned in the grass, overlooking the pond and the sea beyond. Eli adjusted the chaise flat and patted the cushion. "Lie down," he said. "May I unzip your dress?" Remy nodded and stretched out on her stomach, stiffening as Eli pulled down the zipper and peeled away the sides. "I can't do anything if you tense up like that," he said. Remy closed her eyes, took a deep breath, and tried to relax. "That's better." Eli ran a hand over her skin, raising goosebumps, before seeking out the knot under her shoulder blade. Then delicious pain as he patiently unwound the muscle.

"I feel much better," Remy said. "Thank you."

"Your whole back is tight," Eli said. "You're just going to get another knot. Shall I keep going? I'm a very good masseur."

She should sit up and get back to work, but his fingers felt too good. Remy reached and unhooked her bra. "Yes, please."

"Smart girl." Starting with her neck and shoulders, Eli worked his way down to her lower back, vertebra by vertebra, his thumbs pressing against her spine, working tight muscles into welcome looseness. Then, time stopped, and there was nothing but the breeze, the soft lap of water, and strong, warm hands on her body.

"You have lovely skin," he said. Eli kneaded Remy's shoulder muscles one last time, then ran his hands down her whole back, stretching and smoothing her like soft warm taffy.

"Done," he announced, hooking her bra and zipping up her dress. "I'd say I've earned another beer. Don't you agree?"

Remy slid her eyes half open to see Eli grinning like the Cheshire cat. "Thank you."

"My pleasure," he said and walked away.

She lay in a daze, melted into the cushion—a puddle of satisfied and unexpectedly horny flesh. Eli's expert hands had pushed a button that had been set to "off" for a long time. Had he wanted to keep going lower, Remy wasn't sure she would have stopped him.

She rolled over and stared at the clouds glowing gold across the blue sky. Had Eli Wolff just tried to seduce her? Possibly, but unlikely. A guy like that would have a comparably spectacular girlfriend. Remy stretched her arms overhead and yawned. He could be gay, with his impeccable clothes and perfectly toned body. Or could be he was just being nice. She turned her head to watch the sun growing larger and redder as it neared the horizon. Remy yawned again and glanced at her watch.

Oh shit. Mike's party.

Seconds later, Remy burst through the kitchen door. "Can I take your tequila? And some ice?"

Eli stood at the counter slicing a loaf of bread, still bare-chested above his beach towel. "Of course. But where are you going? Thought I'd warm up some lasagna for us. I'm starving."

Remy was already at the bar pulling the bottle of Herradura from the liquor cabinet. "I'll replace it in the morning. I'm late for a party. I can't believe I forgot."

"It's a party, you can show up anytime," he said with a beguiling smile. "Stay a bit longer, eat with me, then go,"

"Sorry, I can't." Remy doubled a kitchen bag and started filling it with ice from the icemaker. "Oh, Mike's going to kill me. I was supposed to come early to help set up."

"I'm sure someone else took care of it," Eli said, "Make up an excuse. A client had you do something." He held up a bottle of Barolo. "I need you to open this bottle of wine. And help me drink it."

Remy paused, amazed to see herself turning down such an invitation from the gorgeous, obscenely rich man in the towel. But she was. "Rain check? I really have to go."

By the time Remy arrived at Mike's, the party was at full blast. She searched for the host in the swirl of plaid flannel and hippy ethnic prints, finally spotting Mike over by the food table.

"I'm really sorry, Mike, I got held up with a client," Remy explained. At least that wasn't a lie.

Mike dumped a bag of tortilla chips into a plastic bowl. "That's OK. Glad you made it." Even at his own party, Mike had a certain solid, lumber-like presence, which made his moves on the dance floor all the more surprising.

"I brought some ice anyway," Remy said, holding up the white garbage bag, "And my big cooler is in the car if you still need it."

"I don't. Just dump the ice in the tub over there with the beer. Jodi and Laura ran out and got a couple of bags earlier."

"Remy!" Remy turned around to see her high school friend, Della, moving in for a big squeezy hug. Unlike Remy, sassy Della, with her talent and magnetic personality, had found success even off the Island. Remy hadn't been able to help being a bit jealous when Della had won a full-tuition scholarship to attend Cooper Union, and she was even more so when Della landed a job in a high-end Soho gallery after graduation.

"Della! Welcome home."

Della pulled back and looked at Remy. "I love your outfit. I totally can't do ironic with this hair." She ran her hand along the shaved two inches above her nape; the front of her dyed-black hair swung straight and glossy in an Anna Wintour-style pageboy. "Rickrack!" she exclaimed happily. "And a bow! So retro."

On Remy's bed, seven miles away, sat the outfit she'd chosen for the party: a cute white sundress from her Austin bar hopping days and her favorite strappy sandals. Glowing faint lime in her concierge outfit under the party lights, Remy felt like a giant preppy glow-in-the-dark keychain. Perhaps not quite as unattractive as the one at home with the dead cicada embedded in Lucite, but close.

"Thanks," Remy said, biting off the explanation.

"And oooo, la-la, excellent tequila. Hey Mike, do you have shot glasses? It's time to get this party going!"

Two shots later, Remy was feeling much happier. She said hi to some friends then joined the group around Della, who was telling stories. "Oh, and let me tell you about this guy, this performance artist who keeps sneaking into the gallery with his transvestite puppets…"

"Hey, what did I miss?" Willow said, walking up with a platter piled high with golden-brown balls. "I was baking. I almost forgot I promised Mike my *pao de queijo*."

"Ooo, I'll take one of those," Della said. "Yum."

After passing the platter around, Willow pulled Remy aside. "You've had sex." Willow ran her eyes down Remy, pausing at a spot near the bow, then back up to Remy's face. "No. But a man's hands have been all over you. And you ran out of time to change."

"OK. The clothes are obvious. But how did you know about …?"

Willow interrupted. "Your aura, Remy. You know, like, you're a clear blue? But there's a second color tonight. Red. So either you've exchanged auras doing a healing, had sex, or something else. And the amount of red I see in your chakras." She looked Remy up and down again, pausing at the bow. "Especially your root chakra tells me which it was. Plus, you don't do healings. But you should, people need blue," she added.

Remy laughed and shook her head. She was starting to feel like a string of holiday lights, glowing red, green, and blue. "You're doing your Brazilian shaman thing again."

"No. That's totally different." Willow crossed her arms. "So, who was it? Fess up, Remy."

Remy hesitated, but she never kept secrets from Willow, and Willow never told. "My new client. You know, the guy with the captain's house." Willow raised her eyebrows. "I had this knot in my back, and he massaged it out."

"He's red, Remy. I get it. But that must have been some massage."

"Oh my, yes."

"I gotta pee. Come with me," Willow said, tugging at Remy's arm. "You can tell me about mister red hands and that massage."

"There really isn't much to tell, Wills," Remy said. The bathroom door was closed.

"Shit, a line," Della said, joining them. "Poor Mike. I just heard about him and Margaret."

"Yeah. Can't believe she ditched him for some bartender at the Black Cat." Willow knocked on the bathroom door and heard a faint "in a minute" in reply. "But don't worry. We'll get him dancing."

Remy nodded. "He'll find someone. Mike's a sweetie."

"Good guys are an endangered species. Or maybe I'm just not looking for them. My taste has changed," Della said with a wink. "You should see the guys I date." She laughed and took another sip of wine from her plastic cup, grimacing at the taste.

The door opened and a noticeably wasted but exceedingly happy Teddy appeared. "Remy, the stupendous Sherpa-girl! My marvelous milkmaid! And I'm not naked," Teddy pulled Remy into his arms, then added a big, soggy kiss on the lips. "You know who that was at my shroom stand? Oprah! She wanted my shiitakes and a hug!" He gave Remy an extra squeeze and bounce that lifted her to her toes. "She's the best hugger ever!" he added, "Present company excepted, of course! And Della! Where have you been, my love!" he said, releasing Remy to give Della the full teddy bear.

Remy shook her head and laughed. "Oprah. Dang! I thought I recognized her!" Remy said. Oprah was near the top of Remy's list of favorite Island celebrities, right along with Michelle Obama.

"We're hug buds!" Teddy hooted, spinning Della around. "Can you believe it? Me and Ooooh-prah!"

# CHAPTER 9

The party had gone past full swing and was heading toward sloppy when Jake showed up. Loud, crowded, and boozy wasn't his thing, but he'd promised to drive Teddy home. And Remy, the girl he couldn't stop thinking about, would be there.

Jake fished a Corona Light from the cooler and surveyed the crowd, mostly dancing except for wallflowers like him. There was his brother, now wearing a hat with pink pom-poms, dancing with Willow. And Remy, laughing as she pogoed to an '80s tune with a girl who had an odd haircut. The rest of the faces were unfamiliar, but Jake could guess what kind of friends Teddy hung around with: folks who farmed organic vegetables and worked in restaurants and repaired houses. Not that there was anything wrong with those jobs—Jake wasn't a snob—but it was a far cry from the career path expected of the Madden boys: top liberal arts college (Phi Beta Kappa and summa cum laude, of course), grad school, junior professor at a prestigious university, tenure. While Teddy would never starve (thanks to their grandparents' foresight and generosity), if Jake didn't do something, Teddy might as well paste a big L on his forehead. Teddy, the favorite, the disappointment, stumbling mostly stoned through life. But it wasn't too late.

Remy was different. Starting with much less, she'd had the gumption to launch her own concierge business. Small, to be sure, but Teddy had been telling him with awe about Remy's spreadsheets and checklists and how "Remy has her shit together, man. Her clients want like, a party for a hundred people with, I don't know, a sushi shark, and she does it." Jake knew the security of the stone-and-ivy walls of academia, its steady income and predictable, if somewhat stifling, life. It suited him. He'd get tenure, then gradually work his way up (as his parents had) to be head of his department and, eventually, maybe, dean. The idea of risking it all as an entrepreneur terrified him. But Remy's talents didn't stop there, according to his brother. She was an artist and a chef. And a chicken farmer and a handyman. According to his brother, Remy could do anything. And boy could she dance.

Jake wandered over to the table and grabbed a handful of tortilla chips, watching Remy spin and twirl, shimmy and bop. He couldn't figure her out. Down at the dock, that foggy morning, something had clicked between them. Something real. But at the farmer's market, Remy had been…not quite cold but closed. No boyfriend in the picture, according to his brother. In fact, the bouquet of boiled red crabs (Remy's favorite food) had been Teddy's idea. Jake had been daydreaming about taking her sailing on the pond, to Quansoo beach to swim and read books in the sun and to go for a sunset lobster dinner in Menemsha. And in each daydream, Remy was smiling and laughing the way she did that day down at the dock.

Jake caught Remy's eye and waved. She replied by throwing her arms up in the air and tossing her hair to the beat, looking at him all the while. As Remy relaxed her arms, the movement slid down, first to her shoulders and breasts, then to the long stretch and arch of her abdomen and back, finally in her hips, rotating and thrusting to the beat: sex, set to music. Jake couldn't take his eyes off of her.

At last, the song ended. Remy and the black-haired girl broke away from the dancing mob. Remy picked up a can of beer from the cooler, ran it over her forehead and neck, and leaned over to say something into the girl's ear.

Jake walked over. "Having fun?"

"You bet," Remy replied. Her eyes were bright from dancing and, perhaps, a few drinks. "Mike plays the best dance music."

"I'm Della," Della interrupted.

"Jake. I'm Teddy's brother," Jake introduced himself.

"Right, of course," Della said, with a loopy, drunken grin.

"Having fun?" Jake said to Remy.

"You already asked me that," Remy replied. "I am." She took a long swallow of beer and put the can on the table. "Oh my gosh, thank you so much for the crabs. I meant to write you a note." Her face glowed with pleasure. "They were amazing."

"You're welcome. Teddy said you wouldn't mind picking them yourself," Jake said.

"I didn't. Where did you find them?"

"I'll show you some time."

Remy smiled and gave Jake a little shimmy, then reached for his hand. "Come on, dance with me."

Jake hesitated. "No, thank you," he said.

"Yes, dance!" Della said and grabbed Jake's other hand.

Jake's feet stayed planted. He did not like to dance, never did. Not at parties, not at the dock dances in Edgartown his parents used to make him drive Teddy to, not at weddings. Not since he'd broken that poor girl's nose in high school with his elbow, releasing a torrent of blood and sending her to the hospital. He couldn't feel the beat, didn't know what to do with his arms and legs, and would not now, in front of Remy and her friends, embarrass himself.

"It really isn't my thing," Jake explained.

"Come on," Della urged. "This is a great song." She tugged, then released his hand. "Oh, don't be a poopy-head," she said, then turned to Remy. "Forget him, you and I can dance."

Remy stuck out her lower lip at Jake. "Your loss," she said and followed Della back out into the dancing crowd.

It was, Jake realized, his loss. A major one. But he'd explain, later. No girl wants a bloody nose.

The song had a Latin beat, and Remy's hips moved in complex, sensual patterns underneath her dress. Maybe he should, he could, just step forward and join her, move a little to the beat, keep his elbows safely at his side. She wanted to dance with him. How hard could it be? He started by bouncing his leg to the music, watching how the other guys danced. Step, shift weight, move the hips a bit. Arms would stay down. He didn't need to be a good dancer, just not conspicuously awful—or worse, injurious to others. Jake was on the verge of leaving his wallflower spot when Remy slid into the center of the throng and disappeared.

Jake waited, hoping she would reappear. He'd catch a glimpse of her from time to time, now dancing in perfect synchronicity with her arms around some guy who knew salsa or merengue, or whatever it was. Time passed, and the loud music, the boozy atmosphere, the late hour got to Jake. He'd come to the Island for peace and quiet, not this. He'd told Remy the truth: dancing wasn't his thing. The music shifted to rap, making things worse. She wasn't going to come back out, ask him to dance again. It was time to find his brother and go home.

# CHAPTER 10

Remy's cell buzzed. She opened her eyes and stared at the ceiling, disoriented and thick-headed, with a nasty headache, her frontal lobes throbbing. Memories of the evening came to her in flashcards: late-arriving bottles of cheap tequila, more shots. Ugh. Dancing with an even more plastered Della and good old Mike, the best dance partner on the Island. Early morning wobble with a silly, singing Willow down dark, empty streets to her house and crashing on the couch.

And Jake, arriving late. What a stuffy stick. "No, thank you," he'd said. Why had she even asked him to dance? Remy rolled over on her side and watched Willow's big old mutt chase rabbits in her sleep. It must have been that massage, loosening more than just her muscles. And the music. And, no doubt, the tequila shots. Remy rolled onto her back again. Willow was right, like him or not, Jake was hot. And unattached. And, being honest with herself, Remy had liked the way he had watched her. Remy had been sure that he wanted to dance. Or do more than dance. But instead, he'd rejected her with that snobby "no, thank you."

The words, suddenly, triggered an even worse flashback. Remy pulled the pillow over her face to block it out, but it was too late.

There she was on Quansoo beach, in her cutest bikini, age 18. It had been the summer after she'd returned from France with her chic clothes and her *pouvoir sexuel de la femme*. Despite Jean-Paul, her five-summer-long crush on Jake had come back. But that summer, she had vowed, would be different.

The scene was set. Jake had been reading Proust on the beach. The adorable French film *Amélie*—a perfect date movie—was playing in a retrospective foreign-film festival at the new movie house. She had planned and practiced her lines. It had been a beautiful sunny day, and Willow and Teddy had gone off to look for crabs. Remy had taken a dip in the ocean so that her yellow bikini would cling semi-transparently to her breasts and butt. She returned to her towel and lay down on her stomach, then propped herself up on her elbows, the ideal position for accentuating her assets. Remy glanced over at Jake. He had put his book aside and was staring at the ocean. "I've never understood the fuss about madeleines," Remy said casually as if the thought had just occurred to her. "When I was in Paris, I much preferred macarons," she added, pronouncing the names of both cookies in her best French accent. "You've read Proust?" he replied, and Remy shivered to find interested blue eyes sliding from her face to her cleavage. Remy's script had her anticipating the question. She tossed off what she hoped was a charming laugh. "Only a bit, in French," she replied truthfully, "but I much prefer French films." A seagull attracted Jake's attention, and Remy nearly lost her nerve. "Um, *Amélie* is playing. You want to go?" she blurted out. Jake picked up his book. "No, thank you," he replied.

Remy pulled Willow's throw pillow off her face, fresh mortification of the ten-year-old event coursing through her pain-filled head and already nauseated stomach as if it had just happened. Which, in a déjà vu kind of way, it had. Nose back in his Proust, Jake hadn't noticed how her face had turned deep red with embarrassment. With three words, he'd cracked her new Paris-shaped self and exposed her as a poseur, a fraud. Remy hadn't changed: she was still a dumb, gawky Island girl, his kid brother's beneath-notice friend.

Remy tried sitting up, but her swimming head convinced her that it was not a good idea. Jake was still the same supercilious intellectual as ever—too good for the party, too good to dance with her. She wanted to be home, in her pretty garden, feeding her sweet chickens, not here, waking stiff and pasty-mouthed in yesterday's ugly seersucker dress with a grade nine hangover.

Groaning, she rolled over and grabbed her cell from the coffee table. The first message was from her brother, Solly. *Hey sis, thanks for the crab! Got any more?* The next, from Eli Wolff. *I hope you had fun at your party. Got a special request after all. Forgot to put the smoothie ingredients on the list. Could you drop off some kale and blueberries—a couple of big packages of each? And hemp powder. Thanks.*

*On it! Be there soon,* she typed back and pushed send.

Like a request for another massage, the knot in her back pinged its return, thanks to the lumpy sofa. Remy took a long slug from the water bottle Willow had thoughtfully left for her on the coffee table. She rubbed her shoulders and neck, recalling the feel of Eli's hands, stroking her skin as she purred in the sun. He'd been so kind, offering to have her join him for a swim on his private beach, giving her that marvelous massage when he saw she was in pain. Then that gorgeous man offered to cook her dinner. And she'd turned him down.

Sitting up again, Remy rubbed her throbbing temples. But it was out of the question that someone like Eli Wolff would be interested in someone like her. Delusional, in fact. He'd just been lonely, all week by himself down that long dirt road. Eli would have his pick of stunningly beautiful, intelligent, successful, kale-smoothie-drinking women.

"Oh, oh, Eli Wolff," Remy groaned.

Willow's old mutt struggled to his feet and walked stiff-legged over to rest a gray muzzle on Remy's knee. "Oh, hi, Hendy. You heard wolf and thought I was talking to you, didn't you?" she asked, rubbing Hendy's soft ears. "You do look like you have some wolf in you, but I think it's German shepherd. Or maybe husky. What do you think?" Hendy gave a soft woof. "Both, huh? Well, I have to go grocery shopping for Eli Wolff. A client. A very hot client."

Remy finished her water, peed, and found Advil (thank God) in the medicine cabinet. She peered in at a snoring Willow sprawled face-down across the bed, then jotted a note. *Thanks,*

*Wills. Just like high school, huh. Wish me luck with my interview today! Talk later—got to go. R.*

Hemp powder, blueberries, and kale. And a replacement bottle of tequila, better not forget that. Remy blew out a long breath. It was time to go to work.

"Is that you, Remy?" Eli called from the porch. "Sorry to drag you all the way back here, but I had some paperwork to finish up this morning."

"No problem. I got your superfoods!" Remy replied, doing her best to fake a cheerful attitude. The shower at home had helped, but the morning traffic had been awful and the lines at the supermarket insanely long. The bone-jarring ride down Eli's road had nearly done her in, every pothole and dip in the road torturing her throbbing head and queasy stomach.

"Thanks. I can't get Aqsa out of bed without her kale smoothie."

Putting down the paper bag, Remy felt a pang. So there was a girlfriend, definitely fit and healthy. Also no doubt gorgeous and sophisticated with a closet full of designer clothes. Aqsa. She'd be an international news correspondent or the CEO of a global conglomerate. Something exotic and fascinating that had her jetting around the world. Eli Wolff wouldn't be needing his concierge's company for dinner. That was for sure.

"And I brought a special treat for you. Crab from Tisbury Great Pond. As a thank you," Remy called as she made space in the refrigerator. "I didn't catch them, but I did all the picking and made the salad. It's great with ripe avocado for lunch. And I brought you more eggs, farm fresh."

Eli had come inside. "So how was your party? It was quiet here after you left."

Remy was conscious of her rear end sticking out of the refrigerator. "It was fine—fun," she said, wiggling the vegetable drawer closed. "Lots of old friends, lots of dancing. Oh, thanks again for letting me take the tequila," she added, straightening up and closing the door.

Eli stood leaning on the counter with one of her eggs in his hand, dressed in a dark green polo that set off his blond hair and green eyes. Too good looking, really. He had the self-confidence of a man who knew the effect he had on women, and Remy wasn't immune. "Anytime." Eli held up her egg. "Such a beautiful blue," he said and looked at her.

It didn't seem to matter that he had a girlfriend. Remy still wobbled inside. It had, after all, been less than 24 hours since he'd unzipped her dress and given her that glorious massage. She took a deep breath. "They're from my flock. The chickens are free-range—you know, outdoors, eating bugs—so the yolks are superrich. They make great scrambled eggs. But they're so fresh the shell won't peel if you hard-boil them."

"I'll remember that, Remy," he said with a lift of an eyebrow. "And how is your back feeling today?"

"Much better," she said and bit her lip. Damn, that Aqsa was lucky.

"Good. Let me know if that knot comes back." Eli put the egg down and glanced at his watch—slender, elegant, and undoubtedly very expensive. "Well, time to get to the airport. Laurel is flying Mitchell and Arlene in."

Remy tucked the paper bag under her arm. "If there's anything else I can do for you and your guests, just let me know."

# CHAPTER 11

Remy sat at a quiet table in the corner of the outdoor café and looked for her potential client. Behind the Bookstore café was the prettiest coffee shop (in Remy's opinion) in pretty Edgartown, a town famous for its charming streets lined with graceful white clapboard houses behind tidy picket fences. At one time, a whaling town, Edgartown had one of the most adorable Main Streets anywhere, as well as the Island's best restaurants. Edgartown is where you summer if your last name ends with a III, your closet is full of Lilly Pulitzer and J. Crew, and your trust fund (you have one, of course) covers the rent on your loft and a few weeks in Aspen with enough left over for a new Land Rover.

She checked that the pale pink nail polish she'd applied hadn't smudged. At least it kept her from biting her nails. In her crisp meet-the-new-client outfit and with her marketing pitch memorized, Remy was ready.

Her phone beeped. *I'm here. Black dress, sunglasses.* Remy spotted her immediately: the woman looked way-too-Manhattan for the colorfully preppy scene. Remy walked up and extended her hand. "Mrs. von Spassky, I'm Remy Litchfield from Nest Concierge Services. I'm so pleased to meet you."

"Yes," the woman replied, looking Remy up and down. Without smiling, she allowed Remy to clasp her bony hand, then sat down. "Can you get me an espresso, please? They told me I had to stand in a line."

Remy pasted on an "anything to please the client" look before replying. "Yes, of course. Be right back."

When she returned, Mrs. von Spassky was typing furiously on her phone. Short, dark, and very New York, the woman looked like she'd applied her makeup with a paint-by-numbers kit. Color 3 there, to create the illusion of cheekbones, color 7 here, for the illusion of full lips. A heavy necklace of yellowish stones (citrine, perhaps?) lay around her neck like a lumpy jeweled collar, and Gucci sunglasses sat atop her head.

Finally, Mrs. von Spassky hit send and looked up with small, heavily mascaraed eyes. "I don't have much time. What services do you offer as a 'bespoke concierge' in Martha's Vineyard?"

Remy bit her tongue. It was always *on* Martha's Vineyard, but Remy was not about to correct the grammar of a potential client. Instead, she smiled and launched into her spiel. "Thank you for meeting me. I'm so excited to tell you about Nest," Remy began. "When you hire Nest, you are hiring 24-7, personalized attention to your every need. Our goal is to ensure that you, your family, and your guests have the best possible vacation while here *on* Martha's Vineyard." Remy pulled out a brochure and slid it across the table. "Most of my clients choose the elite package of services," Remy continued, "which includes…"

The woman put up her heavily ringed hand to stop Remy. "What are your credentials?"

Remy went blank. The woman sighed with impatience. "Your qualifications? To be a concierge?"

A small panic-rat clawed at Remy's bowels as she felt her face redden. Credentials? Qualifications? "Um, I have excellent references," she stammered.

"Oh. I was expecting you would have had something formal, a degree in hospitality from Cornell perhaps. No?" the woman said, picking up Remy's marketing materials and flipping through the pages with maroon-painted nails. "No hotel experience? No training?" she asked, tapping her manicured fingers on the table.

Remy didn't even know there *was* such a thing as a degree in hospitality. All she wanted was to flee the café and get away from that painted face and those hard eyes. She struggled to remember the lines from the marketing spiel she had practiced over and over, spin them into an answer, but her mind was a blank.

"No, but…".

"Oh." The woman tsked and let her attention drift around the café's garden.

A lightbulb came on. "I received my training in Paris," Remy said in a stronger voice. She touched the Hermès scarf knotted neatly around her neck. That was true. Madame Julie had trained her—and trained her very well.

Mrs. von Spassky raised one eyebrow. Remy had caught her interest. "Paris. And when was this—under the auspices of what organization?"

"Oh, it was some time ago. And not really with an organization per se," Remy said, pleased with her correct use of "per se" and wondered whether she should drop in a little French. "I was trained on how to choose wines, select the best produce and meats, as well as breads and cheeses, of course. We have some incredible local cheesemakers here on the Vineyard. And the Grey Barn bakes croissants every bit as good as the ones in France…"

"How many years ago?" The painted eyes narrowed.

Remy paused. "12."

"That would have made you, what, 16? 17?"

Remy's composure dissolved like sugar in a demitasse of café. "Yes."

Mrs. von Spassky's face wore a smug little smile. "Let me guess. You were an au pair." She tilted her head and tsked again. "You just woke up one day and decided that because you were once a teenage babysitter in Paris you could be a 'bespoke concierge.'"

Remy pressed her lips together. Dismay flashed to anger. "I am very good at providing concierge services. So yes. I woke up one day and decided to start my own business," she said, immediately regretting the snarky tone that had crept into her voice.

The woman put her hideous purse on the table, pushed her chair back, and stood. "Thank you. I'll be in touch."

Remy sucked in a breath. This interview had gone horribly, awfully wrong. In less than two minutes, the woman had crushed Remy's carefully built professional persona like a paper doll. But she wouldn't give the woman the satisfaction of knowing that.

She stood and put out her hand. "Thank you, Mrs. von Spassky. Despite my lack of formal credentials, I am sure I can provide excellent concierge services for you and your family," she said. "As a native Islander, I have the insider's edge and will do my very best to fulfill your every wish," she added from her marketing pitch. "Please take a look and feel free to call my references," Remy said in a stronger voice, holding out the marketing brochure for Nest. "As I said, you'll find that I come highly recommended."

The woman's cold fish-eye gaze could have frozen seawater, and the set of her mouth said she'd heard all she wanted to hear. "I'm sure you are. There aren't a lot of choices here."

Remy's mind spun as she watched the woman walk away with tight little clicks of her heels. Mrs. von Spassky wouldn't even take the brochure, read the glowing testimonial from the Hartwells, see the beautiful photos of gorgeously stocked refrigerators and perfectly set tables graced with voluptuous flower arrangements, or read the list of the 42 services offered by Nest.

Sinking back onto her chair, Remy put her head in her hands. Her face sagged with failure. The headache from her hangover came back with a vengeance. How could this have happened? She couldn't have been more prepared. But it had.

She stared at Mrs. Paint-by-Numbers-Makeup's untouched, high-price espresso *she* had paid for. Her options sucked. She could advertise, which would cost an arm and a leg. Or try picking up work from the vacation rental agencies. Which meant—*if* she got hired—doing everything: stocking the refrigerator and kitchen cabinets, checking that the beds had been made and rental bikes delivered, setting up the welcome platter, arranging the fruit bowl and the flowers in a one-and-a-half-hour turnover window, for a different client and a different house every week. The idea made her stomach hurt. Remy knew an Island concierge who was under contract with the agencies and did a fabulous job, but she had a whole team of people working for her.

And Remy had nothing, nothing but herself. And that wasn't good enough.

# CHAPTER 12

Jake slid back into his Vineyard life as if he'd never missed a summer. But for the closure of Chilmark Chocolates, very little had changed. Day-by-day, Jake revisited his favorite haunts, starting with Menemsha. The Island's tiny fishing village with its quaint fishing shacks was as picturesque as could be: the film crew from *Jaws* would still feel right at home. He gorged on not one but two lobster rolls (why decide between the hot roll of pure lobster drizzled with butter and the classic cold, meaty chunks of lobster mingled with creamy mayo, when he could have both?) with a chaser of decadent lobster bisque, eaten dockside on a cable spool table.

Today, he'd taken advantage of overcast skies to head into town. There was nothing like a real bookstore, he thought, for a satisfying morning's leisurely browsing: very literary Martha's Vineyard was fortunate enough to support two. Jake corrected his summer goals: *reading*, writing, and sailing. Cooking—he'd bought *Mastering the Art of French Cooking* on a whim—and eating as much seafood as he could. And a lot of beaching.

Jake's next stop would be Mad Martha's for an ice cream cone, then Murdick's for a pound of teeth-achingly sweet, creamy fudge to take home. (Jake was partial to the penuche, tasting like the love child of caramel, brown sugar, and sweetened condensed milk, while nutty Teddy was a rocky road fan. Then off to Granite to buy beach chairs and a new cooler that had not spent the winter as a mouse house. Jake shook his head. Like his brother had noticed that disgusting fact or that the chairs were collapsing from rust.

A tall, elegant blond hurried down the brick sidewalk past Edgartown Books. "Remy?" he called, walking down the bookstore's front steps. "Hey, wait up." Jake's day, already exceedingly satisfying, had just gotten better.

Remy stopped and turned around. "Hi," she replied, looking like it hurt to smile.

"You look nice," he said, checking her out from her sleek chignon to her practical and pretty vintage Ferragamo flats. "I almost didn't recognize you," he said. "You're all dressed up. I thought you were some rich Edgartown lady out shopping."

"I had a business meeting," Remy replied, pressing her lips together.

"Of course. My mistake," he said with admiring eyes. "Remy the CEO. I hope your meeting went well?"

"Fine," she replied in a voice that closed the subject.

Jake paused. Remy seemed, at best, too busy to chat. At worst, unhappy to run into him. "Some party the other night," he said. "I pretty much had to pour Teddy into the car to take him home."

"It was."

"Well, I've just had a very productive morning." He lifted his heavy bag. "Too many good books out this summer. The store manager had some great recommendations. What are you reading these days?"

"Right now, I'm not," Remy said and shifted the strap of her briefcase onto her shoulder.

"Really? Well, I can fix that." Jake set down the bag of books and poked through it. "Hold on, here's one you've got to read. Everybody is talking about it." He handed Remy a thick hardback. "You can give it back to me later. The author will be at the MV Book Festival—maybe we can go together?"

Remy glanced at the cover, then handed the book back. "Thank you, but I have plenty of books at home."

"Oh, sure. I understand." Jake tried to catch her eye, to see if there was any glimmer of warmth in the gray. There wasn't. But he saw another thing. "Is something wrong?"

Remy pressed her lips together as Jake waited, studying her face. "Yes," she admitted.

Jake put his hand on her sleeve. She looked down at his fingers. "Do you want to talk about it?"

Remy shook her head. "No. I don't. I really don't."

"OK. Ice cream then? Black raspberry, Mad Martha's? My treat."

Remy managed a faint smile. "I'd like that."

# CHAPTER 13

"This is Ada Queetie," Remy said, stroking the big hen's buttery soft feathers. "She rules the roost. And over there is Pondy Lilly and Teedla Toona." The Cinches had gone to Nantucket for the weekend, and Remy had learned that her job also included entertaining a sullen teen who (correctly) felt too old for a babysitter. But, for Remy, it meant extra money and as much time in the saddle as she wanted. Her early morning ride, a gallop on Rajah to the end of Far Beach while the girl slept in, had been marvelous, exhilarating, and almost made up for having to deal with 48 hours of teenage Morgan Cinch and her attitude.

Remy hadn't wanted to spend time with Jake Madden, yesterday or any day, yet there she'd been, sitting next to him on a bench overlooking Edgartown harbor, watching the tiny "On Time II" ferry make its way to and from Chappaquiddick Island as they licked their black-raspberry ice cream cones and chatted about the pond, his sailboat—everything except her disastrous meeting. She wasn't sure why she'd said yes, especially after he'd nearly (and obnoxiously) launched into a lecture on books she should read. But she had. And ice cream had been just the thing to make her feel better.

Morgan stood outside the fence, considering Remy's chickens. "Why did you give them such weird names?"

Enid Cinch had left Remy with strict instructions to "get her out of the house or all she'll do is eat. Take her shopping and make her buy some new clothes—whatever she wants. And be sure to get her some fresh air and exercise." And so, Remy had made a list of fun activities for the weekend, including a visit to the alpaca farm, and a shopping expedition to the Island's best (and out of Remy's price range) boutiques. But all she'd gotten out of Morgan was "whatever," "I don't care," or her specialty, the impressive eye roll, leaving Remy no option but to drag the girl around and hope for the best.

Remy laughed. "Have you heard of Nancy Luce? Her headstone is in the West Tisbury cemetery. It's the one with all the plastic chickens sitting around it."

Morgan sighed. "No."

Remy went on despite Morgan's clear lack of interest in the origins of the woman with a chicken-festooned headstone. "Nancy was the original Martha's Vineyard celebrity, back in the mid-1800s. Most people think she was just an eccentric old lady." When Remy put Ada down, she scuttled off in search of bugs to eat. "Nancy was obsessed with her chickens. When one of her favorite hens died, she'd write a sad poem about how wonderful the chicken had been and have it carved into a granite headstone."

Morgan raised her eyebrows. "Weird."

"But Nancy was a savvy entrepreneur. Back then, the tourists went by buggy to the Gay Head Cliffs. They'd stop to meet her and her chickens and visit the chicken graveyard. Nancy would sell them books of her poems and her photo as souvenirs. I'll show you my copy later." Remy loved the quirky portrait: Nancy's large, sad eyes peered out of her impossibly narrow, kerchief-framed face, two fat hens clutched to her breast, *American Gothic* with chickens.

"Right."

Remy could see it in her face: this was about to be the longest weekend of Morgan's life. She wrapped up her history lesson. "My friend Willow—you'll meet her later—thought it would be funny to name my chickens after Nancy's flock."

Morgan twisted a lock of hair. "OK."

"You ever held a chicken before? We can look for eggs. Tomorrow, I'll make you the best egg breakfast sandwich of your life."

The teen opened the gate. Despite the warm day, she wore shapeless gray sweatpants with a baggy oxford shirt. "Will they peck me?"

"Not usually. Sit on that stump and I'll get Ada. She likes to be held." Remy picked up the hen and brought her over. "OK, you want to be careful to keep her wings secure so she doesn't flap," Remy said, handing her the chicken. Ada murmured and fluffed before relaxing with a double-cluck into Morgan's lap.

Morgan's expression softened. "I think she likes me," she said, stroking the hen's back. Ada swiveled her head and fixed a black eye on the girl.

"You want to feed her a treat?"

Remy pulled a couple of dried mealworms out of a bag and gave them to Morgan, who made a yuck face as she fed them to Ada. The hen said thank you with a soft trilling sound. A brief smile broke through Morgan's overcast face when more chickens, attracted by the treats, ran over and clustered around her feet.

"Can I have more of those gross worm things?" Morgan asked. "I think the other chickens are hungry too."

"Sure," Remy said, handing her the bag. All the hens flocked to Morgan, clucking excitedly and tossing their floppy feathered caps.

"Oh, wow. Will you take my picture? No one's going to believe this."

"Sure."

Remy pulled out her cell and snapped away. "Why are they so funny looking?" Morgan asked.

"They're a fancy breed. Designer chickens—Crested Cream Legbars to be precise."

Morgan tossed a few more mealworms to her feathered fans. "I've never met a chicken before. They're pretty cool."

Remy sighed in relief. Maybe the weekend would be less painful than she expected. "I'm going to look for eggs. You can help if you want. Then I thought we'd go to the flea market if you don't mind. I have to drop off a few paintings. Unless there is something else you want to do?"

Morgan stroked Ada and fed her another mealworm. "Whatever."

"You know, when you asked me if I wanted to go to the flea, I thought of bedbugs," Della said, getting into the backseat. "Hi," she added to Morgan, who had retreated back into her cellphone bubble. "I'm Della."

"Hi," Morgan replied, not looking up.

"Morgan and I are hanging out this weekend," Remy explained. "Her parents are out of town." She glanced over at the teen who was frowning at her phone. "What made you think of bedbugs?"

"Oh! I had them in my apartment last month. It was disgusting. I had to send everything—everything—my clothes, sheets, pillows, you name it, to have the repulsive little things baked out of them."

"Baked? Is that what you do?" Remy exclaimed. "No fleas at the Chilmark Flea Market. Or bedbugs. Are you still in Brooklyn?"

"Yup. But I got a new place. Tiny little studio—160 square feet—but it's all mine. I was ready to move out of the hen house. Six women. What was I thinking?"

"I bet Willow's new place is even smaller. She's moving this weekend from her winter rental into her niece's playhouse back in the woods. She was supposed to be out in May, but she sweet-talked her landlord into letting her stay through June."

"Island shuffle," Della said. Rents on the Vineyard rocketed sky high in the summer; landlords hated to rent year-round when, in summer, they could make in two weeks what they could get for six months in winter.

"It's crazy. Her brother rents out his place and moves the family in with his in-laws, but the renters think the playhouse belongs to the neighbors. Her brother ran a power line out and got her a composting toilet. No Wi-Fi, no water either. But it's supercute, like an oversize dollhouse."

"Remember the summer Lauri worked at Alley's and lived in that nasty tennis shed? That was barely big enough for a bed."

Remy laughed. "Party central. We didn't care," she said and turned off North Road into a gorgeous boulder-laden field that housed the Chilmark Flea Market—part flea market, part artisans fair—eclectic, funky, and fun. Church volunteers directed them to a parking spot under a big beetlebung tree.

Remy took a crate of small paintings from the back of the car. "Come on, Morgan."

"OK," Morgan sighed. "I hate shopping."

Nevertheless, Morgan's eyes widened at the jumble of colors and textures at Willow's booth. Old kimonos and Peruvian weavings looked right at home next to Indonesian batiks, vivid Mexican rebozos, and French toile. Willow had sewn stiff fabrics into totes, beach bags, and broad-brimmed sunhats, and the more delicate fabrics into tunics (great as beach coverups), loose shirts, throw pillows, and drawstring bags. Scraps were transformed into Willow's crazy-world quilts that would cause a great-great-granny to faint with shock, African mud cloth picking up the colors of a Harris tweed, bright green and yellow Thai silk finding much in common with Ghanaian Kente cloth, the world pieced together into a harmonious comforting whole.

"Wow," Della said. "This is some great stuff."

"Pretty cool, huh," Remy said. "You can tell Willow went to Japan last winter," she added, pointing to a pile of bags made of repurposed obis.

"Those, I love," Della said, walking over.

Morgan wandered around taking pictures with her phone, then stopped to run a finger over a delicate paisley wrap in shades of soft violet and gray.

"That's very pretty," Remy said.

Morgan handed it to her. "Try it on,"

Remy wound the featherlight cashmere around her neck and shoulders. "What do you think?"

Morgan cocked her head. "Looks good on you."

Willow finished up with a customer then came over to Remy. "Busy day," she said. "Whoa, I see you've still got some red going there."

Remy ignored the comment. "I brought more paintings," she said as she reluctantly folded the lovely wrap and put it on the table.

"What red?" Della asked looking at Remy's flowered sundress.

"My aura," Remy said with a sigh. "What color is Della?" she asked to distract Willow.

"Really great orange—you know, like the sun just before it sets? It signifies energy, creativity, adventurousness. Lots of super-successful people are orange."

Della beamed. "I'll take that. Remy's red?"

"No, blue. Sky blue."

"You really see auras?" Morgan interrupted.

"Of course."

"What am I?"

Willow sucked her lip as she ran her eyes over the girl. "Wow…that's interesting."

"What," Morgan said impatiently.

"You're striped. Yellow—that's very positive, spiritual, playful—and black. That's not bad, it just means you're blocking something. Or depression, sometimes."

Morgan looked displeased. "My aura is a bumblebee."

"Excuse me!" came a piercing voice with a New York accent. A customer waved a beach bag in each hand at Willow. "Which of these would make a better house gift?" she demanded, apparently torn between bright floral and a Turkish stripe.

"Got to go," said Willow to her friends. "Take a look around—friends and family discount, guys."

Della motioned Remy over to the pile of bags. "I almost forgot to ask, Rem. Are you sleeping with Teddy?" Della whispered. "Oh hey, I like this one. What do you think?" She slung a black-and-silver-silk-obi tote over her shoulder.

"I love it with your hair. No, I'm not sleeping with Teddy. Why would you think that?"

"At the party, he said something about being naked with you. And you know what a dirty milkmaid is, don't you?" Remy's baffled expression set Della laughing. "I don't think I want to tell you, miss wholesome Island girl. Look it up if you want. Are you seeing anyone?"

Remy shook her head. "I'm off men this summer," she said. "Too busy with work and other stuff."

Della turned her attention back to the bags. "Me neither. I haven't given up sex of course. That's easy enough to find. Hey, I want to see your paintings. Let's hang them up. Where do they go?"

"Around here, on the side." Remy wrinkled her nose. She was sure Della would find her Island souvenir-style paintings amateurish and kitschy. "They're for the summer people. Not real art or anything," she apologized.

Nervously, Remy began rearranging the paintings to make space for the new ones. Della's eyes narrowed as she examined the small oils. "Nicely done—you've got talent," she said, her eyes still moving from painting to painting. "And the animal portraits are just charming. Look at this chicken," she said, pointing to a portrait of Ada Queetie with her feathers fluffed in a huff, glaring at the viewer. "She's got some attitude, that bird."

Remy let out a breath. "She does."

Della cocked her head and looked at Remy. "But I don't see anything of the artist here. These say, 'buy me, I'm cute.' Do you ever paint what you want to paint, not what you think will sell?"

"Not for ages." Remy took a sip from her water bottle, thinking. "Sometimes, when I'm just waking up, I'll start to see something, not a whole finished painting or anything."

"What do you see?"

"The whole wall is a canvas, and I start in the center…" Remy shook her head. "I can't describe it. There are these tendrils and…" Della squeezed her arm.

"Promise me you'll paint that this winter? When you have time? Go ahead and canvas the whole wall. I want to see what Remy-the-artist can do," she said with another squeeze. "And, in the meantime, I want to buy that one for my mother. She loves goats."

Remy smiled. "Thanks. I'll give you a discount." She looked for Morgan. "Do you want to ride back with me now or later with Willow? I've got to entertain the kid."

"I'll stick around. Do some shopping," Della said.

Morgan had made a stack of hats. "Which one do you think my mother would like me to get?" she asked with a sly look as she flopped a broad-brimmed Mexican rebozo-striped hat on her head. "This?" She switched to a Kente cloth one, "Or this?" Morgan picked up the third, made from a yellow and orange Kantha fabric, and tried it on. She looked at herself in the mirror. "Or this one?"

"Um, they're a bit...perhaps not her taste. Maybe we can find something when we're out in Edgartown tomorrow afternoon?"

"I hate my mother's stores. I kinda like all of these."

"I don't know, Morgan, your mother…"

"She told you to let me buy whatever I want," Morgan interrupted, in a perfect, unwitting imitation of her mother's demanding voice. The change from sullen-and-silent to sullen-and-snotty was not a positive development. "I'll take all three. And maybe some shirts and skirts too. And scarves. It'll be my new buzzy bumblebee look."

"Sure," Remy said, suspecting what Morgan was up to. "Willow has some really fun things. You can try them on if you want," Remy said, indicating the makeshift changing room.

Morgan pawed through Willow's wares to find the most garish colors and prints. The girl had some sass. But the bright fabrics were surprisingly flattering to Morgan's long chestnut hair and dark eyes. Mrs. Cinch would be appalled, which brought a hint of evil pleasure to Remy.

Remy waited as Morgan tried on clothes behind the curtain. Glancing around the flea market, she spotted a familiar blond man near the underwater photographer's booth. "Oh, damn," Remy said as she clapped Morgan's striped hat on her head and ducked into the back of the booth.

"What? Who'd you see?" Della asked, peering around at the mass of shoppers.

"A client. Right there, in the white polo, looking at the fish photos."

Willow and Della turned to look. Della let out a low wolf whistle. "Hoo-ee, I thought your clients were all fat nasty old investment bankers and their stuck-up wives," she said. Della turned to Morgan, now in a midi-length hot-pink-and-gold-sari-print sundress. "Sorry," Della said.

Morgan snorted. "Describes my parents."

"Why are you hiding?" Della asked Remy.

Remy and Willow passed a look. Della took a step out to get a better view. "Naw, Remy. Really? You told me 'no men' at the party, you liar," she teased. Della gave Eli a full top-to-bottom assessment, lingering where she found something particularly to her liking. Eli, sensing her eyes on him, looked over at Della and grinned.

"I like that dress," Remy said to Morgan in an attempt to change the subject.

"Me too," said Morgan, looking at herself again in the full-length mirror before slipping back behind the curtain.

"Look, he's getting pulled now by some skinny-ass girl down to where Sue has her jewelry," said Willow.

She peeked out to watch Eli's back retreating down past the row of booths. The tawny-skinned woman was model-gorgeous with sleek, nearly blue-black hair, and dazzling white teeth. This must be Aqsa of the kale smoothie.

"So. Are you going tell me what's going on?" Della demanded.

"He gave Remy a massage," Willow explained.

Two pink splotches reddened Remy's cheeks. "I had a knot in my back. I think that's his girlfriend."

"That's some client," Della said. She gave Remy a sideways look. "Massage, huh."

Morgan came out of the makeshift dressing room, added a sarong and the purple wrap to a huge pile of clothes, and handed them to Remy. "I'm ready," she said. "And I'm hungry."

# CHAPTER 14

Pizza was unlikely to be on the teen's diet but Remy didn't care. Morgan wanted pizza, not another salad. Besides, Remy was in the mood for a hot slice of gooey margherita herself. As always, the front porch of the Chilmark Store was full of pontificating geezers and sunburned families looking for an easy, kid-pleasing meal.

"Morgan, hold my spot. I'll be back in a sec," Remy said. "And keep an eye out for Amy Schumer. I saw her last time I was here."

"Sure," Morgan said, glued again to her phone.

After a short wait, Remy was back outside with two paper plates covered with oozing slices of hot pizza. "Psst, I think that's Alan Dershowitz sitting over there," she said, handing Morgan a plate.

"Who?" asked Morgan, looking up.

"Who is right," she chuckled. "But I saw Oprah at the farmer's market the other day. Well, I didn't recognize her, but it was her."

"My parents met Oprah over at the Obamas' new place on Edgartown Great Pond," Morgan said in a bored voice. "At some big party." She flopped the point of her pizza over the top and took a bite. "Mother says pizza makes my zits worse."

"She may be right."

"Well, I don't care," Morgan said, taking another bite. "I like pizza."

"Do you want to try a different beach today? Or if you want, we can go back and you can ride Rajah." Remy wiped pizza grease from her chin. "He's so gorgeous. You're a lucky girl."

"No. Not lucky." She looked down and kicked the dirt. "But yeah, Rajah's a beautiful horse."

"I keep meaning to bring back your jodhpurs. I found a pair online. Thank you for lending them to me."

"Don't bother. I don't need them. I don't ride anymore."

"Oh," Remy said, baffled. She chewed on her crust. Was Morgan punishing her mother by not riding Rajah? Or was Morgan being punished? Remy wouldn't put it past Enid Cinch to take the girl's horse away.

"Didn't mother tell you?" Morgan's eyes welled up, and she rubbed them with the back of her hand. "Shit."

"Do you want to talk about it?"

"No," Morgan stood up and dumped her paper plate into the trash can. "I don't. I'm going to buy ice cream."

Morgan came back with a container of Chubby Hubby and two spoons. "You won't tell her, will you? About the pizza, or the ice cream?"

"No," Remy said. "She'd blame me anyway." The girl still looked sad. Remy remembered her teen years, which were not the best, even without a horror show for a mother. "Besides, Chubby Hubby is my favorite. Thanks for getting two spoons." Remy folded over her empty plate. "The cut is open at Quansoo. That's fun. Let's go there."

Morgan dug a spoonful of ice cream and peanut butter-filled pretzel out of the container. "What's the cut?"

"It's a channel between Tisbury Great Pond and the ocean. They literally cut through the barrier beach to let the pond drain and get some saltwater in for the shellfish." Remy finished her drink. "The tide pulls you through, sort of like a lazy river ride at an amusement park."

"I don't go to amusement parks."

"Della and Willow are going. But we don't have to."

Morgan ate another bite of ice cream and handed the container over to Remy. The treat had seemed to restore her mood. "Sure," she said. "I'll go. I can wear my new bikini. Oh, and I need to give you your purple scarf thing."

"You bought that for me?"

"Mother's money. You liked it."

Remy was surprised and pleased. "I love it. Thank you."

After changing and collecting the beach gear, Remy and Morgan pulled up to the Madden house and parked. "We have to pick up the key," Remy explained. Nearly all the Vineyard's beaches were private, down long dirt roads behind locked gates; public access to the Island's beaches was a long-standing sore spot between locals and summer people. "Unless you'd rather kayak down? It's about two miles. I'm sure I can borrow Mary's extra boat."

Morgan made a face. "Two miles? No thank you," she said and opened the car door.

Teddy answered the door and ushered them inside, looking very 1970s in a Peter Frampton T-shirt and too-short gym shorts. "Your timing is perfect! I've hatched a wonderful new idea. Ted-tea!" He swept his hand toward the dining room table covered with jars of brownish liquid of varying shades and murkiness, some made even less appetizing by the bits of stuff floating in them.

"What kind of tea, Teddy?" Remy asked with some suspicion, remembering too well Teddy's carefree naked march through town.

"Reishi. Chinese medicinal mushroom. Powers up the immune system, fixes up your liver and pancreas. All kinds of good stuff." Teddy picked up a jar to examine it. "But it didn't taste very good, so I'm adding flavorings."

"Worth a try," Remy said. "Is it still OK to borrow the extra Quansoo key?"

"Yes, of course," said Teddy. "Gremlins had hidden it in the sugar bowl."

"Not gremlins, Ted," said a sleepy voice from the upstairs living room. Jake's head popped up over the rail from the upstairs living room. "Remy!" he exclaimed, eyes brightening.

"Hi," Remy said, surprised. "Oh, guys—this is Morgan."

"I'm Jake." He smiled and ran his fingers through his sleep-mussed hair. "You're welcome to the key. Or the boat."

Teddy clapped his hands together. "But first, the Ted-tea tasting!"

Jake chuckled, ready to watch the show. "Glad you found some guinea pigs, Teddy."

Teddy ignored his brother and pulled out a chair for Morgan. "Dear ladies, you must give me your honest assessment. I think these are going to be big sellers," he said.

"You got a spittoon there for them?" Jake asked.

"Skeptic," said Teddy. "This is product development." Remy joined Morgan at the table. "First, the ginger-turmeric version." Teddy poured a bit from one of the murky yellowish-brown jars into a juice glass. Morgan waited for Remy to take the first sip.

A loud meow came from the screen door. "Hey, Turk-kitty what have you been up to?" she asked as the cat pushed through the flap in the screen that served as a cat door. Turk jumped up onto the table, stepped around the glass of tea, and settled into Remy's lap.

"You are about his favorite person," Teddy said.

"Bluefish skin," said Jake.

Remy scratched Turk under the chin. "How did you know that?" His purr deepened to a deep, resonant vibration as if he were half motor, half cat.

"Teddy wouldn't let me throw out your Turk-treats," Jake replied.

Remy smiled up at Jake. "Ah. Well, I like him too. Chickens don't purr."

Teddy tapped on a glass with a spoon to get her attention, "Tea-testing-time. Try it, Remy."

Remy steeled herself to try the cloudy concoction. "OK, Teddy, I'll give it a go." With a deep breath, she took a sip. The flavor of the astringent, bitter liquid, made worse by the chalky texture of the powdered turmeric and ginger, nearly made her gag.

Teddy saw her wince, and his face fell. "Not good, huh?" A muffled chuckle came from Jake.

"A little harsh, Teddy. Maybe if you strain it and add some honey?"

Teddy brightened a bit. "That might work. How about this one?" He poured an inch of clear green-brown liquid from a jar into a second glass. "Green-tea version."

Remy looked at Morgan. It was her turn. The teen's face assumed a stoic expression as she lifted the glass to her lips. Remy watched her mouth pinch as she held back the impulse to spit the tea out. "It tastes...." Morgan paused and gave Teddy a weak smile. "Um. I'm sure it's good for me."

Crestfallen, Teddy rinsed out the glasses. "Shoot, I thought that one was a winner for sure. OK, one more." The last was the scariest of all, an opaque brown liquid, with chunks.

"Your turn, Remy," Morgan said, with a sly look. Remy braced herself and drank a tiny bit. The bitterness of the reishi mushroom was still evident but partially masked by the flavor of cocoa and some sweetness.

"I'm not sure I like this one either, Teddy. Sorry. But I think you're onto something with the chocolate." She thought for a moment. "How about you try grinding the dried mushrooms up and mixing them with dark chocolate, maybe some nuts or coconut or something, and make candies? You know, like edibles? It would be super easy."

Teddy's eyes brightened. "That's an idea! I was worried about lugging all these jars around. And dark chocolate is antioxidant too." He sat for a moment, eyes shining. "Choco-Teds, the healing treat." Teddy stood up. "Would anyone like some real tea?"

"Yes, please," Remy said, grateful for something to wash the taste out of her mouth.

"Me too," said Morgan. "With milk and lots of sugar."

"And I'll take a cup," said Jake from upstairs.

"Four teas, coming up," Teddy said. "Morgan, want to see a mushroom farm? I grow sprouts too!"

"Sure," Morgan said.

"Go ahead. I'll make the tea," Remy said, dislodging the cat. Her white gauze shirt looked like Turk had used it for a cat bed.

She filled the kettle and turned on the burner as Teddy and Morgan, trailed by Turk, walked to the old shed that housed Teddy's "farm." Then the sound of feet on the stairs and there was Jake, in a pair of loose drawstring shorts and a blue Tufts University T-shirt, filling the tiny galley kitchen.

"So how bad was that stuff?" he asked, leaning against the counter.

"Truly awful," she chuckled. "I don't know what Teddy was thinking."

The kettle whistled, and Remy took it off the heat. Having Jake so close was disconcerting, to say the least. "Be careful with that," he said. "You have to pour slowly when it's full. Sometimes the lid…"

Too late, the top rattled to the counter, sloshing scalding-hot water on Remy's hand. "Ow!" Remy exclaimed, dropping the kettle back on the stove.

"I'm so sorry, I should have warned you sooner. Did you burn yourself? Let me take a look," he said taking her hand. He bent to examine the reddening skin near her thumb, the area a science-nerd friend called the anatomical snuffbox. "You should get some ice on it."

"It'll be OK," she said, feeling a blush rise to her cheeks.

"Better safe than sorry." Jake opened the freezer and wrapped two ice cubes in a damp paper towel. "Here," he said, handing it to her. "Sit down and hold that on the burn. I'll make the tea. English or green?"

"English, please. With milk."

Jake brought their mugs to the table. "Thank you," he said, sitting down across her.

"For what?"

"For getting Teddy off the Ted-tea idea. I can deal with a dirty chocolate saucepan now and then."

"Oh," said Remy. "Sure."

Jake leaned forward. "Are you feeling better?"

Remy looked down at her hand. "It'll be fine."

"No, I meant since the other day. In Edgartown. You seemed upset."

She looked up into Jake's concerned eyes. "I'm OK now. I had just screwed up an interview with a new client. Apparently, I lack qualifications."

"That's ridiculous," Jake said. "Their loss, if they don't hire you."

"Well, they didn't."

"I think it's amazing, what you've done. Launching your own business. That takes guts and hard work."

Remy gave Jake a wry smile. "Got to make a living."

Jake smiled. "Don't sell yourself short." He reached out across the table. "Let's see how that hand is doing." He took off the damp ice pack, then lifted her hand out of the pool of melted water and held it in his, heat radiating from his palm.

"It feels better now," Remy said. "The ice helped."

Jake examined the burn. "No blistering," he said. Jake turned her hand over. Remy watched her fingers involuntarily open as Jake ran his fingertips down her fingers, resting for a moment tip-to-tip. Her breath caught. His touch was like an electric current, shooting in an instant to somewhere deep inside. Remy's fingers tingled, her heart raced, and she felt almost dizzy. As if she'd just stepped off the teacup ride at the fair.

"Remy…" Jake started and paused.

The screen door banged open. Turk the cat ran in, followed by Morgan holding up two baggies. "Hey look, I picked us mushrooms! Can we cook them for dinner tonight?"

# CHAPTER 15

The great blue heron stood statue-like across the cove. "He's my favorite," Teddy said, a spliff dangling from his lips like a cowboy in an old Marlboro ad. "I've named him Ptety."

"Petey?" Remy asked, walking out to join Teddy at the end of the floating dock.

"No, not Petey. Like one of those dinosaur birds, you know," Teddy said. "Pterodactyl," he explained, stretching out his arms and making flapping motions. The heron took flight, long legs trailing behind his six-foot wingspan, crawking his objection to being disturbed.

"Whoa," Teddy said as the bird settled back into the marsh further up the cove. "Way cool, Ptety. Totally prehistoric." Teddy flapped again and hooted at the bird. "Yo. Come back Ptety! I didn't mean to scare you."

"That tasted vile," Morgan whispered to Remy. "I thought I was going to spew. And when you took a sip of the brown one..."

Remy made a retching sound. Her spell, or fit, or whatever it was when she was with Jake in the kitchen, had passed. "I know, high payment for a trip to the beach," she whispered back. "But you'll like the boat ride. Nice of Teddy to offer to take us all."

"Hi guys," Willow waved as she walked up and added her beach bag and a cooler to the bow of the crummiest of the boats, a 12-foot aluminum skiff with wooden bench seats. "This is a great idea."

Della dropped in a pair of beach chairs. "I think I remember this boat."

"Yup old splinterbutt here still floats," Teddy said. "She's older than me, I think." He relit his joint and took a deep drag. "It's my happy-buzz weed. Perfect for a beach day. Any partakers?"

"Not us," said Remy. She turned to Morgan. "You won't tell your parents, will you?"

"Of course not," said Morgan, probably filing that little piece of potential blackmail away anyway.

Della took the joint, took a hit, and passed it to Willow. Teddy took a final drag then climbed into the skiff. "Remster, you want to run the boat? You're looking like our designated driver." He laid a towel across the bench seat in the bow and stretched out with a floatation cushion under his head.

"Nice and calm today," Teddy said. "Enjoy the ride, ladies."

The small boat skimmed along the surface of the pond, passing bucolic farms, fields, and discreetly hidden vacation homes. Della and Willow sat with matching grins, and Teddy lay with closed eyes and a beatific smile. "Wow, this is really fun," Morgan shouted over the noise of the motor.

"Glad you like it." Remy tut-tutted as a new Whaler with a 25-horsepower motor overtook the boat, leaving them rocking in its wake. New money, obviously. And either clueless about pond tradition and ban on motors over 10 horsepower or simply rude and selfish. Then she spotted the most egregious violator of the Tisbury Great Pond aesthetic, the pontoon "party boat" that motored about as if the pond was in tacky Miami, not Yankee Massachusetts.

"What's that thing?" Morgan asked.

"Crazy-looking, huh," Remy replied. "Showed up a couple of years ago."

They moved closer to the line of dunes toward a gap where the cut opened to the ocean. Various small vessels were scattered along the shoreline: other small skiffs, new-money Boston

Whalers, Sunfishes, kayaks, and even an old wooden oyster boat. Remy slowed the motor as she neared the barrier beach, guessing the channel lay where most of the boats were pulled up.

"Yo, Teddy, wake up. Let me know when it's getting shallow," Remy called. Teddy sat up, yawned, and leaned over the side. "Looking good so far." Remy held a steady course. "Wait, hold it, slow down. The channel's that way, I think," he said, pointing right. Remy adjusted their course. "No! Shit! Danger ahoy! Cut the motor!" he yelled.

Remy yanked the kill switch as the boat ground its hull into the sand bar. "Shoot. Teddy, can you walk us in from here?"

Teddy jumped out into knee-deep water and grabbed the bow rope as Remy pulled up the motor. Like a child tugging his toy boat, Teddy waded across the sandbars to the beach.

"Where do you want to sit?" Willow asked, pulling a beach chair out of the boat. A dozen or so groups of beachgoers dotted the sand. Families with small children sat along the pond where the shallow waters and catchable crabs kept the kids happy. Most groups chose the edge of the cut, while others spread out along the beach that stretched 20 miles from Katama to the east to Wequobsque Cliffs and Squibnocket Point to the west.

"How about there," said Della, pointing to a high spot located equidistant between the pond and the ocean. "We can watch the waves and look at the pond."

Teddy secured the anchor, and they lugged their chairs, bags, and coolers across the hot sand to the chosen spot. "Phew," Remy said, flopping onto her chair.

"Beer for me," said Della, opening the cooler. "I'm on vacation."

"Me too," added Teddy. He spread out a flowered beach towel and sat cross-legged facing the girls, oblivious to the immodest gap in the leg opening of his gym shorts. Remy raised her eyebrow at Morgan, who giggled before turning to look at the ocean instead.

Morgan stood up and took off the sarong covering her new batik bikini. "I'm going to go for a walk," she announced. The girl's left leg bore a long ugly scar on her thigh and three smaller ones around her knee. Remy bit down her questions, afraid of undoing their tentative could-be friendship. And she sensed the girl needed a friend.

"I collect scallop shells, if you find any," Willow said.

"Sure, I'll look."

Remy watched Morgan walk down to the ocean. The girl wasn't overweight so much as square, with a layer of baby fat which Remy recalled all too well from personal experience. Poor Morgan, stuck with Enid Cinch as a mother. It was that kind of situation that pushed girls into anorexia. She hoped Morgan would keep her sass, her new hippy-ish wardrobe—and appetite for pizza.

"Ah," sighed Della, lying back on her towel. "This is what I need. The Hamptons? Fire Island? Phfff!"

"You got that right," Willow agreed, slathering sunscreen on her face.

Della held out her hand, and Willow splooged a white glob onto her palm. "Remy, tell me about that guy you were hiding from at the flea market. Mr. Massage."

Teddy's ears perked up. "Who's Mr. Massage?"

Remy shot Willow and Della a stern look. "We don't need to talk about this—him—now," she said in a low voice.

"Aw, come on," insisted Willow. "The curiosity's killing me. You never called me back yesterday!" She patted Teddy's knee. "Teddy won't tell anyone, will you, Ted?"

Teddy drew a zipper finger across his mouth. "Secret's safe with me," he mumbled through closed lips. "Nap time." Flopping onto his back, he covered his face with his T-shirt.

"I brought popcorn. You want some?" Remy asked.

"Don't change the subject," Willow replied.

No use putting up a fight. Remy recounted the afternoon as objectively as she could. After adding a few details, including the skinny-dipping invite, neither Willow nor Della was convinced that the massage was just a massage or the woman Eli was with at the Flea was a girlfriend.

"I could tell," Della declared. "He was with her but not into her."

"If that gorgeous man lights your lamp, Remy, then have some fun. I mean, whoo hoo. Just be careful," said Willow.

"He does not light my lamp," Remy said. Her fingers still tingled disconcertingly. She looked down at the red spot on her hand. What had just happened, back there, with Jake? Maybe some nerve reaction from the burn—or a reaction to Teddy's medicinal mushroom concoctions? Whatever it was, it was weird.

"Good," said Della. "Mr. Massage may be way hot, and all that money don't hurt either, but it's a bad idea. You get a reputation for sleeping with the clients, you're going to be in trouble. What rich lady's going to hire a bed-hopping concierge?" Della reached into the cooler for another beer. "Best to keep business and bedroom separate. I was doing the gallery owner, just for fun—an older guy, but in awesome shape—until his wife found out. I almost lost my job. It sucked."

Willow shook her head. "Yeah, I could see that if he was married, but he's not. How'd anyone find out? He gives great massages, he's probably great in bed too. Remy hasn't been with a guy since..." She looked over at Remy.

"A long time," said Remy. "You know that."

"It's time," Willow said firmly. "You can't keep making excuses."

Willow and Della continued to argue the pros and cons, each growing surer that she was right, Remy would be making a giant mistake if she slept/didn't sleep with Eli. Morgan was walking back up to the group. This was a discussion she did not need to hear. "Morgan's back. Anyone ready to go into the cut?" Remy broke in.

Teddy opened one eye. "Yup," he said. "Ah am baked and ready."

The sky and water were interrupted only by a narrow horizontal band of beach and sand dunes, a single brushstroke across a blue canvas. Quansoo was, by far, Remy's favorite beach. Other beaches had dramatic cliffs or picturesque boulders, but the broad waters of Tisbury Great Pond on one side and ocean on the other gave Quansoo a spaciousness that sent Remy into beach bliss. And, when it was open, the cut.

"When the pond level gets high," Remy explained to Morgan. "They bring in a backhoe to dig a trench to the ocean." She described the wild 24-hour surge as the pond, dropping three feet, emptied into the sea before settling into nature's lazy-river version of a water park ride that shifted direction with each tide. "So, the salinity is restored, the shellfish are happy, and it's superfun for the kids. Us too."

Morgan tested the water with her foot.

"I wish Solly—he's my little brother—could be here. He loves the cut. He's eighteen—a lot younger than me. Really cute, too. Sorry for making you hang out with us geezers."

"That's OK. I like your friends."

"Maybe you can meet him sometime," Remy said as she waded knee-deep into the pond. "He's a deck hand on the *Shenandoah*—you know, one of the tall ships in Vineyard Haven?"

"Whee! I'm going in," Willow called as she ran past them and belly-flopped into the water with a giant splash. She rolled to float on her back and was dragged away.

"Me next," Morgan called, flinging herself in after Willow, followed by Remy and Teddy.

"Feet up," Willow called as she spun herself around. "It gets shallow here."

Remy's rear bumped along the bottom before the channel deepened again. A middle-aged woman with a beach bag over her head, attempting to wade across the cut, lost her footing in the deepest, fastest part of the channel and tipped sideways, arms flailing, into the water.

"Hope there wasn't a cell phone in there," Willow called before turning over to freestyle against the current, staying in one spot as if she were in a jetted lap pool.

Grinning, Morgan rolled like an otter. "We used to spend hours in the cut," Remy told Morgan. "My parents gave up trying to watch me. Said if I got taken out to sea, I'd have to get myself back in."

"And you had that Weimaraner in the doggie life jacket," Della said.

"Marta! She hated to swim, but she had to follow us in or else she went nuts."

It was like being a kid again. Remy spun lazily in a circle on her back looking at the sky as the sound of waves breaking grew louder. They climbed out where the cut had formed a sandbar in the surf, laughing and struggling for footing on the unstable delta. Running back up the beach, they flung themselves in for another ride.

Finally, sated and waterlogged, the group headed in. "Double-nap day for me. I earned it," Teddy said, stretching out on his towel.

"Doing what?" Willow asked.

"Ted-teas," Teddy replied. "A glorious, hopeful, inspired, experiment. The powerful health benefits of reishi mushrooms were to be transformed into a delicious beverage. I spent hours brewing, mixing, testing, Ah, you missed the tasting, sweet Willow."

"Lucky you," Remy whispered to Willow. "Sorry, Teddy, but that idea sort of laid an egg."

"Indeed, I nailed everything except delicious. But fear not, our brilliant Remy suggested a new idea. Mushroom chocolates!"

"Ew," Della said.

"Oh, ye of little faith. You will see. With Remy's help, they will be fabulous."

"I'll do my best, Teddy," Remy said from her towel.

Remy lay on her stomach, pulled her hat to shade her eyes, and wiggled the blanketed sand into comfortable indentations to fit her breasts. With the saltwater drying into a prickly crust on her skin, Remy soon fell asleep to the sounds of the waves and soothing chatter of her friends.

Buzzz buzzz. Buzzz buzzz. Remy reluctantly opened one sleepy eye and looked at her phone. Oh God. The Bottimores. *Remy, the outdoor showers aren't working. I called a plumber, but he can't come until next week. Everyone is so disappointed! Can you come and take a look? As soon as possible, please.*

The last thing Remy wanted to do was to leave this glorious beach to go to a client's house to spend 30 seconds turning a valve.

Remy texted back. *The water probably didn't get turned on after the winter. It's easy. Just go down the basement and call me and I'll walk you through it.* The reply was immediate. *I really don't think we can do that. Please come. We'll be waiting.* Remy sighed, feeling her mellow beach bliss slip away. *No problem, on my way, but it may take me a little while to get there.*

The gang had gone back into the cut, Willow and Teddy floating on their backs, linked together head to toe, Morgan doing her otter rolls while Della floated on a boat cushion. She hated to make them leave. Remy could take the boat back alone, but they'd be stranded here for who-knows-how-long.

"Hey Remy," came a voice from behind. "You guys had the right idea. Work can wait." Jake flopped down in the sand with a broad grin and eyes that matched the clear blue sky. "Great beach day, huh?"

"Oh, Jake, you're here." His arrival solved her problem. "Can I take your car and you go back in the boat?"

"Sure, no problem." Jake dug his fingers in the sand. "What's going on? I was hoping, um, we could take a beach walk?"

Remy shook her head and stood up. "No, I've got to run. It's a client thing. Have Morgan call me when you get back. And please tell everyone I'm sorry."

Jake's smile faded. "I drove Teddy's Mazda. Keys are under the mat on the driver's side."

Remy grabbed her coverup and flip-flops. "Thanks." She stood up. "I owe you a huge favor. I mean it."

Jake glanced up, then out at the waves. "Like I said. No problem."

Remy broke into a run down the beach, wondering about the odd look on Jake's face. He was probably trying to hide being pissed, and she didn't blame him for that: she had just taken his car and left him with the teenage girl she was supposed to be babysitting. But *whatever*, as Morgan would say.

A half-mile down the beach, Remy veered onto the path that led over the dunes to Crab Creek bridge and the Quansoo parking lot. She spotted the car right away, a dump-yard relic among the expensive SUVs. Not like when she was a kid and a Quansoo key, while never cheap, didn't cost as much as a college education.

The door of the ancient white jeep opened with a loud reluctant creak. The Maddens weren't into replacing anything—boats, cars—so long as it still ran. The Mazda had been bumping down the Island's roads for decades, gradually losing everything—power windows, odometer, hatch latch, fuel gauge—except a running motor. It was an old car when she was in high school, and now it was positively geriatric. Only one AM setting and it didn't pull in a station, so Remy settled in for the 20-minute dirt-road drive in silence, bouncing on shot shocks like a horse-drawn carriage and cursing the plumber who forgot to turn on the water in the Bottimore's outdoor showers.

# CHAPTER 16

Digging his fingers into the sand, Jake stared at the waves. Thoughts of Remy had become a near-constant distraction. He'd be working on his article, in the middle of capturing exactly the right thought, the right sentence, and there she would be, licking a purple drip of black raspberry ice cream from her cone before it ran onto her hand. Or he'd be reading *The Monist* or *The Philosophical Quarterly*, trying to figure what it was that got those articles—and not his—accepted for publication, and he'd be seeing her dancing again: the shimmy of her body moving down from her shoulders and breasts through her arched back and swaying hips.

But it had been earlier today, back in his house, listening as Remy gamely tested Teddy's vile mushroom concoctions, her kind, low voice steering Ted away from the tea idea without discouraging him, that Jake made up his mind. Then, that moment at the table, the current running through their fingertips. Jake was a grown man; he wasn't supposed to have crushes. But he had one now, and it was bad. It was time to stop being chicken and just ask her out.

"Yo bro, you came to the beach! What happened to Remy? You scare her off, ugly face?"

"Looks that way," Jake said with a frown. "She was napping but as soon as I got here, she said she had to leave. Some client thing." Jake looked out over the ocean; his hopes dashed. "Remy took the car. I'm with you guys in the boat," he said. "Let me know when you're ready to go."

# CHAPTER 17

Another pick-up-and-post Monday. Clients or guests—or both—would invariably forget something that they had to have sent to them *right away*. Glasses, prescription medicine (those she got). But for these people, a forgotten book or half-used tube of Glossier lipstick was an emergency as well. This time it was a kid's cell phone and a David Yurman bracelet, but, in Remy's mind, delivering Eli's fresh-from-the-oven coffee cake came first.

He'd called, late, surprising Remy. Not to complain, thank goodness. Eli had sounded lonely, maybe, and more than a little tipsy. "How about bringing me something unhealthy for breakfast—fresh donuts, perhaps?" he'd asked. "I need something hot and sweet and rich and bad for me. Too many kale smoothies."

"Anything else?"

"No," Eli said. "Just yourself."

"Hot and rich" described Eli. Bad, maybe, too. Remy could've picked up a pastry at Bolla's or donuts at Humphrey's, but her mother's crumb cake fit his request to a tee. It was pure morning decadence, a magnificently unhealthy concoction of refined white sugar, butter, eggs, and flour, crunchy and crumbly on top, with soft, not-quite-gooey cake underneath.

Remy pulled into the gravel parking area and carried the warm cake to the door. "Good morning," Remy called brightly.

Eli, in a terry-cloth robe, sat with a cup of coffee at the kitchen table. His blond hair was damp, and his face had the slightly dissolute look of a long weekend's partying. Remy knew, without knowing, that he was naked under his robe.

"Hi, Remy. I heard your car." Eli's smile was all creases and crinkles and a devilish glint in his eye. "Mmm, smells good. What did you bring me? Coffee cake? And the baker?"

"Crumb cake. My mother's recipe. About the best worst-thing-for-you there is."

"Perfect. You'll join me for a piece, won't you? And coffee? I made a pot. Or perhaps an espresso or cappuccino?" He motioned toward the red Ferrari-expensive Italian machine.

"Coffee—I'll get it. And I'd like to go over this week's plans if you have a minute."

"Of course."

Remy cut two big squares of the cake, half buttery sweet crumbs, half golden sponge, set them on plates, then poured her coffee and joined Eli at the table. He took a big bite of coffee cake. Crumbs bounced off of his bare chest and onto his lap. "This is delicious. Exactly what I was craving. A sweet morning treat and the company of my lovely baker-concierge."

Remy cut off a corner of the crumb cake with her fork. "Were your houseguests pleased with everything this weekend?"

"Very," said Eli. "Aqsa wanted to thank you for the crab salad."

"You didn't try it?"

"Nope. She spotted it right away, took a fork, and disappeared," he chuckled.

Remy's chest tightened with jealousy at the thought of the spectacular black-haired beauty devouring her crab. "Oh."

"How was your weekend?"

Remy couldn't imagine why Eli Wolff would be interested, but she gave him a quick and passably amusing recap of the Ted-tea experiment and Morgan's visit to the alpaca farm. "She's a nice girl under all that teen attitude. But I'm happy to be off duty."

"I imagine your boyfriend is happy to get you back too."

Remy shook her head. "No boyfriend."

"Perfect," he said, taking another bite. "You read my mind with the crumb cake. But I guess that is what a good concierge does—reads minds."

"I try," she said. "But it doesn't quite work that way. What would you like me to do for you this week? My goal is to 'fulfill your every vacation desire,'" Remy said, quoting from her brochure.

A half-smile. Remy was sure she saw a thought that wasn't Eli's shopping list cross his face. But he said, "Just two guests this weekend—some old friends from England. They arrive Friday. We'll want dinner reservations and a tee time. No kale this weekend," he smiled. "You've been doing a brilliant job, so I'll leave everything else up to you."

"Thank you."

Eli reached over to brush a crumb from her cheek. "Remy. You're named after the cognac?"

Remy felt herself blush. "No, my given name is Remember. I know. It's odd," she said, disconcerted by his closeness, that self-aware charm. "It's a Puritan virtue name. My brother got Resolved. He's Solly for short. My parents got all into genealogy. Mom's family came over on the Mayflower—there was a Remember on the ship," she babbled.

"Remember Litchfield?" Eli said. "I like it. And much more interesting than being named after a cognac. And how is your back? Any more knots?" Eli said, his green eyes catching hers.

Remy's heart went thump. "It's fine now, thanks."

Holding her eyes, Eli mashed some crumbs with a finger and licked them off.

Remy bit her lip. "I should go now."

"Why don't you come back later for a beer and a swim," Eli said and leaned forward, his robe opening to display beautifully sculpted pecs. "You won't regret it," he added, touching her hand.

Remy drew in a ragged breath. "Oh. Uh. I don't know," she stammered. "I'm really busy."

"Think about it. Off the clock, entirely your choice. I'll be here."

The angel and devil jumped on Remy's shoulders as soon as she was in the car. *He's a client,* whispered the angel in a prim British accent. *You made a promise this summer: work first. No time for men.* Then the devil's Cali-girl voice broke in. *Sure, but that was like before you knew that yummy Eli was going to be in the picture and on offer.* Remy was appalled that her imagination had assigned the roles to a tiny Sister Wendy (from the art history videos) and a bitty Kim Kardashian, breasts overflowing a low-cut red dress. It was like listening to Willow and Della argue on the beach. Only way weirder.

The argument intensified. *I know I sound like a mother hen, my dear, but it's fine to look, just like it's fine to admire a nude painting or sculpture. You know how I feel about Michelangelo's Adam up there on the ceiling of the Sistine Chapel. But not to touch!* Sister Wendy declared. *But he's so incredibly hot, anybody would want him, and you meant no relationships with men, not no* sex *with men. That's, like, a summer without water or food. No one can give that up—oh, sorry Sister, present company excepted.* Remy knew she shouldn't be taking advice from a Kardashian, but neither should she be putting much weight on Sister Wendy's views, given the nature of the question and the nun's decided lack of expertise in the area.

Remy, distracted, missed her turn, so she cut off the argument. *Be quiet, I'll decide later,* she told the two. Sister Wendy pursed thin lips over her buck teeth. Kim, sure she was winning, smiled, licked her top lip, and winked.

Remy stopped at her house to pick up a bikini, the cute one with the tropical print. Just in case.

# CHAPTER 18

Pulling around the circular drive, Remy stopped in front of one of West Chop's rambling, shingle-style summer homes. The door was opened by a stunning redhead in white pants and a flowy silk tunic. Suitcases were piled in the hall. "Hi, Mrs. Hutchinson. I'm Remy—I think Mrs…" Remy paused, she almost said Mrs. Bothermore. "Mrs. Bottimore called about my picking up Buckingham's phone,"

"Yes, of course. Come in," she said with a gracious wave. "I wish we didn't have to give eight-year-olds cell phones. All they do is lose them. But it isn't as if we have any choice! I've got it right here." She picked up the phone from the hall table. "Here you go."

"Thank you," Remy slipped the new-model iPhone into her bag. "Sorry for the trouble."

"No trouble. He left it on the Pier." The woman smiled at Remy with the most perfect white teeth she'd ever seen, a little terrifying in their brightness. "Can I offer you something to drink?"

"I'm fine, thank you." Remy bit down a surge of house-envy. The home displayed the expensively simple lines and driftwood shades of *the* Vineyard decorator, mixed with 19<sup>th</sup> century antiques and tasteful, summer-y tchotchkes. "You have a lovely home," Remy said, taking the opportunity to schmooze a potential client. "Allen Whiting is my favorite artist," she added, gesturing to the huge five-by-seven landscape commanding the entryway. "I recognize that from his last show. I'm so glad it found a good home."

Another flash of white. "Isn't it fabulous? I love how he captures the colors and the shapes of the Island. Oh, that sky. It just makes me happy!" She ignored the sound of boys fighting upstairs. "We're just leaving, but feel free to take a look around if you like. Such a beautiful afternoon, I hate to go. But lacrosse camp starts tomorrow. What can you do?"

"That's very kind of you, but I should be on my way," Remy said.

"Well, if you have a moment, at least go around back. I'm very proud of my gardens—a photographer from *Vineyard Style* magazine is coming next week. There's a path to the beach too," She glanced at her gold watch then walked over to the staircase. "John and George and James and William! Are you packed? We're going to miss our flight if we don't leave soon!"

In contrast to the home's quiet interior, the quarter-acre garden rolling from the house to the cliff was a riot of color and texture, Remy took her time strolling over the stone paths, pausing to admire a butterfly garden planted with clumps of scarlet bee balm and purple gayfeather, edged with a bold statement of magenta coneflowers and chartreuse pincushion zinnias. Hot-pink wild roses tumbled over low stone walls and a charming peaked wooden folly offered a spot to sit, admire the view, and watch the parade of ferries and boats passing in and out of Vineyard Haven harbor. It was the work of a talented master gardener, for sure. Remy doubted Mrs. Hutchinson, with her impeccable manicure, did more than clip a few flowers.

Remy opened the driftwood gate that led to steps down to the pebbled beach. West Chop, with its charming lighthouse, was one of the oldest, (now) wealthiest, and lowest-key of the Island's communities. Originally founded by educators, it had its own club (1889), inn, and casino (not the gambling but the WASPy social club kind), dining, tennis courts, and a host of rules, very much an insiders-only escape. It was, to the locals, a sort of retreat for literary royalty. Serfs, like Remy, got hired to do the cleaning and weeding and the fetching of iPhones.

She left her shoes at the bottom of the stairs to walk barefoot in the sand. A flat rock caught Remy's eye, reminding her that Enid Cinch wanted beach stones as place cards for an upcoming dinner party. Not just any beach stones, of course. Specs: 14; each flat and smooth enough to be written on; approximately four inches in length and no thicker than three-quarters of an inch. Mrs. Cinch was expecting them to come from her beach, but she wouldn't know the difference.

Or Remy could search for them over at Eli's. She imagined the two of them strolling hand-in-hand, laughing as they picked up stones ("how about this one?" he'd ask) before dissolving into a body-meld kiss with the waves lapping behind them, like a scene from a rom-com movie.

With a sigh, Remy sat down and hugged her knees. Why her, when Eli could have his pick of gorgeous, brilliant women? She chewed on a fingernail. Perhaps it was all in her head: the massage was only a massage; the invitation to come by for a swim and a beer no more than that. But it hadn't felt that way. Remy was sure he had more than a swim in mind. Like a fishing line tangled in a reel, Remy's thoughts spun themselves into a bigger and bigger mess. Was that what she wanted too?

Remy took a deep lungful of air and slowly released it. Resting her eyes on the water, she concentrated on breathing in-and-out, the mindfulness focus. The spinning thoughts slowed and an open, pleasant emptiness took their place. Remy noted, with the lovely detachment of meditation, an object in the offshore current moving, strangely, toward her. Her concentration broke. It was…a dog?

The sodden, shaggy beast found his footing on the shallow bottom, took a few steps onto the beach, shook the water from his heavy coat, and collapsed, panting, onto the pebbled shore.

Remy stood and ran over. "Where did you come from?" she asked. As Remy approached, the dog rolled his eyes but didn't move. "You're a tired soggy doggy," she said. "Let's see who you belong to."

The tag on the Burberry plaid collar read "Beaucoup" and a phone number. Remy fished out her cell and dialed. "Hi, this is Remy Litchfield. You don't know me, but I found Beaucoup. Is it OK if he's down here by himself, or should I bring him back to you?"

"The dog?" a woman replied, in one of those airy, high-pitched voices that irritated Remy. "You mean Bo-coop?" Remy winced at the mispronunciation. "The girls were supposed to have him. Can you just bring him here? I'm in the café."

"Which café?" Remy didn't think West Chop had a café unless there was one at the inn, and she was at least two miles from Vineyard Haven.

"I don't know. One of the upper decks?" she responded in an exasperated tone. "Is there more than one?"

Remy blinked. "You're on the ferry?"

"Of course, I'm on the ferry."

Airy-voice lady was in for a shock. "Bo-coop is perfectly fine," she said. "But he's not on the ferry. He's here on the beach with me at West Chop."

"That's impossible," the woman gasped. "It must be some other dog."

"No, it's Beaucoup. Bo-coop. He's got his collar on with the tag. Did you accidentally leave him behind? It looks like he went swimming and maybe got caught in the current."

Silence. Then Remy overhead childish voices. "Mommy, Mommy, guess who's on the ferry? Natalie and Charlotte! And they have two kittens in a kitty bag. We've been playing with them. They're soooo cute."

A clunk. The woman must have put the cell on the table "Where's Beaucoup, girls?"

"I don't know, he was barking and scaring the kittens so we tied him to the rail. But he's not there now. Can we get kittens?" asked a girl's voice.

A gasp. "Oh my God. Beaucoup must have jumped off the ferry."

A half-second later the girls began to wail, voices overlapping and growing louder as each tried to outcry the other. "Where's Beaucoup? Did he drown? Is he dead? Mommy, Mommy, where is he?"

Remy stared at her cell, fascinated. Beaucoup lifted his rear leg, universal dog language for "give me a belly rub." Remy complied and rubbed his wet, sandy fur.

"Girls, quiet down, he's fine." The wailing continued, if anything, at an even higher volume. The mother's reassurance had zero effect on her kids. Remy imagined the passengers watching the drama. Poor airy-voiced woman.

"Beaucooooppp," cried a girl. "Where is he, Mommy?"

"He tried to swim home. Please, please, be quiet," she begged. "I have to think about what to do."

Another voice broke in. "Are things all right, dear? Should I get the purser?"

"Yes, please," said the mother.

"Everything will be fine. We'll find your doggie. Girls, how about we get you a candy bar?"

"Thank you," the woman said, sounding shaky and grateful. "Whatever they want." Then she was back on her cell phone. "Hello? Are you still there? What do I do? I can't come back." She choked back a sob. "Can you keep him, take him to the vet, I don't know? Oh, I'm a horrible mother. I'm a horrible dog owner," she moaned.

Putting on her soothing client-management voice, Remy said, "Don't worry, he's a nice dog. I can take care of him for a few days, and I'll figure out how to get him back to you. It's no problem."

"Oh, could you?" she said. "The ferry is about to dock. We'll be back Friday, I hope. I'll pay you—whatever you want. But oh, dear God, what am I going to tell Tony?" she whimpered. "He'll be furious, blame me for this. I'll call you later. Here come the girls. Thank you, thank you!"

And so, Remy found herself with a new responsibility: a very large, wet, and sandy dog. She pursed her lips and blew out air. "OK, Beaucoup—Bo-coop. Can I just call you Coop? Like the bait and tackle shop?"

Finally recovering from his swim, Coop stood, peed on a pile of seaweed, and walked slowly down the beach. "Coop, come!" Remy called. He wheeled around and obediently trotted back. "OK. So you've got some training," she told him, patting his ears, "Good dog." Coop wagged his tail in reply.

The newest of the ferry fleet, the *M/V Woods Hole*, lumbered past, its sheer sides rising at least three stories up to the passenger deck. Remy looked at the ferry then the dog. How in the world could the dog have jumped from one of the big ferries? She bit her lip, thinking. Not from the passenger deck, someone would have seen him. But if he'd gotten down to the car deck, he might have jumped through one of the hawser holes.

"Is that how you did it, Coop?" The dog lifted his head at the sound of his name. "You didn't want to leave the Vineyard?" Coop gave a soft woof. "Yeah, I get it. I like it here too."

Then the dog spotted a flock of terns and loped down the beach. Coop suddenly stopped, sniffed, and rolled. "Oh no, Coop! Don't! Stop!" Remy yelled at a run. Coop paused, but *stop* wasn't *come*, so he kept rolling. Remy caught up to find a happy beast, and the squelched remains of a very dead, very odoriferous, bluefish. "Oh doggy, you didn't," she groaned. A dead fish presented a dog with a binary decision: eat it, or roll in it. Neither option had pretty outcomes. Coop's thick, shaggy caramel-colored fur had sucked up the fishiness like a cotton mop. Ka-ching, Remy added a $100 dog-grooming bill to airy-voiced lady's bill.

"I can't believe you did that," she said with a frown. "Well, I can. I just wish you hadn't." Coop's ears perked up, and he wagged his tail. He knew he smelled good. "Let's try to wash you off." Remy waved a stick of driftwood at Coop before throwing it out in the water, but the dog had no interest in another swim. "OK. Home with you. Then a dog bath." Coop's head slunk. "Oh, don't look that way. This is your fault, you know. Let's go. Coop, heel," she commanded.

With the dog at her side, Remy looked up at the bluff with another twinge of house envy, wondering which house was Coop's. Smug inside their generous porches, the sprawling, gray-shingled summer retreats sat catching the summer breezes. The woman on the phone sounded like a disaster, unable to deal with her screaming children and losing her dog. What had she done to deserve a place like that? Probably nothing; just lucky enough to be born into that stratum of privileged society in which nearly anything could be solved by money.

Remy took a deep breath and blew out the resentment. She might not have a multimillion-dollar vacation house, but she had a place to live that she loved, good friends, good health, and a good job; an open invitation to hop into bed with a very gorgeous man (probable); and a wet and smelly dog.

After an open-window drive home and a stop at SBS for kibble, Remy was setting up the hose for the dog-washing station when her cell rang. "I hope you plan to come by later?" asked Eli. "I thought after our swim, I might grill a steak, open that bottle of wine I tried to tempt you with the other night. Make an evening of it."

"Sorry, but I have to wash the dog."

"Is that like washing your hair?"

"Yes, only he's going to use up all the shampoo. Wait, no! That's not what I mean." Coop sniffed the garden, then started to lift his leg. "Stop, Coop! Don't pee on the zinnias!"

Remy dropped the phone to chase him. "Sorry, Eli. He's not my dog, but I have to keep him for a few days. He rolled in a dead bluefish on the beach, and he's got all this long fur—oh my God, you smell so bad…." She could hear Eli laughing.

"Wash your dog then. Why don't you come by tomorrow morning—and bring us some scones?"

Relief mixed with disappointment in an unsettling brew, like the vinegary kombucha Willow made. Remy couldn't avoid seeing Eli. A lot. If he was going to start in with daily breakfast requests. "Sure," she answered. "Bolla's has really good ones. 9:00?"

"Perfect. I'll see you then."

At least the dog-excused deferral bought her time. "OK, Coop. Time for your bath." Coop, well and truly hangdog, knew bad things were going to happen with the hose. He shook and sprayed Remy with water and soapy shampoo at every opportunity. It took three latherings with some old Pert shampoo before Coop was sufficiently destinkified to be allowed in the house. A few mats tugged at his skin, so after toweling him off, Remy made him a bed of some old towels and grabbed a small scissors and an old wide-tooth comb. Coop stared at her with adoring eyes as she carefully went through his long, wavy coat with her fingers and the comb, snipping out the small, painful tangles.

As Remy worked, she tried setting the pros and cons of sleeping with Eli on an imaginary scale. The pro side was small but heavy: he was sexy, gorgeous, rich, undoubtedly great in bed—and she liked him. And Remy knew that she really did have to "get back in the saddle," as the old expression went. Willow had talked her into two dates over the winter. The dinner with Jak, the fisherman, was OK-ish, but he smelled like squid. And then there was Duncan, the alpaca farmer. Two straight hours of hearing about his alpacas (their personalities, which ones had the best fleece, his breeding plans) was enough for her. Just as well. He found true love with Remy's favorite caterer, Felicia, who loved alpacas almost as much as she loved Duncan.

Willow said Remy was being too picky and chickenshit, that the divorce had given her not just cold feet but icebergs for feet. Still, sex-for-sex's sake held little appeal on an Island where you'd run into your hookup in the post office line and everyone was everyone else's ex.

Remy then put Della's comment about the risks to her professional reputation and her business on the other. It wasn't like she was a psychiatrist and she'd lose her license or anything, but Della was probably right, sleeping with Eli could ruin her business. The scales shifted. After all the hard work she'd put into Nest, it didn't make sense to risk it. Remy watched the balance tip—and made up her mind.

Finally done with the dog's coat, Remy turned on the outdoor shower, grabbed a towel, and undressed. The hot water and late sunshine beaming through the slats felt splendid. The Bottimores' urgent request to get their outdoor shower working made perfect sense: who would want to shower inside when they could bathe under a clear blue sky? As Remy soaped and scrubbed wet dog off her body with the rose petal bar, she felt her decision settle her mind: keeping the success of Nest her highest priority *was* the right choice.

Deliciously clean, Remy wrapped herself in a fluffy white towel and went upstairs to check her phone for messages. The Soulanskis were out of cold cuts, and Mrs. Bottimore wanted *a bag of decaf coffee beans, medium roast, Chilmark Coffee if they have it*, dropped off by 8:00 a.m. at the latest. After slipping into T-shirt and sweatpants, Remy picked up her tattered copy of *Pride and Prejudice* and carried it to the living room where Coop dozed on his makeshift dog bed.

"Guess you're my date tonight," she told him. "Jane Austen OK with you?" The dog's tail pounded the floor, and his lips went up in what Remy would swear was a smile. "OK. You are a sweetie," she said, bending down to rub his still-damp fur. "I bet your family is missing you like crazy."

Someone rapped on the front door. Coop gave a soft woof and stood up. "Coming," Remy called. A brown paper bag sat on the stoop. "Oh my," she gasped, pulling out a box. Inside rested a bottle of Rémy Martin XO cognac in its distinctive tufted-cushion crystal flask.

There was a note. *Remy for Remy—Eli.* Her first instinct was to return the gift. Remy bit her lip. She didn't want to offend Eli, and it wasn't like he couldn't afford it. Then she heard her mother's advice in her head. *The only proper response to a gift, no matter how cheap—or expensive—is thank you.* Remy smiled. Mom, in her Trader Fred's jeans, probably wasn't thinking about $150 bottles of booze.

The amber liquid caught a sunset ray of light. That decided it. She'd keep the present and have an evening of solo decadence, the prerogative of the single girl: crab, brie and crackers, strawberries—and cognac.

With a smile of anticipation, Remy chose a French chanson playlist (in honor of the XO) and a few candles for atmosphere.

She'd pick up a proper snifter, tulip-shaped, from the jumble of old glassware at Meg's booth at the flea market next week; a wine glass would do for now. Jake's precious crab went into a cut-glass bowl with a tiny spoon, the gooey brie was surrounded by crackers, and the strawberries sprinkled with a tiny bit of brown sugar.

Thus prepared, Remy sat on the sofa and poured the opulent liquor. She'd tasted the XO once before, in a Michelin two-star restaurant in Paris with her French family, where a cart of cognacs (both ancient and new) was trundled to the table after the meal. After much discussion and pursing of lips, having narrowed the options (in honor of Remy) to Rémy Martin, the sommelier subtly inclined his head to indicate that he would pour the lesser stuff (1738) for the young mademoiselle and the finer for Monsieur and Madam. She was allowed a sip of XO from Monsieur's glass, but only after having received instruction on how to warm the glass in her hand, swirl to admire the clarity and color and release the vapors, then sniff the nose—the heady floral and spice—in search of jam and vanilla. Only then, was Remy allowed to sip.

She cupped her hand over the top to mimic the capture of the fumes as she swished the exquisite liquid, admiring the color before raising the glass to her nose. "Ummm," she said. Velvety, decadent texture, figs, plum jam, a hint of candied orange peel, hazelnuts, toffee. She took another swirl, sniff, and sip, focusing on the floral, jasmine, and something else white... ripe honeysuckle, sweetness at the tip of her tongue.

Remy took another sip and the warmth spread from her core as Edith Piaf's husky voice crooned "*tant que l'amour…*" That was it, Remy giggled. Maybe she didn't need sex, she could just drink cognac instead.

# CHAPTER 19

Jake stared across Tisbury Great Pond, then reached again into his empty pocket. A futile gesture, his cell was home, safe and dry, on his dresser. He had no idea what made him think Teddy would remember to pick him up after he'd sailed the Sunfish down. Getting irritated (which he was) at his brother was not going to help. Still, Goddamn Teddy.

The steady breeze from the north that had made sailing out to the beach pure pleasure was still blowing. Down by the barrier beach, the pond stretched two miles wide, ruffled by the wind under a clear blue sky. Jake considered his options. Sailing back meant tacking against the wind the whole way back, which was fine until he hit the long, narrow cove above Flat Point Farm and defeated the purpose of leaving the Sunfish down at Quansoo. Walking or hitching the nearly three miles to his house held no appeal. Or he could wait, hoping that Teddy would eventually remember to pick him up.

Jake strolled along the pond shore to kill time. He'd give Teddy 20 more minutes, then decide. A big crab—male, Jake could tell from its dark claw tips (females were red)—scooted through the shallow water. Teddy, the 28-year-old man-child. Jake had taken over the shopping: there was nothing more irritating than making coffee and finding there was no milk. Jake fed the cat, emptied the dishwasher, and took the trash to the dump. Enabling, maybe, but nagging only aggravated Jake—and had zero effect on his brother. Teddy floated through life, mostly stoned, growing mushrooms and sprouts with no plan for the future. Something had to be done to get him back on track, but Jake had no idea what.

Not that Jake's own carefully planned life had gone as it was supposed to. He'd left the university to get away from Liz, his ex-girlfriend, gain some perspective, and build the best case he could for his tenure bid. Not that Jake had any real choice in the matter. He picked up a flat rock and skipped it across the surface of the water. Smart as Jake was, he didn't see it coming. So naïve, never suspecting that a viper hid inside, he'd been taken in by brilliant, sexy, captivating Liz. Tenure, which seemed a certainty, was now a possibility at best. His future loomed like a dark tunnel. And he didn't have a light.

Jake flopped down onto the sand and tried to shake off his gloom. The day was gorgeous, and there were worse places to be stuck waiting. He closed his eyes and listened to the sound of the ocean breaking behind the dunes as the sun warmed his eyelids. It had been a marvelous, relaxing sail down on the old Sunfish. The pond hadn't changed a bit. If anything, it was more beautiful than he'd remembered.

Jake heard a splash and opened his eyes. An osprey, broad-winged and magnificent, rose out of the water. A second glided in lazy circles in the blue, blue sky. Jake had always been fascinated by ospreys: the dramatic 60-foot dive before the last-minute reverse and, with pinpoint accuracy, the talons-first plunge into the water. The second osprey circled then flapped, hovering, before folding its wings in a head-first plummet, emerging victorious with a thrashing perch.

But as the bird struggled to gain altitude, a seagull zeroed in, intent on stealing the osprey's prize. "Yah," Jake jumped to his feet and yelled at the gull. "Catch your own fish."

The seagull dove again and the osprey lost his grip. "Stupid gull, you're as bad as Liz," he shouted as the fish dropped, still wiggling, back into the pond. Jake felt like the osprey, losing everything he'd worked so hard for.

"Why are you yelling at the seagull?" said a voice behind him. "And who's Liz?"

"Remy?" Jake said, turning around in surprise. He jumped to his feet. "What are you doing here?"

"Picking you up. Sorry, I'm late."

"You? Where's Teddy?"

"Oh, the gang decided to go to Philbin beach today. He asked me if I would get you around 3:00. So here I am. Remy's taxi service," she said, flashing a smile.

"I'm sorry. He shouldn't have asked you."

"No prob." She swept her hair back with her hand and looked over toward the ocean. "I'd hoped to get here early and take a swim." Remy slipped her shirt off her shoulder. "See, I even put my swimsuit on. But the Bottimores—those are my clients—decided that they needed salt-and-vinegar potato chips and another six-pack of beer for the beach *right away*. You should have seen the traffic in Edgartown, and the lines in the Stop & Shop were insane," Remy said, rolling her eyes. "So that shot that plan. Have you been trying to call Teddy?"

"Left the cell phone at home." Jake's mood lifted. Having Remy show up was a stiff, fresh breeze clearing away the dirty Chicago fog.

She wandered over to the sailboat. "You got the old Sunfish out after all."

"Took me a while to clean the crud off, put some varnish on the wood, but she's functional. Not going to win any beauty contests though."

"You did a nice job," Remy said as she examined the rudder. "Yup, a brass pin. Just like I remembered. Teddy said you were going to keep it down here instead of at the dock?"

"Saves having to tack in and out of the cove. I bought a trolling motor for *Utopia*."

"Good idea." A gust of wind lifted Remy's hair, reminding Jake of that first morning, down at the dock, when she was transformed by the dawn light into Botticelli's *Venus*. She reached up and twisted her hair into a loose knot.

"I'm in no hurry if you still want that swim." Jake glanced at the Sunfish. "Or—how about a sail?"

Remy frowned at her watch. "I should get back. I'm dog sitting. Though the thought is tempting. Nice breeze today."

A catamaran sped across the far side of the pond. Near the cut, a pair of kite surfers skimmed and flew as if defying the laws of gravity. Jake saw the longing in her eyes. "We don't have to go out for long."

"OK," Remy conceded with a grin. "Coop should be all right for a little longer. And I'm done with work for the day. Just a sec while I put my phone in the car."

Jake dragged the Sunfish back down to the water. Standing knee-deep in the pond, Remy and Jake set the rudder and daggerboard in place. Jake hoisted the sail, then clambered aboard and settled himself toward the bow.

"I'm sailing?" Remy asked as she climbed into the stern and grabbed the loose sheet.

"You forget how?"

Remy kicked at one of Jake's legs dangling in the cockpit. "No." She steadied the tiller and drew in two more feet of line. The boat began to heel as the wind filled the white-and-faded-red-striped sail. "Well, maybe," she teased as she leaned back to counterbalance the boat. "We might tip. You never know." Remy pulled in more line, and the sailboat accelerated.

The breeze and the girl blew away the last shreds of Jake's bad mood. He felt buoyant, hopeful. Happy. Jake leaned back on his elbows. "Having fun?"

"Yes!" Remy exclaimed. The boat heeled more sharply as they sped across the middle of the great pond. The wind turned Remy's blond hair into a gilded flag. Jake slid closer to help balance the boat. "I forgot how much fun sailing is! Let's go check out the Shackteau."

Remy changed course to the northeast and pulled the sail into a close reach as they raced across the pond. Their legs touched in the small cockpit, a casual intimacy. Hers were smooth, long, and tan with a little scar like a smiley face above one knee "Is the old place still there?" Jake asked.

"Yup, but Willow's family sold it to some bond trader or investment banker for a ton of money.... Whoa!" Remy exclaimed as the wind shifted direction and nearly capsized the boat. She adjusted the sail, and they picked up speed again.

"Who built a big house."

"Of course."

The sailboat neared the far shore below Deep Bottom Cove. "There it is," Remy said, pointing to the tiny Monopoly-house-shaped cottage nearly overhanging the pond. A Boston Whaler was tied to what looked like a new floating dock. "I was so lucky Willow's family had that place when we were growing up. It was a long dusty bike ride down there, but it was worth every bump." Remy turned into the wind. The sail flapped as the boat slowed. "Looks like they use the Shackteau as a boathouse now. But at least they didn't tear it down."

"Does Willow miss it?"

"Like crazy. Every summer."

"I used to be jealous of you and Willow, getting to live here year-round."

"And we were jealous of you and Teddy, living in Cambridge while we were stuck on a boring old island with no one around and nothing to do." Remy paused. "But now you're back. For the summer, at least."

Jake leaned back. "Maybe longer. We'll see."

Remy's eyes grew distant. "We used to have so much fun there. It was just a summer camp. No power, so they had kerosene lanterns and an old propane fridge to keep the milk cool. Over there," she pointed, "was the hammock and the horseshoe pit. Now look," she said, glaring at the trophy house sprawled across a golf-course-green lawn. "Jeez, who needs all that for their vacation?"

Jake shook his head. "Not me."

"Or me. I like your house," Remy said, handing Jake the line. "Right on the pond, simple, cozy, great view. I wish my parents hadn't sold our place and moved."

"Where'd they go?"

"The Keys. They run a B&B on Key Largo. Still an island. Lots of fishing, just warmer. Ready to head back?" The exhilaration of sailing had returned a smile to her face. "Let me see if I remember how to jibe. Watch your head."

Jake pulled in the sheet, but not fast enough. He ducked as the boom came swinging across the stern. Remy, with a devilish grin, stayed put, unbalancing the boat. The mast started to tip toward the water. Jake let go of the line but it was too late. They were going over and Remy was enjoying every minute of it.

She came up out of the water, sputtering and laughing. "Oopsy," Remy said. "Told you I wanted a swim."

"You did that on purpose," Jake spluttered.

"Maybe," she teased. "Payback. Now we're even."

"Payback for what?" Jake asked, grabbing a floatation cushion and pulling it under his chest.

The boat lay on its side with the sail rapidly filling with water. "Maybe I'll tell you sometime. Let's get her up before she turtles."

Remy swam off with strong, even strokes around to the hull, followed by Jake. In one swift motion, she reached up for the daggerboard sticking out from the hull and pulled herself up onto it. The counterweight should have begun to lift the sail out of the water, but it didn't.

"Jake, give me a hand here—she's not coming up." Remy dropping back down, hanging from the board. "You try."

Jake reached up on the other side. They dangled, faces inches apart, and locked eyes. "Well, are you going to try or what?" Remy asked.

For a brief moment, Jake thought she'd asked for a kiss. Which, were he not hanging from daggerboard in the middle of a pond, he might have tried.

Remy laughed. "Come on, Jake, get up there!"

Awkwardly, Jake hoisted his body up onto the board, feeling Remy's fingers against his side. Slowly at first, the sailboat began to right itself. But the Sunfish, as if it had a mind of its own, filled its sails with wind and began to sail away.

"Wait, come back," Jake called and started to swim after the boat.

"You're not going to catch it, Jake," Remy laughed. "The line got caught in the tiller. She'll circle back around."

As predicted, the Sunfish sailed in a lazy loop before heading into the wind and stalling in a luff. They swam up and clambered aboard. Remy resumed her position in the stern. Jake couldn't take his eyes off her. Remy's hair, dark and wet, stuck to her cheek and neck in sodden waves. And somehow, the wet shirt clinging to her body made her even sexier than if she had taken it off.

"I haven't tipped a Sunfish since, I don't know, I was 15 or something. Still fun, huh?"

The wet sail dripped cold pond water onto their heads. "Ready to head back?" she asked, putting her hand on the tiller.

"Can I trust you?"

The gray eyes were warm and open again, like that first morning at the dock. Remy pursed her lips as if considering, then leaned forward and kissed Jake. It was a kiss full of promise, the kind that made him want to sit cold and dripping wet in the middle of a pond on a sailboat forever. Then Remy broke it off with a smile and pulled in the line. The sail bellied with the wind.

"Of course, you can trust me," Remy said and set course back across the pond.

# CHAPTER 20

Thoughts of Jake and the kiss fled at the sound of high-pitched barking from inside Remy's house. She sucked air through her teeth. She should not have left flakey lady's dog for so long but there was the Bottimores' beer to buy and drop off, and then she was late picking up Jake.

"Oh no," she said, opening the door. "Oh, doggy. Oh jeez." Coop stood on his hind legs and put his paws on Remy's chest, staring into her face with anxious eyes and panting as if there were no air. "Down, boy," she said, pushing him to the floor. Remy surveyed her stress-dog-bombed living room: shredded pillows, stuffing everywhere, gnawed chair leg, and the barely recognizable remains of a flip-flop.

"What have you done? Bad dog," she scolded in a sharp voice. Coop knew mad, he knew "bad dog," and he knew what happened next. His anxiety turned to fear as he pulled his tail between his legs and groveled on the floor, looking up at Remy with the whites of his eyes.

Remorse quickly replaced anger. "Oh, Coop." Remy sat down on the floor and slowly stroked the dog. Coop, confused, tentatively wagged his tail. "I'm sorry. This is my fault. I bet you need to go out, don't you boy?"

Remy took the dog for a long walk, then sat on the floor and started shoving stuffing back into the cushions. Cute as Coop was, it was time for him to return to his family. Remy picked up another eviscerated cushion while Coop, hangdog, watched her every move.

She wasn't sure what had come over her like that, tipping the Sunfish. Had Jake been mad about getting dunked into the pond, the spell would have been broken. But he hadn't. If anything, he'd looked even more smitten, all wet like that. Remy leaned back with a cushion in her lap. She'd kissed Jake Madden on a Sunfish in the middle of Tisbury Great Pond. And she'd kiss him again.

Remy hugged the pillow, nearly giddy. After they had pulled the Sunfish up on the shore, Jake had stammered out an invitation to dinner.

Remy had a date with Jake, and she couldn't wait.

Coop woke up and stretched, then walked over to nose Remy awake. Warm breath and tickle of a whisker barely registered, but a cold nose in the nape of her neck did the trick. "Oh doggy," she said, "I almost forgot you were here." Coop had a new favorite person, and she was awake. Remy reached a hand out to rub his ears. His clean caramel-colored coat was soft and silky, like unraveled angora yarn. "I better see if Willow can dog-sit you today. I don't want you eating my pillows again."

Remy fixed herself a coffee and some toast and jam and poured kibble into a bowl. "You want to meet the chickens today? Then a walk?" she asked. Coop knew the word walk, and his tail swung back and forth like a windshield wiper. She attached the rope leash and picked up her egg basket. "Let's head to the coop, Coop," Remy smiled at her pun. It was nice having someone to talk to in the morning. "Then I have to get going on the stuff for the Cinches' dinner party."

The early morning was full of wonderful smells down at nose level. As they neared the pen, the dog glanced at the chickens and went back to sniffing bushes. The hens, however, went on high alert. Ada Queetie sounded the alarm, and the flock ran at top speed to the hen house.

Coop, now curious, put his nose up to the fence. This was too much for Ada Queetie. She gave a warning cackle and attacked, pecking Coop smartly on the nose. The dog yelped and hid behind Remy with his tail between his legs. Ada puffed with pride.

"I guess I don't need to worry about you," Remy said, reaching around to pat the dog's head. "You're sort of chicken around all these chickens, huh? The dog gave her a betrayed look as if Remy should have warned him that those feathered things were armed, then tugged on the rope leash to get as far away as possible.

"It's OK, ladies. He's not interested in you. Yes, I know he's a dog," she explained to an outraged Ada Queetie, who fluffed her feathers and glared at Remy and then the vanquished canine. "It's only for a few days. Don't worry."

# CHAPTER 21

The Chilmark Tavern was the sort of expensively casual restaurant Remy sent her clients to, but she'd never eaten there herself. It was buzzing despite the early dinner hour. An older crowd, wealthy in that understated, genteel Chilmark way. The women all looked like they had stepped out of an Eileen Fisher ad: no flash, just quiet, deep-pocket affluence. Remy hoped no one would guess that her dress had come from the locals' favorite "boutique," the Chicken Alley thrift store. But the soft blue dress flattered her hair and eyes, hugged her curves, and made her feel pretty.

A glance told the hostess Remy and Jake weren't "someones," and they were relegated to a table in the back, next to the kitchen door. Jake picked up the menu and gave a low whistle. "Maybe we just should have gone to the Black Dog or something," Remy said, equally appalled by the prices.

"No. I wanted to take you somewhere nice."

It was nice. The interior was spare but welcoming with white walls, tasteful art, real tablecloths, and a handsome bar where the bartender would mix a cocktail with your BYO bottle of booze in the dry town. "We'll split the bill," Remy said.

"Nope. I picked the restaurant, so I pay. Next time, you can," said Jake. "Or maybe I should cook for you. I made some amazing grilled scallops with beurre blanc the other night."

Next time. Remy liked the sound of that—and a guy who cooked French food. "Wow, I'm impressed. I wish that was on the menu." She looked at the prices of the entrées again. "You know, I'm not all that hungry tonight," she lied. "We could split something."

The waiter came by to take their orders, looking less than pleased when they ordered only a salad and the pasta entrée to share. "And can I bring you two wine glasses?" he said, raising one eyebrow at Jake's screw-top bottle of wine.

"Yes, please," Remy replied.

"I wonder if they'll still charge $14 corkage when there's no cork," Jake said after the waiter left.

"Cheaper than buying wine off a wine list."

"True." Jake smiled at Remy. "You look nice in that dress."

"Thank you," said Remy, smoothing the teal blue cotton over her thighs. "You clean up pretty good yourself." Jake's black hair still bore the comb marks from his shower and a tiny nick on his jaw showed where he'd cut himself shaving. Remy was tempted to run her finger along the smooth skin of his cheek.

The waiter brought the wine glasses, twisted the top off the wine, and poured. Jake raised his glass. "I'm celebrating tonight."

"What are you celebrating?"

"Finding a beautiful woman who'll go out to dinner with me. Even if she does have a bit of a mean streak."

"That doesn't sound good. What did she do?" Remy teased. It felt good to flirt.

"She went sailing with me one day and tipped the boat."

"That doesn't sound so mean. Maybe she was just testing to be sure you weren't a stiff old stuffed-shirt professor with no sense of humor."

Jake laughed and clinked glasses with Remy. "Touché. I take it I passed?"

"You did."

Jake leaned back in his chair, looking pleased. "So, what did you do today?"

"Oh, nothing," Remy said with mock modesty. "Just the set up for a *very* fancy catered dinner party for 12. They wanted it alfresco, under a tent, with a jazz trio."

"Impressive."

Remy leaned over and squeezed Jake's biceps. "Then I took the dog I'm taking care of to a friend, fed my chickens, and got ready for our dinner."

Jake broke off a piece of bread and buttered it. "You have chickens?"

"Yup. They were abandoned by some stupid summer people. Long story, but I ended up keeping them."

"I've never met a chicken."

"Ada Queetie—she's my favorite hen—is supersmart and as affectionate as any dog or cat." Jake raised a skeptical eyebrow. "Oh, don't look like that. I'm not making this up," she said firmly. "Scientific studies prove it. Plus, they lay eggs. Get a dog or a cat to do that."

"The only thing Turk's ever given me is a half-eaten mouse," Jake laughed. "How long are you dog-sitting?"

"Only until his owners get back." Remy recounted the tale of Coop's ferry adventure. "Even though he chewed up my house one time, I'll miss him. He's a sweet pup."

"That's an amazing story." Jake took a sip of wine. "You know, there's a pattern here. You rescue things. Teddy, the dog, your chickens. Me, from Quansoo."

Remy laughed. "I would hardly call those rescues."

"You know what I mean. I mean, most people would've just left the dog on the beach, figured he'd find his way home." Jake reached over for Remy's hand. This time there was no mistaking the pull, the course of electricity that flipped a switch, Madame Julie's *le pouvoir sexuel de la femme*. Remy gave a little shudder inside. Jake continued, "I've been thinking about you. A lot. That I'd like to spend more time with you."

Remy laughed, then saw the hurt expression on Jake's face. "I'm not laughing at you—I'm laughing at me. Do you have any idea how long I had a crush on you?"

Jake caressed Remy's fingers. "You did not."

"I did. I even asked you out." Jake's eyes widened. He didn't remember. "To a French movie—*Amélie*. You were reading Proust. On the beach."

"Proust." Jake shook his head. "Was I a jerk?"

"No. You were very polite. You said, 'No, thank you.'"

Jake chuckled. "I guess I was more than a bit oblivious." He turned her hand over and traced her palm, then looked into her eyes. Remy's breath caught. She was 16 again, losing her head over a guy. "I'd change my answer today."

Remy pulled her hand away and sipped her water to steady herself. Somehow, she'd gone from disliking Jake (and more than a little) to wanting to jump into bed with him. But, as Madame Julie had advised all those years ago, *life without men, without le sex, phfff, why bother. It is* un cadeau*, a gift, you should open it, enjoy it*. The evening was like a present. She leaned over and smiled.

"I've been doing all the talking. What about you? How did you spend your day?"

"My usual. I worked on my boat, wrote in the afternoon. Or tried to write. Napped. Read."

"Sounds pretty nice." Remy compared that to her frenzied day, a close call with a tent, then delivery of the wrong table linens, with Mrs. Cinch wound up tighter than an old golf ball.

The waiter brought their salad and an extra plate. "So, tell me about what you're writing," Remy said as she split the salad.

"I'd bore you."

"No, really." Remy frowned. "Unless you don't think I can follow."

Jake looked appalled. "No, not that. Not at all. It's…well. The problem is I'm stuck. I know what I'm looking for is out there, and I get close to capturing the idea, but it slips away."

"Like catching a crab," she teased.

"Yes, a bit. Perhaps that's my problem. I'm trying too hard."

"Um, you said your article was about utopian philosophy?" Remy asked, then immediately regretted it, knowing she wouldn't be able to hold up her end of a philosophical conversation. Maybe she could fake it, just let him talk, and she could nod as if she understood. Remy dug into the grilled Caesar with her fork.

"You remember," Jake said. "Right. I'm building off of one of the themes in Thomas More's *Utopia*—specifically, how the social shapes the natural world. Only with a modern slant." Remy waited for him to continue. "You really want to hear more?"

"Sure."

"OK. I'll give you an example. In More's book, the imaginary Utopians hatch their chickens in incubators so they imprint on humans. That's the social shaping the natural." Remy nodded. "*Utopia* was written before the industrial age, so I'm trying to reimagine how More would have envisioned Utopia if he'd written it today, especially the application of utopian principles to environmental and social issues."

"You always were kind of an egghead, Jake," Remy said half-teasing and glad she'd followed the conversation. Remy wasn't a snob but had always been drawn to smart people, people who liked to talk about ideas, not just shopping and TV shows.

"I know." A small smile crept across his face. "I think ideas—the right ideas—can take hold and…" He paused. "This sounds stupid."

"What?"

"Make the world a better place." Jake stared at the tablecloth. "I don't think I've ever actually said that out loud." He looked up at her. "But it's how I feel. My idea is to build on utopian principles but make them relevant—to counteract the feeling that things can only get worse."

Remy sucked on her upper lip, thinking. "So, if we can imagine Utopia, maybe we can figure out what to do to get closer to it?"

"Exactly." Jake grinned his gorgeous, heart-melting smile. "That's exactly it."

Remy glowed with the compliment. Maybe she'd just been intimidated by philosophy and some of it wasn't so hard. "We can use technology to benefit nature and the environment, not just harm it, right?" She tapped the stem of her glass. "You could use the egg-hatching thing?" she suggested. "That's an easy concept to grasp."

Jake nodded his head. "That's not a bad idea. Not bad at all."

Remy watched Jake thinking her idea over, nodding a bit to himself. "Publish or perish, as they say. Even if I get my ideas down on paper, I still have to submit, address the counter-arguments, revise, and resubmit. If I can get one article to the peer review stage, and another accepted, then I'll be back on track. For tenure. Maybe."

"Oh, I'm sure that'll happen."

"I wish I were sure." Jake stabbed his fork into the salad.

"Tenure's like a lifetime job, right—you can never be fired?"

"True. But no guarantee I'll get it. The process is very, very competitive. I need to be published in the right journals, get excellent reviews for my teaching." Jake's voice had taken on a somewhat lecturer-y tone. "And be backed by the right people in the department." He made a face that looked as if he were sipping vinegar instead of wine. "Politics. There's a lot of backstabbing. I was up for consideration then..." He shook his head.

"Then what?" Remy felt a twang. Maybe she and Jake would have a fun little summer romance, but by fall he'd be back in Chicago.

"I don't want to talk about it." Jake drank more wine and looked past Remy, suddenly morose. "But even with all that, what do I end up with? A couple of articles in an academic publication that no one reads, and a guaranteed job teaching a bunch of 18-year-olds who are taking Philosophy 101 only to fill their distribution requirements."

It was as if a gloomy black cloud had settled over the table. Remy didn't think tenure sounded bad at all: prestige and a fat lifetime salary in exchange for giving a couple of lectures a week at a fancy university, and the hardest thing he'd have to do would be to sit and grade papers at a big, antique desk looking out over the crenelated rooftops of his Ivy League castle. In fact, it sounded pretty great. "Well..."

Jake interrupted her. "And it's not like I'm a brilliant lecturer like my father or a ground-breaking researcher like my mother."

Remy had forgotten that Jake's father and mother were professors at Harvard and MIT, respectively. "So, it's not what you want."

He sipped his wine. "I thought I did. But now I'm not so sure. But I've come this far. What else can I do?"

Remy pursed her lips. "You write. Have you ever thought about writing a book? About your utopian ideas—make them less academic, more popular. Sort of like…" Remy struggled to remember the author of the book on the Bottimores' coffee table. "Like Malcolm Gladwell."

Jake gave a dry laugh. "Ha. If you think it's hard getting articles published in academic journals, try getting a book published."

Remy's hackles rose. "But you don't know if you don't try," she insisted. "Or you could try to get published in something else—the *New Yorker* or *The Economist*. Or do a podcast, or give a TED Talk. You could start a blog."

Jake shook his head.

The date had taken an unexpected and unpleasant turn. Here was Jake, with all his advantages, feeling sorry for himself. Remy wished she had the luxury to consider doing something other than making enough money to afford rent in the winter.

"And I thought I was the idealist." Jake shook his head again. "You don't understand. I've invested too much to go chasing fantasies. I have to keep going."

"OK, sure." That *you don't understand* rankled. What didn't she understand?

"But enough about me." He reached across the table for her hand, his fingertips setting off tingles again despite her irritation. "So, you moved to Austin after you graduated from college."

Remy stiffened. "I didn't graduate. I had one more semester to go."

"What happened?"

"Does it really matter?" She didn't want to go into her parents' ancient money troubles or the sore spot that was her unfinished degree.

"You can always finish, you know."

"With what time, and with what money, Jake?" Remy speared a crouton and it broke. She'd bet he never, ever, stared at a student loan payment and a power bill and wondered how in the world he'd pay both. "And why? What good would it do me now?"

"But you're so close. A college degree might open some doors for you. Don't you want to graduate?"

Remy was ready to change the subject. Maybe she was just being sensitive, but she couldn't help but assume a veiled criticism of her, both her academic failure and her job. "Of course, I do. But I can't. OK?"

Remy's cell buzzed.

"Don't answer it, Remy. It's Friday night. Whatever it is can wait," Jake said, lightly stroking her hand. "I'm sorry if I hit a nerve. I didn't mean to. Really. And you're right. I should think outside the box. Let's talk about something else. I was working on the rigging today. The catboat is nearly ready for her maiden voyage. I'd like you to go with me."

With that touch, Remy felt the pull, the tug of the body that overrode the thinking mind. Jake turned her hand over. Her breath caught as Jake ran his fingertips down rest tip-to-tip with hers.

The phone buzzed again. He slid a finger up along her wrist and looked into her eyes.

Remy hesitated. She didn't have to answer. Did she?

Another buzz. Reluctantly, Remy pulled her hand away and tapped on her phone. "Sorry. I have to check. It might be a client."

It was Enid Cinch. Remy's gut clenched. *Remy, the dinner is ruined and it is* all *your fault. I told you no soy sauce in the chicken. The caterer claims she never got the instruction.*

"Oh, shit," said Remy under her breath.

"What?"

"Dinner party disaster." *Don't worry*, she typed back, *I'll take care of it.*

*You had better. We'll be sitting down to eat in a few minutes.* Remy put her head in her hands. She had instructed the caterer, twice—once in writing, once on the phone—about the gluten and soy sauce issue. Not that it mattered now. No way could Eric come up with a replacement entrée just like that.

"Remy?" Jake said.

"I'm thinking," she snapped. Chicken, what was the chicken entrée on the Tavern's menu?

Remy physically grabbed their waiter. His offended look lifted when he heard her request. "No, there is no soy sauce or gluten in the Chicken Milanese. It is excellent. And yes, we can have a dozen portions ready for you in 15 minutes. Was there anything else you'd like to add to your order?"

"No, nothing. Just the check. Standard 20 percent gratuity, please." She pulled her credit card out and gave it to the waiter. "I'll bring my car around back to pick it up."

The waiter smiled as he took the card. "I'll put the order in right away."

"What was that?" Jake asked.

"Me, doing my job."

"What happened?"

"The chef I hired for the Cinches' party messed up."

"Can't they fix it? Isn't that what they are hired to do?"

Remy pressed her lips together. The flash of desire had been squelched by reality. Jake didn't get it. Maybe he didn't get anything. "No. The caterer can't fix it, not in time. And I can't afford to get fired."

"But it's their mistake, right? Not yours. You wouldn't get fired, I'm sure." Jake reached out for her hand.

Remy crossed her arms, taking her frustration out on Jake. "Sure, are you? I'm not. You screw up one lecture, what happens? Nothing. I screw up, I can lose a client and a quarter of my income, just like that."

"But we haven't even gotten our pasta yet."

"I know," she said. "I'm sure it will be delicious," she said with more snark than she intended.

"Remy…"

"Don't pressure me, Jake. I've got enough already."

Remy's mind was already racing ahead. If she loaded the chicken into the cooler and wrapped a blanket around it, it should still be hot when she arrived at the Cinches'. She'd better let the caterer know she was coming. Poor Eric must be frantic. Remy clenched her fists. She should have insisted that Felicia be hired, but Enid Cinch had insisted on Chef Eric.

"Sorry, but I have to go make some calls and wait for the order. You can get yourself home?"

Jake crossed his arms. "I'll call Teddy."

Remy knew she'd dodged a bullet, and by bare minutes. She'd texted Morgan to be on standby to help her and the caterer plate the chicken Milanese. The guests had dawdled over the first course, grilled local miniature summer squash served with a basil-and-olive tapenade, whipped lemon feta, and garlic oil rice cracker crostini. And the chef thankfully had concocted a parmesan crisp and baby tomato amuse-bouche to give the team more time for the switch.

Still, it took Remy half an hour that night to calm the chef and another 30 minutes the next day to mollify Enid Cinch. "Do you know who I had at that dinner? Bill Clinton. When I said no gluten, no soy, I meant it."

Remy knew better than to throw Eric under the bus. "I take full responsibility for the mistake. It won't happen again." Somewhat appeased, Mrs. Cinch had admitted that the substitute entrée was "quite good," and Remy went home with a dozen servings of soy-sauce-adulterated chicken fricassee.

And to think she'd nearly not answered the call. At least things were now clear. The last thing she needed was a boyfriend—especially one like Jake—in her life.

# CHAPTER 22

She was due at Eli's at 9:00 a.m., this time with croissants from the Grey Barn. Remy wasn't quite sure how people in a dairy farm and bakery in the middle of rural Massachusetts managed to produce croissants that rivaled the best she'd had in Paris, but they did. Remy brushed the crumbs of her chocolate croissant from her lap and licked the butter from her fingers, still tasting the warm flakes of the crispy pastry that blanketed the exquisite chocolate interior. Eli was sure to be pleased.

It was easier than expected to get Jake out of her head. She wrote him a nice message explaining that *it was now clear that her business had to come first this summer,* and *while he was a nice guy, she couldn't see things working out, but wished him the best.* Jake had wanted to meet, to explain, but Remy put him off. Besides, Eli Wolff was posing more of a distraction than Remy had expected. A bedtime glass of his exquisite cognac had prompted a shocking sex dream starring Eli and her hens' blue eggs so vivid that she woke panting and convinced that he'd done that—oh my God—first with the egg, that frisson of risk, then with his fingers and tongue.

And there he was. "Hey, you," Eli called from the door of the barn. "Right on time. I'm ready for a break."

Remy greeted him with a broad smile, reminding herself that *it was just a dream. He had* not *really done any of those things.* She handed him the bag of croissants. "A special treat today. Freshly baked croissants. I brought both chocolate and plain."

"Mmmm." Eli peered in the box, broke off a corner, and popped it into his mouth. "Marvelous," he said, reaching out to brush a crumb from her cheek. "But I guess you know that."

Remy reddened and dropped her eyes. "I ate mine in the car. And thank you so much for the Rémy Martin XO," she said with a passable French accent.

"*De rien.* It's nothing," he replied. "I'm glad you enjoyed it. I wasn't sure. I knew you liked beer," he teased.

She looked up. "Oh my gosh, yes. I love cognac. I had some again last night. It was phenomenal." Remy opened the tailgate of the 4Runner to pull out a set of recycling bins. "But I'm going to have to hide it from my friends. They might pour the cognac in orange juice or something."

A look of mock horror crossed Eli's face. "Hide it well then. It's a special gift for you. I've said it before, I like having a concierge. I want to keep her happy."

"Oh, it's hidden. Don't worry." Remy started to carry the plastic bins to the house. "These'll make it easier for the dump. We sort the recycling here. Paper in one bin, plastic, cans, and glass in another. I'll get going on your trash."

Eli rested his hand on her bare arm, his fingers slick with butter from the pastry. "I was about to take a walk. Join me—I've got something I'd like to show you." He grinned. "Or sort my trash. Your choice."

They walked toward the woods down a sunken granite-fence-post-lined road that was once the driveway to the house. Remy turned around to glance at the house, so lovely sitting on its bluff above the sea. A never-to-be-satisfied yearning, tinged with frank envy, rose in her chest. She'd probably never be able to buy a house on the Vineyard, let alone a place like Eli's. But at least she got to work there, even if it meant sorting the trash.

"Want to split the last croissant?" Eli asked.

"Sure."

Eli handed Remy her half of the pastry, mostly crust, keeping the soft inside for himself. At the edge of the woods, a trail opened through the trees. As Remy ate, crisp buttery flakes fell to the path like Hansel and Gretel's breadcrumbs. She thought of Jean-Paul, her first lover, and how he would feed her croissant morsels in his flat, licking the flakes that would drop between her breasts.

"I'm nearly finished clearing the path. You're the first person I've brought here," Eli said, interrupting her pleasant reverie.

"Where does it go?" Maybe the trail led to a pretty view or the ruins of an old farmhouse. Or perhaps to an erratic, one of the massive boulders, remnants of the Ice Age, that were scattered around the Island like a giant's marbles.

"You'll see."

The woods were thick with twisted white oaks, their lichen-covered trunks pale green through the leaves. Tumbled-down stone walls drew improbably straight lines through the trees. "It's hard to imagine this was once all bare sheep pasture," Remy said to Eli's back as she followed him down the trail.

"Hmm, yes," Eli said. "It wasn't just the views that convinced me to buy my house, it's the history too. I've been doing a lot of reading, all these lonely weekday nights. The Wampanoags, the whaling era, that sort of thing. At night, with the wind blowing, it's almost like going back in time. The house creaks like an old ship."

Remy shivered, imagining herself in one of the four-poster beds as a gale buffeted the Captain Abel house on its windswept point.

"Quite atmospheric," he continued, "though several of my friends deemed the old place haunted."

"Is it?"

"Who knows?" he responded with a wink. "Stay the night sometime and you can help me look for ghosts."

It was a tempting invitation in more ways than one. Remy couldn't help but run her eyes down Eli's perfect body. No harm in looking, after all. After a time, the trail began to rise steeply up a hill. "Is this still your property?" Remy asked.

"Yes. The past owners bought this piece from Carly Simon some years ago."

"You're So Vain" began on Remy's earworm playlist at the mention of the singer's name. "Oh. I forgot her place was near here." Remy tripped over a root and Eli put out a hand to steady her. Eli slowed but kept hold of her hand as they stepped over branches and logs.

"Watch out. I have more work to do on this stretch."

A few minutes later, a pond, a near-perfect circle, became visible through the trees. The path ended at a rickety wooden dock with a ladder at the end. A miniature cottage, like a fairy's house, sat at the edge of the water.

"Welcome to Thimble Pond," Eli said with a look of pride. "The purest water in the whole world. It bubbles up from the aquifer. No streams in, no streams out."

Remy stood next to Eli at the end of the dock and peered down. Aquatic grasses swayed in the crystalline water, steeply dropping to indigo depths. "I had no idea this was here. The water's so clear."

"It's a secret. Promise you won't tell?"

Remy nodded. "I'm good at keeping secrets."

"An admirable quality," Eli said. "So am I." He arched one eyebrow, unbuttoned his shirt, then slid off his shorts, then—oh my—his boxers. "Coming in?"

Naked, Eli's gorgeous body gave off the undeniable aura of sex. Remy had no idea if this was Eli's idea of seduction or he just really, really liked swimming in the nude. Either way, her breath quickened with a sudden surge of desire.

Eli gave her a sly smile then dove in with barely a splash. He popped to the surface with seal-slick hair. "Come on, you really should join me. The water is simply marvelous. You won't regret it."

The internal debate, cohosted by Sister Wendy and Kim K., picked up where it had left off. There, perched on a bench near the end of the dock, stood tiny Sister Wendy in her tidy nun's habit. Kim K., on the other end of the bench, unwrapped her sarong to expose a gold lamé bikini clinging to her hourglass curves. *Now, are you ready to have some fun for a change, Remy?* Kim wagged a French-manicured finger at Remy. *Why you went on that date with Professor Stuffypants, I'll never know. But here's your chance to hit the jackpot.* Kim raised an arched eyebrow. *Seriously, what more could you want?*

Sister Wendy pressed her lips together over her buck teeth and shook her head. *You know what's right, Remy,* she said in her prim British accent, then turned to watch Eli floating on his back in the water. Her eyes widened. *Oh my,* she whispered under her breath. *Yes, I do see how that would be tempting, dear. But as I said, it's fine to admire male beauty. But like art, no touching!*

Kim K. clapped her hands to get Remy's attention. *He's not art. He's a superhot guy.* She cast a longing glance over her shoulder at Eli. *I'd be in there in a flash if I could.* Kim put a hand on the swell of her hip and caught Remy's eye. *Opportunity is knocking, girlfriend. This isn't a* boyfriend*, this is sex! Take those clothes off and get yourself into the water. What are you waiting for?*

"What are you waiting for?" Eli echoed.

Maybe it was the egg dream, the memory of Jean-Paul and the croissant, Eli's magnetism, Kim's urging her, or pure impulse to feel that crystal-clear water on her skin. Remy didn't know—or care. She stepped out of her shoes, undid the zipper of her dress, and let it drop to the dock as Eli grinned like the Cheshire cat. In a second, Remy was naked and in the pond. The pure, soft water flowed against her body, priming every nerve ending.

Remy swam out to where Eli floated on his back. "I'll race you to the other side," she said. Eli reached the other shore first and stood up in the thigh-deep water, relaxed in a classic contrapposto pose. Sister Wendy was righter than she knew. Eli was Michelangelo's David in the flesh (and reduced from 17 feet to 6-2). Like the Dress David magnet set Remy had had on her dorm fridge, this David could never keep his pants on. Remy suppressed a giggle.

"Beat you," he said.

"Maybe this time."

Remy's breasts floated weightless in the clear water. It felt wonderful to do just what she wanted, which was skinny-dipping in Eli Wolff's pond. They swam back in silence. Reaching the other side, Remy could feel Eli's eyes on her as she climbed up the ladder.

"I have towels in the shack," he said, climbing up after her. "I can bring one out for you. Or do you want to go inside?" Eli reached over to push a wet tendril of hair from Remy's face, then ran the lightest of fingertips along her jaw. Goosebumps rose on Remy's wet skin. He was so close Remy felt the heat radiating from his skin. Her nipples tightened, and her breaths came fast and shallow. Eli bent and gave her a gentle kiss, then smiled. "No pressure, Remy. I like you. And as I said, I can keep a secret."

"Me too," she replied.

Dripping water, they walked to the deck of the tiny house. Eli opened the door with an ironic flourish, a wet, naked, and very horny doorman.

"Welcome to the love shack, Remy."

"What time is it?" Remy lifted her head with a start from Eli's shoulder, having slid into a blissful, postcoital nap in the narrow bed. Her leg and arm were sprawled over his body, and, embarrassingly, wet had pooled between the muscles of his shoulder. She had, like Turk the cat, apparently drooled in her sleep.

"Does it matter?" Eli replied. She wiped his shoulder dry with a corner of the sheet, then looked around. Earlier, she'd seen nothing but the naked man and the bed glowing white in its cotton chenille bedspread.

The room was simple and cozy, perfect for writing—or secret trysts. The walls were planked with cedar, and four windows, one on each side, let in the late morning light. An improvised kitchen was set against the far wall, a tiny wood stove against another, and old-fashioned oil lamps with wicks hung ship-style from gimbals. An acoustic guitar was propped up in one corner. Did Eli play? She knew so little about the man she had just slept with.

Remy stretched and yawned, then looked back at Eli. He regarded her with warm, satisfied eyes and ran his hand along the length of her side, dipping into her waist then out along her hip.

"Mmm," Remy said, practically purring. "I should get back," she added, sitting up. "Your recycling…"

"Can wait," Eli interrupted. He propped himself up to plant a soft kiss on the nape of her neck.

Remy felt his breath in her ear and shuddered. "But I also have to…" a half-moan escaped her as Eli, shifting position, started moving his lips down her spine.

"It can wait too," he said, his voice muffled into the small of her back.

A few inches lower and raw lust broke over her like an ocean wave, knocking her down and leaving her boiled in the outwash, gasping for air, powerless to get to her feet and leave. *I really should go* was Remy's last rational thought before she was swept back under the sea.

# CHAPTER 23

"Sorry I left you with Willow for so long," she called to Coop in the backseat. "I was, uh, sort of busy." Remy still felt the glow on her skin. No wonder Willow had been nagging her to, if not find a boyfriend, at least hook up once in a while. Adding Eli to her life made things more complicated, but she was nothing if not good at making schedules work.

Remy checked the directions. "You'll be happy to see your family again," she told the dog. A joyful reunion, Remy imagined, grateful owners thanking her for rescuing their dog, and the children delighted to see their beloved pet.

Remy pulled into a driveway off Iroquois Avenue in West Chop. The lovely, gray-shingled colonial sat on a tidy green lawn edged with blue hydrangeas. The waters of Vineyard Sound sparkled in the distance. "Home, buddy," Remy said to the dog, feeling a pang of pain. She'd miss having him around, but it was time for him to go back to his family.

Remy rang the bell with Coop at her side. The door was opened by a young blond girl, about six, Remy guessed. "Beau-coop's back," she screamed then slammed the door in Remy's face. Hardly the reaction Remy had expected. She knocked at the door again. Coop looked up at Remy with doggy-anxious eyes.

"You OK, there?" she asked the dog and rubbed his ears. "You don't look so happy to be home." After a few moments, the door was opened by a wisp of a woman with thin mousy hair. Giant diamond studs weighed down her tiny ears.

"Remy?" the woman asked as the blond girl and a second girl, the two clearly twins, pounded down the stairs yelling at Coop. "Bad dog, you ran away, and we got in trouble."

"Bad, bad dog," said the other, with a mean look in her eye. "We don't want you." Coop looked like he didn't want them either.

Remy ignored the girls. Putting out her hand, she smiled at the woman. "Hi, Mrs. Kemp. Is this a good time to drop Beaucoup off?"

"Audrey, please. Yes, this is fine," she said with a nervous look over her shoulder. "I'll get my checkbook. Has he behaved himself?"

"No trouble at all."

The woman looked skeptical. "I'll be right back," she said.

Remy turned her attention to the girls. "Beaucoup isn't a bad dog. He's a very good dog. Very well trained." A pair of matching blue eyes turned on her.

"No, he's not. He ran away. And Papa punished us." The girl reached out as if to smack the dog on the nose. Whimpering, Coop hid behind Remy.

"Yeah, we had no TV or computer. It's his fault," the other twin said in one of the nastiest tones Remy had ever heard from a child. Coop started to pull on his rope leash to return to Remy's car. Remy began to think he had the right idea. But he was their dog.

Audrey called inside the house, "Tony, dear, do you have the checkbook? The woman is here with Beaucoup."

A small heavyset man with a badly dyed comb-over came to the door followed by his wife. He barely glanced at Coop before fixing Remy with a glare. "Damn dog. What's this going to cost me?"

"Damn dog," the twins echoed in unison. "Papa, we don't want him anymore. We want a shit-poo." The two girls twined themselves around their father's legs. "Please, Papa," they wheedled, looking up at their father with big eyes and simpering smiles. The man shook them off and turned his attention back to Remy.

"I called around, and $80 a day seems to be the going rate. I had to groom him too—he had a lot of mats—so I was thinking $600 would be about right." The man muttered "fucking dog" under his breath as he got out his checkbook.

"Papa, we want a shit-poo," one of the twins started again.

"Shush, dear," her mother said gently. "We'll talk about dogs later."

"Shit-poo, shit-poo, we want a shit-poo," the girls started to chant in a singsong voice.

"Audrey, get the dog, tie him in back," the man ordered as he handed Remy the check. "Stop with that language, kids. You wanted a dog, and I got you a dog."

"Not this dog. We wanted a little dog, a shit-poo. Like Carol's," one girl insisted.

"You know, Smokey?" Audrey explained in a soft voice. "That cute white dog with the gray spot? The one with all the little coats?"

The twins started to chant, louder and louder, "Two shit-poos! Two shit-poos! A poo for you," they sang, pointing at each other, "And a poo for you!"

Remy was appalled.

"Girls, stop that please," Audrey said in a slightly stronger voice. "It's a breed of a dog, Tony, a cross between a Shih Tzu and a miniature poodle. They're quite nice dogs."

"I'll shit-poo you, Goddamn it!" Tony Kemp yelled. He'd balled his fists, and his beefy face was red. Remy could see he was going to blow. "Audrey, I said get the dog. Girls, shut the fuck up!" The twins immediately quieted, looked at each other, and ran back inside. "Those children are a pair of brats. I'm not sure I've ever seen a worse mother."

Stunned, Remy handed Audrey the rope leash. Coop dropped to the ground, a dead weight, and looked at Remy with pleading eyes. The next thing she knew, the man had grabbed Coop by the collar and dragged him to his feet. Coop, to Remy's shock, bared his teeth and growled. The man hit the dog, hard, across his snout, and Coop yelped in pain.

"Stupid what do they call it, positive reinforcement? You hit a bad dog; he learns who's boss." Tony let go of the collar and Coop dropped again to the ground with his tail between his legs, eyes begging Remy. Before Remy could say anything, the ugly, angry man had landed a firm kick into the groveling dog's belly. Coop yelped, stood up, and made a dash for Remy's truck, pulling the rope out of the woman's hands. With a flying leap, he scrabbled his way through the open backdoor window.

Remy's shock turned to fury. "I think he'd be better off at the animal shelter." She could barely control her voice.

"Keep the fucking dog," the man yelled at Remy, then turned on his wife. "A dog was your idea. You can't take care of your own kids. Why did I think you could take care of a fucking dog?"

Audrey cowered, appearing to shrink from a size 2 to a size 0 as her husband ranted and raved, his voice growing louder and more ferocious as he worked himself into a full-blown tirade. Without a word, Remy dropped the check on the ground, walked back to the car, and, trembling, drove Coop home.

# CHAPTER 24

The episode with Eli Wolff seemed like a dream, but her body told her it wasn't. One hop in the sack could be written off as an impulse—a mistake. Hours of trying to rid herself of the poison inflicted by her encounter with the horrible, horrible man (and his awful children) and a sleepless night with a large, traumatized dog on the bed while the arguments why she should *not* sleep with a client ran through her head, had left her exhausted and in no condition to decide what to do about Eli. She couldn't even decide what she thought about just seeing him. But his weekend guests were arriving, and Eli needed groceries.

Remy dropped Coop off with dear Willow and old Hendy and arrived early, hoping to be in and out before Eli awoke. No such luck. "Good morning, Remy. I heard your car." A white terry cloth towel was wrapped around Eli's hips. His hair was wet, and he smelled of fresh shampoo and soap. "What did you bring me?"

Remy tried to stay focused on Eli's face, but her eyes, involuntarily, dropped down to the towel. Eli's smile widened in response, all creases and crinkles and a devilish glint in his eye. She began unloading the bags. "Lots of good stuff. You said your friends liked steak so I picked up some nice New York strips at Edgartown Meats."

Eli raised one eyebrow. "Red meat. That's good. I need to keep my stamina up."

Remy bit her lip. No putting off the elephant in the room. "I think we need to, um," she paused. "Just have a professional relationship. Client-concierge. No more, uh…."

Eli took a ripe peach from the fruit bowl and pressed the flesh with his fingertip. "Fantastic sex?" Eli completed Remy's thought for her. "And why is that?"

"Because you're a client."

"Nothing else? No boyfriend in the picture?" Remy shook her head. "Well. You can always quit, or I can fire you. Not that I want to." His voice lowered and softened. "But you want to sleep with me again." Remy wanted to lie, to say no. Her silence gave Eli all the answers he needed. He leaned back against the counter and steepled his fingers. "Hmm. So, we have a dilemma," he said in a teasing tone. "I assume you don't want to quit this job. And sleeping with a client is a problem because why?"

"My business is built on my reputation," Remy explained, trying to steady her voice. "If it gets out that I jump into bed with my clients, it'll ruin everything."

"But if it doesn't get out? Then it's OK?"

Remy searched her brain for the counterargument that she knew was out there.

Eli bit into the peach. "So, we keep this a secret. No dates, no going out where we'd be seen, no incriminating texts or emails." He stepped toward her. Remy caught her breath. "You'll come here—when I'm alone. That works for me."

"Me too," Remy said, giving in to temptation. "Totally secret, you promise?" she added and tugged on Eli's towel.

*Hey Remy, I wanted to double-check the details for the goat yoga class today? Setup at 11:30, class at noon, Oakheart at the corner of Pennacook and Ocean Ave in OB.* The text from Nate brought Remy back to reality: other clients had needs to be satisfied too. *Yup, see you then*, she texted Nate back. Maybe "secret sex" would simply have to go on the schedule like everything else. Remy grinned.

"What's so funny?" Eli asked, stretching his arms over his head, the hairs catching gold in the sunlight.

Remy rolled over onto his chest and kissed his chin, still dazed that this gorgeous man was *her* lover. Foolish even to think that this might be a bad idea. "I keep this big whiteboard in my kitchen for my schedule," Remy explained. "I think I'll mark this SS. For secret sex."

"You make me sound like a Pilates class," Eli said, pushing her up by her shoulders until she dangled, giggling, above him. "Well, you are quite the workout. Pencil me in for Monday?"

"I'll check my calendar."

"I bet you'll make time for your favorite client." Eli lowered her down and slid his hands down her back. He gave her buttocks a gentle appreciative squeeze. "No stringy chicken here," Eli teased, pressing into her skin. "Supple, a lovely succulent bird. A woman needs a little body fat to keep all the nice bits plump and juicy."

Remy wasn't sure how she felt about being compared to a chicken, no matter how juicy. She rolled off and sat up. "I have to go and help set up some goats for a yoga class."

"Hmm," Eli replied, planting a kiss on her hip. "You're leaving me for a bunch of smelly old goats."

"Baby goats. And they don't smell."

"Do you ever take a day off?" he asked, moving the kisses over to her thigh. Remy willed herself to stand up, lest she stay and start screwing up her business—not by screwing the client but by missing appointments.

"Tuesdays, when I can," she replied, picking up her clothes.

"Good. I've got some ideas for us. SS goes on the schedule for Tuesday too. That is if you're not busy."

"I thought I might ride. But no other plans." Remy had been invited for coffee at her uncle's but she could reschedule that with the convenient excuse of "needing to do something for a client." Well, technically "doing a client," she corrected herself with a smile.

Eli rested his arms behind his head on the pillow and grinned. "I like the way you ride. Bike ride?"

Remy swatted him, then finished buttoning up her shirt. She bent down to kiss Eli. "A horse. One of my clients has a horse that I exercise."

"Mmm, a fine woman in boots, primed by a horse, reeking of sweat and leather. Why don't you come over after that? No shower." Remy shot him a look. "I'm serious. You have no idea how sexy that is."

"Deal. I'll warn you though, Rajah's stiff competition," Remy teased.

"Don't go making any bad bets. The odds are on me."

Glancing up at the round turret of the Hartwells' summer home, Remy smiled at the thought of letting down a Rapunzel braid for Eli to climb. Or perhaps she was Cinderella? That would be a better fit, given her menial concierge duties, though she was missing the evil stepsisters and the slipper.

Mrs. Hartwell greeted Remy at the door with a big hug. But for her gray hair, Remy would never have guessed her age. Or her wealth, judging from her clothes. But the house—a stately gingerbread Victorian painted in subtle (for Oak Bluffs) shades of green facing Ocean Park—and her pedigree (Black intelligentsia) gave that away.

"Oh, Remy, lovely to see you, dear. I'm sure you think this is silly but my daughter-in-law heard about goat yoga and wanted to try it out."

"Oh, they're going to love it. The baby goats are adorable."

"Everyone's at the Inkwell, but they'll be back in time for the class," Mrs. Hartwell said.

"We'll set up in the back?"

"Yes, anywhere, dear." Mrs. Hartwell waved to an area of lush grass. "You're looking wonderful. Life treating you well?"

Remy smiled, thinking of Eli. "Yes. Yes it is." A truck and trailer rumbled down the street. "I think Sky and Nate are here," Remy said. "I'll go give them a hand."

"And I'll get my yoga pants on. My grandchildren convinced me I had to try this too!"

Remy waved at the truck with its Nate-the-Goat-Guy logo. "Hey guys, thanks for fitting this in."

"No problem. Happy to do it." Nate climbed out and started unloading the gates, while Sky unstrapped their baby from her car seat.

"Nate, I should probably feed Gaia before class," Sky said.

Nate ran his fingers through the baby's blond curls then nuzzled Sky's neck. Remy felt a pang of envy. Their story was like a romance novel made real: rich city girl meets handsome local guy and improbably finds true love on a beautiful island.

Remy peeked inside the trailer. The three baby goats ran over. "Mehhh. Mehhhh," they bleated then went back to bouncing around and butting each other. "How's the cheese making going, Nate?" Remy asked.

"Pretty good. Peggy over at the Grey Barn—she's their master cheese maker—has been giving me some tips. I think I'm going to stick with the easy kinds this summer—you know, ricotta and fresh chèvre and feta."

"First dibs on the lavender ricotta if you make that again."

"Sure thing," Nate replied.

Gaia had finished eating and was drooling milk out of the corner of her mouth. "Remy, do you want to take Gaia while I help Nate?" Sky asked. "She might have one more burp in her."

"Are you kidding? I'd love to hold her."

Sky untangled the baby's fingers from her hair and handed her to Remy. "Watch out, she likes to grab things."

Remy carried the baby over to a wicker chair on the front porch and sat down. Sticking her nose into the blond curls, she inhaled the sweet, milky baby scent and sighed. Had things been different, would she be holding Adam's child? Sure, sex with Eli was great, but what Nate and Sky had—true love and a baby— seemed a nearly impossible dream.

After burping Gaia, Remy carried her around back to watch Nate and Sky attach the gates to form a circle like a giant playpen. Released from the trailer, the baby goats bounded around like fuzzy wind-up toys, launching themselves sideways and up with all four tiny legs flailing in different directions.

"I can take her now," Nate said, walking over. "C'mere, stinky."

Reluctantly, Remy handed him the baby. "She's a cutie, Nate."

"That she is." Excited voices came from inside the house. "Sky, you got the yoga mats? Better shake a tail feather. I think your students are ready."

# CHAPTER 25

Remy parked in the beach lot at Menemsha and began to unload the Toyota. The picturesque fishing village was famous for being the location of Quint's shack in the movie *Jaws,* the Island's freshest off-the-boat seafood, and the best sunsets on the Vineyard. The Bottimores had decided that they wanted a sunset lobster dinner on the beach, and Remy, as always, was expected to make it magically happen.

After staking out a prime spot with the beach chairs and a cooler, Remy stopped at Larsen's Fish Market to confirm the order for ten 2-pound cooked lobsters, cracked, with butter and lemon. But she deserved a bit of lobster too. No dis on Larsen's, but the hot lobster rolls with melted butter at the Menemsha Fish Market were her favorite.

Remy was staring at the menu, trying to decide if she wanted to go double lobster with lobster bisque as well (so good) when she felt a hand on her shoulder. There stood Jake in a Red Sox hat and navy polo. His blue eyes were warm and smiling.

"Jake? What are you doing here?" she asked.

"Same as you, I bet." He pointed at the whiteboard menu. "Lobster roll special?"

"Of course. Hot or cold?"

"Hot, of course. You?" Jake asked.

"Oh, I'm hot." Remy felt a flush creep up from her collarbone. "Hot lobster roll," she stammered.

Jake chuckled. "Lobster bisque or chowder?"

"That one's close. Bisque," Remy answered, pressing a hand to cool her cheek.

"That's what I was thinking too."

"Are you together?" asked the cashier.

"Yes," said Jake.

"No," said Remy.

After a short wait, the cashier called out their names. Jake and Remy picked up their paper bags. "Shall we eat out on Dutcher Dock?" Jake asked.

Remy hesitated. She might not want to date Jake, but there was no reason to be rude. "Where else?"

The wooden dock behind the market was lined with boats. Pleasure craft tied up at the end by the jetty, local commercial fishing boats in the middle, and fishing charter boats closest to the creek. A row of decrepit-but-picturesque shacks edged the harbor, truly looking like a movie set. A sport-fishing boat slowly putt-putted past the white clapboard Coast Guard boathouse.

Remy put her bag onto one of the weathered cable spools and sat down on the bench. "I've seen this view like a zillion times, but it never gets old."

Jake joined her and opened his bag. "You got that right," he agreed. "This is great. But I still miss The Bite."

Remy puffed a sigh of relief. If Jake wasn't going to bring up their Chilmark Tavern date disaster, she certainly wasn't going to. With luck, he'd come to the same conclusion she had: they simply had nothing in common. "And the *Quitsa Strider*," Remy said. "Remember that old rust bucket with the chopped off bow?" She pulled her food out of the bag. "I like that Menemsha's still a working fishing port. Have you had the scallops they sell off the *Martha Rose*?"

Jake shook his head. "I've been meaning to."

"You should. They're awesome." Remy's mouth was watering as she unwrapped her lobster roll, the hot dog bun barely containing the chunks of red-and-white lobster meat.

"I will." Jake prized the lid off his bisque and took a sip. "I remember you and Teddy would nag our parents, begging them to bring us to Menemsha to get burgers at the Galley. And they'd make me babysit while they went to the Homeport."

"And after you got your driver's license, we'd nag you. You were the biggest grouch." Remy took a bite. The lobster was warm and tender, and the melted butter had made a delicious, soggy mess out of the bun. "Yum."

Jake chuckled. "I didn't mind doing the driving. Though you guys were pretty annoying. What was that song you'd sing?"

Remy thought for a moment. "Oh no. Oh geez, I remember." She started to sing in a gravelly voice as she waggled her shoulders. "I'm too sexy for my fish, too sexy for my fish...."

Jake shook his head, laughing. He leaned back against the weathered gray-shingled wall. "Still annoying. And no thanks for the earworm!"

"You brought it up," Remy said. "We totally used to do that to bug you. You were so serious all the time."

"Sullen teenager, more like it." Jake unwrapped his lobster roll, "Wow, they don't skimp on the meat, do they?"

The phrase "too sexy" sent Remy's thoughts drifting to Eli. Who was too sexy for any of his clothes. Not that he kept them on for long. She dipped her plastic spoon into her bisque. It was delicious, the essence of lobster in a paper cup. Decadent and rich. Just like Eli.

"What's your plan for this evening?"

Remy was startled out of her reverie. "Oh. I am responsible for the perfect sunset lobster dinner for one of my clients. Of course, they don't realize how hard it is to eat a lobster out of a beach chair. I won't bore you with the details."

"Bore me."

"All right. You asked for it." She outlined her plan for the party, from the crates she'd found to use as tables to the champagne bar (because Mr. Bottimore insisted on American—local lobsters, after all—while Mrs. Bottimore drank only French) to the menu: grilled corn, lobsters, stuffed clams, chowder, and brownies and blondies for dessert.

"Blondies," Jake said. "I haven't had one of those in years."

In a rush, Remy slipped back into her teenage crush-addled self, baking yet another pan of Jake's favorite cookie as she dreamed of his kisses, his fingers caressing her skin, the day he'd realize that Remy was his true love. An echo of adolescent infatuation rose inside as she watched Jake dab melted butter from his lips. All those summers—and all that sugar and butter—wasted pining after him.

"I made them from scratch. Really yummy. I'll save you a couple." Remy scraped the last of the bisque out of her cup, willing her adult self into control. "So I do all that, then wait around, and clean up their mess. Oh, and I get to valet park their cars, like that's going to work," she said, rolling her eyes. "You remember what it's like trying to find parking here at sunset."

"I do." He ate the last of his lobster roll. "You need some help?"

"I'll figure it out," she sighed. "Thanks for the offer, though."

"If I'm here, we can give them both our parking spots when they arrive," he said, wiping his fingers with a napkin. "I'm not doing anything tonight. And it'll give me an excuse to stick around for the sunset."

Remy bit her lip. Jake's plan solved her problem. Otherwise, she'd have been running around like a chicken with its head cut off parking the cars. "OK. That would be a huge help."

Jake balled up his napkin and stuffed it into the empty paper soup cup. "If I'm sticking around, I might as well help set up too."

Remy laughed. "Offer accepted."

Dinner finished, they walked down the dock to the parking lot and started to pull the party supplies out of Remy's truck. Lingering teenage crush aside, what Remy felt—did—with Eli was decidedly more adult. Remy's thoughts drifted pleasantly to the morning's frolic in his bed. She'd arrived early and had snuck upstairs while he was still sleeping (naked) to join him (naked) under the sheets. She'd let her hand slide down his chest to wake up the part she was particularly interested in.

"I'm too sexy for the lobsters, too sexy for the lobsters," Remy sang and wiggled her hips as she dragged out a heavy cooler of ice from the truck. "Too sexy for the lobsters…"

She heard Jake's breath catch behind her. Remy spun around. Two bright pink circles grew warm on her cheeks.

"Let me help," Jake said, reaching for the cooler.

Close up, Jake's blue eyes glowed with unmistakable desire. He put his hand over hers, and Remy's heart jumped. Jake's fingers were warm, and his breath brushed her neck. He was close enough to kiss. Which was exactly what she wanted to do.

"It's OK. I've got it under control."

And Remy hoped she did. Shaky with suppressed desire, Remy lugged the too-heavy cooler and set it up on the beach. Had sleeping with Eli opened some door that made her hot for any guy who came close? Or was it something else?

# CHAPTER 26

An hour later, Jake helped Remy put the final touches on the setup. Her red cooler made do as the bar, matching the red napkins and red-and-white gingham tablecloth on the appetizer table, while another cooler kept the boiled lobsters hot. She'd found, thanks to the internet, stick-in-the sand beach champagne glasses. And, if the party went late, Remy had a dozen lanterns ready to be lit. A portable speaker was set up with a beach-themed playlist, and a lobster cracker and mallet and a container for discarded shells sat on each crate.

"You know, this looks really nice," Jake said.

It was pure serendipity, running into Remy like this. Jake had been having an especially shitty day. His ex-girlfriend, spiteful thing, had mailed him a copy of the journal featuring her published article, the one he'd spent so much time helping her put together. Jake told himself it didn't matter, but he knew it did. His writer's block now felt like a 12-foot wall, and his ex was standing gleefully on the other side.

But Remy's bright gray eyes had dispelled his Chicago gloom. She glowed, and not just from the hard work of setting up the party. Jake's hopes had been rising, inch by inch. Their date at the restaurant had gotten off on the wrong foot, probably two wrong feet, but tonight he had a second chance.

"Yup, it does." Remy flopped onto one of the beach chairs. "Sit down, take a break." She took a deep breath and exhaled. "Jeez, I'm not sure I would've finished in time. I owe you," Remy said, watching the sun, now an orange disk, backlight the clouds above the horizon.

"Nothing I'd rather do," said Jake.

Remy's cell buzzed. "We finished just in time. My clients are here."

Jake and Remy relinquished their parking spots, moved their own cars to Robby's driveway by the crossroads, then walked down the hill back into Menemsha. Low bands of clouds promised a spectacular sunset; Remy's clients had lucked into a great night.

"I think we deserve an ice cream from the Galley," said Jake. "My treat. Want to split a frappe?"

"Chocolate malt?" Remy asked.

Jake nodded his agreement. "You read my mind."

"Then to the jetty to watch the sunset?"

"Of course."

Sipping their milkshake like teenagers on a date, they strolled through town, peering into windows of shops and galleries as they made their way to the rock jetty that protected the mouth of Menemsha harbor. Remy was so easy to talk to. She made him feel... lighter? Perhaps, though that wasn't exactly it. Jake thought. She took him out of his head. With Remy, there were sunsets and singing and chocolate malt frappes. And work—real work—the kind that brought a sense of satisfaction in a job well done. She made people happy. She made him happy. And, oh my God, when she sang the sexy song and wiggled her hips...

Remy sipped the shake. "There is something about the malt that makes this so addictive. Here, take it before I drink it all." Remy handed Jake the paper cup as they paused in front of the window of a small art gallery. "I'd love to see if Joan would take any of my paintings on commission. I'd like to do a painting of your catboat—if I can ever find the time, that is."

"Sure," said Jake. "*Utopia*'s nearly ready for her maiden voyage." And if he played his cards right, Remy would be on it.

They took the steps down to the dock and followed it along the harbor to the jetty. Picking their way from rock to rock, Jake followed Remy to the end just in time to watch the sun slip below the horizon in a glorious blaze of orange and red.

"Gorgeous," Jake said.

"You got that right."

Remy's face and hair shone gold in the fading light. She was so close, so lovely. An Island girl, steadfast and secure. A rock to anchor his life to. If she'd let him. Jake wanted to take Remy in his arms and kiss her, feel the softness of her lips, the press of her breasts against his chest, to bury his face in her salt-scented hair. But first, he needed to apologize.

"Remy…"

She gave him a look as if she knew what was coming. "Better go check on my clients." Before Jake could stop her, Remy had darted down the jetty.

When he caught up, Remy was pulling out garbage bags to clean up the rather impressive mess her clients had left behind. Napkins, lemon wedges, and bits of shell were scattered everywhere, and an empty champagne bottle sat next to almost every chair.

"Looks like they enjoyed their party."

Remy grinned. "They loved it. Mrs. Bottimore texted me and said it was 'perfect.'"

"That's because you're awesome at what you do."

"I try," Remy said, appearing pleased with the compliment.

Jake reached for a bag. "You don't have to clean up too," Remy said. "That's my job. Get yourself to a beer if you want. There's plenty in the cooler."

"It'll go twice as fast if I help."

"Glutton for punishment," she teased.

Jake started on the lobster debris. He picked up a huge, uncracked claw off a paper platter. "What did they do, only eat the tail?" Jake said and waggled the enormous red claw. "I mean, look at the size of this."

"Guess the claws were too much work. Just put it in there," Remy said, pointing to a box on the table. "They won't go to waste. I make a mean lobster salad. And there's a whole giant lobster left," she said. "Why don't you take that home. As a tip. And the rest of the blondies."

Jake wiped his hands with a paper towel. "Blondies. I'll take one of those now," he said and picked up a golden-brown square. Studded with chocolate chips, the sweet, buttery, chewy treat triggered a long-buried memory. "My favorite. Didn't you and Willow used to bring these to the beach all the time?" he asked through a mouthful of cookie.

"We did. This is my old recipe."

Jake licked a crumb from the corner of his mouth. "Absolutely delicious." He gathered his courage. Out with it. "The other night, at the Chilmark Tavern. I shouldn't have tried to make you stay."

"Not a big deal."

"I was an idiot. But I didn't want you to leave." Jake reached for her hand. "Can we try again?"

Remy slipped her fingers from his grip. Her lips drew together in a thin line as she looked out at the water. A sick feeling rose inside Jake as his hopes slipped away.

"Jake, honestly, I'm too busy to date anyone." She turned back to look at him with what might have been pity. "Friends. OK?"

# CHAPTER 27

Vivaldi played on Remy's stereo as she laid out the bag of beach stones and a black Sharpie on the kitchen table. Time to focus, first on the place cards—place stones—if she was to pull off a perfect event. Enid Cinch had been driving her nuts all week to ensure "the careless mistakes you made last time" would not be repeated. The caterer had refused to work for the Cinches again, so she was trying a new chef, which made her anxious.

Writing in cursive on the uneven, curved surface was harder than it looked: *Marie-Claire* took two tries to come out right. Remy had just finished *Adrienne* and was concentrating on *Eden* when someone knocked on the door, nearly causing her to flub the loopy "E."

Morgan stood on the doorstep, hiding underneath one of Willow's floppy hats. "I can't stand it anymore," said Morgan. An angry, new pimple reddened the teen's chin. "I can't stand her. You have no idea." She rolled her eyes. "She's even more nuts than usual."

Coop wagged and woofed at Remy's side. "Morgan, what are you doing here?"

"You have a dog? Can I pet him?"

Remy opened the door and let Morgan in. "This is Coop. Does your mother know you're here?"

"Nope. She thinks I took the bus into Edgartown 'to buy something appropriate' for her snooty dinner party." Morgan looked up from petting the dog with an evil grin. "She hated that I showed up at her last party in that pink and gold sari sundress I bought from Willow. I think I'll wear it again."

"I don't know. Maybe you should go buy something, uh, quieter. I can drop you off."

Morgan frowned. "Whose side are you on?"

"Your mother will not be happy with me if she finds out I knew about this."

"Then don't tell her. I won't. I just need a place to hang for a couple of hours. I'm tired of the beach."

Remy sighed. "Fine." Her cell rang. "Just a minute, Morgan, I need to answer this."

"I'm sorry, I hope I'm not bothering you," said Audrey Kemp in her soft airy voice. "I wanted to explain. To apologize."

"It's OK, really. But if you're calling to get your dog back, I can't do that," Remy said as a residue of anger bubbled up.

"No, no. I think things will be better here without Beaucoup. It seemed like a good idea to get a dog, but I'm afraid it didn't work out as I'd hoped. Like most of my ideas," she said in a dejected voice. "But I was wondering if you still had him or if he's at the shelter. I'd like to say goodbye. I'm going to miss him."

Anger was replaced with a rush of sympathy. Poor cowed woman with a horrible husband and brats for kids. The dog was probably the only one in the house who was nice to her.

Remy glanced at Coop, who was in the process of getting a belly rub from Morgan. "He's still with me for now. Feel free to drop by for a visit."

"Are you sure it's no imposition?"

"No, of course not. I'm in West Tisbury, a few doors down from Alley's General Store."

"Would this morning be all right? I'm about to drop the twins and the nanny at the beach at Black Point, so that's not far. Or I could come later or tomorrow? I don't want to be a bother."

Remy rolled her eyes: first Morgan, now Audrey Kemp. "Not a problem. Come by anytime, I'm home for a while."

Remy gave the woman directions to the house and turned back to Morgan. "OK. You can stay, but I've got to work on stuff for your mom's party. And I'm not changing the music."

"I'll be fine," said Morgan. "I've got my phone. You won't even know I'm here."

Remy turned back to her calligraphy. She finished the final two stones, so *Elisabeth* and *Nigel* would know where to sit, then considered the flowers. Enid Cinch had specified something "Japanese-inspired" and "beachy" using white orchids. She bit her lip in concentration. She could do a voluptuous English-garden style arrangement in her sleep, but this was hard. "Here we go," Remy sighed.

She filled one of the shallow oval containers with small beach stones and set a metal florist's frog off to one end. She'd googled the principles of ikebana. Heaven, the tallest point, would be a tall, twisted twig inserted almost upright into the tines of the frog. Then a shorter twig, representing man, would come in at a steep angle. The big butterfly-shaped phalaenopsis orchids were the lowest element, earth. Remy added two pieces of driftwood on top of the pebbles. It was OK. Not great.

"What are you doing?" Morgan was at her side.

"Trying to make Japanese-style beach-themed floral arrangements for the table." Remy chewed on a fingernail. "But it needs something."

Morgan picked up two long stems of beach grass. "How about adding these?" she suggested. Morgan made loops out of the grass and held them in place.

"Yes. That's it!" exclaimed Remy, fixing the grasses in place.

Morgan snapped a couple of photos of the arrangement and Remy. "You're really photogenic," Morgan said as she handed Remy her phone. "I wish I was. OK if I go visit your chickens? I want to take pictures of them."

"You can look for eggs, too. Basket's by the door."

Remy placed the arrangement in the middle of the table. Morgan's inspiration was just what the design needed. The loops of beach grass drew the eye up and back around to the gorgeous orchids. She puffed out a breath of air and relaxed. One more thing off the list. She'd make herself a cup of tea, do the second arrangement, then start folding napkins into origami.

Remy was in the kitchen when she heard a car pull up. Coop woofed and his tail circled like a propeller when he heard Audrey's voice calling hello. Remy opened the door. "Come in."

"Oh, Beaucoup," Audrey cried, dropping to the floor to hug the dog. Coop, ears back in joy, licked her face as his tail beat the floor.

"Can I get you something? I was about to make myself some tea."

"Tea would be lovely, but I don't want to impose."

Remy went to check the kettle, and when she came back, she found poor Audrey softly crying into Coop's coat. "I'm going to miss you so much," she sniffled, "Our beach walks were the best part of my day."

Audrey's birdlike shoulders shook under her light shirt. She was slender—not in a diet-and-exercise-thin way, but in an I'm-too-nervous-to-eat way. "Um, as I said, I haven't decided if I'm keeping him, but if I do, you're welcome to take him for walks."

Audrey looked up with wide wet bush-baby eyes. Strands of mousy-brown hair were stuck to her tear-dampened cheeks. "Really? That would be wonderful." She turned back to the dog. "Oh, Beau, if only you hadn't eaten Tony's loafers and pooped in the house."

The kettle whistled. Remy went to the kitchen, poured the boiling water over the tea bags, then hit her freezer stash of saltine cookies, piling the chocolate-and-nut-crusted butter bombs on a plate. The woman needed some calories. "What do you take in your tea? It's English."

"Just some milk, please. If it's no trouble." Audrey wiped her tears, stood up, and walked over to Remy's arrangement. "This is lovely. You're a florist?"

"A concierge," Remy said, setting the tea and cookies down on a table between two armchairs. "I do shopping, reservations, flowers, party planning—pretty much anything my clients want." She raised an eyebrow. "Emergency dog-sitting, for example."

Audrey managed a wan smile. "You must be very organized. I could never do all that. I write things down then lose the list. Tony gets so mad." Coop walked over and laid his head in Audrey's lap. "You sweet dog. I think you missed me." She stroked his ears. "Oh, I almost forgot. You left your check." She rummaged around in a giant messy Coach bag until she found the slip of paper. "And you're sure we don't owe you for anything else? He didn't eat any shoes or anything?"

"The first day he chewed up a sandal. And part of a chair leg. But that was my fault for leaving him here alone too long."

Audrey looked horrified. "You have to let me pay for that."

"It's OK. It was an old flip-flop, and my friend can fix the chair leg."

"I insist." Audrey dove back into her purse until she found a blank check and a pen. She wrote a check for $200 and handed both checks to Remy. "I feel terrible as it is, please take these."

She accepted the checks. The woman could afford it. And that meant Remy could pay Mike for repairing the chair. "Thank you."

Morgan banged through the back door. "Remy, I found a bunch of eggs! Oh, hi," she said to Audrey.

"Thanks, Morgan—just put them in that bowl. Morgan, this is Mrs. Kemp. Coop used to be her dog."

"Nice to meet you," Morgan said automatically and zeroed in on the plate of cookies. "Can I have one?"

Remy held out the plate. Morgan took three cookies and retreated to the sofa. "Thanks."

Audrey settled into the armchair with her tea. She took a delicate bite of the cold cookie and smiled. "Oh. These are delicious. Tony won't let us have sweets in the house. Except for his secret stash of Oreos. My mother used to make cookies all the time."

"This is my grandmom's recipe." Remy couldn't imagine a childhood without homemade cookies, warm from the oven. No wonder the twins were so unpleasant. She took another bite, savoring the buttery crunch. Crack cookies, Willow called them. "I keep them in the freezer and try to forget that they're there, so I don't eat them all at once."

"Is that your grandmother on the mantle?" Audrey asked.

Remy glanced at the framed photo of the kerchiefed woman clutching two hens and snorted a laugh. "Oh my gosh, no. That's Nancy Luce."

"She's the famous crazy chicken lady," Morgan informed Audrey from the couch.

"A friend gave it to me as a joke. I keep a flock of hens in the backyard."

Audrey looked around the room and sighed. "It's so peaceful here, the music, the flowers, tea and cookies. A bowl of fresh eggs from your very own chickens."

"Thank you." Remy sipped her tea. "What kind of dog is Coop? That's my nickname for him"

"Coop. That's cute. He's a Barbet—it's a French hunting dog. The girls wanted a little dog, something they could dress up in coats. But my husband insisted on a 'real' dog."

"I've never heard of a Barbet."

"Oh, Tony's big client has a Barbet on his estate on the Eastern Shore of Maryland, you know, for goose hunting. So, Tony had to get a Barbet too." A worried expression crossed Audrey's face. "He's started to hunt, but I don't like it." Remy was horrified at the idea of that angry, out-of-control man having access to firearms. "Anyway, Bo-coop came from a breeder in France, can you believe it. Yes, I know it should be pronounced *beaucoup*," she said with a perfect French accent. "But Tony insisted." Audrey reached for another cookie. "I can't stop eating these."

"Help yourself—there's lots more." Remy took another herself and munched it. She was starting to like Audrey, so sweet and open, yet so cowed. "What happened with your husband and Coop, if you don't mind me asking? He's such a good dog—very well trained."

"Oh, he went to doggie boot camp. You know, where you send him off to a boarding school and they do all the work? But then the owners need to get trained, learn the commands. But Tony didn't have any patience for that. He didn't grow up with dogs, didn't know they chewed things and had accidents." Audrey looked down at her hands. "All that money for training, but Tony wouldn't listen. He'd say, 'get over here,' and the dog would ignore him. I'd say, 'come,' and Beaucoup would obey. It annoyed Tony so much." She looked down at the dog and stroked his ear. "And when you ate Tony's favorite loafers, those tasty Italian custom-made ones, that was very bad." Audrey looked up, sad. "It went downhill from there. Tony would yell at Beaucoup, even hit him, and the next thing you know, there's poop on the carpet. I think it was an anxiety thing. I didn't know what to do." She was about to cry again. "So that's why I said I think it's for the best, giving him away." Audrey unearthed a Kleenex and dabbed her eyes.

"You're doing the right thing," Remy reassured her.

"Oh, he loves cheese. It's his favorite treat." A tear ran down Audrey's cheek. "And Beaucoup—Coop—does get anxious being left alone too long. I used to take him with me to run errands. He's very, very good at waiting in the car." She stood up and took a deep breath. "I should go. The girls will wonder why it's taken me so long to get sandwiches."

"No trouble, really."

Coop followed Audrey to the door. "Oh my gosh, I forgot to show you his best trick." Another rooting around in the giant bag and Audrey pulled out a dog treat. Coop perked his ears. "Bang," she said, pointing her fingers like a gun.

Coop slid to the floor, rolled onto his side, slid a paw across his face like a dying drama queen, and lay still. Audrey dropped the treat near his nose and he gobbled it up.

Remy laughed. "You taught him that?"

"He's very smart. You can teach him anything." She stroked Coop's soft furry side. Audrey turned to Remy, eyes again filled with tears. "I can't thank you enough. You'll let me know what happens to him?"

"Of course. I'm glad you stopped by," Remy said, meaning it.

The car door slammed and Audrey's sobs drifted through the open window. That poor woman. All that money and Remy wouldn't switch places with her for the world.

"Wow," said Morgan. Coop had returned to the sofa and laid his sad head in Morgan's lap. "That's messed up."

"Hey, Remy-sweet, who's this fine furry beast?" said Teddy as he dumped a shopping bag on the counter then bent to pet Coop.

"Long story. But I've ended up with a pedigreed hunting dog, all the way from France. Know anyone who wants a dog?" Remy peered into the bag. "You only brought reishi mushrooms, right? Not the magic kind?"

Teddy pretended to be offended. "Mushroom master am I," he intoned sounding like a cross between Yoda and a BBC newscaster. "Shroomies I never mistake. Hrmmm."

"OK, OK," Remy laughed. "How about the other stuff?"

"All right here." Teddy patted the shopping bag. "As instructed: two bags of Ghirardelli chocolate chips, two bags of Dove dark chocolates. A bag of almonds, slivered not sliced, and a bag of shredded coconut." Teddy looked pleased with himself for remembering everything. He bent to rub Coop's ears. "So, where'd you find the pooch?"

"I'll tell you. Here, let's start unwrapping the chocolate." Once again, Remy recounted Coop's rescue story. "Then I went to take him back and found an absolute shit show at the house. The kids didn't want him, the wife was all meek and scared. Then the husband showed up, went psycho, and started abusing Coop. He hit and kicked him, right in front of me. The poor dog ran and jumped into my car, and the man told me to keep him. So he's mine—at least until I figure out what to do with him."

"So you pulled off a canine coup d'état?" he asked, pleased with himself.

Remy laughed. "Very punny, Teddy. But I don't know. What do you think I should do? He's a great dog, but it's a big responsibility. He'd get adopted out of the shelter, no problem."

"Ask him. Hey Coop." The dog's ears perked up. "Do you want to live here, with Remy?" Teddy asked in a bright wanna-go-walkies voice. Coop thumped his tail on the floor, then stood up and put his head in Remy's lap. "There's your answer," Teddy said with a grin. "Dilemma solved. Chocolates unwrapped. What next?"

Remy stroked Coop's ears. "OK, Coop, we'll try it out. No promises though." She turned to Teddy. "Uh, I guess we try putting the mushrooms in the Cuisinart, see if we can pulverize them."

Teddy picked up the bag of dried reishi. "Oh hey, I told Willow, and she's going to come over with her shake. She wants to make some edibles."

"Oh geez. OK. We better be supercareful to keep them separate." Remy opened a cabinet. "Two bowls, obviously. I think I have some candy cups in different colors we can use." The Island had always been home to an above-average number of stoners. Since the changes in Massachusetts law, marijuana had gone mainstream—as a more-or-less all-natural antianxiety, appetite, and mood booster. Poor Audrey Kemp could use a few pot-laced chocolates, Remy decided.

"Hellooo…" Willow called. "Hey, have you guys started already?"

"Just now—come on in," Teddy said and hugged her.

Coop bounded over to Willow, wagging his tail. "Thank you again for dog-sitting him so much," Remy said.

Willow waved her hand. "He's a doll. Hendy loves having another dog around." She reached into her patchwork bag and pulled out a half-pint jar with an inch of greenish-brown flecks inside. "I've been collecting shake a while. I have no idea how strong it is, so we'll have to experiment!"

Teddy nodded happily. "Sign me up!"

Remy took the jar and shook the contents. "You'll want to toast the shake, right? I'm about to put Teddy's superduper mushrooms in the Cuisinart and see what happens."

Teddy had wandered over to Remy's giant whiteboard where she kept her client calendar. "Who's SS, Remy?" Teddy asked.

Remy hesitated as she searched for a plausible lie. Willow, once again, simply read her mind. Willow's eyes widened "No. No way. I thought his name was… "

"Don't say it. We're keeping it quiet," Remy said with a warning look.

"What?" Teddy asked.

"Remy's got her sex life scheduled on her whiteboard. SS."

Teddy studied the board, then whistled through his teeth. "Whoa…"

"I know. I can't believe I told you guys."

"You didn't tell me, I figured out," Willow said.

Remy swatted Willow. It was time to change the topic. "I thought you wanted to make chocolates."

Willow and Teddy were not done yet. "What's SS stand for?" Teddy asked. "The guy's initials?"

"No."

"Super Sex?" Teddy offered.

"Steamy Sex." Willow countered.

"Spectacular Sex."

The guesses rained down as Remy sat with her face in her hands.

"Sultry Sex."

"Summer Sex.

"Safe Sex."

"Slippery Sex."

"Sassy Sex."

"Splendiferous Sex."

Remy sighed. Her friends were annoying but not vocabulary challenged: they weren't going to let this go until they ran out of s adjectives. "Secret sex. OK?" She smiled at her friends then raised one eyebrow. "But all those other things too."

Willow and Teddy grinned and high-fived each other. "OK, where's that cookie sheet?" asked Willow. "Let's get started."

Willow had started with half a marijuana chocolate candy and, an hour later, pronounced herself buzzing nicely. Teddy had started with a full edible, plus two of the Choco-Teds and was a happy camper indeed. The experiment had worked. With plenty of coconut and nuts, you could barely detect the reishi mushroom bits.

Teddy surveyed the mound of chocolates on the plate. "So what d'you think? $1 a Choco-Ted?"

"Five bucks, if you get some cute little boxes to put them in," Remy suggested as she washed out a bowl. "It's the Vineyard.

People are used to paying through the nose. You want me to design a logo?"

Remy's cell rang. She dried her hands to answer.

"Remy, I hope I'm not bothering you? I want to thank you again," said Audrey in her tiny voice. "You have no idea how nice it was to see Beaucoup and have a quiet cup of tea in your peaceful house." The twins argued somewhere in the background. "Is this a bad time?"

"No. It's fine," Remy said, wondering why Audrey was calling.

"I've been thinking." She paused and let out an airy little sigh. "Could I hire you? I mean, not officially like you'd come to my house. But you could help me with planning and stuff, so everything will be how my husband wants it."

Remy hesitated. While she needed another paying client, she didn't want to have anything to do with Tony Kemp. She reached over for a chocolate and popped it into her mouth. The candies were, she noted with surprise, pretty tasty.

"You wouldn't have to deal with Tony. I wouldn't even tell him." Audrey added. "I'll just use my own money. Please think about it. It would help me so much."

The voice sounded so pathetic. And after almost getting fired by Enid Cinch over the soy sauce incident, she knew she shouldn't turn work down. "Sure. I can find some time. And I think I've decided to keep Coop, so we'll meet here instead of your house, and you can visit with him."

"Thank you, thank you!"

"Why don't you text me Monday, and we'll set a time to meet. See you then." Remy clicked off her phone.

Willow giggled. "You know, you just ate one of my chocolates, not Ted's. Did you mean to?"

"Oh shit. You're kidding me." Remy looked at the empty wrapper. Blue, not white. She looked at Teddy who had finished cleaning up and lay on the floor next to the dog, who was patiently allowing Teddy to turn his ears inside out.

"Hey, I can make Coop into a bear. See?" Teddy said.

Willow joined him on the floor. "You got anything to eat, Remy?"

Remy rubbed her eyes, poured some coffee, then looked for the waffle recipe. "OK, let's get the eggs," she told her dog. "You know to stay away from those chicken beaks, right?"

Coop trotted at her heels, stopping a safe distance from the fence and lying down. "Hey ladies, did you have a good night?" Remy chirped to her chickens.

After shooting a fierce warning look at the dog, Ada Queetie fluffed her feathers and dashed over to Remy. The rest of the flock followed. Remy tossed the wilted remains of her vegetable drawer onto the ground: sagging lettuce, dried up carrots, and some shriveled sprouts. As the chickens pecked at their bonanza, Remy poked around in the straw for the day's eggs.

Remy hadn't been so stoned in years. She wondered if Teddy had slipped some magic mushroom dust in with the shake. The evening started with a silly walk to Alley's General Store for junk food and pints of Ben & Jerry's. Mike dropped by with an invite to a dance party and found the trio on the sofa watching a *Bob's Burgers* cartoon, surrounded by empty pint containers of Chubby Hubby and Phish Food and open bags of potato chips. Then it had been Teddy's most excellent idea to take the boat to watch the stars come out. The pond's mirror-still surface shone pale pink as they set out, fading to twilight gray as the last streaks of sunset left the sky. The boat's wake spread in broadening, shimmering, mesmerizing vees. After cutting the motor in the middle of the pond, they lay on their backs to watch the darkening sky. Conversation stilled, and all was silent but for the lapping of water against the sides of the skiff and an occasional wisp of sound: the low roll of the surf, faint laughter from a dinner conversation, a goat's annoyed bleat. A fingernail moon rose in the east along with the first planets, rusty-red Mars the easiest to spot. They watched with stoned fascination as the sky deepened to black ink and the stars pinpricked through, eventually revealing the density of stars that was the Milky Way, a broad, glorious arch smeared across the black vastness of the sky.

Something opened inside Remy as she floated in the amniotic dark with two of the people she loved most in the whole world.

She sensed vastness and connection, drifting in the universe yet tethered to people and place: a warm bliss in the cool air. The trio's meditation of the heavens was broken when Teddy announced he needed to pee. He stood up and did so, splashing with great vigor and lengthy duration into the pond, an event which Willow, clutching the side of the rocking boat, found immensely, infectiously funny. On the ride back, moon jellies lit their wake with a phosphorescent glow, spreading behind them like a liquid comet's tail.

Egg basket filled, Remy cuddled Ada Queetie and headed back to the house. She plugged in the waffle maker and cracked two hen-warmed eggs into a bowl and whisked in the rest of the ingredients. The syrup was a gift from a friend's farm in Vermont, and a can of Reddi-wip would guarantee the pinnacle of waffle perfection: a crisp, hot homemade waffle topped with whipped cream and real maple syrup.

Remy pulled out the first two waffles, put them on a plate, and headed upstairs. Teddy and Willow were asleep upstairs in the guest room bed, fully dressed and cuddled like a pair of puppies. "Get up, you two," Remy said, waving the plate under their noses.

"Murf," Teddy replied, yawned, and opened one eye. "Is that a waffle?"

Willow tried to roll over but was pinned. "Ted, you're on my arm. Wait, hey, what are you doing in my bed?"

"Remy's sofa was lumpy and cold." He pulled the quilt up and smoothed it over them. "Soft and warm here."

"C'mon, guys," Remy reminded them with another waffle wave. "It's 10:00. Time to get up."

"OK, OK," Teddy said and snuggled back against Willow's side. "In a minute."

"Oh my God, your breath, Teddy. I'm up."

Willow freed her arm and followed Remy downstairs. "So, no SS on the calendar today?" Willow teased.

"Nope, no SS. Eli's had houseguests all weekend. I can't wait until they leave."

Willow added whipped cream to her waffle and took a bite. "You really thought you were going to keep SS secret from me," she pouted.

"No, not from you." Remy tried to give a bare-bones account, but Willow, as usual, cross-examined Remy with questions until she got what she wanted, eyes widening at the particularly salacious bits.

Teddy's footsteps sounded upstairs. "I almost forgot Teddy was here," Remy whispered. "I'll tell you more later."

"Any waffles left?" Teddy called down the stairs.

Remy plugged the waffle iron in. "Plenty of batter."

"Hey, something smells good," called a voice through the screen door. "There you are, Ted," Jake said, pushing the door open. "Hi, Remy. I was just picking up some milk from Alley's." Jake shot a look at his brother. "Someone had drunk all ours again. And I was wondering if you knew where my brother had spent the night,"

"Here, with Willow-pillow," said Teddy.

Willow swatted at Teddy. "I'm not your pillow."

"You were last night," Teddy replied. "Waffle chef, might you be able to produce an extra waffle for my bro?" Teddy asked.

"Sure," said Remy. She poured the batter into the waffle iron. It bubbled and sizzled as she closed the lid. Friends. Remy had told him she wanted to be friends, and she meant it.

"Remy and her waffles are the best," said Teddy.

# CHAPTER 28

Remy pulled the waffle out of the iron and put it on a plate in front of Jake. "Here you go, steaming hot homemade buttermilk waffle." Remy's hair was tousled by sleep, and she was still in pajamas. Jake couldn't help noticing her breasts bouncing gently beneath her Up-Island Automotive T-shirt.

"Thank you," Jake said and picked up the syrup. He'd spent the evening reading and thinking. Overthinking probably. Mostly about Remy. Then he'd recalled that sharp stab of envy when he'd heard the trio of laughing voices making their way in the dark to the dock.

"Purple," Willow announced, throwing a non sequitur into the scene. "No, actually more lavender than violet. But it is kind of undulating. Hmm," she added, staring at Jake with an uncomfortable intensity.

"Willow can see auras," Remy informed him.

Willow tilted her head and continued to stare. It was quite disconcerting.

"Try it with both maple syrup and whipped cream," Remy said. "That's my favorite."

Jake prepared his waffle as instructed and took a bite. "Delicious," he said. "Maybe the best waffle I've ever had."

Remy smiled and sipped her coffee.

He turned back to Willow. "Auras," Jake said, trying to sound like he took the idea seriously. "That's interesting,"

"It is," Willow said. "And accurate. Don't you want to know what yours means?"

"I'm pink," Teddy volunteered. "Time to tally the Choco-Teds." He got up and pulled a Tupperware out of the refrigerator, then took the lid off and started counting chocolates.

"Lavender. OK. Sure. What does that mean?" Jake asked. He'd planned to tempt Remy into going sailing with him. A friend would do that, right? It promised to be a perfect day, with a steady stiff breeze from the east. The catboat was rigged, repaired, and ready to sail. More than anything else, Jake wanted Remy on the maiden voyage of *Utopia*. But in the meantime, he'd make small talk about auras with Remy's flakey friend.

Teddy continued counting under his breath, "47, 48, 49, 50."

Willow's eyes watched not Jake but the area around him. "A true violet is a very spiritual color: visionary, associated with the crown chakra. Lavender is more idealistic, intuitive, and creative, but it's less connected than violet to wisdom and mystical or psychic abilities."

Jake didn't know what to say. "Um, thank you."

Coop barked from outside. "Hey, anybody home?" called a male voice. The back door opened. In bounded Coop, followed by Mike's big brown Lab.

"Hi guys," said Mike, following the dogs through the door. As always, he wore his tool belt and a Cottles lumberyard cap. "Here," he said, handing Remy a paper plate loaded with cake. "We had a ton of *tres leches* left over from my niece's birthday party."

"Thanks," Remy said and leaned over to kiss Mike's cheek. "It's my favorite. Vineyard Grocer or homemade?" Jake felt a pang of jealousy. It was Remy's dancing partner from the party, the one with all the Latin moves that Jake could never hope to master.

"My sister made it."

Remy pulled back the plastic wrap and took a bite of the gooey cake, rich with heavy cream and sweetened condensed milk. "Yum. Can you ask her for the recipe?"

"Will do. Hi, I'm Mike," he said, extending his hand to Jake. "You must be Teddy's brother."

"Jake." His hand felt like it was trapped in a vise.

"Nice to meet you."

"Jake's a professor," Teddy said proudly. "Of philosophy at the University of Chicago."

"Great," Mike said.

As if sensing Jake's discomfort, Coop walked over and laid his shaggy head on Jake's lap. He patted the dog's head. Teddy, the mushroom farmer. Willow, the aura-seeing artisan. Remy, the concierge. And Mike, the carpenter. Jake felt terribly out of place. Here, on Martha's Vineyard, he was Teddy's off-Island brother, the professor that nobody knew how to talk to.

"You want a waffle, Mike? There's enough batter for one more," Remy said.

"Naw, I'm good. I'll take some coffee if you have extra though."

"...82, 83, 84," said Teddy. "84 Choco-Teds!"

"That's terrific, Ted." Remy poured coffee into a mug for Mike. "Black, right?"

"Thanks," Mike said. "You all back on earth this morning? You guys were flying high last night."

"We were," Teddy said, eyeing the cake. "Remy and Willow cooked up a primo batch of edibles!"

"And I accidentally ate one," Remy laughed. "It made for a most interesting evening."

Mike sipped his coffee. "You missed a good dance party."

"Next time," Remy said. "Who was the DJ?"

Jake ate his waffle in silence as he listened to Mike and Remy talk about the party she'd missed. Willow had started looking at him again.

"Hey, I think I'll take a look at your chicken pen while I'm here," Mike said. "Make sure it's secure. Did you hear about what happened last night over on Panhandle Road?" Remy shook her head.

"Somebody's kid forgot to bring in their chickens." Mike's black eyes were sad. "A dog or maybe a raccoon got a couple of them."

Remy looked stricken.

"Oh, that's awful," said Willow.

"Most got up in the trees. Could've been worse."

Teddy reached over and patted Remy's shoulder. "Don't worry."

Remy blew out a puff of air. "Thanks, Mike. I'd appreciate that. Sometimes the latch doesn't want to catch. Are you working on the house again today? I'll be out, so I won't be in your way."

"Not today, no," said Mike. "But the windows are coming in this week. I'll try to stack them on the side of the house so they don't mess up your garden. It's going to be a push, but I think we can get this old place ready to go on the market by Columbus Day."

Remy stiffened. "What? What do you mean, 'on the market'?"

Mike shifted his weight. "Uh," he said, refusing to meet Remy's eyes.

"Like, for sale?" Remy said. Her face had gone white.

Willow put a hand on her arm. "That can't be right."

"Maybe you need to talk to your uncle, Remy. Maybe, uh, I misunderstood him," Mike stammered. He put down his mug. "I'm really sorry, Remy. I'll go check that latch. Then I have to go. Thanks for the coffee."

# CHAPTER 29

Remy stood, staring through the window, unseeing, as Mike backed his truck down the driveway. "Your uncle must have meant the rental market," Willow said. "And Mike got it wrong. You know, so there'd be pictures of the finished house for summer rental listings?"

Remy put her face in her hands. "I thought I had until spring," she said. Remy looked up to find Jake and Teddy both staring at her with matching blue eyes.

"Even if your uncle is selling it, with all the empty vacation houses, it should be easy to find a winter rental," Jake said reassuringly. "Someplace nice."

Willow gave him a look. "You're wrong there, Jake. Owners would rather close their houses and leave them empty for ten months than rent. You should see Edgartown. It's a ghost town."

Remy put her face back in her hands. "I need to call Uncle Danny." Willow refilled their coffee cups. "What am I going to do. I thought if I made enough money, I could even cut a deal on a year-round lease here. But if he's selling it, where am I going to live?" Remy's eyes filled with tears. "I love this house."

"You don't know he's selling it. Call your uncle. Now," Willow said, handing Remy her phone.

Remy tapped the numbers. Her heart was pounding. "Hi, Uncle Danny," she said. She took a deep breath. "Mike was here. He said something about the cottage having to be finished by Columbus Day."

"I was going to call you soon, Remy," said the voice on the phone. Remy felt queasy. "I was talking to Albie about the real estate market—it's picked up—and I think it makes more sense to sell than rent. Don't worry about the painting, I know you offered to do it, but I'll bring in a crew to take care of that."

Fresh tears sprang to Remy's eyes. Willow patted her arm. "Oh." Jake and Teddy looked at Remy with concern.

"But don't worry, once it's under contract, I'll look for another fixer-upper, happy to cut the same deal with you," Uncle Danny said. "Might take some time to find one though," he added.

Mike was right. She was going to lose her house.

Remy worked to get words past the giant lump in her throat. "Remy, are you there? I know this is a surprise."

Remy felt she'd been gut-punched. Fighting nausea, she found her voice. "Oh. I understand. Of course. That makes sense."

Uncle Danny's voice was sympathetic. "I'd offer to let you stay here again but, you know, Jackie. You understand." The last thing Jackie, her uncle's new girlfriend, would want was an adult niece underfoot. "I'll keep an eye out for a winter rental for you. Sorry to pull the rug out, but you've got time, I'm sure you'll find something."

"Plenty of time," Remy said.

The garden was as serene and lovely as ever. The zinnias and cosmos planted against the picket fence bloomed in sumptuous July profusion, the basil grew fat and happy, and the cherry tomatoes reddened ripe as the heirloom varieties plumped on their vines. Coop rolled in the sun on the grass. A vine of some sort had begun to twine itself over the lichen-covered stone wall under the old apple trees. Remy gazed around her garden, her little paradise. Destined to become someone else's.

Her stomach was balled in a knot. Ridiculous to get so upset. Perhaps the house wouldn't sell right away. Perhaps she'd still be here to pick the apples and grapes and beach plums and would be able to make all those jams and jellies. Perhaps it might take until next spring or summer, or even longer, to find a buyer. That happened. Sometimes.

Or perhaps the cottage would be snatched up. Just like that. Remy would buy it in a second if she could. Taking a deep breath, she wiped away tears. She wouldn't be homeless. There would be a rental. Somewhere. Worse comes to worst, Remy could couch-surf with Willow and other friends. It wasn't the end of the world.

Down the path, the hens clucked in a fuss over something before settling down. Her chickens. Fresh tears filled Remy's eyes. The flock needed a place to live too. If finding an affordable rental was hard, finding one that would take a dog and also had land for keeping Ada Queetie and the rest of the ladies would be nearly impossible. But the idea of giving her hens to some farmer, no matter how kind, broke Remy's heart.

She stood and walked down the path to the chicken pen with the dog at her heels. Coop waited patiently outside the fence as Remy went inside, picked up Ada Queetie, and cried.

"Hi, this is Linda Fletcher from the *MV Times*. Do you have a minute?"

"Sure. How can I help you?"

A long chat with Willow and a visit to Eli's bed had Remy feeling better, but much as she tried, it was hard not to brood over her housing woes. A call from a reporter was a distraction if nothing else.

"Well, I understand you found a wonder dog," she said. "We'd like to talk to you; get some more details for our article. Some pictures, if you are OK with that. Everybody loves a good dog story, especially with a happy ending."

"Dog story?"

"Maybe I don't have the right number. Didn't you rescue a dog that jumped from the ferry?"

"Coop? Oh. Yes." At the sound of his name, Coop stood up and padded over. "But how did you find out?" Remy asked.

"You haven't seen the Instagram post? My sister showed it to me. Let me see…. It was posted by a MorganGorgon. Then it was just basic investigative reporting to track you and the owners down." The reporter chuckled. "Pretty amazing, that dog!"

"I guess so."

"Where exactly did you find him and how did you know he jumped from the ferry? What condition was he in after his adventure?"

Remy opened her Instagram account as the reporter talked. Morgan had made a minivideo of Coop in midair leaping for a ball superimposed over a cartoon of a ferry boat, and she'd also posted a selfie of herself with Coop, captioned *Fabulous furry dog flings from ferry to flee family, finds friend.*

"Oh. I found him on the beach at West Chop." She ran through Coop's story again.

"I bet the family was happy to get him back. What was their reaction?"

Remy paused. "Have you talked to the owners?"

"They refused to talk to me. Rude man. I'm going to write the story anyway. The Steamship Authority confirmed that a report had been made that a dog had jumped, likely from the car deck."

"Coop's a great swimmer. He's a Barbet, which is a French hunting dog. How about I send you a couple of pictures of him swimming?"

"That would be great."

"I've got to run. Bye." Remy hung up before the reporter could ask more questions.

Remy texted two pictures of Coop swimming in Tisbury Great Pond, one of him shaking water from his coat, and another of him standing in her yard, looking very handsome.

"You're going to be in the paper. How do you like that?" Coop wagged his tail. She glanced at her watch. "Speaking of swimming, how'd you like a swim in the pond? We have time. And your old owner is coming over later."

Audrey Kemp arrived promptly at 11:15, yoga clothes snug on her birdlike frame. After an enthusiastic greeting from her ex-dog, the three went to sit in the garden.

"I can't thank you enough, Remy," Audrey said. "Beaucoup—Coop—seems like a different dog. He seems so happy with you."

Remy sipped her tea. "I got a call this morning from a reporter at the *MV Times*. They're writing a story about Coop jumping from the ferry."

"Oh, isn't that nice?" Audrey nibbled on a cookie. "I once thought I wanted to be a reporter. But I think I was a better editor. But that was all before Tony."

Remy debated whether to bill Audrey for chitchat. "At a newspaper?"

"No. My family was—is—in publishing. We own a publishing house. It's small but prestigious. But, unfortunately, not very profitable." Audrey broke off a piece of cookie. "I did everything—fiction, nonfiction. It was a wonderful job."

"I imagine your children are big readers," Remy said, trying to figure out how to steer the conversation around to scheduling.

"Not one bit." Audrey rolled her eyes. "The girls take after their father. In so many ways."

"Food too?" Remy opened her notebook. "Shall we start with the shopping list?"

They eventually agreed on a trial schedule for the week: two restaurant reservations, two prepared dinners (Batty's lasagna and pot roast), three nights dining at the Inn. She quizzed Audrey on Tony's favorite foods (yuck, Pringles, canned ravioli, Slim Jims), drinks (more yuck, box wine, Natty Lite), and activities (mulligan golf). Money appeared to be no object: the more Remy offered to do; the happier Audrey seemed to be. Remy would put the reservations in Audrey's Outlook calendar; Audrey, using her classes at the Yoga Barn as a subterfuge for the visits up-Island, would stop by Remy's to pick everything up.

After Audrey left, Remy estimated her hours and what she'd bill the Kemps and smiled. At last, she'd make the target in her business plan. It was as if the last tumbler in the lock had fallen into place, opening the door to a realization of her many blessings: a successful business, a shaggy dog, good friends, a lovely-albeit-temporary place for her and her hens to live—and, of course, a gorgeous, passionate lover.

Life would never be perfect, but she was a very, very lucky girl.

# CHAPTER 30

Tuesday. Remy's day off. Enigmatically, Eli had asked her to "dress up a bit, wear some sexy shoes" and promised her a surprise. Remy had dropped Coop at Willow's and was almost wiggly with eagerness.

She'd picked her shoes first. An easy choice: vintage Yves Saint Laurent red sandals with a heel and ankle strap, hand-me-downs from Madame. She'd wobble but they made her legs look fantastic. After some deliberation, she'd decided on a snug black dress. Hair up in a loose bun and a careful application of French red lipstick, *naturellement*, and pearl drop earrings. Remy started with a simple silver necklace but exchanged it for a narrow red silk ribbon tied around her neck: she would come wrapped with a bow. The red ribbon had a ghoulish fashion past, the post-French Revolution style *à la victime*, but it looked sexy and went with the red sandals and lipstick.

Remy swayed and lurched on the uneven granite path to the house and let herself in. "Just a minute," Eli called from upstairs.

She walked over to the living room window and gazed out over the lawn sloping down to the boulder-edged pond. Beyond that, the beach ran for miles in broad sweeping curves. A cormorant sat on Lone Rock, and the waters of Vineyard Sound were clear and nearly Caribbean-blue in the sunshine.

Eli came up from behind and kissed her neck. Remy turned around and wrapped her arms around his back. In her heels, they were nearly the same height. She let her hands slide down his backside.

"You own whale shorts," she said, eyeing his pink Bermuda shorts embroidered with small spouting cetaceans.

"Ah, but we're going to Nantucket for lunch. This is my disguise—I'm in camouflage. Now for yours." Eli went into the closet and pulled out a shopping bag.

"Wait. I can't go off-Island. What if one of my clients needs me?"

"Come now, Remy. You deserve a few hours off," Eli said, smiling.

"I do, but…"

"We're flying—need be, we can have you back here in a flash."

Remy bit her lip as she weighed the risk. Eli's offer was tempting—so very, very, tempting. And she would have her phone, after all.

Eli opened the shopping bag. Inside was a pair of huge dark sunglasses and a large-brimmed black hat. "Now, for your disguise. I've decided on Italian contessa. Or Spanish marquesa. Your choice. Your outfit is perfect, by the way."

"What?"

"As I said, I'm putting you in disguise—we can't have anyone recognizing you, right?" Eli walked over and caressed Remy's shoulders. "Aqsa left these behind. She won't mind you borrowing them.

Remy pushed down a jolt of jealousy. "Oh."

He slipped on the sunglasses and hat and led Remy by the hand to a mirror. There, looking back at her, was a sleek, wealthy, European woman, eyes enigmatic behind dark designer glasses, nose transformed into an aristocratic beak, glossy red lips parted in surprise. "Oh, I almost forgot this." Eli reached into his pocket and pulled out a small box. Remy held her breath as he pulled out a narrow rope bracelet of woven matte gold. "A little subdued for the contessa, but I thought this was more your style," he said, fastening it around her wrist. Eli stepped back and assessed Remy from head to toe. "Perfect."

"But Eli…" Remy finally said, looking at the bracelet and willing herself to give it back. "It's too expensive."

"You've been a cheap date. Indulge me." He smiled, clearly pleased with himself. "You look incredible." Remy looked again at the elegant, unknown woman in the mirror, then back at Eli. He glanced at his watch. "Time to go," he said and reached for her hand, "Contessa."

Remy returned his smile. "Can I be a French comtesse instead? I don't speak any Italian."

"*Oui, absolument*," he replied in impeccable French.

As she wobbled down the path on Eli's arm to his Land Cruiser, Remy felt like Cinderella. Was she destined to be a princess? Remy snorted at the idea, a very uncomtesselike noise. She should feel a fraud in her costume, like a child playing dress-up, but, somehow, she didn't. No one would call her out, especially with Eli as her arm accessory. Remy was, for the afternoon, his perfect match.

"I haven't been to Nantucket since high school. We'd take the ferry over for sports," Remy said, holding onto her hat in the wind. "This'll be fun. I've never gone out in disguise." She looked out the window. "Eli, you just missed the turn."

"As I said, we're flying, Comtesse."

"But the airport is back that way."

"I keep my plane at Katama."

"You're a pilot?"

"A good one. Don't worry. And we have perfect weather. Bluebird skies."

Remy's heart started to pound. She'd flown to the Island only once before, on Cape Air. The ridiculously expensive round trip to Boston meant that real people took the ferry and the dreaded Peter Pan bus. That one time, she'd been assigned to the copilot seat to properly balance the weight in the nine-seat plane, where she sat fascinated (and a bit terrified) as the pimpled pilot flipped switches, revved the two propeller engines, and lined up—a toy among the jumbo jets—for takeoff from Logan.

Eli looked over. "You're quiet. You're not afraid of flying?"

"No. Just excited. I've flown in a little plane only once."

"You're in for a treat." They trundled down past the Farm Institute and pulled in at the small grass airfield.

"There's Trixie. She's an old Cessna 206."

Remy's spike heels dug holes in the turf as they walked to the plane. "Why Trixie?"

"Her tail number ends with a T. See? And I have fond memories of a Trixie in the back room of a London pub when I was 15." He waggled his eyebrows suggestively. "Not quite elegant enough for a comtesse—you should be arriving in a private jet—but she'll do."

Eli buckled Remy into the copilot's seat then spent several minutes walking around the plane, working down the preflight checklist: windscreen wash check, rudder cables, brake lines, flaps, and static ports. Then he climbed onto the struts to inspect the fuel tanks, antennas, and wing surfaces. Satisfied, he climbed in and plugged in their headsets before doing mysterious things with switches and knobs and fussing with a tiny screen.

"A-OK. Ready for takeoff?" Eli asked. Remy nodded and gripped her seat. "How about a sightseeing tour around the Island first, then head over to Nantucket?"

"Sure." Remy's heart beat a tattoo in her chest. She understood why planes needed to be light, but Trixie felt uncomfortably like a tin can with wings. The fuel pump groaned as Eli pulled on other knobs and turned the key. Then the engine sputtered and caught, the hum of the motor sounding more like it was powered by cicadas than aviation fuel. As Eli turned a red-handled knob, the propeller smoothed into a blur.

"Area traffic, Niner One Six Three Tango taxiing to runway 15 for takeoff to the West." Working the rudders right and left, Eli steered Trixie to the end of the field, lowered the flaps, and turned her into the wind. The plane bumped along the grass runway eager to launch. Within seconds she was airborne and climbing. Eli raised the flaps, banked the plane west, and leveled off.

He reached over and rested his hand on Remy's knee and winked. "Doing OK?" Remy nodded again and grinned as the exhilaration of flying kicked in. The Island, so familiar from the road, was laid out below her in clear blues and greens. Parallel lines of breakers rolled across the full length of the south shore. Soon Tisbury Great Pond came into view, its narrow coves like the tentacles of a jellyfish. Remy spotted Teddy and Jake's house, but hers in town was hidden by trees. Next, Chilmark Pond—there was the Bottimore's house, down at the end—and Squibnocket Pond edged by the stretch of Far Beach. Then the brightly colored Gay Head cliffs rose at the end of Aquinnah. Eli waggled the plane's wings at the nude sunbathers at the very end, and they waved back.

"This is incredible," Remy said over the roar of the engine.

Eli nodded. "I got my pilot's license at 17. Trixie was my birthday present. Look, there's Menemsha." Remy looked down at the cluster of small houses and fishing shacks surrounding the docks. "Katama Airfield is one of the reasons I bought the house here. I take off whenever I want, go wherever I want." He turned and grinned at her. "Ultimate freedom, weather permitting." Eli banked and followed the north coastline of the Island. "And there's my place." He reduced altitude to give Remy a better look. There was the point with the house and barn and the freshwater pond. Remy saw the glimmer of a tiny circular pond set in the trees.

"Is that Thimble Pond?" she asked.

Eli nodded. "Shall we pay another visit to the love shack this week?"

Remy placed her hand on Eli's thigh and danced her fingers. "Oh yes."

But Eli was not done with his surprises. "*Nous sommes arrivés, chère comtesse,*" he announced upon landing at Nantucket's small airport. A black Audi was waiting for them at the airport. Remy did indeed feel like royalty.

"Is this the right place, Eli?" Remy asked, looking at the sign on the adorable clapboard house. "It says it opens at 6:00."

"Come this way." He led her by the hand to the back of the restaurant and knocked on the door. "To keep your cover, I've arranged for a private lunch."

"Just us?"

"Just us."

"The whole restaurant." Remy shook her head. "Wow."

A bowtied waiter opened the door and ushered them inside. He nodded respectfully to Remy and began discussing the proposed menu with Eli in rapid French, too fast for Remy to catch much other than *foie gras, coquilles avec caviar, homard, et île flottante.* That was more than enough to make Remy's mouth water. The waiter led them upstairs to a small table overlooking the harbor and disappeared.

"This OK, or would you rather be having a grilled cheese back at my place?" In reply, Remy leaned over to give him a lingering kiss. The waiter soon reappeared with two flutes and a bottle of Laurent-Perrier champagne.

Remy wiped red lipstick from Eli's lips. "Champagne?"

"I prefer this to Dom. I hope you aren't disappointed." Remy took a sip of the champagne and fell in love.

"I wouldn't know, but this is beyond delicious." She took another taste, trying to identify the flavors in the bright yellow liquid. Hazelnuts, perhaps, something sweeter than bread—brioche. Remy sighed with pleasure. She looked at the astoundingly handsome man across from her and realized that besides his money, fantastic taste, and top-notch bedroom skills, she knew next to nothing about him. "How come I couldn't find out anything about you online?"

"I use a program called Incognit. Developed by a friend of mine. It's like an invisibility cloak. I got tired of every computer science, software engineering and information systems major in the country asking me for a job."

"So if you took off your cloak, what would I find?"

Eli laughed. "Not much. The usual prep schools. Mostly in the U.K. My parents were in Hong Kong when I was young, and they got brainwashed about the superiority of British public schools.

That's what they call their private schools." He paused and took a sip of champagne. "Mine looked like Hogwarts, but I was miserable. All boys, of course, though I made do." He winked. "I finally convinced my parents to send me to school in the States for the last couple of years. Lawrence Academy, in Massachusetts. The British accent helped with girls, they were something new; the guys gave me shit, called me a twit. I never want to hear another Monty Python routine."

Remy bit her tongue; she was just about to ask him if he could do dead parrot. "Oh. That explains your accent. It reminds me of James Bond."

The first course arrived: a single perfect scallop, topped with black caviar, in a pool of beurre blanc. "Oh wow. Do you always eat like this?" Remy asked.

"No. But when I do, I indulge myself. I'm a hedonist, in case you hadn't noticed."

Remy smiled. "I've noticed. And I don't mind. College?" She dipped her fork into the caviar and let the salty, fishy beads roll around in her mouth before bursting them with her tongue.

"Yale. That's where Wolffs go. Elihu Yale—I'm named after him—was my great-great-great-grandfather or something. I nearly didn't graduate. Then, with my useless history degree, I decided to ski bum for a while. My parents have a sweet little cabin in Aspen. I was there, goofing around when this prep school buddy of mine—brilliant guy, Carnegie Mellon grad—calls me up with this idea. That was DataSee. He did the tech, and I found the start-up money and did everything else. The company ate up the next ten years, then we sold it, and here I am. Figuring out what to do next."

"Any ideas?"

"None. I think I'm going to split my time between here, New York, Aspen, and Paris—I have a flat there—until I figure it out." Remy's eyes lit up.

"Paris? Where?"

"Île Saint-Louis. You know Paris?"

"A little. I spent a year as an au pair in St. Germaine en Laye before going to college."

"What made you decide to do that?" Eli had looked bored telling his own story but now fixed his eyes on Remy with curiosity, charisma pouring out like the heady champagne.

"You know the children's book, *Madeline*?"

"Of course."

"Well, I loved it so much I made my parents let me take French instead of Spanish. Then I saw the movie *Amélie* when I was in high school and fell in love with Paris. I wanted to be Amélie, you know, working as a waitress and living in Montmartre." Remy colored pink. "Oh, that sounds stupid."

"Not at all, ma comtesse," Eli said warmly, taking her hand. "You follow your passions."

The waiter cleared the plates and brought the next course, *foie gras* served simply *en gelée* with toast. "Oh, oh, I haven't had *foie gras* for ages." She took a bite and swooned as the buttery goose liver melted in her mouth.

"Glad you like it. I wasn't sure. So, tell me about your French family."

"Four girls. Mostly well behaved." Remy took another bite. "And Madame was wonderful. Well, sort of a tyrant. But a well-meaning one. I think I was her project. She taught me how to shop, how to cook, how to eat, how to dress—these are her hand-me-downs," Remy said, sticking out a red sandal-clad foot. "She'd approve of the hat and sunglasses. They're exactly the chic sort of thing she'd wear." Remy smoothed her dress over her legs. "Tell me about your apartment."

"You'd like it. It's got a rooftop terrace with a view of Notre Dame. So tragic, the fire."

Remy nodded. "It was. Heartbreaking." Remy scraped the last bit of *foie gras* onto her toast point. "I know where that is. Berthillon—the ice cream place—was the children's favorite. And down the street, there was the most incredible hot chocolate."

"Chocolat De Neuville." Memories of the tiny cups of silky rich chocolate were interrupted by Eli leaning over to run a finger along Remy's lip. "I love *chocolat chaud*. Ladurée on the Champs-Élysées is my favorite. And th*eir praliné mille-feuilles*, fantastic."

"Voilà, Mademoiselle," said the waiter, interrupting. "Special, for you. *Homard à l'Américaine*." He poured a tablespoon of cognac over the next course and lit it with a match. "Lobster flambé in a tomato-wine sauce."

Wide-eyed, Remy watched the blue flame. The waiter served the lobster and refilled her champagne glass. Eli held his finger over his glass to indicate he'd had enough. He had the natural curiosity of the best conversationalists, and Remy found herself recounting everything from high school to college to her failed marriage to the launch of Nest as they savored their way through the lobster and, *enfin, île flottante*, a fluffy, egg-rich dessert.

It wasn't just champagne that was spinning Remy's head.

"What next—a walk around town? Some shopping?" Eli asked over cups of espresso.

"I don't think I can manage the sidewalks in these shoes," she said. "Not to say my food stupor." Remy sat back and groaned. "And too much champagne. That was—no exaggeration—the best meal I've ever had."

"Then let's head back. Unless you want to get a room here?" Eli asked with a wink. "There's an inn next door."

"*Non, je préfère ta chambre.*" Remy was beginning to hatch a plan, a surprise of her own.

No check arrived—Eli had already taken care of the bill. He merely handed Remy her hat and sunglasses and escorted her downstairs where she waited as Eli, in gorgeous French, complimented the chef. Outside in the bright sunshine, the car waited to take them back to the airport.

"We don't check in, go through security?" Remy asked as they bypassed the terminal.

"We get to go straight to the plane. One of the perks of flying myself." Eli opened the door and helped Remy inside. "I'll be back in a minute. I need to pick up a quart of oil. Trixie's running low."

Remy got straight to work. Wiggling in her tight dress, she scrambled over the two middle passenger seats to the back of the plane with her props. She pulled the sleeping bag from Eli's crate marked "Emergency Supplies." Unrolling the bag, she spread it over a big quilt to pad the floor, then patted the bed down—a little lumpy, but it would do—and got ready.

Wearing naught but Eli's leather bomber jacket, her sandals, a scrap of panties, and his aviator Ray-Ban sunglasses, Remy lay down on the sleeping bag like a WWII pinup: knee raised, cocked hip, bent arm beneath her head. She'd never done anything like this before. Eli better not laugh; she'd die of embarrassment.

Minutes, maybe, but it felt like an eternity before Eli returned to the plane. Licking her freshly lipsticked mouth, she tried to convince herself that she was a sexy French comtesse, not a personal concierge from dinky Martha's Vineyard.

At last, Eli opened the door and looked inside. "Remy?"

"Back here." He peered over the row of seats and grinned.

Remy tapped the clipboard with her pen. "Ready to fly?" she asked, letting the jacket fall open.

Eli climbed back to the tail of the plane. "Roger Wilco, captain."

The next day, Remy landed on her real-life runway with a jolt, like a tiny plane bouncing along Katama's lumpy grass airstrip. Her day started, oh joy, with a call from the Soulanskis: their renters had put lobster shells down the garbage disposal and jammed it. Would she please fix it? If not, call the plumber? (Bump.) Then Enid Cinch emailed (bump-bump): their weekend guests had changed plans, would Remy push everything—the reservation for dinner at the Beach Plum Inn, tee times at Farm Neck and Mink Meadows, the sailing charter on *Tigress*, appointments for private gallery showings, the catered dinner—back a week?

Garbage disposal first, an hour pulling sharp bits of shell and stinky salad from the blades. The sides of the disposal coated Remy's hand in black slime. It was about as far as one could get from silky bites of *homard à l'Américaine*. The memories of the day before, the flight, the exquisite lunch, the sex, seemed unreal, like scenes she'd read in a romance novel. Had she really sat sipping $150 champagne and eating cognac-flamed lobster chunks while flirting with her impossibly rich lover? Wasn't her lobster reality this? Smelly shells in a garbage disposal? She tugged on a thick piece of wedged claw. The blade (or the shell, did it matter?) sliced the side of her finger, deep and long enough to need stitches. Yelping in pain, Remy bled all over the white marble countertop. (Bump-bump-bump.)

Then at 4:00, the sitter for the Hartwells' grandchildren canceled. Remy called Mrs. Hartwell and got the daughter instead, who begged her to please fill in, even if she could find another sitter, they didn't want a stranger with the kids. It was the Hartwells' anniversary, Remy knew—she'd made the restaurant reservation, after all—and she couldn't disappoint her favorite client. There went Remy's plans with Eli, Chinese takeout and a sunset beach walk inevitably followed by some SS. But Eli seemed not to care: he was about to cancel on *her* in favor of a cocktail party hosted by some literary grand dame in Vineyard Haven.

So Remy spent her day at the clinic waiting for stitches and making calls, and her evening with five beastly children who didn't want to play a game, didn't want to watch the same movie, didn't like their dinner, and liked being told to go to bed not at all. Remy's finger throbbed and her patience was worn to a thread.

But the worst was yet to come.

Remy woke up, looked at the bandage on her index finger, and vowed to put her crappy Wednesday behind her. She was due at the Hartwells' in the morning, but free afterward to make a surprise visit to Eli. She'd planned a redo of Chinese-food-then-Thimble-Pond for the evening, but there was no reason not to drop by earlier too. Willow would say that the karma balance had been restored—one crap day to counterweight magical Nantucket.

Remy leaned over to pick up the gold bracelet from her bedside table, then flopped back, dangling it from a finger. It really was perfect. Bangles banged your wrist, and cuffs, well, they suited Wonder Woman but not her. The brushed gold was braided like a ship's rope, with a nearly invisible clasp and a tiny double-latch to keep it secure. The sun set the gold aglow with an inner, molten light. Remy clipped it to her wrist and smiled.

Nantucket had been real. The bracelet proved that. She had dressed up like a comtesse, eaten a superb lunch, and seduced Eli in the back of his plane. (Had the other pilots noticed Trixie bouncing on her shocks?) Impossible fantasy, but she couldn't help but imagine what it would be like, if sex evolved to love, if she were to join his world where no one worried about paying the bills or satisfying picky clients, a world where she'd just get on a plane and fly to Paris for the weekend simply because she wanted to.

After her morning tasks, Remy changed into a barely-there top and tiny shorts for her surprise visit to Eli's. She added a dab of Dior J'adore, which she loved for its heady fresh jasmine and hint of citrus, between her breasts. This trip was for pleasure, not work.

Remy could almost drive the dirt road to Eli's blindfolded. She knew every rut and patch of washboard. She'd ask Eli for another French lesson; there was something so sexy about speaking French in bed. Then her mind drifted to Paris, imagining the two of them strolling down Rue Saint-Louis en l'Île, scarves around their necks like true Parisians, for silky liquid *chocolat chaud* on a blustery fall day. They'd make their way along the Seine, then head back up to Eli's pied-à-terre to make love, simply to pass the time until dinner at Eli's favorite bistro, where the waiter knew to seat them at the best table and bring out Eli's favorite dishes (no need for a menu!) with a special bottle of vintage Bordeaux.

To make her arrival a surprise, Remy parked in a pullout up from the house, walked the last 20 yards, and snuck inside. Remy heard footsteps above and crept up the stairs, walking carefully on the edges to avoid a giveaway creak. This would be a silent ninja attack. The door to Eli's bedroom was ajar. A rustling of sheets. Perfect. The lazy man must be about to take a post-lunch nap. She slid the strap of her top off her shoulder, put a seductive smile on her face, and pushed open the door, ready to ambush her napping lover.

What she saw caused Remy to recoil in heart-stopping shock. Eli wasn't alone. The color drained from her face as she stared first at the naked breasts of a blond woman sitting up in the bed, then at a slight, dark-haired man with his hand on Eli's bare chest. The room smelled of fresh salt air—and sex.

"Remy, these are my dear friends Olivia and David," Eli said as easily if he were introducing them at a party. "They decided to surprise me by coming a day early. I was going to call you, but we got distracted. A little ménage-à-trois, as you see."

"Pleased to make your acquaintance, Remy," David said in a BBC-worthy British accent. He cocked one eyebrow at Eli.

"Well, hello," said Olivia in an equally posh voice. "And you are...?"

"Remy's my personal concierge."

"I hope she remembered to bring that cheese you were raving about," Olivia said, getting out of bed to look out the window. "Perhaps she can bring it up for a snack."

Remy stood, aghast, heart sprinting against her rib cage, unable to believe what was before her eyes. She knew that she should just leave, but the shock had glued her feet to the floorboards.

"Eli said he wasn't lonely up here all by himself. I guess you're why," David said.

Remy looked again from the woman to the man back to Eli, registering Eli's glazed, satisfied eyes. "David's an old friend from Charterhouse in England. The boarding school that I told you about," Eli said.

"Close friend, you know, no girls within 50 miles. But we made up for it later. Still, old friends are the best," David added, caressing Eli's chest.

The words barely registered. Remy's shock was turning to nausea. She remained glued to the floor. Her mind urged her to flee, leave this horrible tableau behind. Olivia returned to the bed, looking at Remy as if wondering why the help was just standing there.

"David's an investment banker now, of all things, in the City," said Eli.

"Oh, New York," Remy said stupidly.

"London," corrected David. "And Olivia is at the Tate. So, you see we've come a long way to see our dear friend Eli."

"Not just 'at the Tate'," said Eli. "Olivia is the director."

Eli put his arms behind his head and considered Remy in her skimpy outfit. "I have an idea. Why don't you join us, Remy? Today's lesson can be *partie carrée*, a foursome. What do you think, *ma chère? Ça serait merveilleux,* marvelous, I promise. David, Olivia, don't you agree?"

Olivia raised her eyebrows, more interested now. David made a slow head-to-toe perusal of Remy, lingering on her breasts, clearly visible through her thin top. Then, smiling, he ran the tip of his tongue lightly across his upper lip. He patted the bed, looked at Remy's stunned face, then turned to Eli. "I think we've shocked her."

"Come on, Remy, don't look so surprised. I didn't take you for a prude." Eli put on a reassuring smile. "If this is your first time in a foursome, we'll take it slow. You said you like new things."

"No," Remy almost whispered. "I can't."

Olivia stood again and, smiling, took Remy's hand, and gave a little tug. "Come. It'll be fun."

"I don't bite, love," David added. "Two blokes for the price of one, eh?" He slid his hand down under the covers in case it wasn't 100 percent clear what he meant.

Remy's eyes darted from the bed to the dark red polish on Olivia's perfectly manicured hand. "No. I can't," she repeated, shaking her head.

Olivia gave Remy's hand a gentle squeeze before releasing it. "Later, perhaps," she said. "Think about it. You're a lovely girl."

"I hope you aren't upset, Remy. It's not a big deal," Eli reassured her. "I'm going to show Olivia and David around the Island today. Why don't you come back for dinner tonight, now that they are in on our little secret? But let's upgrade from Chinese to Italian. Can you pick up the scallop gnocchi—that was fabulous—and spaghetti *alle vongole*? And tiramisu for dessert."

There, seared into her brain, was Eli in his ménage-à-trois with that unfocused post-sex look in his eyes, while the innocent daisies she'd arranged sat in their little glass jar on the bedside. Then the appalling proposal. David's lascivious lip-lick, as if she were a morsel he anticipated tasting. Olivia, with her seductive smile and taut nipples, tugging her into Eli's bed for a little *partie carrée*.

Remy wasn't a worldly, sophisticated comtesse. She was a simple Island girl who needed to go home, crawl into bed, and put her head under the covers.

But hiding there hadn't made it any better. Remy rolled onto her side and slowly stroked Coop's silky ear. Stupid, to be so upset. Had she begun to think that Eli Wolff would be her boyfriend, that he'd fall in love with her and sweep her away like some Prince Charming? She'd relaxed when Eli had said it was only one couple coming for the weekend, some old dear friends for a "hedonistic weekend," and not that gorgeous, kale-smoothie-drinking Aqsa. Never, ever, would she have guessed what he meant. Remy pulled the covers back over her head and moaned.

But Coop didn't understand naps or crying. He nosed Remy's ear with doggy concern and softly woofed. She pulled the sheet from her head to face reality: her dog, her unfaithful lover, and a long list of undone concierge tasks. Including, she thought with a punch to her gut, grocery shopping for Eli and his "dear friends." And bringing them dinner. The hour in bed hadn't changed anything.

A knock on the door. Remy rolled out of bed, dragged herself downstairs, and opened the front door. "Jake," Remy said dumbly.

Jake tilted his head in concern, taking in her red-rimmed, swollen eyes, and pasty face. "Remy, are you OK?"

"I'm fine," she lied.

"Sorry to bother you, but you don't have the second Quansoo key, by any chance? We can't find it again." Remy shook her head no. Jake stepped forward and put his hand on her shoulder. "Are you sure you're OK?"

"I don't know. Maybe I'm coming down with something," she replied feebly.

"Can I bring you some chicken soup or something? I've got some homemade in the freezer." Jake peered into her face, catching Remy's look of revulsion. "Oh, your chickens. That was the wrong thing to offer, I guess."

"No, it's not that. I eat chicken. I just have no appetite. Don't worry, some tea and toast and a nap and I'll be fine."

"How about I fix something for you now and bring it up?" Jake said.

"I'll do it myself. Really."

Jake looked unconvinced. He gave her shoulder a gentle squeeze. "I've got a friend from Boston here—she's waiting in the car. I'm taking her to Aquinnah, but I'll send Teddy over to check on you later. Take care of yourself, Remy."

"Have a nice time." She padded into the kitchen and put on the kettle for tea. The sight of her whiteboard more than pricked. It stabbed. There in red marker, with three exclamation marks, was Thursday's SS, underlined. Twice.

Finally, Remy felt a welcome flash of anger as she picked up the eraser.

# CHAPTER 31

The gods had smiled upon Remy: Eli, Olivia, and David were out when she'd returned later with the weekend's groceries and who-cares-if-it-gets-cold Italian food (though the smell of the seafood combined with the bumpy road and the appalling prospect of seeing them again nearly undid her). Teddy dropped by later with soup, Choco-Teds (the healing treat), and sympathy, promised her a big hug when she didn't have germs, and like his brother, patted her shoulder with concern. That helped.

The next day found her seesawing up and down. Remy forced herself to keep busy with work. She had no choice; she could erase SS but not her clients. But with the force of will, she (semi-successfully) shoved thoughts of Eli to a corner of her mind where she *might* deal with them later. Then, with tears, leftover chicken soup, and wine, she realized that she had been mourning the bursting of her little imaginary dream bubble.

Remy, a girl from tiny Martha's Vineyard, was a college dropout working as a concierge to pay her bills. Her best friends grew mushrooms, sewed bags to sell at a flea market, and repaired houses. She wasn't going to start jet-setting around, visiting Paris and Aspen with Eli and his friends, an investment banker "in the

City" and the director of one of the most prestigious art museums in the world. Remy wouldn't even have met Olivia and David if they hadn't arrived a day early. The only thing they had in common was Eli—and his bed.

Then Eli called. No way would she answer. It was bad enough listening to the message later, his voice apologizing for upsetting her. It had nothing to do with the two of them. Just a little experiment. He cared about her and hoped she'd be over for Sunday night leftovers.

Remy doubted what she interrupted was an "experiment." Or that he really cared for her. Gorgeous, charismatic Eli Wolff was used to getting what he wanted, and Remy was sure he wanted to keep his concierge conveniently available to hop into his bed.

She was smart enough to have known what the deal was. And stupid enough to let herself dream that it could be anything else.

"No. Don't flop that way. Stand up!" Remy ordered Willow's canopy tent contraption. It was supposed to pop open, easy as an umbrella, but instead, Remy found herself dealing with supports and legs that were all going the wrong way until the leatherworker guy in the next booth gave her a hand. Then, she had to deal with the tables and racks, unpacking crate after crate of bags and shirts and hats. Remy was happy to do Willow a favor, but it would drive Remy nuts if she had to set up and break down the booth twice a week, Wednesdays and Saturdays, all summer long.

The morning was cool and overcast, perfect for shopping, and the hours passed by quickly. "Hey, Remy-sweet," Teddy called, walking up with a plastic cup. "I'm ready for my shift. Jake dropped me off. How's it going?"

"Busy." Remy made a face. "I overheard that couple over there call my paintings 'kitsch'," she said, turning her head to glare at the offending tourists.

"Aw, poor Remy. Nasty old summer people."

"It's ok. So long as they spend money," Remy said. "Willow just sent me a text. She says thank you and that she's having a great time in Maine."

"Willow-pillow deserves to get away." Teddy picked up his lemonade and offered it to Remy, who took a sip and handed it back. "Besides, I'm looking for reasons to get out of the house. I mean I like Jane and all, but it's like having an icicle around." He stretched his arms overhead, exposing a stretch of chubby Teddy-tummy. "I'm lying on the sofa in my boxers and she comes in and gives me this look. Hoo-ee! It's like my nuts got froze." Teddy tugged on his shorts. "I've been walking on eggshells. And she and Jake. It's like they're speaking a different language, hybrid consciousness and ethical ambiguity and shit."

"Who's Jane?"

"Over there with Jake. She's a women's studies prof at Tufts. Our *houseguest.*" Teddy pointed down to where Jake stood at a jewelry booth with a tall, slender woman with striking pale-blond hair. "I don't know how long she's staying, but our little house just got *way* too small. Man, what a pair," he added, shaking his head.

The blond picked up a silver necklace, and Jake leaned over to clasp it around her neck. This must be the "friend" Jake had taken to Aquinnah. The woman placed her hand on Jake's shoulder. Remy felt a twinge of jealousy as Jake leaned close to examine the necklace then pulled out his wallet to pay.

Remy turned back to Teddy. "OK. Do you know how to make the credit card reader work? And calculate tax?"

"Nope," said Teddy. "Look, here they come."

"Hey, guys. Jane, this is the handicraft place I was telling you about." Jake said.

Jane lifted her sunglasses to the top of her head and extended a narrow hand to Remy. "I'm Jane Booth," she said in a cool voice. Close up, she looked like a Nordic goddess, with pale, almost colorless hair pulled back in a thick braid, gorgeous cheekbones, and light blue eyes. The new silver necklace Jake had just bought for her gleamed around her slender neck.

"Remy Litchfield. I live around the corner from Jake and Teddy. That's a lovely necklace," she said, feeling Jake's eyes on her, probably comparing her (unfavorably, Remy was sure) with Jane.

"Thank you. Everyone is so, um, crafty here on the Island."

That's us, quaint and crafty. "Yes," Remy said, "My friend Willow sews everything here by hand."

It was very strange how Jake was looking at Remy, not Jane. Remy crossed her arms, trying to hide the silly cartoon chicken on her T-shirt.

"Except for the paintings," said Jake. "Remy's an artist. You're feeling better?"

"Much better."

"How about a new beach bag, Jane," Teddy said, handing Jane a large red-and-orange patchwork tote. "This one holds lots of stuff. Or a hat?" he suggested and plonked a yellow batik hat on her head.

Jane blinked and gave Teddy a weak smile. She took the hat off and handed the bag back. "Oh, no thank you." She glanced at her watch. "Jake, did you forget about our reservation?"

"Don't you want to see Remy's paintings first?" Jake asked. "She's very talented."

Jane looked supremely uninterested. "Yes, of course. But then we have to go. Nice to meet you, Remy," Jane said and rested her hand on Jake's arm.

"Nice to meet you too," Remy lied.

Jake gave Remy a crooked smile as they walked around to the side of the booth where her paintings hung. Barnyard animal art, suitable as a joke gift, would be no more Jane's style than Willow's "crafty" bags.

"Like I said, Jane is some icicle. Brrr," Teddy whispered. He hugged Remy into his side. "Not like you."

"Thanks, Teddy."

With a wave, Jake wandered off with Jane on his arm. They looked like the perfect couple. Jake's thick black hair set off Jane's pale shining braid, matched in attractiveness and nearly in height. Lucky Jane, sailing across the pond with Jake in *Utopia*, relaxing on the beach as they read their serious books, joining Jake for lobster rolls and chowder in Menemsha at sunset. Even their names went together, Jake-and-Jane. Remy thought about getting the story from Teddy but changed her mind. She knew everything she wanted to know.

# CHAPTER 32

"You're sure it's OK, my always dropping in like this?" Audrey apologized again as she rubbed Coop's ears.

"It's absolutely fine. I'm just about finished up here," Remy said. "Iced tea?"

"That would be wonderful." Audrey wandered over to the table where Remy was putting final touches—a spiral of olives—on an arrival platter. "This looks fantastic. Almost like a painting, only with cheese and charcuterie."

Remy was pleased with herself. "A bit. The swirls were inspired by Van Gogh's *Starry Night*. I did a *Sunflowers*-inspired one last week that came out really well too." Remy stretched plastic wrap over the platter and slid it into the fridge. "My favorite client gets one of these every week. They're fun to do." She pulled out the pitcher of tea. "I'm glad you stopped by. I'll get my notebook."

"Such a nice article in the *MV Times* about Beaucoup," Audrey said when Remy returned with her binder. Coop rolled over onto his back and closed his eyes in bliss as Audrey rubbed his belly. "But the girls were furious when they heard Tony refused to meet with the reporter. They wanted their picture in the paper too. Did you see it?"

"No." Remy handed Audrey her glass. "I forgot to pick up a copy."

"Oh, I've got it here," Audrey said, rummaging in her big bag. "Here you go."

Remy scanned the article. They'd printed two of the photos she'd sent. No mention of the Kemps, only (incorrectly) that the dog had been happily reunited with its family. "He looks cute," she said and opened her notebook. "Let's see. Something different for the salad greens this time? Tabor Farm has a nice mix with a little arugula."

Audrey wrinkled her tiny nose. "Tony only likes iceberg. But get the other for me." She turned back to stroking the dog and Remy jotted down a note. "Oh, he asked for shrimp scampi."

"No problem. I'll pick up the ingredients."

"Oh, could you? Enough for two—the twins won't eat it. And some extra for shrimp cocktail."

Unexpectedly, Remy flushed with a wave of hot, sad emotion as her mind flashed back to a plate of fat juicy shrimp with spicy cocktail sauce brought to her by Eli wearing nothing more than his most devilish, charming grin.

"Are you OK?" Audrey asked in a gentle voice.

Something in the tone of her voice, so empathetic, released Remy's tears. "I'm fine. It's just boyfriend problems."

"Do you want to talk about it? I'm kind of an expert in man problems, even if I don't take my own advice."

Remy looked at the kindness in Audrey's eyes. She did want to tell someone. Badly. Remy hadn't wanted to burden Willow while she was away on her minivacation, but the need to talk was about as hot as a pot ready to boil over. She took a deep breath. "I caught my…." Remy paused as she decided what to call Eli Wolff. "My guy in bed with another woman—and a man. I didn't even know he was bi. Or into that sort of thing."

Audrey caught her breath. "Oh my."

"And to make things worse, he wanted a foursome." Remy gave a bitter laugh. "I said no."

"I've been there. Well, not exactly, but Tony with other women. Yes." Audrey brushed her hair out of her face with her hand. Her sleeve slipped down, exposing bruises, shaped like fingers, on her thin arm. "Have you two been together long?"

Remy paused, dismayed at the bruises. "No, not long I guess I don't know him that well. We're very different people."

Audrey reached over to pat Remy's hand. "At least you found out early what he was like. Not like me, married to a serial philanderer. My marriage certainly isn't everything it was cracked up to be." Remy glanced up. She couldn't imagine Tony's appeal to any woman. Audrey read her look. "You'd be surprised, he can be very charming and generous. I can't fault him there." She fingered her designer purse. "Though his taste…." Audrey looked at Remy. "Tony has a weakness for a pretty face, big boobs, and a tiny brain, so far as I can tell. I'm not sure how he ended up married to me," she added, glancing down at her flat chest.

"And you're OK with that?"

"I didn't find out until after the twins were born. It was a tough pregnancy. Months in bed, and it took me a long time to recover. So we weren't, you know, intimate for a long time." She took a deep breath and raised her eyes. "Then there were babies to take care of, and I didn't have the energy. He's discreet. Mostly. Then, somewhere along the way, I just got used to the idea. He says it has nothing to do with us, and I believe him. He yells at me sometimes—he can't help it—but he loves me."

"Eli doesn't love me." Remy stopped. She hadn't intended to mention Eli's name, but Audrey gave no sign she recognized it. "He claims he cares for me, but I'm sure he was just in it for the sex. Like me," she added, trying to convince herself. "I'll get over him. I just have to stay distracted with other stuff. Like work." Remy took a deep breath. She picked up the binder and pen. "OK. Garlic, pasta, shrimp, and parsley. Anything else?"

"Some cold cuts for lunch? And some more Cheese Nips. Tony finished the box the other day," she said as Remy's cell rang. "Do you need to get that?"

Remy glanced at the phone. "No. It's my friend Nate. He's probably just checking the schedule for next week. His wife does goat yoga classes."

"Goat yoga?"

Then a text. *Remy, call me asap. I think your chickens escaped.* "Oh no." Remy quickly hit redial. "Sorry, Audrey, I may have a chicken crisis on my hands."

"Chicken crisis?"

"I'll explain." She tapped his number. "Hi, Nate. What's this about my chickens?"

"Are they kind of gray with striped feathers and a clump of feathers on their heads, sort of like a chicken pompadour?"

"Yes. Oh geez. I told my neighbor her grandkids could visit them. The kids must have left the gate open. Where are they?"

"They're wandering around the Field Gallery, mostly. Guess they like art." Nate laughed. "It's pretty funny, actually. I've got Nan—you know my dog—keeping an eye out so they don't cross the road. Hey, I got a joke for you. Why did the chicken cross the road? To get to Alley's."

"Ha, ha, Nate. I'll be there in a sec with my car, and I'll bring the crab net." Remy turned to Audrey. "Sorry, I got to go catch my chickens."

Audrey's eyes lit up. "Can I help? I'm fast—lots of practice chasing twins!"

Three hens were still in the chicken pen. Remy grabbed the cracked corn and mealworms and secured the gate. That meant 25 chickens were on the wing somewhere between her house and the Field Gallery. She'd chased her chickens before but never the whole flock. They were crafty little birds, letting her get within an inch of grabbing them before taking off at top speed in a zig-zaggy dash.

The lawn in front of the gallery was chaos and laughter, full of people taking photos and little kids running after the chickens. Two hens perched on the outstretched arms of a dancing Tom Maley sculpture. The rest pecked in groups of three or four in the garden and on the edges of the field. Remy parked the Toyota, rolled down a window, opened one door, and slammed it on a towel to make a curtain. She'd have to use her car as a holding cell.

"Hey, Nate. What a mess. Thanks so much for calling," Remy said, walking over. "And thank you, Nan, for keeping the chickens out of the road," she added as she patted the black-and-white border collie mix.

"No problem," Nate said with a smile, adjusting baby Gaia in her sling. "I've had a lot of experience with this sort of thing." They watched a hen escape the outstretched hands of a little girl. "I think chickens are even faster than goats."

Audrey stood by the car with a big grin. "So, what's the plan?"

"Let's round up some volunteers and I'll explain." There was, fortunately, no shortage of helpers. Remy armed one group with mealworms and a battle plan: sit on the ground, get a hen interested with mealworm number one, gain her confidence with mealworm number two, and go for the grab with mealworm number three. The rest she'd use as a human net, she hoped, to trap chickens in the corner of the L-shaped gallery building. Any birds that failed to fall for either technique would have to be chased the old-fashioned way.

An adolescent voice cracked behind Remy. "I caught one! I caught a chicken!" The pimpled stock boy from Alley's jumped to his feet with a chicken clutched to his chest. "I can't believe I caught a chicken!"

Remy walked over. "Thanks, Zach. I think that's Pinky. Just put her in the car through the towel there," she said pointing to her Toyota. "One down, two dozen to go."

"Chook-chook-chook-chook," Remy called, shaking the coffee tin of corn to attract the hens' attention before pouring it on the ground by the gallery. Audrey was handing out mealworms to a bunch of kids who had wandered over from the library. They might have to use a crab net on the chickens that were on the statues, but already eight or nine of them were moving in on the cracked-corn bonanza.

"Remy," called a voice. She turned to find Jake walking up. "I was picking up the mail from Alley's and saw the commotion over here. Your flock, I take it. Need more help?"

Jake gave her a wide, open grin. Remy felt the tug of attraction. But Jake was with Jane, so that was that. "Um, you can help us grab that bunch."

It was time to make a move on the chickens pecking at the corn. The giggling line of people slowly moved closer until Ada Queetie figured out it was a trap and gave an imperceptible chicken signal to dash. Jake managed to scoop up Ada but the rest of the hens ran between and through legs, dodging and pivoting like wide receivers with a football. Hooting, Remy's helpers started a chase, scattering chickens everywhere. Remy sighed in frustration.

"What do I do with this beautiful girl?" Jake asked as he stroked Ada Queetie's ruffled feathers.

"Ooh, look at that. She's mad at being caught. Just put her in the car, push her through the window with the towel." Remy sighed. "We're never going to catch them all."

"You just need to reinforce the line. It's a battleground: man versus chicken," Jake said. "Yo, Nate. Can your dog help herd?" The irresistible corn had already lured a half-dozen hens back to the corner.

With General Ada Queetie captured and Nan, in her herding crouch, holding the back line, the second corner attack was more successful. Jake had fast hands and, with an intuitive sense of which way the chickens were about to run, he captured two more birds. A third, a wily foe, led Jake on a merry dance across the field. The mealworm kids had some success, but after a time Remy's volunteer army lost interest and began to peel away, lured by the beach and other nonchicken Vineyard attractions.

Audrey came back from counting chickens through the car window. "We're still missing six.

That looks like another helper," Nate said, pointing to Mike's truck.

Mike's dog leaped out after his owner. "Buddy, no," Mike ordered. "Stay in the car." Too late, the hens sensed dog-danger and had all taken flight. Buddy stood by Mike's side with his eyes fixed on the nearest bird. "Sorry about that. Now they're all up in the trees. How'd your chickens get out?"

"Neighbor kids left the gate open," Remy replied.

"Let's give it another go." Audrey's eyes were bright and her cheeks pink from running. She was, Remy realized, absolutely lovely, in a delicate china teacup way. "Where's the crab net?"

"I'm not sure," Remy said. She turned to Mike. "Can you put Buddy in your truck? I don't think the chickens will come down if they see him. I'll go find the net."

"Hi, I'm Audrey," Audrey introduced herself. She, not the chickens, now had the guys' attention.

"Nate. And this little cutie pie is Gaia." Nate adjusted the sling so the baby could peep out.

"Jake. I'm a neighbor. And, hello, Gaia," Jake said, offering the baby a finger to grab.

"And I'm Mike," Mike said, putting out a huge paw to gently shake Audrey's doll-like hand.

Audrey grinned. "I can't remember the last time I had this much fun."

Remy returned with the crab net. "So, here's the plan. Mike and Audrey, you're a team."

# CHAPTER 33

The agitated, flapping chickens had turned the inside of Remy's Toyota into a feathery, poopy mess. Unwilling to risk letting any of the hens escape, Remy had climbed through the towel-flap, setting the entire flock into a frenzy of feathers and a cacophony of chicken noises.

This day would not be a highlight of Remy's avian-farming career.

Jake stood chuckling outside the car. His trip to Alley's for the mail had taken an unexpectedly entertaining (and pleasant) turn. Jane's arrival had done nothing but emphasize the difference between Remy and the insular group of his friendly academic rivals—and his ex-lover—back in Chicago. All Jane's talk of tenure—Tufts was as vicious as Chicago—had picked at the scab on his memories.

But today, he hadn't thought about any of that once.

"Ow, ow, ow, don't peck me," said Remy.

Jake peered through a window. "You doing OK in there?" Chickens were on the dashboard, in the seats, perched on the headrest. Remy wrestled one unhappy bird to the cargo area to have it immediately flap back over the seat. Jake guffawed.

She lifted a corner of the towel. "Jake Madden, is that you laughing at me?"

"Who me? No, no," he chuckled. "Just waiting to see if I can help you get all those pissed-off chickens back inside the pen."

"You can," Remy said as she tried to climb into the front seat. "I'll drive back if—geez, you guys are not making this easy—I can just get the chickens out of the driver's seat!"

"That reminds me of a joke. Why did the chicken drive the car?" Jake said.

"Not helping, Jake."

Back at the house, Remy began handing chickens to her waiting helpers. "Toona, oh my God, just stay still," said Remy. "You guys are the most uncooperative chickens ever. OK, here comes another." Remy thrust the annoyed chicken through the towel to Mike's waiting hands. He took the hen and, careful to hold her wings down, carried her down the path to the pen. Buddy, stuck inside Mike's truck, watched the chicken handoff like it was the best TV show ever.

"Got a chicken for me, Remy?" called Jake.

Remy crawled over the backseat to have her quarry all flap to the front. "Darn chooks! They won't stay where they are and let me catch them!" Jake peered through the window as Remy's rear end disappeared over the seat.

"It would be easier if you put all the seats down," he suggested.

"You want to help? Get in here!"

"Naw, you're doing a great job, Remy. What are there, only like 15 in there?"

"More! 18!" Oh, you stay still now, Pinky, let me catch you!"

Audrey was next in line. "I can't believe I've spent my morning chasing chickens!"

"Believe it," said Remy. "Argh, come here!"

At last, Remy emerged from the car clutching the last bird. Her hair was tangled and dotted with feathers and smears of poop, and fluff decorated her legs and arms. Jake thought she looked adorable.

"Oh my gosh, this was a mess. I'm a mess. Thank you so much. There's no way I could've done it by myself." Remy stroked the large hen in her arms. "You chickens are a big pain sometimes, but I do love you," Remy said to the bird.

"I was telling the guys I haven't had so much fun in a long time," Audrey said, brushing some fluff from her shirt. "But I've got to run. I'm late picking up the twins. They're going to be so annoyed with me."

"I'm going too," said Mike. He grinned at Audrey. "Thanks, partner."

Audrey beamed. "We made a good team, didn't we?" she asked, laying her hand on Mike's arm.

"We sure did," he replied.

"Thank you so much, guys," Remy said. "I really mean it."

"Is there anything else I can do?" Jake asked, reluctant to leave. "Fix the latch?"

"I think it's OK, it was just left open. But we can double-check."

Remy carried the last hen up the path to the chicken run. "OK, Beauty Linna," she said, putting the hen into the pen. "You're the last one home."

Jake closed the gate and tugged on the latch. "Seems good." Jake wandered over to the hen house. "You got some pretty luxe quarters here, you chickens. Nice little saltbox. Mike build this for you?"

"I did it all myself," Remy said proudly. "Well, Mike helped a little. The walls and roof are made out of pallets." She pulled a drawer out that once came from a dresser. "See, these are the nesting boxes for the eggs. A solar panel on the roof runs a heating pad for the winter. And I've got my hawk defense," she added, pointing out the wires strung overhead. "Totally secure, except when the gate's left open." The chickens had gone back to pecking at bugs, their bird brains having forgotten their grand adventure.

"I'm impressed," he said. "You know what Frank Lloyd Wright said. The architect?"

Remy nodded. "Fallingwater, right?"

"Right. He said to 'regard it just as desirable to build a chicken house as a cathedral.' And something about character being what counts, not size or money."

Remy gazed at her chicken house as she considered the quote. "I agree. And a nice way to insult people who build big, expensive, ugly houses." She stretched her arms overhead and sighed. "That was hard work. Ready to head back?"

"Let me guess, all the nutty names came from Nancy Luce's flock," Jake commented as they walked down the path.

"What, Teeddla Toona and Levendy Ludandy are nutty names?" Remy teased, looking up at Jake.

He flushed warm inside. "Well, yeah."

"How did you know that?"

"I saw an exhibit about her at the Martha's Vineyard Museum. Did you know she was a poet and an entrepreneur? She was quite famous back in the day."

"I did know that." Remy seemed pleased. "It's a great exhibit. I love that museum. The names were Willow's idea. She told me I was turning into a crazy chicken lady like Nancy."

"I think you've got a way to go before that happens," Jake said. Remy, with her flushed cheeks and bright expression, bore not an iota of resemblance to skinny, sad-eyed, pinch-faced Nancy Luce.

They reached the house. "Thanks again, Jake," Remy said, resting her hand on his arm. "I'm going to go shower all this disgusting chicken stuff off me. But I'll see you around. Tell Teddy he missed all the excitement. And say hi to Jane."

# CHAPTER 34

"Thanks, Teddy. It's a huge favor and I'll pay you—don't forget to keep track of your time. I overbooked myself, and it takes me forever to get out there to Eli Wolff's house." Remy hated to lie, but it wasn't a big one. "It's just stocking the house with groceries and beer and stuff. I'll do all the shopping; you'll just need to drive it out and put it away."

"Nada problema. Nice place?"

"Incredibly nice. But kind of hard to find."

"Don't worry. I have an unerring sense of direction, you know."

That Remy doubted. She envisioned Teddy, lost, driving around dirt roads as Eli's ice cream melted all over his bananas. "I'll draw you a map. No cell service on the roads there." Remy walked over to the whiteboard. "If you come by here around noon on Monday, I'll load you up. And he gets another delivery on Thursday afternoon."

Teddy joined her at the whiteboard. He tilted his head. "Hmm. Where did SS go?"

"Mistake, Teddy. A big one." For a moment Remy panicked that Teddy would put two and two together.

Teddy's face brightened. "Sorry about that," he said with a half grin, not looking sorry at all. "You going to tell me who he was now?"

Remy shook her head. "You don't know him. I guess I didn't know him either. OK if we don't talk about it?"

"Of course," Teddy said. "You want to hear my love-life news?" His face took on a happy, impish look.

"Sure."

Teddy waggled his eyebrows. "Willow."

"Willow? My Willow?"

"Our Willow. Remember waffle morning?"

Remy nodded, eyes bugging out. "But how?" she sputtered.

"Choco-Teds and Willow's chocolates, consumed together, have magical powers. Like a love potion."

"They do?" Remy well knew her best friend's taste ran to tattooed bad-boy chefs. Hot in front of the stove, hot in bed, was her theory. Ending, always, with Willow getting burned. Dear, sweet, Teddy was about as far from that as one could get.

"Willow and me, we never hugged lying down before. It was like," Teddy paused and wrapped his arm around himself. "Like she fit me, I don't know." He bit his lip, eyes soft and bright. "We fit each other," he said at last.

She gave Teddy a sly look. "*Everything* fits?"

"You have a dirty mind," Teddy said reprovingly. "We're not *there* yet. But I think we might. What do you think?"

"I think," Remy paused. "I think I can see you as a couple. You'd be good for Willow. She's dated way too many losers."

"You'll give her a little hint?"

Remy nodded. "I will."

"And I'll bring by some Choco-Teds for you. I bet they work on a broken heart too." Teddy started to push open the screen door then stopped. He slapped his forehead in mock exasperation. "I almost forgot!"

"Forgot what?"

"Jake wanted me to give this to you." Teddy searched the pockets of his ratty shorts. "Here," he said handing a folded piece of paper to Remy. "Toodles," he said and left.

Remy unfolded the note.

*Free at last from our pen-itentary*
*The scholars will write, "the escape of the century"*
*We cluck and we walk and we peck at new ground*
*We squawk and we flock on fresh earth our feet pound*
*For we must evade she who taketh our eggs*
*Running tall and proud on our hen legs*

Remy was in a good mood when she arrived at the Cinches' property. She spread the poem out on the steering wheel, chuckled over the line "she who taketh our eggs," then refolded the note to put it in her shirt pocket, amused to find stuffy Professor Madden had a sweet, silly side too.

Enid Cinch was in the ring, riding Frederik. Remy crossed her arms on the top rail and rested her chin. Enid and the big bay executed a series of flawless pirouettes, the horse and rider fused as one, the barest movement and shift of weight directing the horse's next move.

Morgan wandered out of the house eating an apple. "Hi, Remy," she said. "They're going away again. I can't believe they make you babysit me."

"It wasn't so awful last time, was it?"

"No. Except for Teddy and his mushroom tea." Morgan made a gagging noise.

Remy laughed. "Agreed. That was awful." Enid and the bay cantered around the ring, then shifted to a piaffe, nearly floating in air. "Look at that. Beautiful."

"I know. Doesn't make her any less of a bitch," Morgan said.

Enid finished her routine and guided the horse over to the rail. She looked down her long nose at Remy and Morgan. "Mathew and I have decided to go to Belgium next Thursday. There's a horse I want to look at there. And we've been invited to Lord Clarke's estate for a few days. Remy, I need you to stay here again and take care of Morgan." Enid's eyes narrowed as she looked at her daughter. "I also want her to go with you when you exercise Rajah. She's still being stubborn." Enid turned to Morgan. "I thought you would be grateful after what I went through to talk the owner into selling me a Marwari."

Morgan's face had turned to stone. She looked up at her elegant mother sitting ramrod straight in the saddle. "I'm not riding anymore. You know that. And I don't need a babysitter, Mother."

Enid ignored her and spoke to Remy. "We'll be back from Europe the following Friday. I assume that's no problem. Like last time, you run your errands or whatever it is you do during the day and check in on Morgan from time to time, make sure she's not sitting around eating potato chips and playing on her computer all day. Please cook healthy low-calorie meals. I think she's gaining weight."

"I'm not and I can cook healthy meals for myself," Morgan said. "What do you think I'm going to do if you leave me here? Start having sex with the local goatscaper or something?"

"You are not staying here without adult supervision," Enid declared. "Remember when I left you by yourself? The trash was full of empty Ben & Jerry's cartons."

Morgan rolled her eyes. "That was a long time ago."

"I don't trust you. And you still don't drive."

The teen glared at her mother. "Like that's my fault."

"You're 16?" Remy asked.

"Yes. And I have my permit. But someone," she said, still glaring, "is too busy with her horses and parties to teach me to drive."

Remy turned to Enid and put on her best client-pleasing smile. "I'm happy to house-sit again," she said. "But I'd need to bring my dog."

Enid's mouth pinched tight. "I don't allow dogs in the house. He'd have to stay outside or in the barn. Or have someone else take care of him for you."

"I like dogs, Mother." Morgan looked sideways at her mother. "He's a purebred, a Barbet. It's a kind of French water dog. He doesn't shed."

Enid considered her options. "All right," she said, ignoring Morgan. "But I don't want to find a single dog hair in my house."

She wheeled the horse around. "Remy, do you have time to exercise Rajah?" It sounded more like a command than a question.

Remy looked at her watch. "Yes, I can do that."

"McGraw, saddle Rajah, please," Enid shouted toward the barn.

"That's OK, Enid. I can do it."

"Take Morgan with you."

Remy held the barn door open for Morgan and walked inside. She took in the welcoming hay-and-horse scent. Rajah nickered and lowered his head with pleasure at seeing Remy. "If you don't mind me asking, why don't you ride anymore?" Remy asked as she collected the pad and saddle. "I mean, this is the best part of my job."

"I used to. Steeplechase, some show-jumping." Morgan slowly stroked Rajah's long nose, then reached up to rub the curled ears. Rajah dipped his head and chuffed. "I was good."

Remy waited for her to continue. "But you stopped."

"I was stopped." Morgan turned, looked Remy, and pointed to the long scar on her leg. "My horse and I fell going over a jump in a race. I snapped my femur in half, broke my arm and some ribs. Dinkins broke his leg too."

"And then what happened?" Remy asked gently.

Morgan's eyes flooded as she tried to compose herself. "You really want to know?" she said. Remy nodded, feeling tears prick behind her own eyes. "They were afraid to move me until the ambulance came, and they couldn't move my horse. He was on top of my leg. Dinkins," her voice broke, "was looking at me when they shot him. It was so loud. I watched his eye go dead." Rajah leaned over the gate to move his nose closer to Morgan as if he understood what she was saying. He puffed a horse breath into Morgan's face as she resumed stroking his face. "Why won't she understand that I can't have another horse, I can't ride. I can't."

Morgan's face broke Remy's heart. "I'm so sorry," she said, wiping a sleeve across her eyes. Remy finished saddling Rajah in silence. "You don't have to come to watch."

"No. It's OK. I should go for a beach walk anyway. Mother's right, I need more exercise," she said making a bagel out of her belly fat. "It doesn't bother me to watch other people with their horses." The anguished look was gone, but Morgan still looked sad. "And it's OK you're staying here. I didn't really want to be all the way out here by myself."

"Well, we'll try to have some fun," Remy said as she gathered up Rajah's reins. "Your mother doesn't need to know everything."

"How'd it go?" Remy asked Teddy. "Did Eli Wolff seem to mind you doing the drop-off?"

"Naw, I don't think so. He said something like I'm supposed to tell you Trixie misses you." Teddy stacked the empty crates on the floor. "But hey, I think that Eli dude is gay. And man, that is one long dirt road."

"Why do you think he's gay?" Remy asked with an uncomfortable twinge.

"Well, it seemed like he was putting the moves on me, asked me to go swimming with him, no bathing suit needed."

Remy's guts twisted. She couldn't believe Eli would have asked Teddy—Teddy!—to go skinny dipping. "Really," she said.

"Yah, I was getting big ole horny vibes off him. He kept staring at my junk." Teddy tugged on the waist of his gym shorts and peered down. "I mean, I guess it's pretty special," he said, pulling out the waistband further to get a better look, then let the elastic snap back. "But I don't swing that way."

Teddy's story removed all doubt: Eli was a sex addict. And none too particular. "Oh my," she said.

He looked back up at her. "So I told him thank you, but I was late meeting my girlfriend. Well, maybe my girlfriend. Did you talk to Willow?"

"Ah, I'm sorry, Teddy. Not yet. But Mike and Willow were talking about catching a movie in Vineyard Haven tonight, and I was going to invite my brother. Want to join us?"

Teddy grinned. "Can you hint around that it can be a date-date, if she wants? But not like, to make it weird if she doesn't want a date-date."

"I'll drop a hint, I promise."

Remy returned from dropping groceries at the Hartwells' to find Willow in the kitchen munching on crack cookies from the freezer stash.

"I'm glad you're eating those," Remy said. "I keep snacking on them at night." She recounted the story of Eli making a play for Teddy. "Unbelievable, huh?"

"Well, only sort of." Willow tilted her head. "I'm sorry, Remy, but looking at it objectively, I think Eli's ..." she paused, searching for the word. "...opportunistic. Just an old horndog, as my Alabama roommate would've said. And a narcissist, too, I bet. I mean, I get the appeal—the hot sex, that gorgeousness, the fabulous house. But that's not you, Island girl."

Remy made a wry face. "So I've been a fool."

"Hardly. I mean, you certainly got something out of it too. And not just that gold bracelet. But he was too red for you. And you got burned. I'm sorry." Willow reached over to pat Remy's hand.

"Eli did say he was a hedonist."

"I bet a banana peel would do for him," Willow said, trying to tease Remy out of her mood.

Remy raised her eyebrows. "A banana peel."

"It's a thing. Remember Archie? We got bored one rainy day. You nuke a banana—not too much—so the peel gets nice and warm and slippery. And you know how much I like bananas."

"TMI, Willow!"

"And you thought I called him the 'big banana' because he was tall and had that yellow hair..."

"Oh please, stop!" Remy interrupted, laughing. "And I'm not sure I like being told I'm interchangeable with a microwaved banana peel," she added. "Or as sexy as Teddy."

"Oh, Teddy's not so unsexy," Willow said. "It was kind of sweet waking up with him the other morning. Other than the morning breath."

"I don't think Teddy minded waking up with you either." Remy gave her a sly look. "I invited him to the movie tonight."

"Teddy, huh." She paused. "I'll have to think about that." Willow took another big bite of the crunchy cookie. "I don't need these calories if I'm going be eating popcorn too," she said, licking chocolate off her lips.

Remy watched Willow consider the idea.

"Teddy. Hmm. Maybe."

Willow and Teddy shared a tub of popcorn, interlacing their greasy fingers afterward, Remy noted with approval. As Remy's punishment for choosing a foreign language film last time, Mike picked a comic book superhero flick. But if Mike could make it through a movie with subtitles, Remy could sit through two-plus hours of actors in rubber suits, especially if it meant she got to see her little brother.

"Awesome flick," said Solly. His generous mouth, so much like Remy's, broke into a wide grin. "And thanks for paying, Sis."

"Glad you liked it," Remy said. "I hardly ever get to see you. You're working too hard. Are you eating enough?" she asked, running her eyes down Solly's lanky teenage frame. "Let's get some food at the Black Dog—my treat—and you can tell me what you've been up to."

"Sorry," Solly said, looking at his cell. "I'm meeting up with the guys in OB. Rain check?"

"But all you had was popcorn."

Solly pushed his flop of blond hair out of his eyes. "I'll get something to eat later."

"But Solly…"

"I promise, Sis."

Remy sighed as she watched her little brother stride down Main Street. "Cute kid," said Mike. "A bowl of Black Dog chowder sounds good to me."

Willow and Teddy looked at each other. "I'm kind of stuffed with popcorn," Teddy said.

"Me too," said Willow, patting her tiny waist. "But I've got some Girl Scout Cookies back at my house if you're interested."

Teddy's eyes lit up. "I am."

Remy turned to Mike. "OK. I guess you're my date."

"Will you be mine?" Teddy asked Willow with a hopeful look.

Willow cocked her head at Teddy "Maybe," she replied and took his hand.

Pleased with her matchmaking, Remy tugged on Mike's arm. "C'mon, let's see how long the wait is for a table."

The Black Dog Tavern was packed, as usual. Restaurants came and went, but the Black Dog never changed. Massive beams held up the plank ceiling, like the interior of a ship, and the walls were hung with old photos of schooners under sail. Captain's chairs and nautical antiques continued the seafaring theme, and a row of windows overlooked the Black Dog's own tall ships and the smaller sailboats moored in the harbor. It was touristy in the summer but in a comfortable, Vineyard-casual way.

Several groups were settling their checks, and Mike and Remy quickly found themselves seated at a window table. After scanning the menu, they ordered beers, clam chowder, and Mike's favorite, a massive (and excellent) serving of fish and chips.

"You know, it was really good, but I think maybe the first *Ant-Man* was the best," Mike said. He swallowed a big slug of ale and wiped his mouth with the back of his hand. "Good beer."

"I didn't see that one," Remy said. "I didn't expect there to be a love story. That was kind of sweet." It had been Willow's idea to start a movie club over the long winter, successfully getting Remy out of her Netflix rut. Remy's taste ran to British costume dramas set in manor houses, even though they were not anyone else's cup of tea (literally). But everyone got a turn to pick.

"I don't know. They were enemies. I don't think they would have fallen in love. But the fight scenes were excellent. I hope they have another sequel planned." Mike looked out the window at the harbor. "Nice to see Solly. How's he like being a deck hand on the *Shenandoah*?"

"He loves that boat." Remy frowned. "I was hoping he'd stick around so we could catch up."

"He's a teenager, Remy. He's not going to spend his night off hanging out with his big sister and her friends." The waiter dropped off a loaf of the restaurant's way-too-good fresh-baked country bread. "Did I see what I thought I saw? Willow and Teddy?"

Remy nodded as she pulled off a slice of bread and slathered it with butter. "I think so. They're such old friends. I never thought of them as a couple," she said. "It kind of makes sense though. Don't you think? Old friends into lovers?" She smiled at Mike.

Mike looked surprised. "I'm sorry, Remy," Mike said. "As much as I like you…"

Remy nearly choked on her bread.

"Are you OK?" he asked.

"Fine." She drank some water. "Oh my. That isn't what I meant!"

Mike reached over and took Remy's hand. "Good. I wasn't sure there, for a moment." He laughed. "I did meet someone. But she's out of my league. And married."

"Oh, Mike. Don't even think about it," Remy said, squeezing his fingers.

"I know. You don't need to tell me that," Mike said. "But you can't help who you're attracted to."

A flash of pale-blond hair caught Remy's eye. There they were again, professor and professor, the perfect couple. Remy felt like she was running into them every time she turned around. The Vineyard was small, but not *that* small.

Jake and Jane made their way over. "Hey Remy," Jake said. "Teddy said you'd be here after the movie."

Remy pulled her hand away from Mike's. "Teddy ate too much popcorn, so he bailed on us. Mike, you remember Jake? From the chicken roundup? And this is Jane."

A new light tan enhanced Jane's Nordic beauty, and her hair hung straight in a shimmering curtain. She'd paired a simple blush sleeveless shift that displayed her toned arms with the silver necklace from the Chilmark Flea Market and dangly earrings. She was overdressed for the Black Dog, yet perfect.

"Hello," Mike said. "Nice to meet you, Jane." He stuck out his hand, nearly swallowing Jane's, slim fingers in his square calloused mitt.

"They lost our reservation at Garde East," Jane explained. "Or maybe Jake here," she rested a perfectly manicured hand on his shoulder, "Forgot to make it. A friend recommended it."

"My clients all report that Garde East is excellent," Remy said. "It's worth trying again."

"We will." Jane scanned the room as if hoping to see someone more interesting to talk to.

"Remy and I just saw the new *Ant-Man* at the Capawock. You guys seen it?" Mike asked.

Jane smiled, but Remy could tell exactly what she was thinking.

"It was good, but Mike was saying the first *Ant-Man* was better," Remy said defensively.

"Oh," Jane said with a hint of condescension, a smirk playing at the corners of her mouth. She turned to Jake. "You'll have to take me to the Film Center next week," Jane said. "They're live-streaming *La Bohème* from the Met. It's one of my favorite operas."

"Sure," said Jake, "We can do that."

Teddy was right. Jane was like one of those fake freezer icicles that you can slip into an open bottle of white wine to chill it. Remy wondered whether that frigid exterior trapped heat from a passionate interior, like that volcano that erupted under an Iceland glacier.

"I loved my chicken poem, Jake," Remy said. "It made me laugh."

Jake gave Remy a weak smile. "Sort of a secret hobby of mine."

Jane raised an arched eyebrow at her date. "You write poetry?"

"I'm not sure you'd call it poetry. Sometimes I jot down a couple of lines when the mood strikes."

Jake kept looking at Remy, and an awkward silence descended. "Would you like some bread, we have plenty," Remy said, holding out the wooden board. "It's so good, I'm afraid I'll eat it all."

"No thank you. I don't eat bread," said Jane.

But of course, the ice queen would be a no-carbs woman. "Jake?" Remy asked.

"Thanks," he said, taking a slice. "I'm starving."

Remy forced herself to smile at Jane. "So," began Remy. "Have you been enjoying the Island?"

"I love it here. I could stay forever," Jane said, smiling at Jake as she ran her fingers through her pale hair. "Except for the deer ticks, of course, and my dog getting skunked," she added with a cool laugh. "Even so, it is exactly what I was looking for this summer."

"That's nice," Remy said weakly. She glanced over at Mike, sitting like a log and now gawking at Jane's movie-star looks. No help from that quarter. "What have you two been doing?"

"Some work, some play. Oh, Jake, look, I think our table is ready. Nice to meet you, Mike, and see you around, Remy."

Mike watched the pair walk to their table. "Teddy's brother is like a professor or something, right?"

"Philosophy, University of Chicago. She's a professor too. At Tufts," Remy said. She was kicking herself for that *Ant-Man* comment. Way to make herself look like a cultural idiot. Of course, Jake-and-Jane would like *opera*.

"They make a nice couple. Jane seems nice. Really pretty, too."

"Very," Remy agreed.

The chowder arrived, a welcome distraction. "Oh yum," Remy said, dipping her spoon into the hot creamy soup, topped with a giant pile of crunchy croutons. "So, what should we pick for our next movie? Unless you'd rather go see opera?"

# CHAPTER 35

"Mike, this is weird. Coop's not barking. You don't think the dogs got out?" Remy quickened her pace up the front walk, Mike close behind.

"They probably just tired themselves out playing and are asleep," Mike said.

"Coop? Buddy? Doggies?" Remy called, opening the front door.

Coop lay on the living room rug, shaking from nose to the tip of his tucked tail, eyes rolling, white with anxiety. Buddy was nowhere in sight. "Oh my God, what happened? Did you and Buddy get in a dog fight?" she asked as she searched through Coop's dense caramel coat for signs of injury.

"Buddy, come," Mike called, "Now!" He walked into the kitchen. The back door was still secure, but there were claw marks on the windowsill and a dog-sized hole in the screen. "Oh shit. Remy, is Coop OK? It looks like Buddy got out through a window. I'm going to go look for him."

"I can't find any puncture wounds. There's a flashlight on the counter."

Mike flipped on the porch light and opened the door. Buddy stood at the edge of the yard. He looked at Mike then picked up something at his feet and started down the path. "Buddy, come!" Mike ordered. The dog paused, looked over his shoulder, and dashed away.

"I think something happened to Buddy too. He's acting really weird. He just ran away from me down the path."

Remy joined Mike at the backdoor with Coop glued to her side. "What do you think could've happened? Coop's terrified of thunder, but it's clear tonight. I wonder if some kids lit off firecrackers or something."

"Maybe," Mike said. "Oh, shit. That path goes to your chickens."

A sudden fear gripped Remy's insides. "You don't think…"

"Buddy, come! Mike called again. "Now!" The dog ran up, the thing still in his mouth. "Drop it," Mike ordered. Buddy dropped a pile of feathers at Mike's feet and sat.

"No, no, no," cried Remy.

"It's one of your chickens, Remy. Oh my God, Buddy. How could you do that," Mike gasped. "Remy, I'm so sorry. All the times I've taken him hunting, he's never gone after the birds. Not until I tell him too." He shined the flashlight at Buddy, then leaned over and pulled his dog's lip back. "This is weird. There's no blood on Buddy's mouth or around his muzzle. Something took this hen's head off. But it wasn't him."

Remy shuddered beside Mike. He laid a hand on her shoulder. "Do you have a flashlight? How about you wait inside with the dogs and I'll go check on the rest."

"No. I need to know."

The flashlight lit a deathly tableau of feathers and lifeless lumps. Remy gasped when she recognized the pale shape of Beauty Linna. It was like a horror movie made real.

Mike dragged Remy back to the house. "I'll look for survivors. Please, Remy, stay here."

In shock, Remy sat in the kitchen, trying to unsee the glimpse of the nightmare that lay inside the chicken pen. Coop lay his shaggy head on Remy's lap, shaking so hard that his teeth chattered. She dug her fingers into his fur, not believing that this was really happening.

Mike returned ten minutes later, ashen faced. "Whatever got them broke down a fencepost. Your hawk wires trapped the chickens inside." Mike pulled a chair around, sat down, and put his arm around Remy. "I counted the bodies, including the one Buddy brought back. Twenty-seven. I am so sorry."

Remy was too stunned to cry. "Twenty-seven?"

"How many were there?" Mike asked gently.

"Twenty-eight."

"Maybe one hen escaped." Mike tilted his head and looked into Remy's pale face and dazed eyes. Her lips were colorless. He took a breath. "But more likely it was carried off. We can look tomorrow."

"No, now." Remy stood up, opened the door, and started blindly down the path in the near pitch black. "Chook-chook-chook-chook," she cried.

"Dogs, you stay here," Mike said and went after her. "Remy, slow down."

Mike caught up and put a restraining hand on Remy's arm. "We're not going to find anything in the dark."

Remy tried to shake off Mike. "No. I have to look now. Chook-chook-chook-chook," she called in an increasingly desperate voice. "Chook-chook-chook!"

"Please, Remy. There's nothing we can do," Mike said. "We should go back to the house. Please."

"Chook-chook." All was silent but for the barest rustle of the leaves and the frantic barks of Coop from inside the house. "Chook-chook," Remy called, her voice breaking. "Chook-chook."

The barking stopped, and a moment later Coop dashed past her down the path. "Coop, no," Remy yelled. "Come!" she shouted as she ran after him. "Coop! Come!"

Mike caught up with the flashlight. Coop had stopped fifteen feet down the path. He was frozen in an odd posture, staring at a low tree. One front leg was bent and his head, body, and tail drew a stiff, straight line.

"Remy, that's a point," he said. "He's spotted something."

Mike scanned the tree with the flashlight. Remy gasped when the beam hit a round shape perched on a branch.

"The missing chicken," said Mike, astounded. "I can't believe it. Coop, you found her."

Remy moved slowly, murmuring reassuring noises. Her heart leaped when she recognized the striped feathers.

Ada Queetie, her escape artist, her smartest bird.

Her dear heart.

Remy woke at dawn to find Ada nestled against Coop's side. Ada looked better. Alert. The hen rustled her feathers and looked around, clucked, and started exploring the bedroom looking for food.

Remy felt a moment of relief, then the horror returned. Ada was proof that it hadn't been a nightmare. What happened was real. Grief hit Remy like a body slam. Her lovely, lovable, hens. All gone, but one.

"Oh, Ada." Remy lifted the hen and buried her face in the soft feathers. "Ada, how can I bear it?"

The chicken made a reassuring cluck in reply. When Mike and Remy had brought her inside, they had thought her nearly dead of shock. Ada's comb and wattle were pale, and when Remy had put her down on the kitchen floor, the chicken had tipped over on her side, legs sticking out like matchsticks. Remy had wrapped her in a fleece blanket and hoped for the best, willing dear Ada to live.

"You're OK, right?" Remy asked.

Ada flapped her wings, ready to go back to exploring.

The phone rang. "Remy, this is Mike. I'll be over just as soon as I can to, uh, take care of things in the chicken pen. A pipe burst over at one of my sites, and the owners are freaking out. How are you? Is the chicken OK?"

"She's better. I'm…I'm dealing," Remy said in an unsteady voice.

"Crap, the Wangs are calling me again. This might take a couple of hours, I don't know. Just wait for me. OK?"

Remy took a deep breath. She couldn't let the—bodies—sit for hours in the sun. She could do this herself. These were her chickens, her responsibility, not Mike's.

After steadying herself and drinking a cup of coffee, Remy got a shovel, work gloves, and a black plastic trash bag. She willed herself to be strong. "You two stay here," she told Ada and Coop as she put on the gloves and headed out the door.

A striped feather lay in the grass. Remy's heart stopped. The thought of what lay waiting for her in the chicken pen was too much to bear. Leaning against the handle of the shovel, she began to sob, choking with cries that shook her body and hammered her brain. Then giving in to grief, Remy collapsed to the ground.

She couldn't do it.

# CHAPTER 36

Jake set a chair in his favorite spot on the deck, sat, and propped up his feet on the rail. Across the field, the pond sparkled in the morning light. The resident pair of swans, followed by three ugly-duckling cygnets, paddled down the cove. Jake took a deep breath of fresh air. The day promised to be sunny and warm. A beach day. He had been working hard—having Jane around to bounce ideas off had been helpful—and he deserved a break.

Jake took a sip of coffee and picked up the newspaper. The fight over building more affordable-housing units in Vineyard Haven was heating up again, and a dead seal had been found on the south shore with shark bites. Reading the local news, where a real crime was as rare as a hen's tooth, was one of the little pleasures of his day.

Jake's phone rang. His heart lifted to see Remy's number pop up. "Hi Remy," he said.

"Jake, is Teddy there? He didn't answer his phone," Remy said unsteadily.

"He didn't come home last night. Said he might spend it at Willow's. Don't worry." For the umpteenth time, Jake felt a flush of irritation at his brother. "Is something wrong?"

"I need help." Remy's voice broke.

"I'm on my way." In a panic, Jake put on his sneakers and ran to Remy's, cursing Teddy for having taken one car and Jane the other.

He burst through the front door. "Remy? Where are you?" he called, panting. He found her kneeling in the backyard with her face in her hands. Jake put his hand on her shoulder. "Remy. I'm here. What happened?"

Remy shook her head. "Last night…" her voice choked. "Last night, Mike and I came back from dinner and then…." Her face dissolved. "Something got in the pen and…killed my chickens."

"Oh my God, no," Jake murmured. He dropped to the ground and wrapped his arms around her. "Shhhh." Jake gently rocked her back and forth. "It'll be OK," he said, knowing it would not. At last, Remy's shuddering sobs eased into hiccups.

"Help me up."

Jake pulled her to her feet. Remy stood on wobbly legs and picked up the shovel. "I have to clean them up. The bodies. But I can't." She motioned to the black plastic bag. "I can't. Put them in a garbage bag."

Jake felt a flash of anger. Where was that boyfriend, Mike? What a shit to have left her alone. "We could bury them properly. Would that be better?"

"Yes," Remy said.

Jake took the shovel, then slid the work gloves from Remy's limp fingers and put them on. "I'll take care of it."

With dread, Jake walked the path to the chicken pen. In the light of day, the carnage was unspeakable, unbelievable. How could Remy think that she could do this by herself? She was strong and brave. But this? This was too much.

Feeling nauseous, Jake picked a shady spot in the farthest corner of the pen and began to dig. He dug steadily, the shovel crunching against the soil to form a wide, deep hole. At last, it was time. With a deep breath, he walked over to the first body and gently picked it up. Bereft of life, it was as light as a small feather pillow. Near tears himself, Jake gently laid the hens side-by-side, like fallen soldiers, then swept the loose feathers into a tidy pile.

Remy called to him from the path. "I have to say goodbye," she said, stepping through the broken fence. Her face was red and puffy from crying, and she carried a small bunch of flowers.

Jake took her hand. "Is this OK?" he asked, pointing to the grave.

Remy nodded. "Yes. Thank you."

"Should we say, um, a prayer or something?" he asked.

"If you would," Remy replied, voice cracking.

They stood together over the poor, sad bodies. Jake racked his brain. He could quote utopian philosophy until the cows came home but was blanking on anything religious. There was something about green pastures, but it slipped away. "I'm sorry. The only thing I'm coming up with is 'now I lay me down to sleep....'"

Remy joined in. "I pray the Lord my soul to keep. If I die before I wake, I pray the Lord my soul to take." She leaned against Jake's side and rested her head against his shoulder. "My grandma taught me that."

Jake put his arm around her. "Mine too."

Remy gazed with sad, brimming eyes at the grave. "Goodbye, my chooks, my loves," she said, tears flowing again. "I'll miss you."

# CHAPTER 37

Teddy and Willow stood at the end of the floating dock, making ripples in the dark pond. "Remy-sweet, how are you feeling?" Teddy called.

Remy walked into his open arms. "I don't know," she said. "Not good, though talking to my mom helped. Then I went for a long walk today with Solly. And my uncle came by to talk about the house. He said at least I don't need to find a place with a big yard now. Uncle Danny meant well but..." Remy added, tears streaming down her face

"It'll be OK," Teddy said, squeezing Remy tighter.

Willow wrapped herself around them. "We'll take care of you," she said, stroking Remy's hair. Their sympathy made her cry all the harder.

"How's Ada Queetie doing?" Teddy said when Remy had settled down.

"She'll be all right, I think," Remy said. "She ate a mealworm this afternoon." Remy hiccupped. "I think she knows Coop is her savior or something. She won't let him out of her sight."

"She's right," said Willow.

Remy wiped her nose on her sleeve and sat down on the blanket. "I still can't believe it happened." Willow sat down next to her and put her arm around Remy's shoulders. "It didn't take long for the news to get around. I've been getting messages all day. Everybody is so thoughtful and kind. I've never cried so much in my life. I wish I could stop."

Willow shook her head. "My *avó*—you remember my grandma—said you should never hold back tears. You should cry as much and as loud, as you can. Be as sad as you want. We're here."

Remy leaned into Willow's side. It didn't take much to get her going again. Remy started to bawl in earnest, cathartic sobs. "I'm just going to miss them so much," she wailed.

Teddy patted her back. "Now, now," he soothed until Remy stopped, with one last shuddering whimper.

She took a deep breath. Teddy pulled a bottle of bourbon and a pencil-thick joint from a bag. "We just got to fix you up, sad girl."

"Ugh," she said, leaning back on her elbows. "I feel broken. Thanks for getting me out of the house." Even when she wasn't crying, sadness tugged at Remy's cheeks and lead-weighted the corners of her mouth. "And thank Jake again for me. I couldn't have made it through this morning without him."

"I will. Now, what'll it be?"

Remy forced a wan smile. "A little bourbon, Teddy."

"You got it," he said.

Teddy's good bourbon took the edge of Remy's grief. Snuggled between Willow and Teddy, she lay back on the blanket and stared at the stars. "Remember that night we took the boat out in the middle of the pond? That was pretty magical."

"Indeed," Teddy said. "I've been thinking a lot about stars. You know, I like the idea that every time a spirit passes, a star is born."

"Oh, Teddy. It's interstellar fusion or something," said Remy.

"Oh, ye of little imagination," Teddy said, patting Remy's arm. "Science, schmience. Right, Willow?"

"Right. You just need to open your eyes, to believe," Willow said.

Teddy relit the joint and pondered the sky. "Look, I think that's a new star. I don't remember seeing one there before," he said pointing to a dense cluster. "It must be Beauty Linna."

Remy gave a little laugh-sob. "Chickens, too? I thought you were talking about people."

"Chickens have spirits, don't they, Remy?"

"I guess."

"Oh look, there's another new one, right next to it. Who's that, do you suppose?" Teddy asked.

"Could be Bebbe Pinky," Willow volunteered.

"I think you're right," said Teddy. "And there—that little one by the bright one. Tweedle? It was definitely not there the other night."

"And Lebootie Ticktuzy?" said Remy, "Over there?"

Willow snorted. "Sorry, her name always made me laugh." With giggles and fond memories, they worked their way through Remy's flock, one by one, finding their stars in the dark skies.

Remy sighed and sat up. "I should get back. Make sure Coop and Ada are OK," she said, getting to her feet.

Teddy slid over to Willow and pulled the side of the blanket over them. "Come down anytime you want to say hi to your chickens, Remy. I'll remember where they are."

Remy arrived home from the dock to find a pile of chicken poop in the middle of the living room rug, an anxious, panting dog— and a missing hen. Panic, like a quintuple shot of caffeine, raced through her body.

"Ada Queetie!" she called. "Where are you?"

Remy told herself to calm down. The doors and windows were secure. The chicken was somewhere. "Coop, where's your new friend?" Coop cocked his head, then flopped on his side. He didn't know.

Remy wandered around the house calling Ada's name. Fear wrapped tight hands around Remy's insides. Chickens could die of shock, she knew. That, she couldn't bear, not after what had happened. Downstairs, upstairs, no sign of Ada Queetie.

Trembling, Remy forced herself to search more carefully, looking under furniture and inside wastebaskets, behind the dryer, anywhere a PTSD chicken could fit. Still, no sign of the hen.

"Now what do I do?" she asked Coop. "I've looked everywhere. Twice." She stood up from the sofa. "I guess I'll look a third time. But first, I need to pee."

Remy sat on the toilet and looked up. There, near the ceiling on the shower rod, perched Ada Queetie, sound asleep. Remy's heart leaped. "Ada!" she called. The hen opened one eye, looked at Remy, and closed it. It was nighttime, she'd found a safe place to roost, and she was not to be disturbed.

A double cognac (or was it a triple?), then a second, seemed a good idea to settle her nerves. Warm, blurry drunkenness numbed her pain. Hours later, however, the alcohol residue had pooled thick and heavy in Remy's head and belly like poisonous sludge. She rolled over onto her back—not a good idea—and pulled up the covers.

In the silence, Remy's head pounded dark blue and black on a keyboard, notes but not melody, audible warning of the inevitable hangover. It would be a doozy, she could tell. She pushed thoughts of the massacre from her mind, but the scale of her loss was only beginning to settle in. No more strolls through the pink early morning fog to hunt for warm eggs in the hay. No clucks and trills of excitement as her flock ran for wilted vegetable rejects from the local farm stands. Her chickens had been her family, part of the pattern of her days. Fur baby, feather baby, the loss had left Remy kneecapped with pain.

But she still had Ada Queetie. Remy was hit with a sudden fear that Ada could have fallen from her roost into the bathtub and was lying there injured. It could happen. The rod was round and smooth, and Ada was used to a flat roost. The pounding became a hammering as she stood up, nauseous and wobbly. Carefully, Remy made her way downstairs, Coop at her heels.

The round hen hadn't moved from her perch. With a sigh of relief, Remy climbed back upstairs to bed.

"Hey, Remy. I got a solution to your chicken poop problem," Willow said brightly.

"Go away. I'm not here," Remy said, burying her head under the covers.

"Yes you are. You're not hung-over again, are you?" Willow patted Remy's shoulder. "Come on. You can't spend another day in bed. Teddy keeps messing everything up. You're going to piss off all your clients."

"I know, I know. They're already mad," said Remy's muffled voice.

Willow tugged on the blanket. "He thought your stinky cheeses had gone bad so he tossed them and made the arrival platter with cheese sticks and onion dip from the supermarket. 'Artfully arranged' he said, 'with a pile of sprouts.'"

A voice came from under the sheets. "Don't tell me he threw away all the Mont d'Or. It was perfect."

"I think he gave it to Coop. That dog's a cheese fiend." Willow wrinkled her nose. "But he may have thrown it up—or maybe it's Ada, I don't know. But it smells really bad downstairs. I'd stay and clean up for you, but I'm late setting up at the Flea Market. But look," Willow pulled two blue fabric-and-elastic slings from her bag. "I made chicken diapers."

Remy poked her head out. "You made what?"

"Chicken diapers. I found a YouTube video." She hung the contraption over her arm. "You see, this part goes underneath her and the Velcro here secures the back. This part," she held open the bag-shaped end, "hangs under her butt. And you take this," Willow pulled a panty liner from her purse and pulled off the plastic strip. "Stick this inside the bag. Ta-da, chicken diaper!"

"Wow," Remy said, trying to generate enthusiasm as she examined it. "It's very, uh, innovative."

"Teddy was convinced I was sewing him a codpiece. I mean, he's generously endowed but, really!" Willow said, sticking her fist into the bag and swinging it between her legs.

Remy managed a wan smile as she pulled herself up into a sitting position in the bed. She turned the diaper over. "Pretty fabric."

"Indonesian batik, from Lombok. My favorite." Willow smiled and patted Remy's knee. "Ada's a hippy chick, I think. She deserved something way cool."

Willow opened the blinds. The bright light made Remy squint. "But she—and you—need to get outside. You're the one that told me chickens need fresh air and sunshine and to eat bugs and stuff. You, too." Willow tried to yank the covers off Remy, but she held fast.

"I know," said Remy. "All I need to do is eat some bugs and I'll be fine."

"You know that's not what I meant," Willow said, giving another tug before giving up. She cocked her head. "I'm worried about you. Your aura is like superfaint. And you should take a shower."

Remy lifted an arm and sniffed her armpit. "I know. I stink, and the house stinks."

"But seriously, Remy. It's not fair to keep Ada cooped up. I'll come back later and help you set up a fence for her in the backyard. I bought a roll of chicken wire." A small, sad frown crossed Willow's face. "I get you won't want to use the big pen and the henhouse."

Remy ran her fingers through her hair. She did need a shower. "No need. I'm moving out for a week. Got to babysit Morgan again. You know, Mrs. Pinchy-Cinch's daughter. I'm taking Ada and Coop with me, so I'll bring the chicken wire with me too. Thanks," she said, sincerely grateful for Willow's thoughtfulness.

"Good. You need a change of scenery. Something to do. You want me to get Ada, try her diaper on? She'll need it if she's going up-Island to fancy-smanchy Squibnocket Farm."

It took another two hours before Remy could force her feet to the floor. She tried, once, after Willow left, but the sweet oblivion of sleep drew her back to her pillow. But Willow was right. She had to get up and deal with life, no matter how sad she was.

Downstairs was as bad as Willow had said. Maybe worse. A barnyard smell had begun to permeate the house. The bathtub, over which Ada had been roosting at night, looked like a chicken Jackson Pollock. She found the cheese that Coop had thrown up and cleaned the floor.

Ada strutted past in her new apparel, rear dragging on the ground. "Oh girl, what you got in there?" Remy asked. "Time for a diaper change, I guess. Then, I've got to clean the tub." She undid the Velcro and pulled an egg from the bag end. "Oh, sweetie. An egg. Thank you."

Remy attached a clean panty liner and rinsed the egg in the sink. She held the warm oval in her hands, running her fingers over the blue shell. One chicken. One egg. The rest, gone. Sadness slid down a dark shade, and a lump formed in Remy's throat as she began, once again, to cry. Remy wanted to go back upstairs, bury herself under the covers, and pretend none of this was real.

A knock at the back door startled her back into what was. Oh, shit. It must be Mike. She wiped her face with the tail of her shirt. But the shape on the stoop was too tall to be Mike, too broad-shouldered to be Teddy.

"I guess you really have been sick," said Eli Wolff as she opened the door. Remy took a step back in shock, self-conscious of her red eyes and lank hair. "Is it so awful to see me?" he said, oozing charm out of every pore.

"How did you? Why are you?" Remy sputtered. "Here."

"Come now. You aren't hard to find. I asked the fellow at the liquor store where you lived. I told him I wanted to deliver this in person." Eli held up a bottle of Veuve Clicquot. "Mountain to Mohammed, eh? And don't worry. I parked at the gallery and came in the back way. No one will know I'm here."

"Teddy was supposed to drop off your groceries this week," Remy said dumbly.

"He did. And a case of kiddie juice boxes. But no beer." Eli waggled the champagne. "Are you going to invite me in? Or are you horribly contagious? I hadn't thought about that."

"I'm not contagious," she said, sagging against the door jamb.

"Dear Remy. I've missed your visits," he said. "You look like you need some TLC. When have you eaten last? Let me at least cook you an egg," he added, looking at Ada's egg in her hand. "You just go back to bed, and I'll take care of everything."

"I'm not sick," she said. "I'm sad."

"I can fix that, too."

Remy was past caring. A week ago, she would never have let Eli Wolff, client, ex-lover, in her house. Remy opened the door and, without a word, showed him into the kitchen. His eyes widened at the sight of the chicken strutting across the floor.

"I'm serious. You go back to bed," Eli said.

What difference did it make, Remy thought as she climbed the stairs. A minute later, Eli was at her bedroom door with a glass of orange juice in his hand. "Here," he said, setting the glass down on the bedside table. "Drink this. And how do you want your egg? Scrambled? Fried? Poached?"

"I'm not hungry. Really."

Eli sat on the side of the bed and stroked her arm. Remy felt a tingle. His hand moved up to caress her breast. "Not hungry for anything?"

Remy's body responded, longing for the mind-obliterating mindlessness of sex. Not lovemaking. Sex. He touched her cheek. "You've been crying," Eli said. "Tell me about it?"

"No," she said.

Eli drew her into his arms. Remy shuddered as his tongue found a pocket of dried tears behind her earlobe. "Poor, sad Remy," he murmured into her neck. "Let me make you feel better."

An hour later, Remy stood in the outdoor shower, soaping Eli's kisses from her neck so hard that her skin stung.

She had almost made a horrible mistake.

Remy had been plummeting into the chasm, barely able to grasp a broken limb before hitting bottom. She was horrified at how close she had come to letting Eli back into her bed, how easy it would have been to let sex take the sadness away, even if only for a brief moment.

But it was time to pull herself together, to climb, branch by branch, toward the light.

She had to try.

# CHAPTER 38

A change of scenery, as Willow had said. And the scenery was as stunning as anywhere on the Island. Remy could ride Rajah as much as she wanted, anytime she wanted. And with miles of private beach right there. She would be living in a house that was fancy enough to have been featured in *Architectural Digest*. And she would have dear, sassy Morgan for company. Forcing herself to focus on these positive thoughts, Remy cleaned her house until all the stink was gone, showered again, and packed the car.

Remy left her bags in the guest room, inserted a fresh liner into Ada's diaper, and went to find her charge. Luckily, Morgan, absorbed in texting on her phone, hadn't batted an eyelash when Remy showed up with both a dog and a hen.

"Morgan, can I leave Coop and Ada Queetie here with you? I've got to do a bunch of things, but I'll be back later."

"OK," Morgan said, thumbs flying over the screen. "Leave me here in this boring house. How long are you gone?"

"Pretty much the whole day. I was out sick this week so I've got to catch up. Don't worry if Ada starts to act weird. She probably needs to lay an egg."

"Then what?"

"Take it out of her diaper and rinse it off. Cook it if you want."

Morgan wrinkled her nose. "Ew. She poops eggs?"

"Not exactly." Remy picked up her keys. "Well, sort of. It's all the same vent. How did you think eggs came out?"

"No idea," Morgan replied. "Never thought about it." She heaved a sigh, sat up, and looked out the glass wall at the drop-dead gorgeous view. "Can I come? It's superdull here."

"Sure, if you want," Remy said. "But let me tell you first what I'm doing. It's not very exciting." She picked up her notebook.

"I can't believe you write things down like with a pencil? That's so oldster," Morgan said.

Remy gave her a look. "Don't be giving me a hard time about my checklists. I do them with my laptop but, yeah, I use a pencil. And I read books. Made out of paper." She was barely holding it together, and Morgan in a snarky mood was the last thing she needed. "Do you want to hear or not?"

The classic Morgan eye roll. "Yes, I want to hear."

"My clients all have weekend guests coming in, so today is a lot of running around." Remy took a deep breath. "First, to my house to do the flower arrangements and pick up the groceries for a client on the North Shore." She rattled on through her list: Shirley's Hardware, Cronig's, the Net Result, Our Market. "Last stop is my client in Edgartown."

Morgan twisted a lock of her thick chestnut-brown hair, looking for split ends. "Remy, the errand girl."

"Concierge, Morgan. I do whatever my clients ask. It's my job." Remy put down the notebook. "You don't have to come. Or I can drop you off in Vineyard Haven or OB and pick you up later."

"You know I don't like shopping. That's my mother's thing. Spending money. Oh, and horses. Spending money on horses," she sneered. Morgan looked out the window again and sighed again. "Sounds pretty boring but OK." She turned on the selfie feature on her phone to examine a pimple on her chin. "I hate zits."

"That'll heal better if you put a warm compress on it. I'll make you one."

Remy wet a clean dish towel with water out of the hot water dispenser and handed it to Morgan. Ada Queetie wandered into the living room, looking for something to peck at on the immaculate floor. "Mother freaks out if there is a speck of sand in the house. I can't believe she let you bring a dog *and* a chicken," Morgan said, holding the cloth to her chin.

"She doesn't know about Ada. You won't tell her, will you?"

"Of course not," Morgan said, shooting Remy a look. "But why'd you decide to make Ada an indoor chicken? Doesn't she miss being with the others?"

A wave of sadness passed over Remy. "There are no other hens. A dog, or a fox, or raccoon, I don't know," Remy explained as tears threatened. "It got into the pen last week and killed the flock. Except for Ada."

Horror crossed Morgan's face. "No."

Remy put her face in her hands and took a few deep breaths to compose herself. "It'll be OK."

Morgan's lower lip quivered as if she were about to cry. "I'm really sorry, Remy."

"Thanks. I know you liked them too. But I'd rather not talk about it."

"I understand," Morgan said, wiping her eyes.

Remy took a deep breath. "Are you ready to go? We'll take Coop and Ada with us. I don't want then getting into trouble."

Remy's battered Toyota looked like the poor stepsibling to the Cinches' immaculate his-and-hers Mercedes SUVs. "I'm sorry I called you an errand girl," Morgan said as she got into the passenger seat.

"It's OK. That's what I am. Have you been practicing driving at all?" Remy asked as she put the truck into reverse.

"No." Morgan made a face. "My parents don't want to teach me. I mean, I don't want them to. That would be horrible."

"You want to grab your permit? There's a dirt road down near a client's house that never has any cars on it. You could practice there."

"Really?" The girl's face broke into a lovely smile. "Thanks."

Remy gave Morgan driving tips as they drove to Remy's house. She let Morgan inside and went to get her clippers. "Make yourself at home. I have to cut flowers."

"OK," said Morgan, flopping onto the couch.

After cutting an armload of zinnias and cosmos and filling a dozen pint jars half-way with water, Remy began to clip the stems for her easy-peasy arrangements. "I usually do these with flowers from Morrice Florist or my clients' gardens, but I'm taking a shortcut today."

"Right," Morgan said, back to staring at her phone. "How long until we go where I can drive the car?"

Remy grabbed a handful of flowers and placed them in the jar. "Not too long."

Morgan heaved herself off the couch and sat down at the table. "Can I help?" she said, brushing her fingers across a peach-colored zinnia.

"Sure. The stems should be about this long," Remy said, handing Morgan a cut blossom. "About eight inches. I'm skipping the arrangements for your house this week. That OK?"

Morgan put down the flower and started to twirl a deep rose-pink zinnia. "How come we never get pretty flowers?"

"Your mother is into white. I give my clients whatever they want."

"White flowers, white sofas, white rugs, white bedspreads, white pillows, white walls," Morgan said, frowning. "It's like living in Antarctica. I hate it."

Remy pushed the finished arrangement to the side and started another. "Your house isn't very cozy; I agree with you there. But it's stunning."

"I wish Mother would let me live in Beetlebung Cottage. She hasn't gotten around to ruining it. Yet."

"Is that the guest house down by the little pond?"

"Yeah. The caretaker moved out so Mother could start 'planning the renovation.' So, I've been hanging out there. I'll show it to you." Morgan got up and wandered around the room. She picked up a framed photo of Remy and Willow together at the

Flying Horses Carousel holding a golden ring. "I like the way you decorate. It looks like a real home."

Remy looked up from her project to survey the hodgepodge of bargain box furniture scattered around the living room. The best thing she owned was a faded (but still lovely) antique Persian rug she'd found at a yard sale in Edgartown. Her oil paintings, mostly student work, filled the walls. Remy had done her best to tie everything together by painting the furniture a driftwood gray and sewing (with Willow's help) cozy throw pillows in the same soft shades as the rug. As always, clutter abounded. Every flat surface had a bowl of beach stones or a stack of glossy lifestyle magazines rescued from a client's recycling, and a big pile of folded laundry sat in a chair waiting to be taken upstairs.

Ada wandered across the room clucking. "Not sure most people would call this decorated," Remy said with a wry smile. "And I'm sort of a slob. But it's home, for a while. I have to move out in September."

"Why?" Morgan held up a giant yellow zinnia. "Can I help?"

"Sure." Remy got out an extra pair of scissors. "You don't have to copy me though. Do whatever you want."

"Why are you moving?" Morgan asked as she selected blossoms from the pile.

"This is my uncle's house. He wants to sell it once he's done with the repairs," Remy said. "I'm trying not to worry about where I'm going to live."

Morgan bent her head and, biting her lip in concentration, began to snip flowers and arrange them in one of the jars. "Why don't you buy it? My father says real estate on the Vineyard is a very good investment."

Remy snorted a laugh.

"What's so funny?"

"I'll never be able to afford to buy a house on the Vineyard. I'm lucky I've been able to live here as long as I have. Hey, I like that." Deep pink zinnias overlapped at the top of Morgan's jar in a flat, flowery saucer. In the center, the cosmos on longer stems bobbed above like a cloud of butterflies. "I think I'm going to copy your design."

"If you want." Morgan picked up a fuchsia cosmos and bounced it on its stem. "You know, you should start a lifestyle blog."

"A lifestyle blog."

Morgan pointed to an egg carton on the windowsill. Tiny basil plants in blue eggshells leaned toward the sun. "Like that is totally bloggable as a DIY project." Morgan took a picture of the basil, then Remy holding a pale pink zinnia. Ada strutted across the living room then nestled in next to a sleeping Coop. "And your chicken, your dog, your flowers, you *live* a lifestyle blog."

"I need to make money, Morgan, not start a website."

"I was making, I don't know, two, three thousand a month before I shut my horse blog down. After the accident," Morgan said. "Damn, I cut this one too short."

Remy finished one arrangement and started the next. "Do you mind if I turn on WMVY?"

"Oldster music?"

Remy looked up. Morgan was teasing. "Ha ha. Are you getting hungry? How about some sandwiches from 7a?"

"Liz Lemon?" Morgan asked. "That's my favorite."

"Get two," said Remy as she got out her wallet. "And a peanut butter cookie."

Remy was setting a finished flower arrangement in Eli's crate when she heard a car door slam. Audrey, as waif-like as ever in a flowered beach coverup, burst through the door.

"Oh Remy, thank goodness you're here. I had to get out of the house, to talk to someone. This is the only place I could go."

Coop ran up, tail rotating at top speed. Audrey dropped to her knees and buried her face in the dog's fur. "Oh, Beaucoup, you have a much better life away from Tony. You smart, wonderful dog. Of course, I'd never make you leave here."

"He's not leaving me," Remy said.

"You don't understand. The Boston news station, they heard about Coop and the ferry and wanted to do a piece on Beaucoup's adventure. And film the 'happy reunion with his family.'"

"What?"

"Tony told me to bring him back home. The twins want to be on TV." Audrey took off her sunglasses. A black eye in shades of ripe plum-purple ringed her china-blue eye. "I refused."

Remy sucked in a breath. "Oh, Audrey."

"If I don't bring him back, he says he'll tell the police you stole him. That we only wanted dog sitting, which we paid for."

Morgan would be back any minute with the sandwiches. Remy turned to Audrey, who had buried her face in Coop's fur again. "Let's take Coop for a walk. We need to talk."

Remy jotted a note for Morgan to eat without her and let Mike in if he came by. She clipped a leash to the dog's collar and opened the door. "First, don't worry about the police. We're not giving Coop back. One of the perks of living on an island is you know everyone. Including the chief of police. Now about Tony," Remy said as they turned down the path. "First time?"

Audrey shook her head. "No."

It was worse than Remy had thought. She took a deep breath. "Have you thought about leaving him?"

"Yes, of course," Audrey said, eyes welling up. "But the twins. They need their father."

"They may be in danger too."

"Oh no. I don't think he loves me anymore, but he loves them. He yells, but he'd never hurt them," Audrey said.

"You don't know that."

Audrey looked down. "But divorce." Her chin quivered. "It's admitting I made a mistake. Everyone said I was. Except for Granny. She understood. Tony was so generous back then. If I hadn't married him, I don't know what would have happened."

"You probably wouldn't be running around with a black eye."

"Remy, I know how this looks. But you see, our family, well, we used to have money." She twisted the lima bean-size diamond on her finger. "We hid our 'genteel poverty.' Our family still had social status—our good name. But that was all. We'd run out of paintings to sell. The houses would be next. But Tony took care of everything."

Remy shook her head. "It doesn't matter why you married him. He punched you. That's abuse. Battery is a crime."

"But it isn't his fault. If I had done what he said, he wouldn't have gotten so angry, I'd…"

Remy cut her off. "No excuses. Ever." She grabbed Audrey by her tiny bird-boned shoulders. This was like a bad TV drama. Not knowing what else to say, she followed the script. "Stop. This is his fault. 100 percent. There is nothing—nothing—you could have done or said to give him any reason to hit you. Or for the verbal abuse either."

Audrey's eyes welled with tears.

Remy sighed, then gave Audrey's shoulder a gentle squeeze. "Do you want to be married to him? Honest answer. Yes or no?"

Audrey stared at the ground. Remy waited, silent. "It was different back when it was just the two of us. Maybe it'll be better, once the twins get a little older."

"Come on, Audrey. Do you want to stay married to Tony?"

She shook her head. Wisps of hair stuck to her face. "No. I don't love him. And I don't think he loves me, but he loves the girls. That's why I can't leave him."

"Audrey, he hit you. And he'll hit you again. Next time it could be your kids." Remy could easily envision that man's anger turning on his bratty daughters. No way could their weak mother protect them. Or herself. Remy felt a wave of fierce, protective anger. "I'll help you if you want. And I'm sorry, but I need to take a picture of that black eye. We need to start collecting evidence." Before Audrey could object, Remy snapped a photo on her phone and showed it to her. "That isn't OK. It just isn't," she said.

Audrey looked at the image, aghast. "It's gotten worse."

Remy could almost see the steel harden in her spine. "Is there anything else? Any other bruises?"

Audrey pushed up her shirt to show Remy the black finger marks that encircled her upper arms. "Wow," Remy said as she clicked.

"And the house. He made a hole in the wall with his fist. I'll take a picture of that too."

"Good. Anything and everything."

Remy cocked her head. "What leverage do you have? Other than pressing charges for assault and battery?"

Audrey's blue eyes narrowed. "Oh. I know things." She pulled her sleeve down. "I have to think it through." Audrey lifted her eyes and tilted her head. "Thanks, Remy. I'll be OK. He's gone off-Island for business. I'm supposed to have Coop home when he gets back." She shook her head. "But I won't do it."

Mike's truck was parked in the drive. Morgan had finished her sandwich and was working on a giant version of her design in one of the tall glass vases. "Mike's here." She added another bobbing cosmos to her arrangement. "Some other guy, Jack or Jake or something, stopped by too. He left you something. It's over there, on the coffee table." She snipped a fat pink zinnia. "Is it OK that I'm doing a bigger one?"

"Yes, of course. It looks fantastic."

Boots clumped down the stairs. "Remy," Mike said, folding Remy in a hug. It was nice, like being hugged by a barrel-chested stuffed bear. "Hey, I've been worried. How're you doing?"

"OK, I guess."

Mike noticed Audrey standing behind Remy. His eyes widened as he took in the shiner. "Hi," he said.

"Mike. I remember you. We chased Remy's chickens together," Audrey said with a smile, her white, perfect teeth incongruous in her battered face. "That was such a fun afternoon. How are the chickens doing?" Audrey looked from Mike to Remy. "Did something happen?"

"A dog or a fox got into the pen and got all Remy's chickens," Morgan volunteered. "Except one."

Audrey wrung her hands. "What? Those lovely chickens?"

"It was horrible," Remy said. "As Morgan said, something killed the flock."

Mike rested a work-toughened hand on Remy's shoulder. "You should know. They caught some fancy purebred dog—a Giant Schnauzer—going after those free-range chickens over on Panhandle Road. The owners had been letting him run off-leash." He shook his head. "Stupid summer people. They knew he'd been harassing the neighbor's horses and wandering all over but 'had no idea he'd ever kill anything.'"

Remy's relief that the culprit had been found was quickly replaced by anger. *Stupid summer people* was right. "I can't believe that. How idiotic and irresponsible can you get?"

"They slapped them with a big fine and ordered the dog to be leashed at all times. They'll take him away if he's caught again."

"But that won't bring my hens back," Remy said as sadness returned. She was ready to change the subject. "Mike, I've got a job for you. Audrey's got a hole in her wall that needs fixing. Is that something you could take care of for her?"

Mike's expression brightened when he looked at Audrey. "Sure. I could take a look now."

# CHAPTER 39

Morgan's flower arrangements rattled in the back of Remy's Toyota. The teen had been fascinated by the stream of people coming through Remy's living room. "What's the story with that Audrey lady's black eye?"

"Abusive husband," Remy answered as they neared the turnoff for Eli Wolff's.

"I wouldn't stay with a boyfriend who hit me."

"Then you've already got more sense than she has. Watch out for verbal abuse, too, it can be as bad. Audrey's husband dishes out both." Remy slowed down to look for the nearly hidden road. "You remember, that's the family I got Coop from. Took him from. The husband beat the dog too."

Morgan's eyes went wide. "Wow. That's so fucked up."

"Morgan. Language."

"Sorry. No way you're giving Coop back, right?"

"Are you kidding? Never in a million years." Remy turned the wheel. "OK. Here's that dirt road I told you about. I'll take us down, then you can drive back." She steered around a pothole. "You'll want to go slow, especially around the corners in case there's another car. And watch out for ruts. They haven't scraped this road in a while."

The Toyota bucked across a patch of washboard road. "What happens if there is another car?" Morgan asked.

"Island etiquette is the first car that reaches a pullout will wait for the other to pass. A lot of summer people don't do that. Then you get stuck backing up. Watch out for cars with New York plates, especially if it's a new fancy car—they're the worst."

"Like my parents'?"

"Yup," Remy replied. Morgan laughed. "And never speed up. No playing chicken on these roads."

"Duh." Morgan watched a branch scrape along the side. "It's OK to scratch the car?"

"You can't help it. That's why you're learning in mine."

They bumped along. "What was in the bag that Jack-Jake brought? He seemed really disappointed you weren't home."

"A book of chicken poems. It's out of print. It was sweet of him to find a copy for me." Remy appreciated the gesture, but she wasn't ready, not yet, to read Nancy Luce's mournful poetry about dead hens. In time, perhaps, it might bring some comfort.

"Is he your boyfriend?" Morgan asked as if the question bored her. "He seemed nice. Pretty cute, for an old guy. He has, like, really blue eyes."

"No. He's a friend, I guess." Remy sighed. "OK. We went out on one date."

"And?"

The corners of Remy's mouth turned down. "It didn't work out."

"Why not?"

"Because we have nothing in common. And he's got a new girlfriend now."

"That sucks."

Remy nodded. "Yeah."

Remy got increasingly nervous as they neared Eli's house. Thanks to Teddy's semireliable delivery service, Remy hadn't been there since finding Eli in the horrible ménage-à-trois. She drove the Toyota carefully down the last steep stretch of road before going around the corner to the drive, willing the parking area to be empty when they arrived.

No such luck. Remy pulled next to Eli's Land Cruiser and hoped for the best.

"Morgan, can you put four of the small and two of the large arrangements in a crate? I'll get the groceries."

"Wow. This is nice," said Morgan, peering through the windshield. The property was as picture perfect as ever, like the cover of a magazine. "It looks really old. That's cool. Not like my house." She sighed, then her eyes widened as a man stepped out of the back door. "Whoa. Who's that guy?" Morgan asked. It was Eli, naked under an open robe. She stared, eyes wide and glued to the unexpectedly visible sausage of flesh. "Is *that* your boyfriend?"

Remy lifted her head. "Oh, shit," she muttered. "No, he's not."

Morgan's eyebrows shot up. "You mean, like, that," she pointed to Eli's groin, "Like that's one of your services? Whatever your clients ask for?"

Remy put her head on the steering wheel. "No. That is not one of my services. I'm not a prostitute, Morgan." Eli was heading down the path, robe flapping. "We used to, uh, date. I'll explain later." Remy opened the car door.

"Remy, love," Eli called. "You're finally here. I've missed you."

"Eli," Remy said. "I've got a helper with me today. This is Morgan."

Eli smiled even more broadly when he caught sight of Morgan's long dark hair through the windshield. He closed the robe and loosely belted it. "Nice to meet you, Morgan. Can I give you ladies a hand?"

"No. We've got it." Remy turned to Morgan and whispered, "I'm sorry I brought you. We'll make this fast."

"Hey, at least I'm not bored," Morgan said, shooting Remy a sassy look.

Remy lifted the tailgate of the truck and handed Morgan the crate. "The small arrangements go in the bedrooms upstairs and the big ones in the dining room and living room."

Eli held the door open for Morgan and Remy. The teen's eyes stayed wide as she passed close to the man in the robe who'd just had his dangly bits on display. "Thanks," she said, still smirking.

Remy almost dropped her groceries when Eli's free hand dropped to caress her rear end. Morgan snorted. Of course, Eli would assume they were picking up where he thought they'd left off. And now Morgan knew about Eli and their "dating," she'd tell her parents, and Remy's business would go down the tubes. Remy hadn't thought things could get any worse, but they just had.

"Take a look around. Decide what bedroom you like best," Eli called as Morgan's long legs climbed the stair to the second story.

"OK," Morgan replied.

Remy emptied the grocery bags onto the counter under Eli's gaze. "Why the long face? I thought you'd be glad to see me. Still sad?" he asked.

"A bit. But we need to talk." Remy picked up a stack of boxes to put away in the pantry.

Eli strolled over and leaned against the door jamb. "If you want," he said.

Remy, trapped in the narrow pantry, held a box of Honey Nut Cheerios over her chest like a shield. She felt…nothing. No twinge of lust, no attraction at all to the man who, just a few weeks earlier, could make her heart pound through her chest with a glance. Eli was just a handsome, rich, hedonistic man looking for an easy lay. She'd been swept away by the sex, the gifts, the house, the plane. All of it. He'd taken what he wanted, and so had she, but she wanted no more.

"No, Eli." Morgan's footsteps clumped overhead.

"Why?" asked Eli. His tongue licked his upper lip. "Still too sad to 'be in the mood'? I promise I'll make the sad go away."

Morgan walked back into the kitchen. "OK. What else can I do?"

Eli turned and smiled. "Hi, Morgan. I'm glad you came with Remy." Eli's nimbus of sexual charisma shifted its focus to the girl. "You have lovely hair," he said. Eli stepped forward and lifted a long glossy lock to his nose and sniffed. "Umm. Coconut shampoo?" he asked, his eyes dropping to her breasts. Morgan gasped and backed away.

This was beyond worse. This was appalling. Morgan looked at Remy with a what-the-hell look on her face. "Morgan, please wait in the car while I finish up here." The teen nearly sprinted out the door.

"Oh my God, Eli. Morgan's 16. I'm babysitting her. She's my client's daughter."

"Too bad. I'd have guessed 18, 19." He turned his attention back to Remy. "Sorry about that. I can't help admiring beauty," he said. Eli ran his eyes down Remy's body, stripping off her prim white shirt and khaki shorts.

Like Willow had said, he was just an old horndog. But a horndog client. Who had just maybe made a pass at a teenage girl, the daughter of a client. The whole thing was a giant mess, and it was all her fault. Remy donned her professional demeanor. "I brought everything you need for the weekend. I'll finish up here and be on my way. Morgan's waiting," she said, opening the refrigerator to put away the milk and butter.

"Everything?" he asked. "You know, I leave soon for Cap d'Antibes. I'll be gone for ten days, maybe more."

Remy took a deep breath. "No. I mean no, Eli. No more," she insisted. "It's not the right time for me—for us—to be together." Her heart pounded. She didn't want to sleep with him, but she didn't want to get fired either. "I'm sorry."

"Ah, I see. The girl. Stop back later then. I'm sure I'll remember something I need you to bring me."

"That's not what I mean, Eli. I mean not again."

"We'll see," he said.

Minutes later, Remy returned to the car. Morgan sat in the driver's seat fiddling with the side mirror. "Did that ancient dude just try to hit on me? I mean, like, ew—he's almost my dad's age, I bet."

"Morgan, I am so, so sorry," Remy said. "He thought you were older. Not that that's an excuse."

"But why?" Morgan stuck her tongue out. "That was so gross. I mean, he was all yum, coconut shampoo. I'm not using that stuff again."

"Eli Wolff is like a lot of men—and most boys. He's just more upfront about it. And a lot of women respond to that." *I did,* she admitted to herself.

"Upfront, yeah. When he came out of the house with his dick hanging out like that, I thought I was going to shit," Morgan giggled. "Upfront, in front, oh yeah."

Remy put her hand on Morgan's shoulder. "You cannot tell anyone about that—or him and me—please," Remy said. "Especially your parents."

Morgan gave her a sideways look. "Tell my parents? Are you kidding? I don't tell them anything. Ever." She straightened up in the seat and wiggled the steering wheel. "I'm ready. Let's get out of here."

The days passed quickly. Eli's unseemly display of his privates unlocked the privacy filter on Morgan's thoughts. Out poured all the minutia of teen angst: zits, weight (too much), hair (too boring), boobs (too small), friends (all of them having a much better summer than Morgan), clothes, boys (and more boys, Morgan had a seemingly endless list of questions about sex), the ice cube mother, never-there father, SAT scores, her place (low) in the intricate social hierarchy of Milton Academy, the latest awesome music, and more.

It took some planning, but Remy found time to take Morgan kayaking on Tisbury Great Pond and to see the tiny gingerbread cottages in the Campground in Oak Bluffs, followed by a ride on the Flying Horses Carousel and a black raspberry cone at Mad Martha's. They jumped off the Jaws bridge at Sengekontacket Pond, visited the alpaca farm to see the new baby alpaca, and ate hot red lobsters with melted butter and lemon on wooden crates on the dock outside Larsen's in Menemsha. An evening beach fire with s'mores was followed by camping out under the stars. Remy had even enticed Morgan into enjoying the pleasures of farm-to-table cooking and eating with stops at the Beetlebung Farm and Mermaid Farm, where they bought the freshest vegetables and best yogurt lassi the teen had ever tasted. And, for their last night together, Remy finagled them a spot for the sunset cruise on the tall ship *Shenandoah*.

"I think I told you that my little brother's a deck hand. He lives on the boat," Remy explained as they searched for parking in Vineyard Haven. "It's a private cruise, so there will be only about ten other people. Like I said, technically, we're on board to set up the buffet and drinks and do the cleanup, but I'll do that. Solly will show you around. He's crazy about that ship."

"Is that a real job, being a deck hand?"

"Solly doesn't earn much, but yeah. He's doing that instead of college." Remy fiddled with the radio. "Nice kid. I think you'll like him."

Morgan flipped down the visor and looked at herself. A week's worth of fresh air and sunshine (and application of warm compresses) had cleared her complexion, and her "crew whites" set off her thick chestnut hair and glowing tan. Not only that. Morgan looked, Remy decided, happy. "That was fun this afternoon, playing with your makeup," Morgan said. "This is way better than how I was doing it." Out came the phone to snap a selfie.

"Happy to pass along Madame Julie's lessons." She glanced sideways. "You look gorgeous." The two had sat in Morgan's white room (much improved by a pile of Willow's most colorful pillows), putting on makeup and doing one another's hair, giggling as Morgan prized out every detail about Madame Julie's other lesson, on *le pouvoir sexuel de la femme,* and Remy's success with Jean-Paul, the handsome waiter. "So that really works," Morgan had said. "Just check them out, then hold their eye and let your power rip?"

"It does," replied Remy. "Just pick better than I have recently."

"Eli the dick?" Morgan had volunteered before convulsing with laughter. "Oh, oh, I will never, ever be able to forget that guy!"

"Oh please, I wish you could," Remy moaned in mock despair. "Ah, heck, where are we going to find parking?"

After finally finding an almost-legal spot on Drummer Lane, they hoofed it down to the dock. "Hurry up, Morgan. We're running late. Solly's going to be pissed."

"OK, OK," Morgan said, hurrying to catch up.

They sped past the Black Dog and pushed open the gate to the boat pier. A lanky teen with unruly blond hair stood leaning against a piling. "Hey, Sis, we better get a move on. What took you so long?"

"Parking. Sorry," Remy said. "Solly, this is Morgan."

Morgan ran her eyes up and down the young man. "Hi," Morgan said, extending her hand as she pushed out her boobs. "I can't wait to see your ship."

Remy did a doubletake. As did Solly.

Oh no, the lesson. Morgan locked eyes with Solly, looking like she was ready to climb aboard more than his boat.

"The *Shenandoah*'s awesome. Let's go." Solly leaped into the motor launch and held out his hand to Morgan. She stepped onto the gunnel, wobbled, then fell against Solly's chest.

"Whoa there," he said, holding her upright. "I guess you need to get your sea legs."

Remy pursed her lips. Morgan had balanced like an acrobat on the top rail of Jaws bridge. That stumble climbing into the launch was no accident. Morgan saw her look and winked.

It was easy to see why Solly had fallen in love with the *Shenandoah*, a square topsail wooden schooner with two massive masts. Skimming along with all sails out—three triangular Bermuda jibs, top, and mainsails—there was no prettier sight.

Poor Solly. Morgan's eyes had moved down to his shorts. "What's that?" Morgan asked, lightly touching a finger to the knife sheathed at Solly's hip.

"My sailor's knife," he said, pulling it out to show her. "Sailboats can be dangerous. I need to be able to cut myself out of the rigging if I get tangled in a line."

"Oh," said Morgan. "That would be scary." Solly shared Remy's wide gray eyes and generous mouth. A season of hauling ropes had tanned and muscled his arms and broadened his shoulders. He was, Remy had to admit, pretty cute.

"It's useful for other things too," Solly added.

"Like what?" Morgan asked, fortuitously taking an interest in Solly's prized possession.

Remy listened with half an ear as Solly explained the uses of the blade and marlinespike as he piloted the small boat alongside the *Shenandoah*.

"Sis, let me help get Morgan on board then you can hand the coolers up." Solly secured the launch then danced up the wood and rope ladder. He leaned over the side to help Morgan. "Just step on the gunnel there," he said. "Get your balance, then grip the rope there."

The lever was still set to full flirt as Morgan climbed up and stepped on board, holding onto Solly's hand much longer than was necessary. She leaned back and looked up the foremast. "Wow," she said. "The mast is so big and tall. Do you have to climb to the top?"

"Of course. It's my job. You can help hoist the mainsail when we get underway if you want

"That sounds great," Morgan said. "I'd love to learn how to sail."

"Uh, Solly?" Remy called up from the launch. "The coolers?"

# CHAPTER 40

As spectacular as the Cinches' house was, Remy couldn't shake the feeling she'd been living in a high-end art gallery for a week. True, the immaculate surfaces and glossy white floors did make it easy to sweep up Coop and Ada's fur and feathers. Like Morgan, she much preferred the Beetlebung Cottage, a cozy one-story Cape that had been the original house on the property. It had cedar-plank walls, a huge beach-stone fireplace, and not a single shiny white surface. They'd had a sleepover there one night, cooking fish and vegetable hobo packets in the fireplace and finishing with toasted marshmallows for dessert.

Remy missed the teen's happy, distracting chatter, which after the sail on the *Shenandoah*, had shifted to everything Solly. Morgan had been a shameless, successful flirt. Their first date, a sailing lesson in the Maddens' old Sunfish, ended with (as reported by filterless Morgan) a kiss and a caressed breast, both of which were very much to Morgan's liking. Such a long time ago, that day Remy and Jake had taken the Sunfish across the pond, and she'd tipped it, for fun, just to see what Jake would do. Back then, that sail had ended in a kiss too.

Remy was pulling into the post office parking lot when her cell phone nickered (horsy ringtone installed by Morgan, of course). Remy picked it up, expecting a report on date number two, a surfing lesson at Katama Beach. *I hate them, I hate her,* read the text. She sighed. It was only a matter of time before Morgan and her mother clashed again. *Can you talk?* Remy texted back.

"Hey, what's going on, Morgan? Is your mother upset about you dating Solly?"

"No, not that. I mentioned something about him teaching sailing, and she thinks he belongs to the Vineyard Haven Yacht Club," Morgan said in a dead voice. "She's selling Rajah. I saw the contract on the desk. I can't believe she would do that to me."

Remy's heart sank. "Oh, I'm sorry."

"He's my horse. She gave him to me. She has no right to sell him."

Of course, Enid Cinch would sell a horse that only the concierge rode. "It probably makes sense from her perspective. It's expensive to keep Rajah. And you don't ride him, Morgan."

"But you do."

Remy sighed. "I don't know that there's anything you can do. I'm truly sorry."

Morgan made a snuffling sound. "Will you come get me? I don't want to be here in this house with her."

"Of course. I need to come out there anyway to drop off some stuff. See you in an hour?"

Remy arrived to find Morgan lying face down on her bed, eyes red rimmed from crying. "C'mon Morgan. You'll be OK," she said, sitting on the edge of the bed and rubbing Morgan's back.

"You don't understand," Morgan said into the bedspread.

"Probably not," Remy said as she stroked her hair. "Do you want to explain it to me? Why you're so upset?"

Morgan rolled over and looked up at the ceiling. "You remember about my accident, right?"

Remy patted her shoulder. "I can't imagine how awful that must have been for you."

"I couldn't ride. And I couldn't bear losing another horse. But when I watch you ride Rajah, it's almost like I could pretend I was you. Only without the fear." She sat up and rubbed her eyes.

Remy gave her a fond smile. "I'm glad all three of us were getting something out of it."

"Will you take him out for a ride now, so I can watch?" She bit her lip as tears filled her eyes. "It may be the last time."

Remy hugged the girl and battled her own tears. "Of course. Let's go."

Rajah snorted and tossed his head at the sight of Morgan and Remy. "Hey! Happy to see us, aren't you, beautiful?" Remy said, as the horse leaned over to nuzzle Morgan.

Morgan stroked his neck, then reached a finger out to touch the tip of one of his curled ears. "I come out here and visit him when I get lonely. He makes me feel better."

"Animals are good at doing that," Remy said.

"You, Solly, and Rajah are my only friends." At the sound of his name, Rajah took a breath and snorted again, flapping his lips. "You see why she can't sell him? He's happy here."

"He'll probably be happy in a new place, with a new owner too," Remy said as convincingly as she could.

Morgan shook her head. "Mother is selling him to some rich woman in New Jersey. She collects rare breeds and wants a Marwari." Rajah puffed a breath into Morgan's neck. "He'll be stuck being ridden in a ring. He'll hate it. I just know."

Remy didn't say anything. Privately, she agreed with Morgan. Rajah, bred on Chappaquiddick, would be miserable confined to riding circles in a ring.

"Will you ride him bareback? I can't. He'd like it, I know."

Remy paused as she adjusted his bridle "I don't think I know how. I haven't ridden without a saddle since I was your age."

Morgan looked downcast. "That's OK."

Remy gathered her courage. "But I'll try if you want me to. The muscle memory is probably still there, somewhere." Remy reached out to lift Morgan's chin. "Is that something you used to do with Dinkins?"

"You remembered his name." Morgan nodded and a tear fell. "Whenever I could. I still dream about it sometimes."

Morgan took the reins and led Rajah out of his stall. Remy stood looking up at the horse's back. "Uh, I forget how to get on without a stirrup."

"I'll bring him over to the rail."

Remy put on her riding helmet, climbed up the fence and, with a deep breath, swung a leg across Rajah's back. Morgan handed her the reins and stood back, longing clear in her eyes. "He's just beautiful. The most beautiful horse I've ever seen."

Remy adjusted her weight, the warmth of the horse unfamiliar between her thighs. "He is. I'm going to miss him too. Very much."

Remy moved easily with Rajah's gait, even without the security of a saddle, as if his muscles carried the message into her own. They walked single file down the path through the dunes to Far Beach, empty as usual but for one family of beachgoers. "You'll pick me up if I fall off?" Remy joked, tightening the strap on her helmet.

"I don't think that'll happen," Morgan said. "Have fun. I'll be watching."

Remy loosened the reins, and Rajah slid like silk into his four-beat ambling gait. Remy shifted her weight almost imperceptibly, and the horse shifted into a canter. The sand on Far Beach was flat and hard, ideal for riding. She dug her fingers into Rajah's mane, then urged him into a gallop. With his hooves beating a tattoo on the sand. Remy felt transformed, horse and rider fused into a single entity. It was, truly, like flying.

At Squibnocket Point, she slowed Rajah and turned to canter back to Morgan. Remy hoped to find Morgan in better spirits. Instead, the girl sat with her head between her knees, crying again. She raised her head to look at Remy atop Rajah. "It's my fault he can't stay here. I hate myself."

Remy leaned forward to get a good grip on Rajah's mane, then brought her leg over to slowly slide off his back. She knelt next to Morgan. "It's not your fault. It's no one's fault," she said wrapping her arms around the girl.

Morgan buried her face into Remy's neck and sobbed. "But it is."

# CHAPTER 41

Jake walked around the side of Remy's house, a shy smile creasing the corners of his mouth. He was wearing a hoodie despite the warm day. One arm was pressed awkwardly against his abdomen and the other balanced a Styrofoam cooler against his hip. Remy sat on a folding chair with a glass of iced tea, watching Ada take a dust bath in her makeshift chicken pen, the book of Nancy Luce's chicken poems on her lap.

"Oh! Hi," said Remy, surprised but pleased to see Jake. "Thanks again for the Nancy Luce book," she added, holding up the slender paperback. "Her poems are awfully sad—she goes on and on about how she tried to nurse her 'poor little hearts' when they got sick. And it so broke her heart when they died." She put the book back in her lap. "But in a weird way, it's a comfort. Where did you find it?"

"Oh, I'm pretty good at finding things I want." Jake's smile widened. "I brought something else for you," he said, jostling the cooler against his hip. "Can you get the door for me?"

"You brought me a cooler? Or are there some goodies inside? More crab?" she asked hopefully.

"You'll see," Jake said. Remy held open the back door. "I haven't seen you around for a while."

"I was housesitting for one of my clients out in Chilmark. And keeping their daughter out of trouble," Remy said, pulling the screen door closed with a click. "Though I'm not sure I did that. She's now dating my brother." Jake's arm was still held protectively across this midsection. "Is your stomach OK?"

"It's fine. Was that the girl I met when I dropped off the book?"

"Oh, right. Yup, that was Morgan. Teddy let me borrow your Sunfish so Solly could give her a sailing lesson. And teaching her a few other things, I suspect. Or maybe she's teaching him." The house was dim after the bright outdoor sun and Remy flipped on the overhead light. "I mean it's OK, she's almost 17, and he's only 18."

"Nothing wrong with a summer romance. I'm sure Solly's a nice kid."

"He is. But her parents are not going to be happy when they find out he's a local. They think she met him at the yacht club." Remy made a face. "Here, let me take that," she said reaching for the cooler. It had an odd pane of glass set in the lid and something inside made a metallic clunk.

"Careful," Jake warned.

"What do you have in here?

A smile played at Jake's lips as he started to unzip his hoodie. "You'll see. Are you ready for your present?"

Remy's eyes widened as Jake's jacket opened to expose two rows of raised lumps protruding from what was clearly a woman's tight pink tank top. "What?"

Carefully, Jake started to roll up the bottom of the top with one hand, exposing a strip of curly black hair running down from his belly button. He reached under to pull out a green-shelled egg. "They're fertilized, so I needed to keep them warm until I could get the incubator set up." He pulled out a second egg with a turquoise shell. "I couldn't find your kind of chicken. These are Easter Eggers."

Stunned, Remy stared at the eggs cradled in Jake's hand, then raised her eyes to his face. "Why?"

His look of happy anticipation disappeared. "I knew I should've asked. I'll take the eggs back to Sherri, the farmer. No big deal."

Remy looked out the window at Ada Queetie, now pecking with gusto on a melon rind, then to the Styrofoam cooler. "That's for hatching chicks?"

"Yeah," he said, carefully putting the eggs back under his tank top. "It's like one we made in elementary school. Long, long time ago," Jake said as he reached for his hoodie. "I thought maybe you'd want to raise chickens again. But I guess that's like people saying 'get a new puppy' when your dog dies. I'm sorry."

"Wait. It's not that." Remy put a hand on his arm. "I just hadn't thought about it." Something warm and glowing expanded in her chest at the thought of hatching chicks, then shrank. "But I won't have a place to keep them, come October. I have to move, remember?"

"We could set up a pen behind Teddy's mushroom operation."

Remy's mind was racing to match her heart. "Baby chicks, oh, Jake," she said, eyes filling with tears. "That would be so wonderful." She could see them, tiny balls of fluff peeping and pecking, with Ada ordering them around like a general, keeping them out of trouble.

Jake's face lit up. "It'll take a couple of weeks."

"I'll keep the incubator on the kitchen counter." Remy moved a pile of tomatoes. "Let me help you get the eggs out."

"I feel a little like I'm wearing a suicide vest," Jake joked as Remy reached under the pink top. Her fingertips grazed his skin. She could feel his heart beating fast to match her own. "One mistake, and boom," he said in a husky voice.

"I'll be careful." Gently, one by one, Remy slid her fingers for the eggs, then laid them under a towel to keep them warm.

In a hot rush, Remy realized what she wanted was right there, under her fingers.

Jake, still Jake.

"That's seven." His voice caught as Remy's hand slid an egg down his breastbone. "The tank top was Jane's idea, to keep them snug and warm," he said.

Jane. Of course, there was Jane, the ice queen. Jake was claimed, off limits.

"OK," she said, "That's the last one." He was so close. The force of attraction tugged on her like a magnet. *You had your chance and blew it. Give it up, Remy. Jake has everything in common with Jane—and nothing with you.*

"How is Jane?" she forced herself to ask.

"Fine. We both have articles due. Hers is going well. Mine, not so great." Jake tugged at the top. "Let me get this silly thing off. Pink's not my color."

Remy pressed a hand to cool her cheek. She did not need Jake Madden taking his clothes off in her kitchen (or maybe she did), but in either case, she had no choice but to watch. His chest was tan, his stomach flat. She couldn't help but notice something, right there under his zipper, that wasn't an egg. So, it wasn't just her, he wanted her too. Or maybe not. That wasn't always under the guy's control, after all, and she'd just had her hands all over him.

Jake folded the pink top, then slid on his sweatshirt and zipped it. "We'll need a bowl of water and a sponge," he said, adjusting his shorts. "You need to keep the temperature at 100 degrees and the humidity at 50 percent for 18 days, then up to 70 percent for the last 3 days. That helps the chicks hatch."

Remy tried to focus on his instructions. "OK, 100 degrees at 50 percent for 18 days. I'd better write this down." She tore a piece of paper out of a notebook. "How do you know all this?"

"I took a book out of the library. I'll bring it by later and make sure everything is working OK." He set the eggs on the egg holder, a minimuffin pan, put on the lid, and turned on the light. "The temperature is automatic—the light bulb will turn on and off—but you'll have to adjust the humidity by adding or taking away a sponge."

Remy peered through the window into the glowing box. A dozen eggs in shades of blue, green, and buff set off a wave of anticipation. Soon, little beaks would be pecking their way out to life, fluffballs peeping in her kitchen. "And that's it?"

"Pretty much. We'll candle the eggs in about a week and see if the embryos are growing." He checked the position of the light bulb in the incubator and shut the top. "I almost forgot. Do you have a Sharpie?"

Remy handed him one from the kitchen drawer. Jake carefully marked one side of each egg with a smiley-face. "The eggs have to be rolled three times a day for the chicks to develop properly." He set the lid back in place and looked inside. "I know you're usually busy during the day. I can do the midday roll for you if you want."

Remy's gray eyes were bright with excitement. "That would be great."

Jake paused. "And one more thing." He took a deep breath.

"OK." Her heart pounded in her chest.

Jake hesitated. "You were right."

"About?"

"A lot of things." Jake suddenly looked uncertain. "I've written a book proposal. The first chapter and an outline. For real people, not academics. It was your idea." He pressed his lips together. "I haven't shown it to anyone, not even Jane. She called the idea pop philosophy. Obviously thought it was beneath me."

"Writing something that people might actually want to read is beneath you?"

Jake took a deep breath. "I'd like you to read it first. And tell me, honestly, what you think."

"Sure."

His phone buzzed. "Oh, no. It's Jane. Geez, not again. Sorry, Remy, I've got to run."

# CHAPTER 42

"I'm shaking like a leaf," said Audrey, opening the door to her West Chop house. The fading black eye had gone technicolor, purple mixing with shades of yellow and pale green. Per Remy's instructions, she wore no makeup and a short-sleeve shirt. Tony would be forced to look at what he'd done, what he was capable of. And she wanted Audrey reminded of what he would do again if she didn't get him out of her life.

Remy stepped inside. She hadn't been to Audrey's house since the day she took Coop away. The interior evidenced Audrey's genteel good taste—and the expenditure of a lot of money. Unlike the houses of Remy's other client, it didn't look "decorated." Instead, freshly upholstered sofas and chairs sat on a scattering of antique oriental rugs, and a gorgeously detailed model of the Charles W. Morgan whaling ship graced the mantle.

"You're lucky the house is in your name," Remy said, admiring a formal oil portrait of a young woman with Audrey's large eyes. Jake's visit had left her wobbly, unable to untangle the strings of intense attraction and regret twisted around her heart. Touching Jake, so close that she could feel his breath on her hair and the beat of his heart under her fingertips had discombobulated her. But he had Jane, and Remy had a job to do.

"It was my grandmother's idea to leave the house to me," Audrey said. "That's Granny in the portrait. I think it was her way of trying to make it up to me after convincing me to marry Tony. But that's all water under the bridge."

"And the girls are off to their friends' in Nantucket with the nanny?"

"Yes." Audrey bit her lip. "I've asked Mike to be here too. I hope that's OK."

"Mike?"

"He came over, remember, to repair the hole Tony had punched in the wall? He's been back to fix some other things." Audrey looked down, shy. "We've talked a lot. He's been a help. And I thought, with his uncle being the police chief, having him here would keep Tony in line." Mike was a cupcake, but he didn't look like one. Audrey's eyes flashed welcome ire. "Let Tony know what he's up against. That I'm serious."

"Good idea."

They sat at the dining room table. Remy, anxious, chewed on her thumbnail. "Let's practice what you're going to say again. And you've downloaded everything?" she asked.

Audrey nodded. "And I made three copies. I gave one to my lawyer and the other to Mike to hold, just in case."

Mike arrived as they were going over the script a final time. Audrey looked at him with grateful eyes. "Hi, Mike," she said, "Thank you for being here."

Remy sat, suddenly invisible, watching Mike's and Audrey's eyes lock. The looks they gave one another were unmistakable. Mike reached for one of Audrey's hands and clasped it gently between his own. "You can do this," he said. Remy's baffled eyes darted back and forth between the two, frozen in a tender tableau. What the hell? Audrey and Mike?

"It's good you're here, Mike," Remy said, not sure that either of them had noticed she was there.

"Sure," he said, glancing at Remy, then sat down next to Audrey, still holding her hand. "You ready?"

She nodded, seemingly fortified by his presence, as if some of Mike's physical strength flowed into her. Audrey sat up tall and took a deep breath. "I'm ready."

The clock ticked closer to 7:00. Audrey wanted to confront Tony on her own. Remy didn't like the idea, but she insisted that Remy and Mike watch from the kitchen and only come out if things started to get out of hand.

The minutes crept by. At last, the slamming of a car door signaled Tony's arrival. Remy and Mike took their positions in the darkened kitchen.

"Where are you? Where's dinner?" Tony bellowed, walking through the hallway into the dining room. He looked even more porcine than ever, his eyes small, red, and angry.

Audrey sat stock still at the empty table, eyes wide with fear.

"I told you I wanted to eat when I got in," he bellowed. You know I don't eat airport food. Did you forget or something?"

"No."

Audrey looked down at her hands as the tirade continued. "How fucking hard is it to have dinner ready for me?" he yelled. "You wanted to go out tonight? Well, I'm not in the mood. Ceneron wouldn't sign the contract. Claimed they needed to do more due diligence. Whole trip was a waste of time. And where are the girls?"

"Away for a couple of days with Tamara's family on Nantucket." Audrey pressed her lips together.

*Come on, out with it,* Remy urged silently from the kitchen. *You can do it.* Audrey glanced at the kitchen door before fixing her eyes on Tony.

His pig eyes narrowed in his fleshy face. The hairspray securing his comb over had loosened, and a slice of pink skull glinted through the dyed hair. "Shitty cook, shitty mother," Tony said, his mood turning even nastier. Tony's mouth turned up in an ugly leer. "Shitty in bed, too. Had to call Kayleigh for a decent fuck."

Remy winced. *Come on, Audrey.* Remy had a moment of panic. Audrey once said that Tony hunted. There could be a gun in the house.

"And where's that damn dog?"

"Tony, I…" Audrey froze.

"What. You what?" Tony said, banging his hand on the table. Audrey jumped. "You want to say you're sorry? For being useless?"

"I want a divorce," Audrey said in a barely audible voice.

"You want a divorce," Tony said with a nasty smirk on his face. He crossed his arms over his gut. "Isn't that rich. No. You're married to me until I decide *I'm* done with *you*."

Audrey trembled. "I want you to leave my house. Tonight." She bit her lip. "Now."

"Your house. The only reason this is *your house*," he sneered, "is because I bailed out your family, saved all your pretty antiques from the auction house. I'm not going anywhere. You've gone nuts. Batshit crazy. Just like the rest of your family." Audrey gripped the edge of the table, cringing. Tony made a move toward her. "You're going to get in the kitchen, make me my dinner, and shut the hell up."

"If he lays one hand on her," Mike whispered.

"Who's that?" Tony's face turned evil, and he balled his small hands into fists. He turned his head to look into the kitchen. "Don't tell me my pathetic little wifey has found herself a lover boy? And he's hiding in the dark." Tony rocked on his toes like a boxer. He was enjoying himself. "Come out, come out, whoever you are," he called in a singsong voice. Then Tony's voice turned mean. "Is that who that is? I want to see who's been fucking my *wife*."

Before Remy could do anything, Mike had stepped into the room. "He's a friend, Tony," Audrey whimpered. "He's been fixing the house."

Remy stepped into the room. "Get out. She told you to leave," she told Tony.

Tony ignored Remy, fixing his eyes on Mike. For all the flab, Remy could see the power gathering in Tony's shoulders and arms. "Friend, are you?" Tony asked. "My wife doesn't have friends."

"If you don't leave now, we're calling the police," Remy declaimed in as tough a voice as she could muster. "Mike's uncle is the police chief."

Tony swung his attention to Remy. He cocked his head. "I remember you. You stole my dog." Fear gripped her insides.

Police chief or no police chief, this was a dangerous man. "I'll have you arrested," he growled.

"Let's calm down here," Mike said, stepping forward with palms facing forward. In a split second, Tony's arm shot out in a blur, connecting with the side of Mike's face. Mike staggered back. Tony raised both fists like a boxer, planning his next blow. "Come on little friend, defend yourself," he taunted.

Less by thought than instinct, Remy swiftly moved behind Tony and wrapped her arms around him in a bear hug, pinning Tony's arms to his sides. "Make the call, Audrey, like we practiced. Now."

After a moment of surprise, Tony started to fight against Remy's grip. It was a horribly intimate experience. Remy could smell his musky cologne and feel his flabby ass pressed against her body. She concentrated on holding him with all her strength. "I'll fucking kill her," Tony growled as he tried to wrest himself from Remy's grip. "Let go of me," he hissed. "I'm not going to hit him again. He's too sissy to hit, letting a girl do his fighting."

"Hello? This is Audrey Kemp. Please send the police. My husband just threatened to kill me," she said in a quavering voice. She gave the dispatcher her address.

"I'm not going to hit any of you. Let. Me. Go," Tony snarled, wrenching his body free. Tony shrugged his shoulders and adjusted his jacket. "Call the police back. Tell them you were joking," he ordered.

"But I'm not, Tony," Audrey said. "I'm serious." Then Audrey, tiny behind the mahogany table, gathered her courage and pulled out her secret weapon. In a clear, steady voice, she said, "I have it all, Tony. I can ruin you. I can smear your reputation if that's all I want to do. Or I can destroy you. You shouldn't have left your laptop behind."

Tony stood stock still. "You don't have shit. You're bluffing."

She shook her head. "I couldn't get into your files, but I think the DA would be interested in your emails. The Feds too, especially the ones with your Russian friends. Even stupid little me could figure out what you were up to."

The color drained from Tony's face. Then an awful reset as Tony calculated his next move. "Now, sweetie, you wouldn't do anything like that," he said as a false, affectionate smile transformed his face. "Not to our little family."

"I might not. If I get what I want. I want a divorce. I want you gone. I've already got a restraining order."

"But you'll need money, honey. You know where that comes from."

"I've got that, too. I cleaned out the joint accounts. My lawyer will get the rest for me." Remy was amazed as Audrey sat and executed the script in a clear confident voice. "You can't touch me, Tony. But you might want to leave before the police get here."

Tony grew red as he stared at Audrey. "You fucking bitch," he said, before turning and walking out the door. "You too," he said to Remy. "I'll get you back."

"You won't," said Audrey. "You make one move against me or my friends, and it all comes out." She held Tony's gaze. "I think I forgot to tell you. I made copies of all your files."

The rain had settled into a steady downpour by the time Remy had returned the next day to the sprawling colonial. She had forgotten that her yellow slicker leaked, and a clammy dampness had seeped through to the inside of the oilskin. Audrey swayed ever so slightly as she opened the locked door.

For better or worse, Audrey had started drinking early. "Such a long day. I've been afraid to leave the house. And it's raining. Thank you for coming."

"Have you heard from Tony?" Remy hung her soggy raincoat on the coatrack, tugged her damp shirt from her shoulders, and followed Audrey into the living room.

"He's left messages. He sounds so angry." Audrey took the last sip of wine from her glass. "But he said he's gone back to New York to talk to his lawyers." She looked at Remy with her bush-baby eyes, bruised and now slightly unfocused. "Do you think he's really left?"

"I imagine he did. I'll ask my friend Jessie at Cape Air to check. Or maybe the police have to ask, I'm not sure," Remy said. "Unless he took the ferry."

"No, he would've flown. He never drives."

Remy had a thought. "I know. I'll go to the airport parking lot and look for the car. What does he drive?"

Audrey put her head in her hands. "Audi R8 Spyder. Two-seater sportster, red and black, New York tags."

That was about as un-Vineyard a car as Remy could imagine, though hardly a surprise. "That should be easy to spot," she said, trying to keep her sarcasm in check. "Did he say anything else?"

Audrey looked at her empty wine glass. "A lot of cursing. That I'd better not tell anybody anything."

"Well, you won't. If he gives you what you want. If he hasn't realized that yet, he will soon." She patted Audrey's arm. "You're safe here. How did you sleep?"

Audrey shook her head. "I had a nightmare, Mike came upstairs, to calm me down. He was still here in the morning. He and that wonderful big dog."

Remy took a moment to register that. "That was nice of him to spend the night."

"It was." Audrey cast her eyes down. "Mike's not like other men."

"He's not like Tony, that's for sure." Remy's instincts were right. Improbable as it may have seemed, something between lovely, fragile Audrey and the carpenter had clicked. It made sense, in a way: kind, strong, gentle Mike was the human embodiment of a safe space.

"Is it wrong to have feelings? I may have…" Audrey blushed. "I may have kissed him, just a little to say thank you, but then it turned into something else."

Remy nearly groaned. Poor Audrey. For all Mike's fine qualities, she'd heard through the grapevine that he kissed like a wet squid. But a smile played at the corner of Audrey's mouth. "He was so gentle—like I was a china teacup. That's what he said, what I reminded him of."

"Of course, it's not wrong to have feelings. Mike's about the best guy ever. But you, um, you kind of run in different circles."

"I realize that."

At least Audrey wasn't a snob. Remy bit her lip. "And you should know he and his long-term girlfriend broke up not too long ago. This could be a rebound for both of you."

"Margaret. He told me all about it. It's a sad story, but he says he's over her."

So far as Remy knew, Mike hadn't said more than five words about his ex since she left him for the bartender. "Glad to hear it."

"And how can I rebound when I didn't have anything to rebound from?"

"True."

"Mike might stay here again tonight. Did you know he was a wonderful dancer? That was a surprise. I love to dance." She glanced at her empty glass. "Do you want some Chablis? I can open another bottle. Mike will be here soon, he'll want some."

Remy almost said, "Mike only drinks beer," then stopped herself. If Mike had taken to sipping wine and kissing Audrey like a fragile teacup, who was she to say anything?

"No, thanks. I'll take a pass."

"Please? In a way, you get credit for bringing us together. I hope you don't think it's a bad idea?"

"No, of course not. But I've got to run. I just wanted to make sure you were OK and give you the name of a divorce lawyer. I got it from one of my clients—she's on her third husband."

Finally, Remy had found a use for Mrs. Bottimore. Remy opened her bag. "It's in here somewhere. Putting her client folder and Jake's book proposal on the table, she searched the bottom for the scrap of paper. "My client said the lawyer is as sharp as they come. It'll cost you, but what she gets out of Tony will more than pay for it."

Audrey's eyes suddenly focused, and Remy got another glimpse of the steel that must have held her together all these years. "Yes. I think I would like to make him pay. I'll call her first thing tomorrow."

Remy handed the paper to Audrey. "That's the way. You've done the hardest part. I'm happy for you."

Audrey sat taller. "I'm happy too. And relieved." She picked up the stack of paper held together with a binder clip. "What's this? *Unearthing Utopia*?"

"Oh. A friend of mine gave it to me to read—it's the first chapter and the outline of a book he wants to write. He's a smart guy." Remy had an idea. "I think it's really good. But I don't know if a publisher would be interested."

"Can I look at it?" Audrey looked Remy straight in the eye. "That's something I know how to do."

# CHAPTER 43

Remy was sitting in the traffic jam at Five Corners in Vineyard Haven when her cell rang with an unknown number. "Nest Concierge," Remy said, expecting another telemarketer. Mike had given her the schedule for when the house would be finished, and she'd been fretting all day. The stress had been building gradually. Each task completed—the trim around another window finished, the bathtub regrouted—added more weight to the stack. Remy had been asking around about rentals, but, so far, she'd come up dry. She chided herself: she knew that she wouldn't be homeless-homeless, like the people sleeping on city streets with their shopping carts. She had plenty of places she could couch-surf.

"Remy? This is Jane Booth, Jake's friend," said the voice on the phone.

"Jane," Remy said. "How are you?" she asked automatically. "Have you been enjoying the Vineyard?"

"Very nice, very productive. So kind of Jake to let me stay while the kitchen was being renovated. And my dog has been having the best summer of his life." Jane chuckled. "The only problem is he's developed a vendetta against skunks."

Jane wanted to chat about skunks? "I can give you my magic skunk juice formula if you like—for de-skunking. It works way better than tomato juice or the stuff they sell at the pet store."

"Yes, I'd love to have that!" She laughed again, a low, cultured chuckle. "But that's not why I'm calling. I'd like to hire you for a commission to do a painting. Two paintings, actually."

Remy moved ahead a few car lengths. She didn't really have the time, but she hadn't held a paintbrush in weeks. "What did you want painted? And what size?"

"Oh, two of the small animal ones," Jane said. "One would be of Kip—he's my dog with the skunk problem—for me, and one of Turk as a thank you to Jake and Teddy."

"I'd love to do that."

"Take your time, no rush. I assume you can ship the one of Kip to me in Boston?"

"Of course," said Remy.

"I'd like the one of Kip to have the pond in the background. He loves the dock. And you can do whatever you want for Turk's."

"I'll need to come by and take photos, maybe do some quick sketches. I could come by this afternoon, 4:30? 5:00? The light will be nice then."

"Perfect."

The day sped by, Remy in the usual frenzy of errands and calls. As if in payback for giving Remy the name of the divorce lawyer, Mrs. Bottimore had insisted that Remy come by to reorganize all the linen and towel closets. Horrors! Beach towels had migrated into the bath towel closet and vice versa; the king sheets were hanging out with the queens, and Mrs. Bottimore would be appalled if she knew what the pillowcases and tea towels had been up to.

At last, Remy was done with that and was ready to head over to the Maddens'. She looked at her watch. It was 4:30. Right on time. "Hello?" Remy knocked and called through the screen. "Jane?" Turk ran from the field at the sound of her voice. "Oh, hello there, kitty," she said, picking up the chubby black cat. "I wanted to see you too."

Jake's head popped up over the half-wall of the living room. "Come in," he said. "I was just, uh, relaxing here with a book."

Remy bit her lip. Suddenly, she felt school girl shy. Remy recalled her fingertips on Jake's chest as she slid the eggs from under the silly pink shirt. She took a breath and composed herself. "I hope I didn't wake you from a nap or something. Is Jane here?" Remy asked, opening the door while juggling purring cat and sketchpad. "I was supposed to meet her here."

"Jane? No, she's out," Jake said, stifling a yawn. "But come say hello. You're welcome to wait."

Remy climbed the half-flight of stairs. Jake was stretched full length on the sofa in a Tufts T-shirt and shorts. His long legs were bare but for a pair of white crew socks on his feet and his black hair was mussed as if he'd been asleep. Next to him, a huge book in a dark blue cover was splayed spine up on the coffee table.

She put Turk down and sat in an armchair. After meowing a complaint, Turk jumped up onto Jake and started kneading Jake's belly with his paws. "Yo, kitty, watch it with the claws," he said, petting the cat. "Everything seems to be working OK with the incubator. I stopped by earlier today when you were out to do the roll."

"I can't thank you enough."

"*De nada.* It's nothing. Just hope they hatch."

"Me too." Remy glanced at the book. Some massively incomprehensible academic tome, no doubt. "What are you reading? A philosophy book?"

"Ah, but you've caught me at my guilty pleasure. It's *Outlander*," he said with a sheepish look, holding the book up. "Pure, mindless escapism. Time-traveling lovers."

"I binged-watched the show this past winter," Remy said, blushing at the memory of the sex scenes between Jamie and Claire. Jake bore little physical resemblance to the strapping red-haired Scot, but one never knows what's under a kilt.

Jake appeared to read her mind. "Yup, the book's the same way," he said, faking a salacious grin. "Almost makes me want to get a kilt. My grandfather had one made, my uncle has it now. Full regalia, dirk, sporran—that's the furry purse thing—the whole nine yards."

"Willow tried making man skirts but they didn't sell. She's probably still got a few in a box somewhere if you want to try one."

Unconsciously, Remy's eyes ran down Jake's body, imagining it naked under a kilt.

Jake laughed. "Maybe I should. It worked for Jamie." He crossed his legs. "What did you want Jane for?"

"She wants me to paint her dog's portrait. I came over to take some photos and maybe do a quick sketch or two," Remy said, recomposing herself. Jake scratched Turk under his chin. The cat's eyes were closed and his purr deepened to a low rumble of pleasure. "Maybe I'll take some pictures of Turk too, while I'm here, try a painting of him as well. Cat pictures sell, though it is hard to paint black fur."

"Be my guest. He's a pretty cooperative subject." Turk's back arched in pleasure as Jake ran his hand down the length of his body.

Ridiculous, to be jealous of a cat. Remy looked at her watch. "Maybe I should get started."

"Sure. Kip's probably under his bush. He's never far." Jake sat up and dislodged the cat. Remy quickly held up her phone to catch Turk's look of displeasure. He jumped up onto the coffee table, stuck out a leg, and started to groom himself. She clicked away, hoping to catch the glossy self-satisfied look of a well-loved, well-fed cat. "Besides, it's time for me to get off my sofa."

"He's a great looking old kitty," Remy said. "With that big square head."

"On top of a very round body. We feed him too much. I think he's sneaking Kip's dog food too," Jake said, poking the cat in his soft underbelly and getting a paw swipe in revenge. "Ow. I guess I deserved that," Jake said with his familiar, warm, blue-eyed smile.

Jake stood and stretched his arms over his head, flashing a strip of flat stomach. Remy pulled her eyes away and picked up her sketchbook.

Lucky, lucky Jane.

# CHAPTER 44

What kind of dog is Kip?" Remy asked as Jake held the door open for her.

"Irish setter. Handsome beast. Terrified of Turk," Jake said. "Yo, Kip, here boy!" Remy's arrival had discombobulated him. And it hadn't helped that the chapter he'd been reading in *Outlander* contained an exceedingly passionate love scene. Could love like that between Jamie and Claire, the kind that overcomes all obstacles, really exist? Or was that only between the covers of a book?

Within a few seconds, a very happy and muddy dog came bounding out of the bushes at the edge of the pond.

"Hi there. You must be Kip," Remy said, patting his head. He had a glossy red-brown coat, long, aristocratic nose, and two of the longest ears she'd ever seen on a dog. Kip was covered in pond muck up to his belly and smelled to high heaven—a very Vineyard combination of pond bottom and skunk. "You are a good-looking dog, even if you do need a bath."

"He always needs a bath," said Jake. "That's pretty much the only thing—other than working—that Jane did all summer: she was continually washing mud off that dog."

"Oh, the two of you must have had more fun than that."

Unhelpfully, Kip gave a big shake, loosening some of the dirt hanging in strings from his fur feathers. "Ah," Remy said, taking a step back as the mud flew. She wiped at the spots on her leg, succeeding only in spreading them into brown smears.

"Sorry," said Jake. "I'll go get a towel."

Remy laughed. "Don't bother. I'm fine. I'll take a shower later." She looked at her legs. "I guess he really is a pond dog. I wonder if Jane wants him painted au naturel or clean?"

After weeks with fastidious Jane, Jake found it a relief to spend time with someone who didn't mind a bit of pond muck. "Good question," he replied.

"Jane said she wanted water in the background. Should we take him down to the dock?"

"Sure."

On hearing Remy say, dock, the dog turned and raced back down the path. Remy and Jake followed, walking along an ancient stone wall past gnarled oaks fuzzed green with lichen. At the dock, water stood in the bottom of most of the aluminum skiffs tied up in their slips. Jake climbed into the ratty Madden boat and picked up the gallon-jug-converted-to-bailer floating in the water. "Good I came down. Teddy was supposed to bail, but I guess he forgot. Again."

"That was some rain the other day. Has Jane been enjoying being out on the pond?"

"Not really," Jake said. "Kip loves the boat, but Jane says it's too small and too wet. The engine got flooded down at the beach one day, and that was enough for her."

"That's too bad. Remember 'choke in, throttle up, and crank it!'" Remy said in a broad Massachusetts accent.

Jake chuckled. "I do. That crotchety old guy, back when we were kids. I'm not sure what he liked better, watching the summer people run aground on the sandbars or seeing them flood their engines."

Remy called Kip, sat him at the end of the dock, and took a series of shots from different angles. She found half a Pup-Peroni in her pocket and let Kip sniff it. "Jake, would you hold this above my head while I take a few more pictures?" she asked. "I want to get him looking into the camera."

Jake stopped bailing and climbed out of the boat. The dog's gaze lasered in on the treat as Jake moved it in little circles above Remy's head. "This got his attention," Jake said, leaning forward. The scent of Remy's hair mixed with the meaty aroma of the treat: one delicious to Jake, the other to the Irish setter.

A long thread of drool dripped from Kip's lips onto the dock. "OK. I think I've got enough," Remy said, suddenly standing up and bonking her head against Jake's chin. "Oh, sorry!" she exclaimed. "I didn't realize you were right there."

Jake rubbed his chin but made no move to step back. The space between them was charged. He resisted the impulse to wrap his arms around Remy and bury his face in her hair. Instead, he said, "The boat is almost bailed out. Want to take a ride with me and Kip?"

# CHAPTER 45

"Yoo-hoo! Willow, are you home?"

Remy stepped through the turquoise door of the playhouse. Inside, it was nearly bursting at the seams. Choco-Ted production sat on a folding table that took up a quarter of the room and housed Hendy and his dog bed underneath, and Willow's sewing machine and boxes of fabrics and bags filled another. The mussed twin bed was pushed against the far wall, leaving a postage-stamp-size bit of empty floor in the middle. The room looked like something from *Storage Wars* and smelled like a chocolate junkie's wet dream.

Willow sat on the bed pinning fabric squares together. "Hi-ho, Remy," she called in a cheerful voice. "I'm so glad you came by! Where have you been?"

"Oh boy. Do we have some catching up to do." Remy looked around. "Wills, how do you live like this?" She looked for a spot to put her bag then reached under the table to pet the dog. "Do you have both Teddy and Choco-Teds living here?

"It's only until Labor Day. Then I get my winter rental back." Willow set her sewing on the floor. "Or at least I hope I will. I haven't gotten the lease from the owner yet. But I can stay on here for a while. Or maybe move in with Teddy after Jake and Jane leave." She patted the spot beside "Come, sit down. Oh, and I've made Ada another diaper." Willow reached under the bed and handed a scrap of fabric to Remy

"Thank you." Remy propped up a pillow and leaned back against the wall, holding up the batik sling. "Cute. She'll look good in the red. You are clever. And kind." Remy leaned against her friend's shoulder. "It's so good to see you."

"Same here." Willow leaned her head against Remy's. "How about I make us some tea and we can catch up."

Remy's stories tumbled out. Willow's eyes widened at the tale of Morgan and Eli, Morgan and Solly, Audrey and Tony, Audrey and Mike. Then it was time to bring up Jake. "And Jake of all people brought me an incubator—and fertilized eggs."

"Baby chicks. That's a superduper idea!" Willow exclaimed as Teddy came in carrying a paper bag.

"Hey, Teddy," Remy said, getting up for a long, welcome, fuzzy hug.

"You feeling better?" Teddy asked.

Remy's "yes" was muffled in his chest. Teddy released her, kissed the top of Willow's head, and started to unpack chocolate bars and coconut from the paper bag. His arrival shrank the dollhouse to even more Lilliputian proportions.

"No, don't tell me you're doing another batch already?" Willow said.

"Yup, nearly sold out at farmer's market today," Teddy said.

"Ugh. I'm starting to dream about chocolate." Willow took a sip of her turmeric tea and turned back to her friend. "Now tell me about hatching chickens."

Teddy looked up. "Those eggies all staying toasty-warm? I think Jake went to every farm on the Island," he said, squeezing in between Remy and Willow on the bed.

"You're too big, Teddy," Willow said.

"First I've heard you complain about that," he replied, waggling his eyebrows.

"Teddy, stop," Willow said, giving him an affectionate swat. "I've been working all day, and it's too crowded in here. You guys want to go for a beach walk? The rain stopped."

Remy looked at her watch.

"Just a short one," Willow cajoled. "Come on." Teddy moved to stretch out on the bed. "You too, Teddy. Uppy-puppy," she said, dragging him to his feet.

The dollhouse's best feature was its proximity to Lambert's Cove, West Tisbury's public beach. As they walked down the long path, Willow insisted that Remy recount her tales to Teddy as Willow chimed in with her own commentary. "And Mike is all kissy-face with the wife now," Willow said. "Can you believe it?"

Teddy's eyes went wide. "Our Mike?"

"Our Mike," Remy confirmed. Teddy blew out a puff of air as he processed that new piece of information. "You know, Jake thought you and Mike might be dating."

Willow snorted a laugh.

"Why is that so funny?" Remy asked. "You like Mike as much as I do."

"Your auras. Blue with green? No way."

The path through the woods changed to sand as they neared the beach. "I'm superexcited about the baby chicks. Jake said it'll take only a couple of weeks," she added as they climbed up the dune and paused at the top. "Oh wow. I always forget how pretty this is."

The view stretched for miles along a long, lovely crescent of sand and calm Caribbean-blue water. To the left, James Pond sparkled through the grasses. To the right, rose the low bluffs of Makonikey Head anchored by Split Rock. Families were scattered in umbrella-shaded groups on the sand, and kiddies splashed in the shallow clear water.

"Indeed it is," said Teddy, striding down the other side. "You and Coop need to come for doggie happy hour. Jane's dog loves it here."

"What's the story with Jane, anyway?" Remy asked, dropping her sandals with the others at the base of the path. "She hired me to paint her dog. Then she didn't show up."

Teddy sighed. "Jane. Put a crimp in my Choco-Ted production. So I leave some chocolately pots in the sink a few days. Big deal." He made a face. "But sweet, generous, lovely Willow," he pulled Willow into a hug and planted a big wet kiss on her lips, "Lets me use her hot plate. I'm making CBD chocolates too. I call them 'Choco-Meds.' They taste kinda funky though. Chocolate with hints of bong. Speaking of which…" Teddy pulled a joint from his pocket.

"Wait until we get away from the little kids, Ted," Remy said. She pointed to the right. "Let's go this way, toward Split Rock."

Low tide and smooth granite stones in subtle shades of tan, gray, and pink dotted the wide band of hard sand, reminders that the Island had been formed by the remnants of an ancient glacier. Remy scanned the ground looking for lucky stones with their unbroken ring of quartz.

"But she and Jake? Two nerdy peas in a pod." Teddy gave Remy a sly look. "Jake's still supersweet on you, you know."

Remy straightened up. "What?"

"Do chickens have lips? Can't you tell?" Teddy said. "He made you an incubator. And I heard you two went for a little boat ride the other day."

"Uh, Jane? Spending the summer?" Remy said.

Teddy looked baffled. "She is, but what's that got to do with it?" Then the light came on in Teddy's brain. "No way. Uh uh. You think they're a couple?"

Remy blinked. "Of course."

Teddy barked out a laugh. "Oh, that's a good one. Like my brother is going to convert Jane or something."

Remy stopped in her tracks. "Teddy, what are you talking about? Convert her to what?"

"You really don't know?" Willow asked.

Teddy snorted in disbelief. "Jane's a lesbian. And married. That's all she ever talks about, Bree this and Bree that. Her wife's off rock climbing on the Eiger or something in Switzerland. Big expedition, sponsored by some fancy outdoor clothing company."

"Gowear," volunteered Willow.

"Gowear. I mean Jake's her friend and all but I wish she'd goweared her icicle-self up that glacier with them. And when she's not talking about Bree, she's writing, so everyone has to be all quiet 'so Jane can concentrate.'" Teddy stopped and looked around. "This is far enough for me," he announced before veering off to flop onto the soft sand. "You ladies walk too fast. Pick me up on your way back."

Leaving Teddy behind, they continued their walk. "You really didn't know?" Willow asked. "Teddy complains to me all the time about Jane. And her skunky dog."

Remy's head spun. If Jane was just a friend and colleague, and not Jake's lover, then...

Willow examined Remy's face as if she could read her thoughts, which maybe she could. "Something happened, didn't it, with Jake. I know what you said about him before, but now, it's different."

Remy blew out a puff of air. "I was standing there, taking the eggs out from under his shirt..." She looked down. "Then I came over, to take pictures of Jane's dog, and he was there."

"But no Jane. That was on purpose. She and Teddy have been scheming. It's the only thing they agree on. But you told Jake you wouldn't go out with him again."

"I did. And I meant it. Then." Remy picked up another stone and examined it. "What the hell. All this time, I'd assumed he and Jane were this perfect couple."

"Phff, Jane. Let's focus on Jake." Willow bent to pick up a plum-colored pebble. "Purple. Of course. You look great in purple."

Another Willow non sequitur. "The only purple I have is my 'I don't give a cluck?' T-shirt." Remy wrinkled her nose. "I do not look great in that."

"Come on, you remember."

"I remember the last time I wore it. I fell asleep on Eli's porch with a beer, and I thought I'd get fired."

"Eli, schmeeli. We're done with him." Willow gave her a look. "We are, aren't we?"

Remy nodded. "We are. Done," she said firmly. "No more Eli."

"Good. That red was too hot for you." Willow clapped her hands together. "You're Goldilocks."

"OK?" Remy waited for her to explain.

"Eli was too hot: you got burnt. Adam, your ex: too cold. Way too cold. But Jake: he's just right. Purple suits you. No wonder Eli got the hots for you after seeing you in that T-shirt."

"This is for you," Willow said, picking up another pebble. "Double rings, double luck, right?" Remy examined where the two rings intersected before slipping it into her pocket.

Back in the dollhouse, Willow rummaged through some of the boxes stacked in the corner. Teddy stretched out on the twin bed to continue his nap.

"I should go," said Remy.

"Just a minute. I have something to give you." Willow rooted around in a different box. "Aha!" She pulled out a spaghetti-strap top striped with shades of lavender. "It's Hmong. I had scraps left from that big quilt I'm making. Try it on. Teddy, don't open your eyes."

Remy pulled off her T-shirt and bra and slipped it on. "It looks great," Willow said, clapping her hands. "Perfect shade. And sexy. Wear that next time you see Jake."

"Willow, you are assuming I want to date him."

"Because you do. Just take it slow. You hear me?"

Remy nodded. "Slow. Got it."

"And hold on. I've got one more purple gift."

"Willow, stop giving me things."

"Nope." Willow crouched and pulled out a round basket from under the bed. "This was going to be your birthday present, but I want to give it to you now." She took off the lid and rooted through a pile of plastic bags, then handed one to Remy. "Barbara and I picked it out at the Pearl Market in Beijing. I would've wrapped it nicer, but here."

Remy pulled out an oval pendant on a silk cord. "Oh, Willow," she said. "It's lovely." She held the necklace up to the window. The translucent stone shone with an opalescent glow as if lit from within.

"It's lavender jade from China. It's a wonderful stone," Willow said. "It purifies your spirit—excellent for meditation—soothes your nerves, clears pathways, and recharges energy. It's especially good after a shock." Willow bit her lip. "Now I feel bad I didn't think to give it to you…" She paused and ran a finger over the beads of her moss jade bracelet.

"When my chickens were killed." Remy slipped the pendant over her head. The stone nestled against her breastbone. "It's beautiful." She leaned over and hugged Willow. "I love it." Remy looked at her watch. "I really have to go. Pick-up-and-post Monday. Baby Dean forgot his blankie at Grandma Baba's house, and FedEx closes at 5:00." She paused at the door. "I love you, you know."

Willow blew a kiss. "Love you too."

Napping pets and the rays of late afternoon sun streaming through the windows cozied Remy's house. She opened the door and dropped her bag. "How was your afternoon, guys?" Remy called. "Have you been sleeping all day? Coop, you must need to go out." The dog stood up, greeted her with a sleepy tail wag, then walked to wait by the back door. "Ada Queetie, let's put you outside for a while too," Remy said, picking up the chicken. She looked out at the slanted golden light. "I think I'll join you."

Remy poured herself a glass of iced tea and set up the folding chair in the overgrown grass. Summer sunshine and the recent rain had encouraged the plants to go crazy. The cutting garden, tomatoes, and herbs grew in tangled abandon, and the path to the chicken run was already overgrown from disuse. She'd better weed whack the path before things got out of control. And pick tomatoes before the birds got any more of them.

But those chores could wait. Remy leaned her head back and let the sun warm her face. She was still gobsmacked by the Jane-is-a-lesbian news. Jane was so lovely and so very, very femme. And so very, very not sleeping with Jake.

Willow, dear Willow, who always had Remy's best interests at heart, thought she should give Jake another chance. Teddy too. Even Jane. And so, Remy would. Not that it was such a hard sell. She closed her eyes. With only the two of them and Kip in the Maddens' boat, they'd flown across the empty pond, the widening vees of the wake ruffling the surface, the sky and water shaded pink and gold and lavender in a presunset display. Remy had been glad that Jane didn't like the boat, that this was something that she and Jake shared. They'd pulled the boat up onto the beach and gone for a long walk along the shore. Once again, the conversation just flowed. They'd known each other for so long that it was like catching up with a long-lost friend. A really gorgeous, incredibly sexy friend who made her tingle inside.

The eggs. Had Jake come by to roll the eggs? With a yawn, she pushed herself up from the chair and wandered inside. There they were, happy-face up in the incubator. He'd left a note.

*Little eggs in a row*
*Add some heat and chicks will grow*
*Dear Remy will be the first to know*
*The sound of their cheeps, then clucks and crows*

Remy smiled. At the bottom, Jake had written a postscript. *Wind will be up the next few days. Want to go sailing in the catboat?* She pressed the note to her chest. Oh yes, she did want to go sailing with Jake. And more.

Jake shared, she realized, Teddy's innate sweetness. But while Teddy hugged, Jake did things like building incubators from scratch and finding out-of-print books of chicken poems. He helped her clean up lobster parties and chase escaped hens, caught her crabs because he remembered how much she loved them, and composed silly poems to make her smile.

Hope burned a tiny, bright flame.

Remy picked up a pencil and went back outside. She'd leave a message for Jake. Something clever. Remy sat tapping the eraser against her chin. "Jake likes philosophy and, apparently, chickens," she told Ada Queetie. "Is there such a thing as chicken philosophy?" The hen, focused on looking for bugs, ignored the question.

Worth a try. Remy took out her phone and typed. She shook her head: 15,800 Google results. Remy clicked the first link. "Why did the chicken cross the road? Aristotle: To fulfill its nature on the other side. Plato: For the greater good."

Uh, no.

Coop lay at her feet then rolled over to warm his tummy in the sun. Remy leaned forward and ran her fingers through his soft, curly coat. "You're such a good boy." Ada strutted to the chicken wire with a loud "tuk-tuk-tuk" and a baleful glare. "Jealous girl, you know I love you too." The hen tossed her silly feathered head-puff in reply.

Inspiration struck. She picked up her pencil and dashed off a quick sketch of Ada staring down an egg, with the caption, *Well, I know who came first! And don't you forget it.* She signed it *Remy* and added *P.S. I'd love to go sailing.* After a pause, Remy added a heart—and smiled.

# CHAPTER 46

The wind blew steady and strong across Tisbury Great Pond. Jake had imagined this so many times. Remy leaned back on her elbows and closed her eyes to the sun. *Utopia* was the prettiest sailboat on the pond, and he was lucky to have the loveliest, most talented woman he'd ever met on board. Trustworthy and kind, she'd showed him what life could be like if he'd only open his eyes.

"Heads up, Remy. I'm going to come about in a minute."

"Aye aye, Captain." She sat up with a deep sigh. "It's Tuesday, my day off, but I still feel like I'm playing hooky."

"You clients owe you a break. You work too hard."

Remy shook her head. "That's just how it is."

"Where do you want to go?"

Remy pulled a wayward strand of hair from her face and stretched her neck. "Um. Let's sail down toward the beach, see if the cut is still open? And then," she motioned to the crab net on the bottom of the boat, "Can we go crabbing?"

"Both excellent ideas. We can try Deep Bottom Cove and maybe Thumb Cove."

"I do love crab more than almost anything else," Remy said. "I've been meaning to go chicken necking off Crab Creek bridge like we used to as kids, but I never seem to have time. I wish I had my summer off, like your sabbatical."

"It's been a good summer," Jake said. "Do you want to take over the tiller?"

"Later, maybe." Remy looked up the mast to the canvas sail billowing full and white with the breeze. "I'm enjoying being taken for a ride."

"Time to tack. Are you ready? Hard alee," Jake called, pushing the tiller away from himself. The keel flattened as the boat slowed and began to turn into the wind. "Watch your head."

The wooden boom swung rapidly across the boat, and Remy shifted to the windward side of the boat as the sail began to fill again. "This is absolutely perfect, Jake. She sails like a dream."

"I was afraid she'd be a bit sluggish, with the broad beam and all, but she's not."

Remy ran her hand over the teak that Jake had so lovingly restored. The fine-grained wood glowed russet gold in the sun. "You did a beautiful job on her."

"I liked doing the work. She just needed some TLC."

"And that's what you gave her." Remy pulled off her T-shirt to reveal a bikini underneath. "*Utopia* was exactly the right name to pick." She turned her gray eyes on him. "Oh, Jake. *Unearthing Utopia*. I forgot to tell you. I loved it. I asked a friend to take a look at it too. She used to be in the publishing business." Remy leaned over and put her hand on his knee. "I hope you don't mind."

The warmth of her hand sent tremors up his thigh. His eyes dropped to her breasts. He didn't want to think about his book proposal, or work, or anything that wasn't Remy. "Not at all. The more feedback, the better."

"Good." Remy sat back and wriggled out of her shorts.

No, this was better than he imagined. Way better.

"Thanks. As I said, it was your idea." Jake ran his eyes up the length of her tall body: the smooth, perfect skin, long legs, and shapely arms. Her softly rounded curves were accentuated by her rose-pink bikini. Remy caught him at it and gave him an equal, leisurely appraisal in return. Jake shifted in his seat and grinned.

Remy grinned back. "So nice." She rested back on her elbows again and propped up her feet. "You know, I've always thought

I'd like to live on a sailboat. Or maybe a houseboat. Not like forever—that's Solly's plan—but just to try it out." She wiggled her toes. "Silly, I suppose."

"No, not at all." Jake let out some line as he corrected their course. "I have a friend who lives parttime in a houseboat in Boston Harbor. He loves it." A gust of wind heeled the catboat. Jake shifted his weight in counterbalance. "He lets it out as an Airbnb. We could..." Jake was about to say, "stay there sometime."

She tilted her head. "Maybe we could. Sometime." Remy peered under the boom toward the beach. "Oh, shoot. The cut is closed."

"I thought it might be," Jake said. "It looked like the pond had started to fill up. Did you want to go to the beach anyway, or are you ready to catch some crabs?"

"Crabs," Remy replied.

Jake set a course east to Deep Bottom Cove, luffing the sail as he nosed the catboat up to the sandbar that nearly pinched off the opening to the cove. Remy jumped off the boat into the knee-deep water and pulled it the last few feet to shore.

"A few more decades, and this cove will be closed off too, like Middle Point Cove."

"Hmm, really?" Jake said. Watching Remy set the anchor interested him more than pond geology.

"Yup. Can you grab the sunscreen too? I should put more on my back."

Jake handed her the crab net, tossed the sunscreen into the bucket, and climbed from the sailboat onto the sandbar. Remy pulled out the tube and handed it to Jake. "Here," she said, turning to offer him her back. Remy lifted her hair and held it loosely knotted in her hand. Resisting the impulse to kiss her neck, Jake squeezed a white glob into his hand. "My shoulders, too, please."

Remy's skin was a marvel: soft and supple but resilient. Like her. Slowly, carefully, he rubbed in an even layer of sunscreen, feeling the muscles of her neck and shoulders relax. Her hair smelled fresh, lemony. The scent, mixed with salt air and the evocative childhood scent of Coppertone, was an aphrodisiac to weaken whatever was left of Jake's willpower. He'd nearly lost it the last time she'd been so close, the day he'd brought the incubator. Her fingers, sliding the eggs from underneath the pink tank top, had been exquisite torture. Jake hadn't been touched by a woman so intimately in so very long. He'd longed for her hands to keep touching him, roaming his body, exploring every inch.

"Don't forget lower down too."

Jake squeezed more cream onto his palm and slid his hands down, feeling her spine under his fingertips. She sighed. He focused on her lower back, then started to spread sunscreen outward toward Remy's waist.

She jumped. "Hey, no tickling!"

"I'm not trying to. I'm just getting the sides." He tried again but her tickle switch had been turned on. Remy jumped again. "OK, OK." Jake slid his hands back down to rest his thumbs in her dimples of Venus, so aptly named. "Do you want me to do your bottom too?"

Remy hesitated. "OK. I always miss spots there."

It was delicious to feel her strong muscles underneath the soft feminine flesh. Jake focused on covering the area by the edge of her bikini, running a finger just underneath. Remy's breath caught, and she stepped away.

"I think that's good." Her eyes were dark and large. She wanted him too. Remy bent to pick up the net. "Thank you. I'm going to catch a crab now."

"Crabs. Right." He pulled his eyes away. If she could wait, he could too. "I've had good luck over there, to the right."

Out of all the pond kids, Remy was the one with the greatest passion for hunting crabs, spending hours with a net in hand, looking to scoop up the wily crustaceans. Only this time, it wasn't a chunky, awkward 14-year-old Remy. It was a fully grown, sexy-as-hell woman. One who set the teen boy inside into a paroxysm of desire.

But it wasn't just that. He'd noticed it all those weeks ago at the dock. Remy had a naturalness that was as clean and pure as the breeze. No artifice, no manipulation, no games. She stood in the shallow water, an intent huntress of crabs. A warm wave of happiness rose in his chest. Remy was, he thought, the puzzle piece he'd been searching for, the one that would fit with a perfectly easy click. His worries about getting his articles published, battling the nasty politics of getting tenure, had faded away. Here and now—that was what mattered.

"Ah, there's one!" cried Remy, splashing knee-deep into the water and lunging forward with the net. Scoop and lift, and she had her first crab. "Get the bucket, Jake. I've got a good feeling about this."

"That's a nice big jimmy," Jake said, inspecting the crab.

Remy banged the edge of the net on the bucket. She banged again, but the crab stayed put. "Give me a hand here, he's stuck in the net."

Careful not to get pinched, Jake loosened the green net from the crab's flipper fins. "There, try again," he said.

Remy did a flip of the net, and the crab was dangling from one claw above the bucket. "Off," she commanded, bringing the net down for another slam. The furious crab skittered around the bottom of the bucket, both claws raised and ready to do battle. "Ha! Got you!" she said in triumph. "You want to take a turn, Jake?"

"Nope. I've done plenty of crabbing this summer. Go ahead, I'll watch you."

Which was exactly what he wanted to do.

The cove was calm and quiet. A heron fished in the shallows. The late afternoon sun lit the fields and trees—and Remy—with a golden light. Jake sat and watched the show. Remy stalked back and forth in the shallow water, splashing and lunging whenever a crab came into sight. After a few unsuccessful tries, her face set into a determined look. She was not giving up, not yet. Strong, dauntless girl.

Three big strides through the water, reach and scoop. "Got you," Remy cried, holding up the netted crab. She took a closer look at the belly. "Oh damn. Female." She shook off the crab and started marching around again. "Ah," she said with another plunge of the net. Remy held up her prize. "Male! Bucket!" she ordered.

Jake got up with a grin as wide as the sun. "Coming."

# CHAPTER 47

"Day eight," Remy said. "This is it." She carefully removed an egg from the incubator. "What if we don't see anything? I lay awake last night, worrying about that."

Infertile eggs weren't the only reason Remy couldn't sleep. She'd tossed and turned in her empty bed, wondering what the heck she was getting herself into with Jake Madden. Sweet Jake had carried her bucket of three pissed-off crabs up from the dock, invited her in for a beer to celebrate their catch, only to find Jane and Teddy arguing about laundry. Even though Jane wasn't in a relationship with Jake, Remy, windblown and just a bit sunburned, was still ill at ease in her icy company.

"If these are duds, I'll get you more fertile eggs," Jake said. "No worries."

"I'm still nervous." She flipped on the flashlight and took a deep breath. "What exactly am I looking for again?" Remy asked, heart pounding. For good luck, she'd worn the purple top and lavender jade Willow had given her.

Jake flipped to the page in the chicken book. "Candling the eggs," he read. "It's supposed to be like this," Jake said, holding the book up. "A dark spot—that's the embryo—with veins spreading out from it."

Remy studied the photo. "Looks kind of gross. OK. Here we go."

They stood together, heads nearly touching, as she held the egg to the light. "Oh my gosh, oh my gosh," Remy exclaimed. "That's it. Just like the picture." Slow, Willow had advised. But slow was so hard when he was so close.

Jake took the egg from her hand. "I'll get the next one," he said. "Here," he said, handing her a second egg.

More confident now, she held it to the light. "This one's growing too. It's like, so amazing," she said. Ada clucked past in her chicken diaper. "Ada Queetie, are you going to like being a mother hen?"

"But I'm sure even if she doesn't, you'll make an excellent mama."

"Mama chook, that's me," Remy said, laughing. "Seriously, I can't tell you how excited I am. That day you came over with all the eggs stuffed in your shirt. I was so surprised. You have no idea how funny that looked."

"My pleasure," he replied. "After what happened, it was the least anyone could do."

"But no one did. Except for you," Remy said firmly. Loads of people had given her sympathy, but only he had done something that would make everything all right again. Not Willow, not Teddy, not Mike, not Solly. Only Jake.

They worked their way through the eggs. It wasn't until they checked egg number 11 that they saw something wrong. Remy turned the egg to check all sides to make sure. "Oh look. Nothing's there. I wonder what happened?"

"Sometimes they just don't grow," Jake replied. "Lots of different reasons, according to the book. Put it aside and I'll get the last one."

Jake's eyes drifted down to the lavender stone pendant around her neck. "That's a pretty necklace."

Remy held it up. "Willow gave it to me. And this top. The stone is supposed to have all sorts of magical powers." She let the stone drop back into place between her breasts. "You know Willow and all her spiritual stuff."

"Saint Willow, bless her for giving Teddy a place to go. He and Jane do not make the best of housemates. Jane does not appreciate his approach to life."

"Or laundry," Remy laughed. Remy walked into the kitchen. She felt Jake's eyes following her. Maybe it was just the success of the candling, but she felt…happy. Happy to be in her house, with Jake, hatching a clutch of eggs.

"I have a special treat for us." Remy pulled out a small glass bowl from the refrigerator. "I almost—but didn't quite—eat all the crab we caught. I exercised a little self-control," she winked, "for a change."

Jake's eyes widened with pleasure. "Ah," he said.

She put the bowl and a box of water crackers on the kitchen table and sat down next to him. "That was a perfect afternoon."

It had been. Watching Jake pull on the lines of the catboat taut against the wind had tugged on something inside Remy too. He might be a stuffy egghead professor, but that was just what other people saw. She loved the way his eyes glowed blue against the sail, bluer than the sky, bluer than the water. Remy couldn't take her eyes off the smooth bulge of his muscles under tanned skin as he held the tiller steady on course. His laughter as she dashed in the shallows after crabs lifted her heart. Teasing, Remy had quizzed Jake on his favorite things, from movies to music to sports, and found their tastes (foreign flicks and rom-coms, indies, everything Sox) perfectly aligned. If only he liked to dance…

Jake reached over to rest his hand over hers and smiled. "It was perfect." His touch flipped a switch. It was different from Eli, who had blown her fuses and left her burnt like a 110-watt hairdryer plugged into a 220 socket. It was a different kind of current, steady and strong, that quickened her pulse and set her thrumming. Under control, for now.

"Can I fix you a cracker?" Remy asked.

"Please."

Her hand shook ever so slightly as she spooned out generous globs of crab cocktail onto two wafers. Jake took a bite, barely catching a falling bit of crab in his hand and licking it up.

"Delicious," he said. "This is hands down, the best thing in the whole world. Fresh-caught Tisbury Great Pond blue crab. Fixed just like this."

A crumb sat in the corner of his mouth. She longed to reach over and remove it but didn't trust herself. Instead, she nibbled her cracker. "I agree," she said after savoring the sweet taste of crab meat. "I love all seafood, but nothing can match this." Remy fixed each of them another cracker. "I only wish I'd caught more."

"We'll go out again. Just tell me when."

"I'll hold you to that."

"Anytime," Jake replied, breaking a cracker in two and dishing out the remaining crab. "Here, last bite," he said, holding the cracker up to her lips.

She opened her mouth and their eyes locked as his fingers brushed her lips. It was going to take all her willpower to take it slow if things kept going like this. She had willpower, but her willpower had its limits. And Jake was pushing them.

Remy's cell beeped. She sighed, wishing it would go away. It pinged with a message. "Oh crikey, not again," she groaned after reading the text.

"What is it?"

"Oh, a client wants me to move her dinner reservations around again." She started to search her contacts, then paused. "Or... we can take their reservation and eat at the Aquinnah Shop restaurant tonight to celebrate?"

"It's a date."

"Come in," Remy called down the stairs, heart beating in anticipation. "I'm almost ready."

For her date. A date with Jake Madden.

She slipped on her sandals and greeted him. Jake, too, had primped for their evening. He wore a blue striped shirt instead of his usual T-shirt, and his wet, black hair had comb marks.

"You look handsome," she said.

"And you look gorgeous." Remy blushed. After trying on four outfits, she had decided on her white gauze shirt and a flowy skirt, paired with the jade necklace and Morgan's paisley wrap (in case they sat outside). A pair of dangly purple wampum bead earrings made by Mike's Wampanoag cousin dangled from her earlobes, and Eli's gold bracelet graced her wrist. The bracelet was pretty, she liked it, and it was stupid not to wear it just because Eli had given it to her.

"Here, I brought you something." Jake handed her a paper bag. "Careful, it's heavy."

Remy took the bag and peered inside. "Oh wow. *What?*" she said as she pulled out a giant egg as long as her hand. The shell was a gorgeous deep teal mottled with jade and forest green.

Jake grinned. "It's an emu egg. Don't worry—we're not going to hatch it."

"I hope not," Remy said, imagining a six-foot bird running around her yard. "But where did it come from?"

"The farmer's market, if you can believe it. It's from off-Island, of course."

Remy ran a finger over the egg. "I've never seen anything like it." She looked more closely. "These colors are just amazing. If I were to paint it, I'd use viridian and some Prussian blue…" She looked up. "Oh Jake, this is one of the best gifts—and definitely the weirdest—I've ever gotten. I love it." Remy rolled the shell over in her hand. "I wonder if you can blow it, like an Easter egg and save the shell."

"Emu omelet—for breakfast?"

"We'll see," Remy replied with a flirtatious look.

After the drive up-Island, and three loops around the circle, they found a spot and parked. The Aquinnah Shop restaurant was perched at the top of the cliff on the westernmost edge of the Island, where the sunset views were phenomenal, the vibe low key, and the prices (for the Island) reasonable.

"I hope we get a table outside for the sunset," Remy said. She wound the wrap around her shoulders and looped her arm through Jake's. "Let's ask."

The teenage hostess seated them at the corner of the deck with a panoramic view. To the west, Gay Head Light flashed its beam across the sea as it had since 1796. They picked the special, a bowl of soft-shell steamer clams—not for the faint of heart—to start, followed by the seafood pasta and the lobster-arugula salad to share, and a New Zealand sauvignon blanc.

"So now we know that we have chicks, what are you going to name them?" Jake asked as the server opened the wine.

"I haven't thought about it," Remy replied. "Maybe I won't, this time. Just call them chook one and chook two, or something."

Jake swished the wine around his glass to inspect the legs and took a sip. "I have some ideas," he said.

"You do?" She put her napkin in her lap. "Like what?"

"Baseball players. Ted Williams, David Ortiz, Manny Ramirez," Jake deadpanned. Remy made a face. "What, you don't like the Red Sox?"

"You know I love the Sox. But I'm not naming my chickens after baseball players." Remy gave him a look. "Or the Pats. No chick of mine is going to be called Tom Brady."

"Hmm. Guess I'll have to change tack here." Jake tapped the stem of his wine glass. "Movie stars. Famous musicians." He tapped again. "Hey, I know, how about great philosophers?"

"You're not serious? That's even worse than baseball players."

"I am quite serious. Kant. Descartes. Socrates. Those are terrific chicken names. We'll encourage them to contemplate great questions of life, like what came first, the chicken or the egg," he said with mock sincerity.

Remy chuckled, envisioning herself chasing a chicken named Socrates around the pen. "You're responsible for the eggs, so I guess you should have a say in naming the chooks." She shook her head. "But I draw the line at Nietzsche."

"Deal. But you're OK with Kierkegaard?"

"Uh, no."

They were interrupted by the server, who set down a generous bowl of steamed clams, their briny, garlicky scent wafting into their noses. "My mouth just started watering," Jake said.

"Mine too." Remy squeezed the lemon into the melted butter. "I haven't had these in ages. I wonder if they are from our pond?"

Jake picked up a clam by its long black siphon, detached it from its shell, and swished it in broth to rinse off the sand. "I remember when I used to dig for these. The black muck would get under my fingernails, and my hands would stink for days."

Remy got to work on her next clam. "Such frustrating little buggers, the way they dig themselves straight down into the sand and run away. Quahogs just lie there waiting to be dug up."

Jake dipped the clam into the butter and dropped it into his mouth, biting off the siphon and laying it on his plate.

"Oh, you still eat them wrong, Jake. You're supposed to eat the whole thing, except this little foreskin piece," she said, holding her clam up to demonstrate. "That's how we do it in my family."

"Uh uh," Jake said, recalling their old argument. "Here. You try it my way and tell me which is better."

Remy patiently waited as Jake fixed her a clam, then held it dangling just above her lips before lowering it in. He held tight as she tried to wrest the clam from his fingers with her teeth before giving up and biting off the neck.

"See," he said. "It's much better to eat only the tender part."

"Hmm," she said. Remy never really did much like the chewy siphon, but she wasn't about to admit that to Jake. "Now, you try it my way." Remy selected her clam, slid off the skin, swished and dipped then held it out to Jake, holding her hand cupped underneath to catch any butter drips. Her gold bracelet caught the light as it slid down her wrist. "Whole thing now," she said as she lifted it to his open mouth, her top falling open as she leaned over. Jake's eyes slid down the opening and didn't come back up. "Eyes up here, Jake," she teased as a flush pinked her cheeks.

"Just looking at your necklace," he lied.

"Sure you are. So, what do you think?" Jake made an exaggerated chewing motion. "It's like eating a rubber band. I'll admit you get more clam that way."

"Let's call this one a tie."

Remy took a sip of wine and looked out over the water. To the west, the sun had changed into a flat yellow disk, half-obscured by deep purple clouds edged with brilliant light. The sky was colored a deep blue that became a band of lavender and rose before warming to orange above the ocean horizon. The bronze light set their faces aglow, giving them both a radiant beauty not missed by the other.

"Look how pretty the sky is getting," Remy said.

"This is beautiful, but my favorite place to watch the sunset is still over Black Point Pond from Quansoo."

"Mine too," Remy agreed. "I'm so busy this summer that I haven't gone once," she sighed. "Keep eating, we've plenty left," she said, pushing the bowl over.

Jake squeezed more lemon into the butter and looked up at Remy. His gaze made her quiver inside. How could she have judged him so wrong? Jake couldn't help getting all nerdy professor sometimes: that was who he was. But so sweet and fun and thoughtful and kind—and very, very sexy.

"You know, I have an emu story," he said.

"An emu story. No one has an emu story," Remy laughed, dipping a piece of bread in the clam broth.

"I do. Back when I was in graduate school, I was visiting my friend Tilden in Philadelphia. She lived in Chestnut Hill, this nice suburban neighborhood. So, we're walking back to her house with some hoagies for lunch, and we hear this really weird noise behind us." Jake swished a clam in butter. "We turn around, and a giant emu is running down the sidewalk toward us. We both freeze, staring at it."

"No way."

"We turned and ran like hell. Those things are huge—at least seven feet tall—and this one looked deranged." Jake wiped his mouth with the napkin. "So, we're running, and I glance over my shoulder and it's catching up. An emu is very fast," Jake said earnestly. His hair had dried in an adorable little curl on his forehead.

Remy started to laugh. "You're making this up."

"I am not. It was really scary. I can hear it hissing and kind of growling at us. I'm terrified, but Tilden starts laughing so hard she can barely keep up."

"Then what?"

"We can't outrun it, so we slip through a gate into somebody's back yard to hide, figuring it'll keep going."

"And?" Remy asked.

"The bird was stretching its neck way out, ready to peck us to pieces or something. He can see us behind this big fence and starts attacking it."

"Maybe it just wanted your hoagies?" she teased.

"I don't know what it wanted. I think it was having a psychotic episode or something. So it's trying to break down the fence, when this lady comes out to the backyard to see what's going on and starts screaming to call the police."

"Then what?"

"It kept pecking and hissing at us through the fence. Then, suddenly, it just changed its mind and ran off. I guess they caught it. Or maybe it ran home."

"I'm doubly glad you don't want to hatch that egg."

"No way. I'm sticking with chickens. And my crazy chicken lady."

Remy poked him in the arm. "Hey, I'm not crazy," she protested. "I just like chickens."

"I know. They're smart and loyal and affectionate. They can even count," Jake said.

Remy poked him again. "I told you that."

"And I remembered," he replied. "You know, I think Ada Queetie is coming around. She used to just give me the hairy eyeball when I'd come to roll the eggs, but yesterday she went up on my lap to be petted." He dipped a piece of bread in the clam butter. "Sort of like a cat, only with feathers."

"That was an honor," Remy said. "I've never seen her do that with anyone besides me."

Jake reached out and ran a finger down Remy's arm, sending a jolt of pleasure. "You know, speaking of cats, last time I saw you in that shirt, it was all covered with black Turk hair."

"When was that?" Remy looked down at her white shirt, unbuttoned to expose just a bit of lacy bra.

"Earlier this summer. When Teddy talked you into testing Ted-teas," Jake said, now lightly running his finger up to the tender, sensitive flesh inside her elbow.

The touch of his fingers was incredibly erotic. Take it slow, she reminded herself. Reluctantly, Remy pulled her arm away and picked up the last clam. "Oh. I was picking cat hair off for ages. What made you remember that?"

"Because I was insanely jealous of Turk."

Delicious anticipation refreshed the pink in her cheeks. Remy finished off the clam and went to pick up her napkin. Jake's hand darted out and stopped her. He lifted her fingers to his lips and brushed the tip of his tongue over her fingertip. The low flame that had been simmering under Remy increased to high. Like a genie let out of a bottle, Remy's *pouvoir sexuel* overflowed its vessel. Every nerve tingled, longing to be stroked, desire set alight. Reason had flown out the window, set sail by a gust of pure lust.

"Jake, what are you doing?" she asked in a low whisper.

"Mmmm," he murmured in reply. "Butter."

# CHAPTER 48

They dropped the bag from the restaurant at the door. The drive back to Remy's had been torture; with her hand resting on his thigh, Jake had forced his eyes to stay on the road as his thoughts ran amok. The hunger that had erupted had made the idea of eating superfluous. They'd looked at each other with ravenous eyes, and Jake had asked, "Should we get the rest to go?" Remy had nodded, then, not caring who saw, pulled Jake into a voracious kiss.

They had barely made it inside when they fell upon each other, lips inseparable as they struggled with buttons and zippers. "Please tell me I'm not making a mistake," Remy said, as her shirt slipped to the ground.

"No mistake," Jake replied, tugging off her bra and burying his face in her breasts. "This is meant to be. I know it."

Remy's body shuddered as lips and tongue met nipple. Jake dropped to his knees and kissed her bellybutton as he tugged at her skirt. He looked up. Remy's hair had come loose and fell around her shoulders, and the jade around her neck glowed as if lit from within. Overwhelmed, he buried his face in her stomach.

Remy ran her fingers through his hair. "Remy, I want you so much."

"Upstairs," Remy said, her breath running quickly through half-parted lips.

Back on their feet, Remy tugged Jake up the stairs and nearly threw him on the bed. "You still have too many clothes on," she said, undoing his belt and pulling down his pants.

Jake moaned as her hands slid down his chest to the strip of black hair below his bellybutton. Remy tugged on a curl. "The day you came with the eggs," Remy said. "You have no idea how much I wanted to do this," she said, showing him exactly what she meant.

The sweep of her feather-soft hair across his abdomen brought an indescribable wave of pleasure. "You are incredible," Jake groaned, as her lips and tongue feasted on his body, tasting and licking her way back up to his neck.

Arms and legs entwined, they sought each other. "Oh, oh," she whispered as his hands slid down to her buttocks. Hard pressed against soft, motion became rhythm, a duet of bodies. Their world became nothing but skin and hands and lips and irresistible urge to make man and woman one.

The universe exploded into a million stars. Sweet Remy. His love.

Jake had been riding high for days. It hardly seemed possible, after all his doubts and dreams, that he and Remy were finally together. Jane's departure had barely registered. Teddy couldn't keep the grin off his face. Jake spent his days planning their evenings. Remy worked so hard; it was only fair he cooked.

Jake sat at Remy's kitchen table and tapped his pencil on the pad. He wanted to get it right, the poem should be about chickens, but it should show his feelings too. A real poem this time, something romantic. *O my chicken is like a red, red rose.* No. Jake tapped his pencil again, then got up and looked through the incubator window for inspiration. A developing embryo, while in some ways an apt metaphor for his growing love, hardly made good fodder for a love poem.

The first night had knocked his socks off. Flat out astonishing. Remy had surfed him like a wave, the saltiest, most mind-blowing sex ever. Last night they didn't make it past the sofa. And this morning, waking in her arms and finding each other all over again had left him blissfully spent. Jake lifted a hand to his nose. He could still smell her, feel her against his body. She was everything he'd ever wanted. Jake leaned back in his chair and counted himself a very lucky man.

A knock then, "Remy, are you home?" asked a male voice carrying a hint of a British accent. The doorknob turned and a blond man stepped into the kitchen.

"Oh hello," Eli said. "I'm looking for Remy," Eli said, putting a bag on the counter. "Do you know when she'll be back?" His eyes dropped to Remy's sundress and bra still lying on the floor.

"She's out for the afternoon. I'm Jake Madden, her uh... friend."

"Eli Wolff." Eli stepped forward, gripped Jake's hand, and shook it just a beat too long. "I just got back from Cap d'Antibes. I thought I'd surprise her with a couple of things I brought back for her." Eli pulled two boxes out of the bag and a bottle of champagne. "I had a friend who wanted to christen her new yacht. Anaka insisted I come. It was quite the party. Nice, but I missed the Vineyard—and my little Island girl," he added, looking up to catch Jake's eye. "Isn't that how that old song goes? Has she been keeping busy?" he asked with a smirking glance at Remy's bra.

Jake stood slack jawed, staring at the confident, handsome man in the Brioni shirt arrange his presents on the counter. "Yeah. She's been busy with work."

Eli raised an eyebrow in challenge. "That's all?"

Had they been a pair of bucks, they would have locked antlers. "Mostly," Jake replied.

"Riding?" Eli asked with a knowing smirk. "She's good."

Jake rarely felt the need to punch anyone, but Eli made a tempting target. "Yes, she is."

"Well, tell her I'm sorry I missed her, but I'll see her later when she comes by with my groceries. I'm looking forward to our reunion." Eli smiled a wolfish grin. "One last thing." Eli walked up to Remy's whiteboard and selecting a red pen, marked "SS" at the bottom of that day and the next. "Nice meeting you, Jake Madden," Eli said, then let himself back out the door.

Jake stood stunned. That could not have just happened. It didn't seem possible. But here was Eli Wolff, with gifts from France, expecting more from Remy than just groceries.

He took a deep breath and closed his eyes, then opened them and looked around. Living room, sofa, chair, kitchen—all as it had been five minutes earlier. But the earth had tilted. A reasonable man would say it was hardly fair to expect Remy to be exclusive after a couple of dates. But Jake wasn't a reasonable man. He couldn't bear to know that she was making love to another guy. The pain stabbed his gut with a long, sharp, familiar blade.

He opened the smaller of the two boxes. Tiny gold ropes were twisted into a pair of small hoop earrings. To match her bracelet, the bracelet Jake had, just hours ago, twirled around Remy's wrist as they lay naked in bed. Inside the other box was a scrap of a scarlet negligee. As if he were committing hara-kiri, the knife sliced through him leaving him bleeding on Remy's kitchen floor.

Not knowing what else to do, Jake went home.

"I don't believe it," Willow said, crossing her arms. "She said she was done with him." Willow picked up her beer from the beach stone coffee table and looked out from the deck. The late-afternoon sun lit the fields across the pond with glowing gold light, a Sunfish was trying to tack up the narrow cove, and the guy with the ridiculous waterbike was taking his daily constitutional. "Remy tells me everything."

Turk, purring, jumped up onto Teddy's lap and started head-butting his chin. "But I saw it, Wills. Right there, on her whiteboard. SS. You remember, Remy's secret sex," he said, stroking the cat. "Maybe she was embarrassed, I don't know. What'll we do, Willow? We got to tell Jake, right?"

Willow shook her head. "I tell you; I don't believe it. She called me yesterday and it was like talking to Little Miss Sunshine." Her forehead wrinkled. "Maybe it's like old, and she forgot to erase it?"

Teddy stroked his beard. "It doesn't seem like our Remy to be having a little SS on the side," he admitted. He shook his head. "But I'm pretty sure it wasn't there before."

"What were you doing over at her house, anyway?"

"Playing Teddy-the-errand boy. Remy hired me again to take the groceries over to that Eli Wolff guy's house," Teddy said. "He's back from his trip. She should pay me more though. That dirt road beats up my car—and my poor old tailbone."

A shade of doubt crossed Willow's face at the mention of Eli's name. "She wouldn't hire you unless she wanted to *avoid* Eli. Maybe it doesn't mean secret sex anymore. It means supersex or something. Supersex with Jake. Don't you dare say anything to him." Willow got out her phone and started texting. "I told her I need to talk to her."

Teddy frowned. "Maybe we shouldn't get in the middle of this. Kind of not our business?"

"She's my best friend, and he's your brother. We're making it our business."

"Yeah, OK. You're right. As always." Teddy said. He leaned forward to grab his beer bottle, dislodging the cat who walked off twitching his tail. "I still can't believe she thought Jake was with Jane all that time." He took a slug and belched. "I must say, I am glad to have the icicle gone and my house back. Big comfy bed again tonight, my love?"

The screen door slid behind them. "Hey bro, what's up? You want to join us for a beer?" Teddy asked. "Why the long face? Oh no, man, you know already."

Willow shushed him. "How's everything going with Remy?" she asked brightly.

A look of pain crossed Jake's face. "Fine. But I don't think it's going to work out," he said in a flat voice. "If she comes by, tell her I'm sorry, I'll talk to her later. I'm heading out."

"Sure thing," Teddy said.

Jake slid the screen half-way and paused. "Since you asked. Yeah. I know."

# CHAPTER 49

Remy had been floating on air all day. The puffy white clouds in the sky had nothing on her mood. She was later than expected; she'd had to run an errand over on Chappaquiddick, and the line for the tiny ferry had taken forever. "Jake," she called, hopeful that he would be waiting for her, but only Coop and Ada greeted her arrival.

The gifts sat on the counter. "Oh, he didn't!" Remy exclaimed. No note, but she knew who they were from—though she never expected Jake to be so extravagant. Or maybe Remy had underestimated his romantic side.

Remy bit her lip in excitement as she opened the jewelry box, then gasped. The earrings were elegant, but not so ostentatious that she couldn't wear them every day. She took out her silver earrings and put them on, then walked to the mirror. She turned her head from side to side. How did Jake find something that matched her bracelet so perfectly? With mounting excitement, she opened the second box. The red silk negligee was, well, sexy. And small. And crotchless. And very not Martha's Vineyard. Remy dangled it from her fingers, trying to figure out how you'd put it on. She'd never worn anything like it, but if that was what Jake liked, she was all into trying something new.

Remy didn't notice the tag until she was putting the lingerie back in the box. It was in French. From a store in Cap d'Antibes. Then she looked at the champagne. It was Laurent-Perrier.

A sick realization took hold. "This can't be," she said.

But it was. Eli had been in her house. Feeling violated—and furious—she unclipped the earrings and threw them into the bag. That arrogant man assumed he could just walk in and woo her back into his bed with expensive presents, like a cheap whore. She'd had enough.

"Remy!" Eli exclaimed, answering his phone. "Did you find my gifts? I enjoy shopping for you." His voice dropped a register. "When will I see you?"

"I can't believe you trespassed on my house," Remy said. "That is not OK."

"Sorry," he said. "I wanted to give you a little surprise. No harm meant. Will you forgive me?" he asked in a disarming tone.

"No. I don't want your gifts or anything else from you. And I've told you before, we're done," she said. Her eye caught the red SS marked on her calendar. Eyes blazing, she rubbed it out.

"Let's talk this over in person. We can't do this over the phone," Eli said. "I like you, Remy. More than I'd expected. And I've missed you."

Remy knew what he was thinking: he'd be able to charm her back into his bed if he could see her. He was wrong. Way wrong.

"No." The only way she was going to get rid of him was to totally get him out of her life. Remy did a quick calculation. She needed the income, but she'd make do. "I'm calling to tell you that I'm quitting. I'll make some calls and find you a new concierge." She looked with disgust at the gifts that had so pleased her just moments before. "I'll get Teddy to drop off your presents. This is goodbye, Eli," she said and hung up the phone.

A burden lifted from her shoulders. Remy stuffed the gifts into a paper Cronig's bag so she wouldn't have to look at them, put them by the door, then picked up her bra and dress. Jake would be waiting. The Eli door was now shut and locked, and a new one had opened.

Jane's departure was evident in the pile of dirty dishes in the sink and wet towels hung over the bathroom door. A case of beer sat next to a pair of dirty white socks on the dining room table. "Jake?" she called, anticipating seeing his dark head pop up over the sofa. "Not here," called a voice from Teddy's bedroom.

She padded downstairs to find Teddy and Willow in bed watching TV. "What are you guys doing inside? It's a beautiful evening."

"Snuggling," Teddy said, wiggling himself into Willow's side. "In my big bed. We're watching *Bridget Jones's Diary.*"

"Do you know where Jake is?" Remy's hair was still damp from her shower, and she'd put on Jake's favorite lavender jade.

Willow paused the TV. "Jake took the boat." She looked at Remy with a serious expression. "Remy, you were supposed to call me back. Have you gotten back together with Eli?"

"Eli Wolff?" Teddy exclaimed. "SS is Mr. Rich Dude?? Whooee, I did not see that one coming."

"Sorry, Remy. Teddy, you're going to forget you heard that. You can't say anything, ever." Teddy pulled an imaginary zipper across his lips.

Remy looked crossly at Willow. "No."

"Told you, Teddy," Willow said.

"Mmmmph, mmmph, mmmm," Teddy said.

"Unzip your lips, Teddy," Willow said rolling her eyes.

"Then why was *secret sex* back on your calendar?" Teddy asked.

"Because Eli wrote that there. He's back from his trip to France and trying to get me back into his bed. I'd had enough: I fired him as a client today." Remy looked out the window at the cove. "I wonder why Jake went out on the boat? We were supposed to go to Menemsha for dinner."

"Tell her, Teddy."

"I think he thinks you're still seeing Mr. SS." He turned to Willow. "See, I didn't say his name."

"Why would he think that?"

Teddy shook his head and said "He's upset. I'm really sorry, Remy."

Remy ran her fingers through her hair. "I was hoping he wouldn't find out. Poor Jake. Well, I guess I better fix it and explain about Eli," she sighed. "I'm borrowing your Quansoo key."

# CHAPTER 50

Jake had hoped getting out of the house would've helped settle his mind, but it didn't. He stared unseeing at the waves. Loser. Failure as a lover, as a man. All the intrusive thoughts that had bedeviled him were back: He would never get tenure. He'd end up being one of those sad adjunct professors who shuffle from one crappy little university town to another, doomed to a pathetic hermit life, never to have a real home. He'd never publish a book. What a pipe dream that had been.

Jake knew he was blowing everything out of proportion, but once he'd started to circle the bowl, it was too late. He put his head in his hands and cursed the fates that gave Eli Wolff looks, money—and Remy.

Brooding, he didn't notice the dog approaching until Coop was nearly in his lap, all sandy paws and wagging tail. Jake turned to see Remy striding down the beach.

"If you wanted to go for a boat ride, you should've called. You know this is my favorite time of the day down here," she said with a bright smile, then flopped down on the sand next to Jake. "But first, I guess there's a little misunderstanding I need to clear up," she said. "Everything's fine—I can explain." Jake flinched as

Remy rested her hand on his sleeve. "Jake, it's me. Don't be so upset."

"I needed some time alone." He stared at the ocean, willing the words to come out. "I don't think we can be together," he said. It was torture having her so close.

Remy dug her toes into the sand. "Jake, don't be stupid. Listen, I don't know why you think I'm seeing someone else, but I'm not." Remy groaned. "Oh shit, did Teddy tell you about SS? I'll kill him."

"Teddy didn't tell me anything." Jake heaved a sigh. "Your lover came by the house today to drop off the gifts he'd bought you in France," Jake said. "He told me to tell you he was looking forward to your romantic reunion." Jake could barely get the next words out. "He's probably expecting you to wear the lingerie."

Remy's mouth dropped open. "You're kidding. That's what happened? I'm so sorry, Jake." She stifled a laugh, imagining the two men facing off in her kitchen. "I guess I should've told you about him, but it was never anything and it's all over. And frankly, I didn't want to think about it—or him." Jake stared at the sand. "He's not used to hearing no. I guess he didn't believe I really meant it." Remy stroked his arm and Jake flinched again. "I have zero interest in ever seeing him again. Jake, look at me."

Painfully, Jake turned his head to meet Remy's eyes. "I don't believe you," he said flatly.

"You don't believe me," she repeated. "You don't believe the truth. You think I'd lie to you?"

Jake didn't say anything. His eyes slid back to stare at the water, and a muscle tensed in his jaw. "You might."

"Why don't you believe me? Tell me!" Remy grabbed his arm and shook it.

He wrenched his arm away. "Listen, I was there, talking to the guy. There was no mistake what he had in mind. I don't know what kind of extra 'services' you offer to your clients, Remy. And I don't want to know."

Remy jumped to her feet. "Fuck you, Jake Madden."

# CHAPTER 51

"Remy, is Morgan with you?"

Remy looked up from her shopping list and rubbed her eyes. She'd been beyond furious at Jake until Willow pointed out that they had no idea what Eli might have said—or implied—about Remy's "concierge services." It was in Eli's interest, naturally, to scare off a rival. After Willow had calmed Remy down, they agreed Jake owed her a huge apology. An immense apology, in fact. He'd get over his jealous fit and realize Remy hadn't been hiding anything on purpose. It just was not information you volunteer on a first (OK, fourth) date. *Oh, by the way, I was sleeping with a client earlier this summer. Knew it was a bad idea, but he was superhot, kind of couldn't help myself, you see.* Like that would've helped to get their relationship off to a good start.

"Oh hello, Mrs. Cinch. Enid. No, Morgan's not with me. Why?"

"I just went to wake her up. She's not in her room."

Remy took a sip of coffee. "Uh, did you call her phone?"

"Her cellphone and wallet are on the dresser."

Remy's heart lurched. Like every other teen, Morgan never ever went anywhere without her phone. It was attached to her hand as if by an invisible magnet. She was constantly taking pictures and checking social media. "Have you looked around? Checked the stables? The guest house?" Guilt swept through Remy. She should have called more often, checked that Morgan was feeling OK about the sale of her horse. "I'll call Solly, see if he's heard from her today."

"Solly? That local boy she's been slumming around with?"

"Solly is my little brother," Remy said in a granite voice. "He's a nice kid. Your daughter needs friends. She's been very upset." Anger started a slow burn. "Call me if you find her."

Morgan hadn't talked to Solly. He had no idea where she was. Panic began to grip Remy's insides. Morgan hadn't seemed like the runaway type, but if she had run without her phone, just hopped a bus to the ferry and gone, she could easily disappear. Or was Remy letting her imagination blow everything out of proportion and Morgan had just taken an early beach walk?

Remy was getting into the Toyota with Coop when Enid Cinch called back. "I think Morgan's stolen Rajah. He's gone from the stable but his saddle is still there. Is this something the two of you cooked up?"

"Absolutely not." Unbelievable that the woman thought Remy would conspire with her 16-year-old daughter to steal a horse. "I bet she took Rajah down to the beach for a walk, not a big deal. Morgan's upset about you selling him."

"That's none of your business."

Remy took a deep breath. "If it has to do with Morgan, it is my business," she said. "I care about your daughter," Remy added and hung up before she'd say something that would be sure to get her fired.

Remy arrived to find Enid Cinch sitting grim faced in the living room. "She's not back yet."

"Have you checked the beach?"

Enid gave her a look. A wave of anger washed over Remy. The woman couldn't be bothered to walk the 200 yards to the beach to look for her own missing daughter. Remy had had enough. "You're coming with me."

Remy marched down the path to the beach, hoping Morgan had just decided to take some private time to say goodbye to Rajah.

Enid, shocked at being told what to do by her concierge, had meekly followed. The sandy path steadily rose between two high dunes. A soft breeze set the grasses swaying like the fur of a giant, gentle green beast. Totoro sand dunes, Remy had told Morgan. When she was met with a look of incomprehension, Remy made her a bowl of popcorn that evening to watch Remy's favorite Japanese anime movie. She'd been surprised at how much it mattered that Morgan liked it too.

Remy stopped at the crest of the dune and looked down the beach. "Oh my God," she breathed.

"What is it?" Enid asked, pushing past Remy. "Do you see her?" Enid clasped a hand to her mouth. "Oh my God," she echoed Remy.

Far off in the distance was a rider on a horse, galloping along the edge of the surf. The horse, unmistakably Rajah. And the rider was Morgan, her long chestnut hair streaming behind her in an echo of Rajah's black tail.

"That horse—I didn't think she would ever ride again," Enid said in a barely audible voice. Enid's features transformed into a look of pure longing, mixed with relief—and joy.

They stood silent as the horse and rider went out of view around the point. Then the moment of happiness, of softness, was gone. "Morgan knows never to ride without a helmet. I'll speak to her when she gets back." She turned to Remy. "Well, you were right. She went to the beach," Enid said.

Remy's eyes were alight. "She rode Rajah. That's amazing."

Enid pursed her lips. "I didn't think she wanted that horse. That changes things," she added, then marched past Remy back along the path toward the house.

Remy walked on to the beach and sat down. After a time, Morgan came back up the beach at a walk, still astride the horse. She ran her fingers through his mane, lost in her world. Morgan looked like a Maharani princess with her ramrod-straight posture and long, loose hair, the same shade as Rajah's glossy coat.

"Morgan," Remy called.

Morgan looked over, startled. "Remy?"

"Your mother couldn't find you. She called me."

"She did?" Morgan asked absentmindedly. She began stroking Rajah's mane again, then leaned forward to wrap her arms around his neck. "He's the most magnificent horse ever, isn't he? He knows exactly what I want." She looked at Remy with an expression of pure bliss. "He can read my mind."

Remy smiled. "Rajah's a special horse."

"I'm never putting a saddle on him."

"You don't have to if you don't want to."

Morgan sat back up and, with a wince, swung a leg over to dismount. The spell broke when her feet hit the sand. Sorrow crossed her face. "But Mother is selling him."

"No," Remy said firmly. "She won't. She bought him for you. Your mother loves you."

Morgan looked doubtful. "She doesn't act like it."

"Some people just can't show it. But if you look carefully enough, you can catch a glimpse. I saw it in her face when she watched you ride. Rajah isn't going anywhere. He's yours."

Teddy dropped the bag of unwanted presents on the kitchen table and went to search for Eli Wolff. He walked out onto the porch. There he found Eli with one—no, there was another one in the water—two topless, top-heavy, leggy blonds.

Teddy marched across the lawn and down the path to the beach, his eyes widening as he drew closer to the display of voluptuous flesh.

"Mr. Wolff, can I talk to you?" he called.

Eli looked up from his task of spreading sunscreen on a round, near-naked bottom. "Teddy, this is a surprise." Eli slowly slid his hand up from thigh to buttock. "I didn't expect to see you again after Remy fired me. Too bad about that, I do quite miss her, but I make do," he said, giving the rear a gentle slap. "That'll do for you, love."

"Can we talk in private?" Teddy asked.

"Certainly," he said, standing up. "We can go for a little walk. And feel free to stay if you wish. As you can see, I'm outnumbered today."

Tearing his eyes from the women, Teddy started his speech. "Mr. Wolff," he started.

"Eli, please."

"OK, yeah. Eli. Um." Teddy scratched his cheek.

"Yes?"

"You really messed things up for Remy."

"I did what?" Eli raised his eyebrows. "What exactly was it that I did to mess things up for Remy?" He paused. "She's not pregnant, is she? And if she has an STD, she didn't get it from me."

"Pregnant? STD? What? No," said Teddy, flustered. "You brought her those gifts. I brought them back. They're in the kitchen."

"I'm sorry, but I fail to see how buying presents for a lovely woman would cause a problem."

"My brother saw them. Well, he saw you. And the gifts," Teddy babbled. "My brother, Jake—you met him—is, was, dating Remy. And then he saw you, with all those presents, so they broke up."

Eli stopped walking. "I'm afraid I don't see where this is going."

"Jake doesn't believe her, that is, that you and Remy aren't, uh, in a relationship," Teddy stammered. "Anymore. I guess you were. Before."

Eli cocked his head at Teddy. "Well, there's not much I can do about that, can I? Please give Remy my regards, tell her my door is always open if she changes her mind." Eli turned around. "Shall we head back?"

Teddy's feet stayed planted in the sand. "You have to call my brother."

A half-smile played on Eli's lips. "You want me to call your brother and tell him I'm not shagging his ex-girlfriend."

Teddy grinned. "Yes, that's it. Exactly!" he exclaimed. He pulled out his phone and dialed. "Just leave a message if he doesn't answer."

Teddy rocked back and forth on his feet, waiting for Jake to pick up. He crossed his fingers. "This has to work," he whispered under his breath.

Eli shook his head, amused at the role he had been asked to play.

"Hello, this is Eli Wolff—no, please, don't hang up, this will only take a second." Eli looked over at Teddy. "You can thank your brother for this. I am calling to tell you that there is absolutely nothing between Remy and me. Hasn't been, for ages." Eli nodded at Teddy. "But you can't blame a bloke for having tried to get her back. I'm quite dejected," he said waving at the blonds. "Now, if you'll excuse me, I should go."

# CHAPTER 52

The dawn broke pink and fresh after a restless, unsettled sleep. Jake should have apologized by now. Remy's confidence that his fit of jealousy would last no more than 24 hours had dissolved the night before with her fourth glass of wine, transubstantiated into messy, drunken tears. What she'd felt with him was real. But so was Jake's willingness to throw it away. Just like that. It was inconceivable that he thought she offered "services" to her concierge clients. Remy realized she'd been balanced on a balloon that had popped, dropping her onto the ground with a thud and a messed-up head.

She unwound herself from her sheets and yawned. Outside her bedroom window, the leaves of the maple, heavy August green, made a patchwork pattern against the pastel sky. Remy opened the window to breathe in the fresh morning air. It had been long—too long—since she'd followed her advice *to take care of herself.* A kayak paddle on the pond. That's what she needed.

The pond was mirror still, the trees and clouds reflected in the water, pretending to be real. The mallows had bloomed in the marsh, and the swamp was cotton-candied with pink hibiscus-like flowers. Remy pulled into the cove with smooth, practiced strokes, loathe to disturb the glassy surface. She tried, as best she could, to let all thoughts drift away with each dip of the paddle, concentrating on the feel of the water under her kayak and the early morning sounds: the gabbling of geese, an early-morning bleat from a goat. The rising sun promised a bright, warm day.

"Remy, wait up," called a voice from a distance.

Remy spun her boat around to find Jake propelling an orange surf kayak with a canoe paddle in a wobbly path toward her. "I saw you from our deck," he called. He looked like an unmade bed—rumpled T-shirt, messy black hair, and beard-stubbled face. "Not sure whose kayak this is, but I figured they wouldn't mind if I borrowed it."

"It's Rebecca's," she said.

"I screwed up."

"Yes, you did."

"I need to apologize."

"OK." She wasn't going to let him off easy. "Apologize."

The sun lit his sapphire blue eyes. "What I said was unforgivable. I was stupid and irrational and jealous, and I should have believed you when you said you weren't with that guy."

Remy balanced the paddle across her kayak. "How do you know? For sure? I could be still be sleeping with Eli. Maybe even being paid for it."

"I have no idea why I said that. I didn't mean it."

"But you did. And why do you believe me now?"

"Because Eli Wolff called me."

Remy shook her head in disbelief. "He did what?"

"Teddy made him."

Remy barked a mirthless laugh. "You're kidding me." Her eyes narrowed. "So, you believed Eli Wolff. But you wouldn't believe me. Why?"

Jake looked so sad, so earnest. Dark circles shadowed his eyes. He looked across the pond, then back at Remy. "I…I'm messed up. Someone did something to me. Back in Chicago. I thought if I just tried to forget about it, pretend it didn't happen, I'd be fine." Jake sighed and looked down at the paddle in his lap. "But I'm not."

Remy's insides roiled with an uncomfortable stew of pity and anger—and desire. "And that's why you thought I was lying about Eli."

Jake nodded. "I spent all night wondering if I should ask you to take me back. But you deserve better, Remy, than a guy who doesn't believe you when you tell the truth." He slumped in the kayak. "It's better if I work it out first. On my own. But I still owed you an apology."

"Jake, you're a real asshole."

"I know."

"You're going to decide what's best for me?" Remy asked. "How about giving me a choice?"

Jake looked at her with puppy dog eyes and nodded. "Yes."

"Will you tell me what this 'something' is that happened in Chicago? Who was she?"

Jake nodded. "My girlfriend. And a colleague. A very close colleague." He smiled a sad smile that melted Remy inside. "I'll tell you everything if you want. No one else knows. It was…is," Jake paused, "painful."

"We've all got baggage, Jake."

He paddled alongside her kayak and leaned toward her, making his boat rock. "Please," he said earnestly. "I screwed up. I can't undo it. But we can start over. If you want to."

Jake waited, sad and mussed, with a tiny bit of hope lighting his eyes.

Remy had wanted an apology, not to break up with him. And here it was, late but sincere. She reached for his hand. "Oh, Jake. I do."

With a look of relief and joy, Jake let impulse overtake seamanship and leaned out of the kayak to embrace her. By the time Remy realized what was about to happen, it was too late. Jake's kayak reached equipoise and started to flip. Like a chain reaction, his weight pulled her kayak onto its side. They fell into the pond and against each other in a graceless, sideways splash.

"Oh no," Remy said, laughing as she began to tread water. She reached to grab her paddle before it floated away. "You're an idiot."

"I know."

Without another word, Remy entwined her body around his and kissed him, sinking them below the surface. They rose to the surface gasping, both wearing the broadest grins their faces could manage.

"Yes," Remy said. "Let's start over"

# CHAPTER 53

It had all sounded so stupid, so trivial, when he said it out loud. His deep, dark secret. Of course, it wasn't the first thing they'd done after paddling back to shore. That was to strip each other of their wet clothes and jump into the outdoor shower at Jake's. It was a pure pleasure to be warmed and caressed by hot water, sweet soap, and Remy's naked skin. That was followed by a makeup sex romp under the sheets, neither caring whether the banging bedframe dinged the wall.

Then Remy made them fresh coffee, sat Jake up in bed, and made him explain. He started with the lingerie. The scanty tiger-stripe panties in the gift bag in the back of Liz's car. She had jokingly told him that it was a present for a girlfriend. It was around Christmas, and Jake didn't think twice about it.

Jake had thought he was in love with Liz and she with him. He'd been so naïve, so stupid, so trusting. They weren't engaged, but neither had ruled it out as a possibility someday. Everyone—Jake's parents, his friends, his colleagues—said he and Liz were the perfect match. So cute, the Machiavellian dating the Utopian. And with so much in common. While Liz technically competed for the same tenure slot, Jake had seniority. He'd make it first, then she'd be next. Franklin, the chair of the philosophy department, thought that her work on feminist interpretations of Machiavelli's writings was very promising. At this Remy put a finger on Jake's lips. "Just tell me what she did to you."

Jake started up again, feeling the hot shame of a secret being loosed from its bounds. So trite, how it had happened. Liz had left her phone on the charger, and Jake saw a message pop up from Franklin. Liz, out for a run, had been anxiously waiting to hear whether she'd finally be assigned a full course load to teach in the fall. Normally, Jake would never have read her messages. But this time, without thinking, he did.

The message wasn't about work. Franklin had asked her to remember to wear "his gift" under her clothes and had added a very explicit description of how he wanted to take the panties off with his teeth and what he would do to her afterward.

Jake took a picture of the message before deleting it. It was disgusting: the idea of that old fart with his saggy jowls and goatee getting anywhere near Liz. The last thing she needed, as stressed out as she was, was to be sexually harassed by Franklin. Jake had heard rumors about him, but this was proof. Egregious, irrefutable proof. It was time for the guy to go.

By the time Liz got back from her run, Jake had done his research. She could file a complaint with the Office of Sexual Misconduct, and the university would be responsible for turning the old lecher out on his ear. Liz could file anonymously if she wished and would be offered complete protection against reprisal.

But that wasn't what happened.

Liz was livid that Jake had looked at her messages. So angry that she screamed and kicked him out of the apartment. Jake had been working in the neighborhood coffee shop waiting for her to calm down so that they could talk about the next steps when the head of the department called him for an urgent meeting.

Liz was there too.

Liz walked behind the desk to where Franklin sat in his big leather chair and laid her hand on his shoulder. "You do understand why we had to keep our little affair under wraps," Franklin had said. "With the tenure decision coming up, we couldn't have any hint of favoritism."

"Franklin helped me so much with my research, Jake. Then, well, things just happened." Liz looked down into Franklin's eyes as he put his wrinkled hand over hers. There they stood together, like a perverted version of a doting father and daughter.

Liz looked back up at Jake. "You really thought you were going to make tenure this year. I'm so sorry, but utopian philosophy is, unfortunately, passé. Franklin agrees. But you might have a chance next year. Or the year after. That is if you are still here." Dead-cold eyes glittered over her smile. "But perhaps a sabbatical might be just the thing, Jake," Liz continued. "You do need time to polish your articles and get them published. What do you think, Franklin?"

"A brilliant idea. Elizabeth, you can take over a few of his classes. The students love you."

Jake was stunned. And trapped. He couldn't believe it. That Liz—his Liz—would resort to sleeping her way to tenure. The oldest trick in the book.

Franklin chuckled. "How about it, Jake? A little paid vacation sounds pretty good to me. Up to you, of course."

Liz tightened the strings of the trap she had set. "It might put to bed those rumors about you and your research assistant. She's an undergrad, isn't she?"

"Rumors?" Jake sputtered. There was nothing between him and his research assistant other than long hours and lots of meetings.

"Oh, well, incipient rumors. They haven't actually gotten out." Liz's eyes glittered again. "Yet."

It wouldn't matter if the rumors weren't true: enough people believed that where there's smoke, there's fire. Not only would it ruin Jake's career, but his research assistant's name would be dragged through the mud as well. No matter which way he turned, Jake was caught. It was all a shit show of the highest degree. His sabbatical wasn't an option, it was his only choice.

With that, Jake ended his story.

Remy had listened with a sympathetic ear. Jake felt sick to his stomach. In the telling, he'd gone back in his mind to the apartment he'd shared with Liz. Her gloating eyes as he packed up his belongings. Liz's lies—so many lies—and her betrayal in the service of ambition had shaken him to the core. Jake had been an idiot to have missed the clues. Matches from a restaurant they'd never gone to. All the evenings she'd go to her office to work and turn off her phone. The showers at odd times, twice in a day.

And, like a nightmare, another pair of sexy panties in a gift bag. And that guy, Eli, so supremely confident that Remy was eagerly awaiting his return. The floor had dropped from under Jake in Remy's kitchen that day, and he'd fallen into a pit of despair.

Jake rolled over onto his stomach and put his face in the pillow.

"Hey, hey, hey," said Remy. "A thousand miles away and, what, six months ago, Jake? You can't change what happened. But you can't let it fester either." She ran her hands along his spine, then back up to work on his tense shoulders. "It sounded like it was an awful time, I agree. But you have to put it into perspective. No one died. You didn't get fired, you got offered a paid vacation, geez. You'll go back, and it'll be all forgotten." She kissed his neck. "But is that what you really want, Jake? That horrible Liz and creepy Franklin? They'll both still be there."

He rolled over and pulled Remy across his chest. Her face was so loving and earnest. "I don't know, Remy. But I know one thing for sure." He kissed her lips. "I want what I've got, right here."

# CHAPTER 54

"I'm so glad I ran into you, Remy!" Audrey exclaimed. She wrapped her bird-like arms around Remy and hugged her. "I have so much to tell you."

Audrey was pink cheeked and aglow. Her voice, while still soft, had lost that hesitant quality that made it sound like she never had enough air in her lungs. "Do you like fried clams? I was getting some to bring back to Mike at the house. He thinks the clams here at John's Fish Market are the best. Join us for lunch?"

"Sorry. I'll have to pass," said Remy. "I need to get over to a client's in OB." She handed her credit card to the woman at the counter to pay for the Hartwells' swordfish. "But we can sit outside and catch up while you wait. You're next in line. Do you mind ordering me an iced tea?"

Remy put the fish in the cooler in her car as Audrey placed her order, then joined her at the red-painted picnic table. "You look wonderful, by the way," said Remy.

"I feel wonderful too. It sounds dorky, but I feel like I've got my life back. I can't thank you enough." Her bush-baby eyes welled up, an echo of the old Audrey. "And thank you for sending Morgan over the other day to babysit. The twins simply idolize her. She's going to teach them to ride. Morgan said she'd look into using the horses over at Pond View Farm." Audrey sipped her iced tea. "I thought it would be harder to take care of the girls after Tony left. They're upset, of course. But now they have to listen to me—or the nanny. No going around our backs to their father."

"That's good news. Very."

"And, if they behave well, I might surprise them with a pair of shih tzu-poodle puppies for their birthday. I've been talking to some breeders. They are adorable dogs. And small enough that you can take them anywhere, even on a plane. Mike said he'll help me and the girls train them."

Remy raised one eyebrow. "And you and Mike...?"

"Mike is a very dear man. A good friend. Nothing more—for now. We had a little flicker of something. It was quite good for my ego. He made me feel...attractive. And interesting. But I need to learn to stand on my own two feet first. Then we'll see."

Remy nodded in agreement.

"And I'll love him forever for helping me face Tony. You too, of course!"

"And the divorce?"

"My attorney is pinning Tony to the wall. Like a bug!" Audrey's eyes gleamed with the prospect. "He knows what I have on him. Jules is one tough cookie. She's been tracking down all the assets he has—legal and illegal. I think he'll be very generous with his settlement offer." The gleam turned to blue steel. "Tony wouldn't want me making a call to the IRS and FBI now. Would he?"

Remy laughed. "No, he would not."

"And Coop is happy?"

"Very. He's inseparable from Ada Queetie. We'll see how he does with the baby chicks—I'm hatching a new flock."

"How exciting! I'll have to bring the twins by to see them." Audrey's was face alight with happiness.

Remy sat back, still amazed by Audrey's transformation. It was as if she'd hatched from her shell too. "I'll let you know."

The door opened, and a man holding two paper bags called Audrey's name.

"Got to run—I need to get our clams home while they're still hot! But I've got more to tell you. I'll call later."

Jake rolled over, snorted, and threw a sleepy arm over Remy's torso. He searched with his hand for her breast, cupped it, and sighed into her neck. Remy stroked Jake's warm arm. Jake. It was…he was…unbelievable.

Remy smiled at the cardboard containers on the bedside table. She'd come over after work with lobster rolls and chowder for dinner to find Jake in bed, already naked, waiting for her. He'd been her appetizer and she his dessert.

Jake murmured and nestled against her side. There was nothing better than cuddling after sex, the contact of skin against skin, feeling your lover's heartbeat, the rise and fall of his breath. Being with Jake felt right. More than right. Blissfully, wonderfully perfectly right. But now it was time to get her lovely, napping man up and going.

"Come on, Jake. Time to wake up. We want to get there in time for the lighting." Remy tugged on his arm. "I can't believe you've never been to the Grand Illumination. We've already missed the community sing."

"All right." Jake stood and stretched. Remy leaned over and paddled his bare bottom with her hand. "Hey that's not helping," he said as he pulled a T-shirt over his head. "We could just stay here instead," he suggested. "I could make you a lantern. I've got some paper and a flashlight somewhere."

"No, no, no. You want to see this. I promise."

Remy drove the back way into Oak Bluffs, parked in the Hartwells' driveway, and nearly pulled Jake's arm from its socket as she rushed him through town to the Campground. At last, they arrived at the neighborhood of gingerbread cottages set in concentric circles around the open-air Tabernacle. Paper lanterns and Asian parasols festooned the porches and eaves of the tiny dollhouse-like homes, sometimes in tidy harmony with the pastel color theme of the house, sometimes in an enthusiastic display of mismatched lanterns from all over the world. The paths were filled with onlookers waiting for the signal to set the lanterns alight. Anticipation filled the air.

"Martha's Vineyard fun fact. Do you know why the houses are so little?" Remy asked.

Jake shook his head. "Why is that?" He looked around. "I mean, these look more like playhouses."

"I looked it up when I was taking Morgan around." Remy squeezed Jake's hand, still amazed that he was here with her. "Back in the mid-1800s, this was a Methodist tent revival, and the attendees rented spots where they pitched their sleeping tents. After a while, they replaced the tents with these little wooden houses. Most were built in the 1860s and '70s. The tent lots were tiny, so the houses are tiny." They stopped to admire a particularly intricate curlicue design on a pink-and-purple-trimmed house. A row of vintage Chinese lanterns with silk tassels hung from the porch and pink-flowered bamboo fans bedecked the rail. An elderly woman in a wide lavender hat sat in a rocker (pink, of course) and waved to the onlookers.

"Your house is wonderful," Remy called.

"Thank you," the woman replied. "Come back after it's lit up."

"Looks to me like there was some competitive gingerbread carving going on back then," Jake commented, looking up at a green-and-white house with lacy trim that looked like a row of delicate icicles hanging from the eaves.

"Oh look, I think they're about to start."

Hand-in-hand, they walked toward the crowd in the Tabernacle. After a short introduction, an elderly woman in an antique kimono lit the ceremonial lantern. Seconds later, the entire Campground was aglow with light from thousands of paper and silk lanterns. Bystanders gasped with delight.

"Wow. OK. I admit it. This is way cool," he said, looking around. The lanterns appeared to float in the air, a firefly glow in the night.

"Told you." Remy rose on tiptoes and kissed Jake's lips. "I think it is one of the most beautiful, the most magical nights of the year."

Jake pulled Remy into his arms and ran a finger down one cheek. "Let's wander around a bit, then go home, and we'll see about magical."

"I've got an idea since we're already here in OB," Remy said. "Johnny Hoy and the Bluefish are playing at the Ritz. I feel like dancing. It'll be packed, but let's go."

"A bar?"

"Yes, a bar. Come on, Jake. It'll be fun. We don't have to stay long."

"If it makes you happy."

"It does." They wandered from the maze of streets onto Circuit Ave. Remy's eyes shone. "I think on Illumination Night, you can really feel the spirit of the Island," she said. "In other places, they would have blown it up into a big tourist attraction. What keeps it special is that it's only for one night, then poof, it's over. Until next year."

"Thanks for making me come."

"For years, I thought I'd outgrown the Island. I was sure I'd move back to France. But now I can't imagine ever leaving."

"I went to Paris last year for a conference."

Remy's eyes lit up. "Oh, lucky you. Tell me about it."

Jake snuggled Remy against his side. "It was my first time there. I'd been to Italy before, and Spain, but never France." His face took on a faraway look. "I stayed in a hotel that used to be a nunnery on the Left Bank with the most amazing old beams. It would be perfect for a honeymoon." He squeezed her hand. "I took a couple of days to go sightseeing. Eiffel Tower, the Louvre, Sainte-Chapelle," Jake said in a ghastly accent. "I think my favorite was Musée d'Orsay," he added, rhyming it with horsey.

"Oh, I could spend days there, just looking at all the art," Remy sighed.

"And, of course, the food was fabulous. There was this tiny bistro by my hotel. I couldn't read the menu, so I just pointed at a couple of things. No idea what I ate, but it was one of the best meals I've ever had."

"Probably sweetbreads or something. They're delicious."

Jake made a face. "Anyway, Paris bumped itself up to my favorite city."

Remy sighed. That would be about the best thing in the world, to travel with Jake. "OK. That does it. I need to go to Paris again."

"You got it." Jake glanced over at her. "I remember that summer you came back from France. You went from being my little brother's annoying friend to a lovely woman."

Remy laughed. "I was Madame's project: take the small-town American and turn her into a Parisian. It was the best year." Remy fell into a reverie, "The house—it looked almost exactly like the one in *Madeline*, the children's book. It was even covered in vines. And the neighborhood was perfectly French, with little boutiques and tiny streets. You could see Paris in the distance over the river. Oh, the food, the markets, it was incredible."

"Sounds wonderful."

She turned her head to look at him. "I didn't think that you noticed me back then."

"Oh, I did. Sort of hard not too, especially the time you forgot you weren't in France and took your bikini top off at the beach."

"Oh, no. You were there?" Remy said, putting her hand over her mouth. It had happened only once, but she had walked halfway down to the ocean before Willow had thrown a towel over her.

Jake laughed. "Lucky day for me. And Richard and Steve and the rest of the guys. I remember it well." He waggled his eyebrows as he ogled her chest.

Remy snorted and batted his arm. They paused in the doorway of the Ritz. Johnny and his band were already in full swing and the bar was packed.

"Today's your lucky day. We're going dancing."

"Nooo…" Jake protested as she dragged him inside. "Let me at least have a beer first."

"Nope." She pulled him onto the tiny dance floor. "You've got to earn it."

# CHAPTER 55

Dancing wasn't so bad when all he had to do was match Remy's rhythm as she pressed her breasts and hips against his body. "Dancing is sort of like making love to music, Jake," she had told him. "Just think about that." Which was something Jake didn't mind thinking about in the least.

At last, the heat and music drove them back outside. Remy fanned herself. "Whoo, that was fun, but I'm tired now."

"Definitely a good vibe in there," Jake admitted. "Are you ready to head back?"

"We could go down to Quansoo tonight," Remy suggested as they walked along Seaview Ave. "It's so warm, and the moon's almost full,"

"Sure." Jake squeezed her hand. "I think the gate key is in the console."

After they got into the car, Remy rooted around in the mess of dump tickets, gum wrappers, and a pack of Teddy's rolling papers. Finally, she pulled the key out dangling from its loop of kitchen string. "Got it."

"To the beach we go," said Jake.

The Quansoo parking lot was empty. Remy stopped in the middle of the Crab Creek Bridge, watching the reflection of the moon in the still water. She took a deep breath of the night air and stretched out her arms. "Come look, Jake." He joined her, carrying a beach towel. "Look at the moon. So beautiful."

"Not as beautiful as you," he replied, reaching for her hand.

The moonlight tinted the scene with an otherworldly blue-white light as beach grasses gleamed like silver threads across the dunes. The air was still and warm with the scent of the sea. They paused at the crest of the dune. Remy seemed lit from within as with her own lunar light. Jake felt a rush career through him— heady, intoxicating. He was in love with Remy Litchfield and was as happy as he'd ever been.

"Oh, wow," said Remy. The quicksilver ocean was calm. Long rolling waves broke softly against the sand, the crest catching the moon's rays in a slippery pale line. Then a mischievous expression crinkled her eyes. "Last one in's a rotten egg!" she called and dashed toward the surf, pulling off her T-shirt and bra as she ran.

Jake took off in pursuit, catching Remy at the edge of the water struggling with the zipper on her shorts. "Need some help," he said, cupping her breasts in his hands and nuzzling her neck.

"That's not helping!" she laughed.

"It's helping me," he said. "A lot."

At last, the zipper gave way, and Remy's shorts and undies dropped to the sand. With a quick twist, she darted out of Jake's grip and into the surf. "Catch me if you can," she called over her shoulder.

Jake stripped off his clothes and followed. Remy dove under a wave, her white buttocks competing with the moon. "It's amazing," she called, standing in waist-deep water, half-mermaid, half-moon goddess. She raised her arms overhead and spun in a circle, waves rolling and lifting up her naked body.

Jake strode through the surf to Remy. "Loser," she teased.

"Winner," Jake corrected as he pulled Remy into his arms.

# CHAPTER 56

At the sound of Remy's car, Morgan bolted out of the stables. "You have to come riding with me. I've finally talked Mother into letting you take Frederik. I've got so much to tell you." She bounced on her toes. "Hurry up and put all that stuff away. I'll get him saddled for you." With that, Morgan turned and ran back into the barn.

After taking care of the groceries, Remy returned to join Morgan in the stables. "You're in a good mood," she said, changing into her jodhpurs in one of the empty stalls. "What's going on?"

"Oh, everything." She looked at Remy with shining eyes. "But the biggest is Solly. He told me…" Morgan bit her lip. "Oh my gosh, I can't believe I'm saying this. He kind of almost said he loved me."

"Kind of almost?" Remy managed a half-smile.

"Well, it came out like this. 'I really loov-like you, Morgan.'"

"That's wonderful. Do you loov-like him too?"

Morgan nodded. "I thought this was going to be the worst summer, but it's been the best summer ever. And you know what else?"

"You've got more good news?"

"I want to keep Rajah here this winter so I can come down weekends from school. I told Mother I can stay with you." The words tumbled out.

"I don't know, Morgan. I have no idea where I'm going to be living. I probably won't have room."

"But there are three bedrooms in Beetlebung Cottage. You'll house-sit for us and take care of Rajah. It totally makes sense. Right?" She gave Remy a sly look. "And I can see Solly too. He's working at the boatyard this winter."

Remy's head spun. The timing couldn't be better. While the Cinches' property was far from the towns, the stunningly beautiful views were more than ample compensation. Remy could see herself watching the winter storms lash the Island from the cozy sofa, a fire blazing in the big beach-stone fireplace as she sipped a cup of hot tea. And maybe, if she was lucky, Jake would visit between academic terms.

"We would need to talk to your mother. She may have other ideas. But yes, that sounds like a very good plan," Remy said. It wasn't just a very good plan; it was an amazingly good plan. "If she agrees."

"She's already said yes. She's almost being *nice*," Morgan said, lifting her eyebrows. "Oh, and you can bring Coop and your chicks too. You *have* to call me when the eggs start to hatch."

"I promise."

"And I told Mother that you might not want to live all the way out here by yourself all winter. She doesn't mind you having visitors, even a roommate." The sly look again. "How's that boyfriend of yours?"

Remy smiled. "Great. But I'm not moving in with Jake. He's a professor, so he'll leave to teach this fall." The words sank her heart. She'd been trying not to think about it, but at least UChicago didn't start classes until late September.

"That sucks. Do you loov-like him?"

Remy laughed. "Maybe. Too soon to tell."

Morgan twirled the reins in a circle. "I started my horse blog up again. You should do one too, on chickens."

"A chicken blog."

"Why not? I'll set it up for you. It's fun. Then we can work on our blogs together on weekends."

The teen's excitement was infectious. "Could be a fun winter project."

"I can help. It's not hard."

Remy took hold of Rajah's bridle. "Come on, let's ride. I'll help you up." She made a sling of her hands and boosted Morgan up onto the horse's sleek back. "You're pretty amazing, you know," she said, mounting Frederik.

"I know," Morgan said. "That's what Solly tells me too."

Frederik seemed less than keen to have a new rider but his ears pricked up as they neared the beach. "Race you," Morgan called as she urged Rajah into a gallop.

The rushing air and pounding hooves took Remy out of her head. All that mattered, for a brief moment, was the duet of rider and horse, the crashing surf, and the pure joy of a flying gallop down a beautiful beach.

"I come bearing wine. And some amazing cognac," said Remy as she walked into Jake's kitchen with her liquid contribution to dinner. The rich smell of beef stew filled the house. "Mmmm. Smells marvelous. What are we having?"

"*Boeuf bourguignon, gratin dauphinois, salade, mousse au chocolat.*" Jake replied with an appalling French accent. "Thanks to a little help from Julia Child," he added, holding up his copy of *Mastering the Art of French Cooking.* "And some littleneck clams on the half-shell to start. I don't need a recipe for those."

"You must have been working all day. I didn't know you could cook like *this.*"

"You deserve a little trip to Paris," he said. "And I've got something even more special in mind for your birthday."

"How do you know about my birthday?" Remy asked as she pulled the bottles out of the bag.

"Little pair of lovebirds told me. And wait until you see the gift that I found for you." Jake stirred the stew, releasing a rich aroma of beef, red wine, and mushrooms.

Eyes glowing in anticipation, Remy joined Jake at the stove and looked into the pot. "That smells fantastic. My mouth is watering,"

"Let me see," Jake said, pulling her close for a kiss. "Yum," he added, pretending to slurp.

The expression was true: Remy's knees went weak as she pressed herself against him. Jake, her soon-to-be-naked chef. She wondered if they'd have sex before dinner or after, or both: no bad options.

"I better start the potatoes," Jake murmured into her neck.

"Oh, yes," Remy replied. "The potatoes."

Jake stepped over to the refrigerator. "And I have a special treat for you," he said, pulling out a bottle of Veuve Clicquot with its distinctive orange label. "You get some glasses and open this, and I'll start slicing."

"Oooh, fancy. I love Veuve," Remy said. "You're spoiling me."

Resting the bottle on the counter, Remy unpeeled the foil then began to untwist the wire cage from the cork. She poured two glasses and handed one to Jake. "*Santé*," she said, raising her glass.

"Cheers," replied Jake and took a sip. "Now to work."

Jake set a potato on the cutting board, slipping into a pitch-perfect imitation of Julia Child as he sliced the potatoes into thin slices and minced garlic. Remy drank her champagne and watched him.

"If you are afraid of butter, use cream," Jake warbled, demonstrated with a generous pour over the spuds for the *gratin dauphinois* before putting the baking dish into the oven.

"You sound exactly like her. How do you do that?" Remy asked.

Jake held up his knife. "I had a college roommate who was addicted to Julia's old cooking shows. Guess I picked it up by osmosis. I'll pop the clams into the freezer while I wash up here. I thought we'd have them first."

Remy refilled their champagne glasses. "I love littlenecks better than oysters until I have a plate of oysters and change my mind, then I have clams again and change it back."

"Clams remind me of the ocean," Jake said as he rinsed the cutting board. "Oysters are soft and, I don't know, sort of debauched. Not that I don't happily eat them too."

"Do you want me to help open?"

"No, I've got it." Jake pulled two clams out of the bag and rinsed them. Confidently, he set the knife-edge where the shells connect, pressed down to separate them, a twist to remove the top shell, then a circle of the knife to release the succulent dime-size clam. Unable to resist, Remy reached out her hand. Jake gave it a gentle slap.

"Patience, Remy," he said sternly. She sat back and licked her lips. So much deliciousness, so close. He squeezed some lemon on the clams.

"Here, I forgot I need to lemon you up too," he teased, taking a whole lemon and rubbing it on Remy's wrists. Jake then sniffed and kissed her palm.

She lifted her hand to smell the fresh lemon oil. As she gazed at Jake, a buoyant warmth radiated from somewhere deep inside as a rush of bliss rose from her collarbone to the top of her head. Could she be falling in love?

Remy wasn't sure she'd ever had a more perfect evening. Remy had Jake choking with laughter as she told tales about her clients, and Jake recounted, to Remy's amazement, the details of his summer-long crush on her. Later, Jake's lovemaking was as tender as the beef, as richly satisfying as the potatoes, as sweet and lush as the chocolate mousse. They'd drunk their cognac naked in bed, Remy attempting to tutor a distracted Jake into how to detect the flavors in the decadent liquor before giving up to taste each other instead.

Remy slipped out of bed and got out the ingredients—flour, eggs, milk, and butter—for her favorite breakfast, crêpes served with jam and powdered sugar. A few minutes later, the smell of fresh pancakes rousted Jake from his bed.

He stretched his arms overhead as he walked into the kitchen. "Mmmm, what're you making?" he asked with a yawn.

"*Crêpes.* No reason to leave Paris yet," Remy smiled. "What are you up to today?"

"My car started making a weird noise. I should take it in," Jake replied.

"You better call first, see if you can get an appointment." Remy ran the end of an unwrapped stick of butter around the hot pan "I keep thinking about your dinner. It was absolutely fantastic." She added a dollop of batter and swirled it around. "So, Julia Child taught you to cook, but where'd you learn to open clams?"

Jake rubbed the stubble on his chin and yawned again. "Teddy taught me."

Remy flipped the crêpes over to brown the other side. "Oh, right. He had that job shucking at the Home Port one summer."

Jake poured himself a cup of coffee. "Hey, I forgot to tell you. Teddy applied for a real job."

"Teddy?" Remy's eyebrows drew together. "What job?"

"Junior sales associate at the Harbor View. Refused to trim his beard or dress properly. Flubbed the interview of course."

Remy slid a plate with two crêpes in front of Jake. "*Voilà*," she said. "Spread some jam on it, roll it up, sprinkle with the powdered sugar. And add a little squeeze of lemon." She turned back to the stove. "What made Teddy do that?"

"Not what. Who. Me." Jake stuck his knife into the jam. "It was like pulling teeth, even though I did everything. The resumé—I had to use a little creative license there—and the application." He sighed. "I need to be doing more about finding him a job. He says he's going to look, but I know he's not."

"Teddy has a job. He grows mushrooms. And makes Choco-Teds." Remy picked up the spatula. "I mean, he's never going to afford a yacht or anything but I think he does OK."

"Ted has a hobby. It's not a career."

A shard of irritation, like a bit of eggshell in the batter, rose to the surface. "A hobby. And everyone else at the farmer's market has a hobby too?"

"You know what I mean. Look at him."

"Look at me. I run errands for a living."

"Ah, Remy." Jake shook his head. "Come on. You've started your own business."

"So has Teddy."

Jake took a bite of crêpe. "I don't want to argue. It's different. Teddy's got a brain, a good degree from a top school, and he's wasting both on a pile of fungi."

Remy turned around from the stove and glared at Jake. The color rose in her face. Jake had forgotten the first rule of holes: stop digging. The crack about it being different for Teddy, with his university degree and brain—and what it implied about her—was galling.

Her eyes narrowed. She adored Jake, but it was time to set Mr. Self-Satisfied straight. "Not everyone is cut out to be a professor, or a lawyer, or to have whatever it is that you call a career. Or have enough money to pay for some fancy private college."

"What I meant is I want Teddy to be happy."

Remy bit her lip as she tried to keep her anger in check. "What makes you think he's not? Teddy's maybe the happiest person I know."

"Maybe now. But not forever. He's going to look back at life, and what will he have accomplished?"

"Making people happy with food and hugs," Remy said, crossing her arms across her chest. How could Jake not see that Teddy would be miserable sitting at a desk in some 9-to-5 job? Was Jake really that clueless?

Jake rolled his eyes and sighed. "Running a seasonal mushroom stand is not an accomplishment."

"Really. And getting some 50-page article published in some obscure academic journal that no one will ever read is. And getting *tenure.*" Remy hit a full boil. "By your standards, Teddy and I will never accomplish anything."

"Can we just leave it?" Jake asked.

"No."

"I just want what's best for Teddy."

"No, you don't. You have no idea what's best for Teddy. You want what won't embarrass you. 'Success' and 'accomplishment' as defined by you and your friends in your narrow little world."

Jake flinched: the barb had struck home.

Anger now flashed in Jake's eyes too. "And your world isn't just as narrow? All of you, on this Island, thinking you have no choice other than to work for summer people. Is that what you want to be doing for the rest of your life?" Jake leaned forward and put both palms flat on the table. "With all your skills, you could take a job off-Island and telecommute. You're not just creative and artistic, you've got organizational and people skills like no one else I know."

"And no degree." Remy watched the fragile bridge between their worlds drop into a crevasse. It had been all in her mind, that they could build that bridge. And that it might be strong enough to hold both of them.

"Finish it, if that's holding you back. Credits don't expire, you know. Take classes online. But instead, your talents are being wasted on a bunch of ungrateful rich people."

The lecture smarted like a slap to her cheek. "They're not all ungrateful."

"But they feel they own you. Like, they can pretend they're the lord and lady at Downton Abbey and you come running when they ring the bell." His voice turned mean. "Or call your phone, like that Mrs. Cinch."

"That's not fair, Jake. It's what I have to do."

"Is it?"

# CHAPTER 57

Jake stared at the email from the publishing house on his computer screen. *Congratulations. We are very interested in contracting with you for your book,* Unearthing Utopia. *If you decide to do so, we are willing to offer an immediate advance in exchange for exclusive rights.* How in the world...?

Remy. The friend she'd let look at his book proposal.

Jake hadn't gone 30 seconds without thinking about her. He pressed the heels of his hands into his eyes as anguish again overwhelmed him. The fight was awful. Jake felt as if he'd been dropped onto flagstones and smashed, the fragile eggshell of their relationship scattered in tiny shards, his heart broken like a yolk.

She hated him. He hated himself. Jake had been given a chance of happiness, and he'd blown it.

In Chicago, Jake had lived his life looking through a spyglass pointed at the top of a university tower. Everything in the small circle was sharp and clear, but he had closed his eyes to the world around it. On the Vineyard, he'd begun to see, to feel. There was the pond, the beach, the pure pleasure of feeling the wind freshen and fill the sail of a boat, setting it skimming across the waves. Of seeing clouds and blue skies, not the four walls of a dusty, dark office. It felt like seeds that had never seen light or water had begun to grow and take root. Then there was Remy, warm and loving, bright as sunshine.

"Yo, bro, what's happening?" Teddy called as he banged the screen door open. "How did dinner in gay Paree go with our dear Remy? Was it ooo-la-la? You were cooking your little fingers off."

"We had a fight. Maybe worse."

"Naw. You're kidding." Teddy flopped down on the sofa across from Jake. "What about?"

Jake rubbed his forehead. What was the fight about? "We don't see things the same way. Big things. I don't want to go into it."

"Well, you better apologize and make up. I'll never forgive you if you break my sweet Remy's heart."

"I'll never forgive me. But I don't know about us." Jake looked out the window at the pond.

Teddy threw a pillow at Jake's head. "Coward. Loser."

"Hey! You could break my laptop."

Teddy's eyes glowed with anger. "That's right. Go hide from life back in your fancy school. You—and our parents—you're all the same." He threw another pillow, and Jake batted it away. "I thought Remy might be able to fix you. But you don't deserve fixing."

Jake stared at his brother. He couldn't recall the last time he'd seen Teddy mad. "We fought about you, Teddy."

"That's even stupider. I don't know what she said to you, but you think about it. Because I know Remy, and I know she's right. And after you do, you go apologize." Teddy stood up. "You think only you know things, Jake Madden. But you don't know anything."

# CHAPTER 58

Remy cried. Then got mad. Then cried again, around and around in an endless cycle that left her drained, only her misery intact. She tried to do the laundry, and that sent her into a fit of weeping as she pulled the dirty sheets from the bed, Jake's warm, unmistakable scent still on them. Rage, sorrow, and hopelessness twisted and caught like an unraveling, tangling ball of yarn, with Remy wound tight in the middle.

She'd left Jake's message apologizing for what he'd said unanswered. And his second message, and his third.

It was over.

Then the world grew gray and dismal. Each interminable day, she felt as if she were slogging through thigh-deep mud. She tried to tell herself that the breakup was inevitable. Jake was going back to Chicago. No way could their relationship have lasted. It didn't help that Teddy reported that Jake was suffering too. This was different from the silly tiff over Eli and his presents. This time, it was the wretchedness of regret, of having the fates dangle happiness in front of her before snatching it away.

But Remy had to work no matter how miserable she felt. Up-Island, down-Island, running from store to store, phone calls, and canceled reservations, the effort of donning her efficient, pleasant concierge persona when all she wanted to do was spend the day hiding under the bedcovers.

Life sucked, as Morgan would have put it.

Remy pulled her car into the Bottimores' gravel parking area and stared at her hands on the steering wheel. In her unhappiness, she had bitten her nails down to the quick. Her fingers were as ugly as her mood. The traffic had been awful and her errand meaningless. This was Remy's second trip to the house that day, this time to drop off two items Mrs. B. had forgotten to put on the shopping list. More than an hour and a half wasted to pick up and deliver a jar of cornichons and smoked bluefish for her cocktail hors d'oeuvres. And it wasn't the first time or the second. It had been like this all summer long.

Mrs. Bottimore, with her perfect hair and immaculate white pants, stood waiting at the door. Remy pulled the bags from Cronig's and the Net Result from the passenger seat and walked up the path to the house.

"Sorry this took so long," Remy apologized.

"My guests are due to arrive any minute," Mrs. Bottimore said. "Leave those on the counter," she ordered. "I'll take care of putting the food out. Just go, we need the parking space."

Remy did as bid, realizing Mrs. Bottimore hadn't even looked at her, let alone said hello.

What he had said was nasty, but Jake was right. Except for the dear Hartwells, her clients acted as if they owned her. Remy had nearly lost it three days earlier, when she was at her lowest point and had forgotten to change Mrs. Bottimore's hairdresser appointment. Mrs. B had lectured her—*now don't you start getting lazy and dropping the ball*—implying that Remy was this close to getting fired, like their previous concierge, despite an entire summer of impeccable service. Remy was in service, a modern version of it, just like Mrs. Hughes and Mrs. Patmore and Daisy. Ring the bell and Remy leaps and runs, responding to the lord and lady's beck and call.

Was she wasting her talents, stuck in the box of thinking it was the only thing she could do? Yes, Remy was an excellent concierge. It paid well. But at what cost?

Remy backed the car from the drive and headed for home, her face set in a frown as the uncomfortable realization settled in. She didn't want to spend the rest of her life driving from one end of the Island to the other, picking up chunks of smoked bluefish. But Nest was her baby, and she didn't hate all of it. While she did dislike the shopping and despised the endless, endless driving, she liked the logistical challenges of scheduling and seeking out exactly what her clients wanted. She loved doing the flowers and creating, like a work of art, a stunning arrival platter of local cheeses and charcuterie. Refining a dinner party menu with the caterer and designing a stunningly beautiful table brought genuine satisfaction.

But anyone could shop and run errands. (Well, maybe not Teddy.) And what she liked to do and was good at, she could also teach. And with that, Remy began to hatch an idea.

The twins started squabbling from somewhere inside the house. "Salvie will take care of them," Audrey said, leaning back in her Adirondack chair. "Did I tell you Tony tried to fire her? She came to me right away, of course." She picked up her iced tea. "I don't know what I would have done without her this summer. You too, of course! And dear Coop," she added, with a fond look at the dog sleeping in the grass. "By the way, how is your business doing?"

"Pretty well. I'm planning some changes for next summer," she said, gazing across the lawn at the ferry boat making its way into Vineyard Haven harbor.

Audrey looked stricken. "Don't worry," Remy said. "Nothing major. I'm going to hire someone to help me. And maybe start teaching classes."

Remy's head had been swirling with ideas. Hiring an assistant—responsible, enthusiastic, maybe Morgan?—to shop and drive next summer would free Remy from the scut work part of her business. With the extra time, she could teach painting, flower arranging, too. Why not compete with the Grey Barn's very expensive-but-popular classes? She could teach people to put together a delicious Pinterest-worthy hors d'oeuvres platter and set a table with creative, charming "Vineyard" table décor—and take it all online too. Morgan's blog idea was a natural fit and, if she was right, would make money too.

Remy bet her clients would love to have their stunning houses used as backdrops for her photos. The list of topics she could blog about quickly grew: throwing a fabulous lobster dinner, planning a perfect Vineyard vacation, stocking a beautiful pantry, even the pleasures of showering with good French soap. Remy could partner with island businesses, have a link to an online gallery for her paintings. She could invite guest bloggers to contribute: Willow on up-cycling textiles, Teddy on his mushrooms, Mike on some easy DIY home repairs. Remy was an expert on frugal living; she could write about being thrifty with a flair. She might have to pay for the design of an awesome website, but she had been building up her nest egg. What better to spend it on?

Remy imagined herself as a younger, hipper, Vineyard version of Martha Stewart (without the blond bob and the jail time). The ideas kept coming. Doing a New England clam bake at home. Canning jams and jellies. Eggshell and driftwood crafts. Living the Island lifestyle with posts on farmer's markets, crabbing, fishing, the best beaches and hikes. Sailing.

No, not sailing.

It wasn't the healthiest way to get over someone, but after days of wallowing in utter misery, Remy had forced herself *just to not think about him*. She'd worked to push every thought of Jake away, not even letting her mind say his name. Still, dark hints of regret and sadness pushed their way to the surface no matter how hard she tried. Teddy and Willow's intervention, well-meaning as it was, hadn't helped.

Audrey picked up her iced tea and took a sip. "What kind of classes?"

"Painting, flower arranging, that sort of thing. I might try offering some this fall, see if anyone is interested."

"What a wonderful idea. There are so many retired people here looking for things to do. I'll let people know at the Chop and put a notice on the bulletin board."

"That would be great," Remy said. "I'm thinking of starting a Vineyard lifestyle blog too."

Audrey's eyes lit up. "What will you blog about?"

Remy ran through her list of possible topics. Audrey's enthusiasm grew with each idea. "And don't forget raising chickens!" Audrey exclaimed, clapping her hands together. "I'd love to help you with your blog," Audrey said. "I'm an excellent editor. Please say yes."

"Spelling and grammar were never my strong suits," Remy said. "But I can't afford an editor."

"Don't be ridiculous. It's the least I can do after everything you've done for me."

Remy smiled. "Offer accepted."

"Speaking of offers, was your friend excited about his?" Remy looked blank. "His book contract—the utopia book? I was so pleased when the publisher accepted it."

"Yes, of course," Remy lied. "Very excited."

# CHAPTER 59

Jake listened to his brother and Willow as they entered the house. "I think we should do something," Willow said. "Remy is stubborn—and miserable. She won't even talk about it now."

"Jake said Remy won't talk to him either. He was trying, but I think he's given up," said Teddy. "You want something to drink before we go?"

"Seltzer, please."

Jake knew he shouldn't eavesdrop, but it was easier than getting out of bed. He adjusted the pillows against the headboard and tried to read his book. Jake couldn't write, he couldn't eat, he didn't want to leave the house. The walk back after dropping the car at Up-Island Automotive had felt like a trek across the Sahara.

A pop-top gave a snap and hiss. "But maybe she's right," Teddy said. "Maybe Jake isn't the right guy for her. Sucks for him. He seemed, like, happy and sort of normal for the first time. In like, ever? Now it's like living with a big old sad black cloud. Day after day, Mr. Doom-and-gloom. He's not even taking his sailboat out. I'll be much happier when I replace him with my sweet sunny Willow. You going to miss the dollhouse?"

"A little," Willow said. "I can do the tiny house thing for a while, but not forever. You sure this is the right thing, me moving in?"

"Absolutely 100 percent-a-roni the right thing," replied Teddy.

"I still can't believe Jake and Remy fought over whether you should get a 'real job' or not."

"Well, at least Jake stopped bugging me about it. Instead, he started asking me about mushroom farming and what I do all winter, you know, my volunteering and stuff."

"Meals on Wheels and the Island Food Pantry? Why would he care about that?"

"Got me. Doesn't seem like his thing. But he got me thinking about my mushroom business. I've got plans to expand," he said. "Farm stands, fancy gourmet food stores. I'm going to sell mushroom merch too. I bet I can get Remy to design me a logo. What about my face as a mushroom?"

Willow laughed. "Not sure that's going to sell stuff, Teddy."

"What, you don't think folks will buy a T-shirt with this handsome mug on it?"

"Uh, better let Remy come up with a design," Willow said. "Still, poor thing. I was sure about her and Jake. Of course, being in love doesn't keep you from doing stupid things."

"Remy loves my brother?"

"Yes, duh," Willow said. "Don't look so surprised. I can tell."

Jake's heart pounded. Could it be true? Did Remy love him?

"If it's meant to be, they'll figure it out," Teddy said.

"I still think we should do something. They can't give up. They have to talk."

"I'll work on Jake. I can be very persuasive," Teddy said. "Got me the best girlfriend in the world."

Willow giggled. "Hey, Leslie is throwing that beach party tonight, BYO weenie and stick. Let's take Remy. Maybe she'll listen if it's both of us."

# CHAPTER 60

Remy peered through the glass of the incubator at the eggs. One had pipped, and she could see a tiny crack visible in the shell. Like a break in a dark, clouded sky, anticipation colored her mood with a sliver of pink. By the end of the day, perhaps, she'd be holding a soft ball of peeping fluff in her hand. A new beginning with a flock of lovely baby chicks.

"What do you think, Ada? Ready to have a pile of babies around?" Remy asked, changing Ada's diaper for the umpteenth time. "I'll be happy when I'll be able to move you and the chicks outside."

As busy as a mother hen, Remy double-checked her set up: humidity level up and temperature steady in the incubator. The brooder, a plastic baby pool set up with a warming lamp and lined with pine shavings, sat ready with chick food and water.

Remy picked up the flyer for her first art lesson, which would be held *en plein air* at Audrey's in September. This was her future. Plus a flock of tiny chicks. A fresh start. She could do anything she wanted.

*Credits don't expire, you know.* The itch she felt thinking of her unfinished degree demanded to be scratched. Remy remembered exactly what she was going to take: art history and French poetry because she loved them, graphic design, entrepreneurship, and linguistics because they intrigued her. "They probably don't even offer them online," Remy told Coop.

She opened her laptop and typed in "UMass online courses." Biting her lip, Remy scrolled through the listings. There they were, her senior spring semester, but for the poetry. But she could take "Love and Sex in French Culture." And wouldn't that be fun? And if Remy took just one or two courses at a time, she could (thanks to her house-sitting/teen-sitting gig) swing the tuition.

She saw herself doing homework with Morgan in Beetlebung cottage on gray November days as chocolate chip cookies baked in the oven. Remy clicked the "for more information" page and hesitated, her finger paused over the keyboard.

If not now, when? Remy asked herself and pressed send.

"Keep working on that shell, baby," Remy said to the egg. "I've got to go out for a while."

Her day went by in a blur. Teddy had promised to stop by and call her if there were any action. At 2:00 p.m., he texted a picture, *Crack is a tiny bit bigger. I think I saw a beak. It's wild, I can hear the little dude peeping in there!* Remy stopped by the house at 3:00, but the hole seemed no bigger. At 5:00, he texted again. *Can you come home? I think things are happening.*

Heart beating fast, Remy unloaded the Hartwells' groceries and dry cleaning and hurried back to her house. She pushed the door open and dropped her handbag on the table. "Come look," Teddy called from the kitchen. "Little peeper's been busy."

"Oh my gosh," Remy said, peering through the glass window of the incubator. The chick had started to unzip the egg, like tapping the top off a soft-boiled egg, only from the inside. A few wet feathers could be seen through the crack.

"She's tried to push, but, man, it looks like a lot of work. I mean, it's hard to crack an egg. And that baby's got to do it from the inside." Teddy wrapped Remy in a hug. "But little Peeper can do it, I know she can!"

Remy laid her head on his shoulder: warm, soft, good old Teddy. "You've been doing OK?" he asked gently.

"Better. I'm working on some ideas for my business that I'm excited about." She stepped back. "Do you want to stick around to watch the eggs hatch with me?"

"Naw," Teddy said. "I got plans with Willow." He looked up at the door as if he expected to see her come in. "It's a Reiki workshop or something. Willow's all fired up. I'm going to take my Choco-Teds, see if I can make some sales." Teddy's eyes slid to the door again. "Yup, I'm off. Three's a crowd," he said and got up.

"Three?" Her heart stopped. Jake was at her screen door.

"Come in, bro. I was just leaving," Teddy said. "Your eggs are hatching."

"Jake," Remy said.

Jake put his hand on the doorknob but didn't move. Teddy must have told him. Remy willed herself to be calm, keep it together. Polite. They were, after all, his eggs too.

"It's OK, you can come in," she said. "Go take a look," Remy added, motioning to the incubator.

"Happy hatching," said Teddy as he stepped past his brother, giving him a hearty slap on the back. "You can do it, dude."

# CHAPTER 61

Jake hesitated in the doorway. A comment from Willow that he'd overheard was Jake's motivation, the hatching egg an excuse. For all his nagging, his brother was right. He had to talk to Remy face to face, to try to right the capsized boat of their relationship before it sank for good.

"Teddy told me about the egg," Jake said. "He also told me that I am an idiot."

Remy crossed her arms. "OK," she said.

"I guess that isn't news to you. And that I should have figured that out on my own." Jake stuck his hands in his pockets, fingering a small silk bag. "I want to thank you for giving my book proposal to your friend."

"Congratulations. Audrey told me."

He took a deep breath. "And to apologize for what I said. About you, about Teddy."

Remy tilted her head and looked at him. "Apology accepted. I'm sorry for what I said too."

"But you were right." Jake's heart pounded with anxiety. It was now or never. "I…I want to ask you to give us another chance. I can't lose you, Remy. I'm only beginning to realize how wrong I've been about a lot of things. But I'm not wrong about us."

Remy stared into Jake's eyes for a minute, then slowly, sadly, shook her head. "Jake, we're too different, who we are. It can't work."

"Is there anything I can do, say, to change your mind? We can work it out. I know we can."

Remy looked pained. "No. There isn't. It's better this way."

Jake looked for a glimpse of warm, loving Remy but saw granite instead. So that was it. He looked down at his feet as a dejection pushed him again to the bottom of the sea. "I told Teddy that's what you would probably say. But here. I want you to have this anyway." He pulled out a small blue pouch, the result of hours scouring the internet, and held it out. "Please don't say no." Remy pulled out a tiny gold egg-shaped charm on a delicate chain. "It opens," he added.

Remy pressed on the clasp to reveal an even tinier chick. "Oh," she exclaimed.

"I was going to give it to you on your birthday," Jake said. "But today is a big day too."

Remy hesitated, as if she were going to hand it back to him, but she said, "Thank you. I'll wear it for good luck."

Jake forced a grim smile to his face and turned to leave. "I hope everything goes well. See you around."

"Wait," Remy stopped him. She sucked on her lip for a moment. "Don't you want to see the egg that's hatching?"

Remy turned from the door, fumbling to secure the clasp of the necklace. Jake walked over to where the incubator sat on the counter and peered in through the window. "Wow. Look at that."

"Teddy's been keeping an eye on it for me all day."

"And it looks like one of the blue ones just pipped too." Jake stepped back to let Remy look inside. The gold charm swung from her neck, catching the light. She was so close it hurt. "The book contract—I can't thank you enough."

"It was nothing. I just let a friend take a look at your proposal," Remy said.

"I'm still in shock. I'm going to extend my sabbatical and stay here to write it."

Remy straightened up, and the corners of her mouth twitched into a small, painful smile. "But I thought you needed to get back to the university, back to teaching and working on your tenure."

"That was the plan." Jake ran his hand through his hair. "But I've been thinking. About what's important. Revaluating..." He looked down. "Everything. Including what I really want. Maybe it's not tenure. I might not go back to Chicago at all."

"Oh," Remy said.

The fight had yanked the gauzy pink curtain from Jake's eyes. Like an old stone wall, a few gray rocks had tumbled, beyond which he could see a bright meadow. Not enough to allow passage without kicking it down, few enough that it would be easy to build it up again. It was as if Jake stood on one side and Remy on the other. He'd accused her of not realizing she had choices. But he did too.

Remy cocked her head. "But remember, everything looks different when you're on vacation. Then you get back to real life and realize what a fantasy it was that you could stay and become a farmer or a painter or..." She hesitated a beat. "A writer."

"I know, Remy. But I want to—have to—try."

With her sad eyes, Remy was even lovelier than he remembered. "I've missed you. I wish I could take back what I said."

Her smile looked like it hurt. "You were being honest."

"But wrong. I've been thinking about what you said, about success and happiness," Jake said. "I've been talking to Teddy. About his life, his business too."

Remy gave him a challenging look. "So, it's a business now. Not a hobby."

She wasn't going to let him off the hook, not that easy. He took a deep breath. "Whatever it is, it's how he wants to make a living. And I suppose you know about his volunteering."

"He doesn't talk about it much. But sure, I know."

"I always assumed Teddy just refused to grow up. Just lay around stoned all winter long. I guess I've never really talked to him."

"Teddy *is* a flake and a stoner, but he's a really good guy."

"I know." Jake felt a glimmer of hope. Remy's eyes were soft, confused—but not angry. "I'll check the egg again, then I should go."

# CHAPTER 62

Jake bent over, looking through the window at the eggs. His face was thinner, sadder than it had been, like he'd been forgetting to eat. "Wow. Look at that," Jake said. "It's rolling around now."

Jake wanted them back together. He was sorry for the fight, for what he'd said. He missed her. He had messed with Remy's head. And banged the hell out of her heart. But it felt right to have him here watching the eggs he'd kept warm against his chest hatch, that unexpected gift in her sorrow.

She didn't want him to leave.

Remy looked at Jake's profile as her emotions battled: desire fought with self-respect in one ring, while hurt set up a knockout round with love. How easy it would be to wrap her arms around him and let desire fuel a wild bout of makeup sex. At last, Remy called the round. Her head, not her feelings—and certainly not her body—would decide what came next.

She joined Jake to peer through the window. "It's resting now," she said, biting her thumbnail. "The how-to-hatch-chickens book says you should never help get the chick out of its shell. It just takes a long time, sometimes."

They stood, side by side, watching nothing happen. Jake leaned in closer and their shoulders touched. Remy felt a quiver, a tug of current running between them. "How long?" he asked.

"No way to tell. Minutes. Hours, sometimes."

Ada Queetie strolled over to Jake and murmured a greeting. He bent to stroke her back. "Hey, Ada. How have you been doing? You ready to be a mama bird?"

She cocked a black eye at him in reply and clucked. Jake stuck his hands in his pockets. "I'm going to head home. You'll let me or Teddy know how it goes?"

Remy should let him leave. But saying goodbye was closing a door that she wanted open, just a crack. "I have a feeling the chick wants out soon. And I need a glass of wine. Stay, if you want."

Suddenly the back door opened with a bang and Morgan flew in. "Are the chicks hatched yet? I wanted to come earlier but I was helping brat-sit Audrey's kids. They wanted to jump off Jaws bridge and she wanted me there to supervise. Then I had to wait for the bus."

"Hello to you too, Morgan," Remy said. "Not yet, but one's getting close. Go take a look."

"Oh, hi," Morgan said, spotting Jake. She turned to Remy, raised her eyebrows, and mouthed, *What's going on?*

"I'll make us some pasta while we wait," Remy said. "Jake, could you pick some basil from my garden? A big bunch, please. And some tomatoes."

Remy joined Morgan at the incubator after Jake left. "I like your necklace," Morgan said.

Remy opened the charm to show Morgan the tiny chick. "Jake gave it to me."

"But he doesn't look very happy. You either. I thought you looov-liked him?"

"We had a fight. Broke up. He came over to apologize."

"And?"

Remy rubbed her neck. "I had decided it was over. But now I don't know."

"What happened?" Morgan listened with rapt ears as Remy gave a very brief and heavily edited account of the fight, leaving out the part where Jake more or less called her nothing more than a lowly, groveling servant.

"Hmm. That sucks." Morgan stared at the eggs. "What are you going to do? Hey, did that egg just move?"

"What do you think I should do?"

Morgan stood up straight, flattered to be asked her opinion. "Well, I don't have much experience, but…. Remember that fight Solly and I had when he got mad at me for always wanting to pay for him?"

"Of course." A flash in the pan, but it had caused Morgan no end of anguish until she and Solly made up.

"He asked me, once we talked everything over, did I want to be with him or not? It was that simple, he said. And if the answer was yes, then we had to work it out." Morgan put her hands on her hips. "I think Solly was right," she added, staring at Remy. Morgan lifted her eyebrows. "So…?"

Remy sat down on the couch and groaned. Out of the mouths of babes. She pulled a pillow over her face. Out came a muffled "Shit."

It was a simple question. With a simple answer, if Remy stripped away the tangle of thoughts that had her hung up and spinning. Here was a man who made her weak at the knees, wrote her poetry, and came by every day to roll the hatching eggs. Who not only wouldn't forget her birthday but would find her the perfect gift. And cooked for her and made love to her as if she were the most important person in the world. Yes, she wanted tender, sexy Jake Madden—cluelessness, stuffiness, baggage, and all—in her life.

Remy uncovered her face. "Yes, I want to be with him. Is that stupid?"

"Nope. Not stupid," said Morgan. "Remember the day you hired me to brat-sit? You sounded soooo happy. You were like, la la la, I just had the best date with the most incredible guy. You didn't say it, but I could tell you had had really hot sex. I bet that's part of it," she added with a smirk.

Jake walked in cradling three fat heirloom tomatoes against his chest with a bunch of basil clutched in his hand like a bouquet. Morgan clapped her hand over her mouth, sure he'd heard her.

"Is this enough?" he asked.

"Plenty," Remy replied.

Morgan looked from Remy to Jake and back. "Well," she announced. "I guess I'm going to go home now. A watched egg never hatches, or something like that."

"Thanks, Morgan." Remy stood and hugged her. "We'll have chicks by tomorrow morning, I'm sure. Come back then."

"Will do. Bye, Jake," Morgan said with a saucy lilt. "Maybe I'll see you tomorrow too."

Remy's realization rocked her back on her heels. Was it really so simple?

She stuck her nose in the basil bouquet and took a deep breath. "Smells so good. Basil lemon pasta and caprese salad OK?"

"Very OK."

Remy busied herself in the kitchen, locating a mystery bottle of Chablis in the back of the fridge. She kept testing the answer out in her head, making sure she'd gotten it right. Each time, it came back the same. Remy needed time to let it sink in. This time, she needed to be sure. In the meantime, they'd have a nice, normal dinner. Well, normal-ish.

"Here, you can open the wine," Remy said, handing Jake the bottle. "One of the perks of buying cases and cases of wine. Sometimes Frank in the liquor store gives me a bottle of expensive stuff they want to move, hoping I'll order a case for my clients."

Jake poured two glasses. Remy drank half her glass in two gulps, feeling the alcohol run warmth through her body, all the way down to her feet. She shouldn't guzzle a bottle of wine this good, but what the hell.

She'd just realized she loved Jake Madden.

With the pasta boiling on the stove, Remy sliced the basil into a chiffonade and grated the lemon zest, remembering how Jake had rubbed the fresh lemon on her wrists. That incredible meal, that perfect evening, a glimpse of paradise before things erupted.

"Won't you miss teaching?" Remy asked.

Jake shook his head. "No. Maybe," he said. "Honestly, I don't know. But Jane says she can get me a position as an adjunct at Tufts in Boston next spring if I want." He walked back to the incubator. "Hey, the egg's moving again and…" he leaned his ear close to the glass. "It's peeping?"

"They've been doing that." The timer sounded in the kitchen. "You ready to eat?" Remy asked.

Dinner started awkwardly. The pot of boiling pasta had teased Remy's hair into curls around her face. She smoothed the tendrils back, conscious that Jake was staring at her with dark, longing eyes. The elephant in the room swelled like a hot-air balloon.

"I watched a documentary about show chickens the other night," Remy said to break the tension.

"Show chickens?"

"You know, dog shows, horse shows, chicken shows. The owners get all obsessed with the 'Standards of Perfection,'" she said. "The perfect beak, wattles, toes, feathers. That sort of thing. I was afraid the show was going to make fun of the breeders, but it didn't. It was sweet."

"Netflix?"

Remy nodded and returned to eating her pasta. In a bizarre twist of imagination, she imagined Jake, naked, illustrating the standard-of-perfection entry for 'academic cock': beak, well-formed; eyes, blue; wattles and earlobes, small; skin, pale; shanks and toes, lean and long; cock, well-hung; plumage, on the head, black and thick, and on the body, dark and lightly haired. Symmetry, weight, and condition would be equally weighted on the scorecard. She smiled and shook her head.

"What?" Jake asked.

"Oh, nothing. Just thinking about a funny scene in the movie."

His eyes dropped to the little golden egg glimmering against Remy's breastbone. "Are you going to enter the baby chicks in the fair?"

"I hadn't thought. But yes, of course," she replied. "They'll win a blue ribbon for sure."

Jake rolled the pasta around on his fork. "I'll pick up an extra fair booklet for you. Teddy wants to enter Choco-Teds in the candy category."

"I guess I'm to blame for those."

"Better than his other idea. Remember Ted-teas?"

Remy faked a gag. "Unforgettably awful."

Jake gave Remy that gorgeous, heart-melting smile. "You should enter your paintings too. They're really, really good."

"Thanks. Maybe I will. The one I'm doing for Jane of Kip is coming out great." Remy sprinkled more Parmesan onto her noodles. Maybe it was the wine or the food, but the tension had gone out of the room. "I want to do more painting this winter. Some bigger works. And Della—remember my artsy friend from Brooklyn?—thinks I can sell my animal portraits at a gallery there if I add hipster glasses."

Jake, midbite, nodded his approval and swallowed. "That's a great idea." Jake ran his fork around the empty plate to pick up the last bits of cheese. "The pasta's great too. And the tomatoes. Thank you."

"I have more basil and tomatoes than I know what to do with. Not quite up to mushroomy pasta standards, but not bad." Jake's hand rested just inches away. Remy longed to run her fingertips across his hand, to reignite the flame that she knew would burst into fire with the least spark. Instead, she picked up their plates and said, "Help yourself to more wine."

"I've eaten enough mushrooms this summer. Mushroomy pasta too. It's delicious, but it's one of only two recipes that Teddy makes."

Remy dumped the plates in the sink and turned on the water. "And the other is sprout salad—sprouts covered in ranch dressing."

Jake joined her in the kitchen. "Yup." He put his hand on her arm. "Here, I'll clean up. You cooked."

His touch was gentle, but that barest of connection, fingertips to skin, the closeness of his body to hers, nearly undid her entirely. She felt the blood rush to her cheeks. Remy forced herself to remember that her head, not her emotions, not her body, would decide the next step.

"OK," Remy said controlling her voice as she dried her hands. "I'll see how the baby chick is doing."

Remy walked over to the incubator. "Jake, come quick. The egg's moving again. A lot."

The blue egg rocked back and forth, and the top of the shell had opened a quarter inch. Another push and a tiny wet wing emerged from the crack. "Come on, baby, you can do it," Remy urged. She clutched Jake's hand in excitement. "Look, there's the head!"

Spellbound, they watched the chick rest before it rolled and pushed its way, step by exhausting step, out of the shell. There it lay, as if dead, half-bald, its feathers still stuck to its body in wet strands.

"What's wrong?" Jake asked.

"Nothing, I think. The book said not to worry if they just lie there at first," Remy said, biting her lip. "But sometimes it's too much—all the work to get out of the shell—and they don't make it."

"Try to get up, little Plato," said Jake. The limp chick lifted his head and staggered halfway up before flopping in a heap. Jake looked worried. "It's not doing so well."

Remy and Jake stood, fingers clasped, nearly cheek to cheek, waiting as they stared through the small window. Minutes later, the tiny chick opened its eyes fully and made another attempt, a few staggering steps, looking more like a drunken baby dinosaur than a baby chicken. "That was a little better," Remy said.

"Do you want more wine?" Jake asked. "I think I need another drink. I didn't realize how nerve-racking this would be."

Remy reluctantly let go of Jake's hand and gave him her empty glass. "Please. I don't know that I can do this another ten times. I guess we're like chicken doulas or something."

Jake's face creased in concern. "Are you sorry I got you into this?"

Remy rubbed the tiny golden egg on her necklace with her fingers. "Oh my, no. I can't wait to have a flock of baby chicks. It was the kindest, most thoughtful thing anyone's ever done for me," she said.

And it was. Jake had known the one thing that would heal her broken heart after her flock was killed. Remy knew in her heart that Jake would always put her first. No one had ever done that before. Not distracted careless Adam-the-ex and certainly not Eli Wolff. Jake might still make her madder than a wet hen sometimes, but what couple, no matter how deeply in love, didn't argue?

They sipped their wine in silence. After an agonizing wait, the chick did another stagger and flop but seemed a little steadier. The tiny feathers on its head and belly were gradually drying into a downy fluff. "The farmer said Easter Eggers can be all different colors, like their eggs. Looks like this little guy—gal—is going to be blond, like you," Jake said.

After a few minutes of rest, the chick rose onto its feet and flapped its tiny wings. This time it didn't fall over but took a couple of unsteady steps before sitting down to look around.

"Look at that, Jake. I think it's going to be OK," Remy said.

Within the hour, little Plato had dried into a ball of pastel yellow fluff. The down covering its tiny body was as light as air, and the bright blinking black eyes took in its new world. The transformation from wet, weak newborn to perky chick filled Remy with relief and joy.

"I'm going to take him out. Oh, Jake, this is so incredible." The chick's birth felt like a miracle. A sign. Carefully, Remy slipped her hand inside the incubator and lifted the baby. She stroked the tiny, downy back. "You are so adorable," she cooed, then handed the baby to Jake. "Here. He's the softest thing I've ever felt."

Jake cuddled the chick in his hand. "Welcome to the world, little Plato." The baby stretched out its tiny wings and flapped, then began peeping, tiny little chirps.

"Oh, my gosh. He likes his name, Jake!"

"Or he—she—doesn't and is complaining," Jake chuckled.

Ada Queetie, hearing the chick, strutted clucking across the floor looking for the source of the peeps. "Is it OK for the chick to meet Ada?" Jake asked.

"I guess there's only one way to find out," Remy said. "The book said many hens do adopt hatched chicks." She turned to the chicken. "Ada, you've wanted to be a mother since you got all broody on me, right?"

Jake carefully set the baby chick down. "Here you go, Plato. Time to meet your new mama."

Ada Queetie skittered across the floor making a beeline for Plato. In a panic, it occurred to Remy that the hen could just as easily injure the fragile newborn chick. "No Ada, don't hurt her," she cried.

But Ada wasn't to be deterred. Still clucking, she stopped, settled next to the chick, and fluffed out her wings. Plato peeped then wobbled over and pushed underneath her. Ada Queetie puffed up and looked at her human in reproach. The message was clear: she was in charge now. Plato poked out his yellow head from under the hen's breast before snuggling back under her feathers.

"I guess everything is OK," Remy said.

Jake looked from the hen to Remy. The yearning in his eyes was unmistakable. "Smart bird. Ada knows exactly what to do."

But did Remy? She thought back to what Morgan had said. A simple question: did Remy want to be with Jake Madden?

With a simple answer.

Yes.

Remy took a step forward no longer able—or willing—to hold herself back. Radiant with hope and love, she wrapped her arms around Jake and pressed her face against his chest. Jake's breath caught as he held her close, his heart pounding a tattoo against her cheek. The newborn chick peeped from under Ada's feathers, and the hen replied with a trill of contentment.

Yes.

*Feathered friend, we meet again*
*Me outside, you in your pen*
*You've served me well, ten out of ten*
*Not just as a hen, but as a friend*
—D.B.M.

# BONUS– A FEW RECIPES!

SWEET

Best Bad-For-You Crumb Cake
"Buttermilk" Waffles
Crêpes
Choco-Teds
Crack Cookies
Blondies


SAVORY

Willow's Pao de Queijo (Brazilian cheese breads)
Crab Cocktail
Jake's Fast Homemade Chicken Soup
Steamed Soft-Shell Clams
Mushroomy-Remy Pasta
True Love Basil-Lemon Pasta

## BEST BAD-FOR-YOU CRUMB CAKE
(One 8-inch coffee cake)

2 cups flour
2 teaspoons baking powder
1 cup sugar
½ cup unsalted butter (1 stick)
2 eggs
¾ cup milk

Preheat the oven to 350 degrees. Grease an 8-inch square pan.

Combine the flour, baking powder, sugar, and butter in a bowl. Using a fork, make small crumbs. Reserve 2 cups of crumbs for the top. Add the milk and eggs to the rest of the crumbs and mix. (It will be a thin, lumpy batter.)

Pour into the prepared pan and top with an even layer of the reserved crumbs. Bake for 30 minutes until the top is slightly brown and the cake springs back when pressed.

## "BUTTERMILK" WAFFLES
*(makes about 5 waffles)*

1 ¾ cup flour
1 teaspoon baking powder
1 teaspoon baking soda
Scant 2 cups milk
1 tablespoon white vinegar
1/3 cup vegetable oil
2 eggs
Maple syrup, butter, whipped cream, and/or fruit for serving

Preheat and grease the waffle iron.

Mix the milk and vinegar and set aside to curdle (or use 2 cups of buttermilk). In a large bowl, whisk the flour, baking powder, and baking soda together. Add the curdled milk (or buttermilk), oil and eggs. Beat until smooth. Pour the batter onto the hot waffle iron and cook until done.

Serve with maple syrup and butter—or whipped cream!

*(Adapted from the 1986 "New Good Housekeeping Cookbook")*

## CREPES
(serves 5-6)

6 eggs
1 ½ cups milk
1 ½ cups flour
¼ teaspoon salt
Butter for the pan
Confectioners sugar, lemon, jam, Nutella, and/or fruit for serving.

Mix eggs, milk, flour, and salt in a blender (or in a bowl with a stick blender).

Heat a crepe pan (or 9 or 10-inch sauté pan) over medium-high heat. Run a stick of butter around the pan, then pour in batter to cover about 2/3 of the bottom, tilting pan to cover the pan in a thin layer. Flip over when brown to cook the other side. Repeat, stacking finished crepes on a plate.

Serve with confectioners sugar and lemon and/or jam, fruit, Nutella, etc.

## CHOCO-TEDS

1 (10-oz.) bag Ghirardelli 60% chocolate chips
1 (8.8-oz.) bags of Dove dark chocolate Promises, unwrapped
2 cups slivered almonds
1 (14-oz.) bag sweetened shredded coconut
½ cup pulverized dried reishi mushrooms (or more coconut or nuts)

Toast the almonds either in a dry fry pan (watch carefully!) or on a cookie sheet in 350-degree oven for 5-10 minutes until light brown.

Melt the Dove chocolates and chocolate chips in a microwave-safe bowl: microwave for 1 minute, stir, then continue to microwave for 10-second intervals, stirring in between, until almost entirely melted. Remove from microwave and stir until the chocolate is smooth. Add toasted almonds, coconut, and reishi mushrooms to chocolate and mix well.

Spoon out into shaggy tablespoon-sized balls on a foil-lined cookie sheet. Chill until firm.

## CRACK COOKIES

40 saltine crackers
1 cup sugar
1 cup butter (2 sticks)
1 (12 oz.) package semisweet (or 60%) chocolate chips
1 cup chopped walnuts or pecans

Preheat oven to 350 degrees. Line a 10 x 15-inch rimmed cookie sheet/jelly roll pan with foil or parchment.

Place crackers in a single layer in the pan. Heat butter and sugar together in a saucepan and spread evenly over the crackers.

Bake for 9-10 minutes. Remove from oven and sprinkle with chocolate chips. When soft, spread the chips over the crackers in an even layer. Sprinkle with the nuts.

Freeze until hard (or chill in the refrigerator at least 2 hours) then break into pieces.

## BLONDIES
*(16 squares)*

1 cup flour
½ teaspoon baking powder
¼ teaspoon salt
½ cup unsalted butter (1 stick)
1 cup tightly packed brown sugar
1 egg
1 egg yolk
2 tablespoons honey
2 teaspoons vanilla
1 cup chocolate chips, butterscotch chips, or both
½ cup chopped pecans or walnuts, lightly toasted

Preheat oven to 350 degrees. Line an 8 x 8-inch pan with greased (or nonstick) foil.

Whisk together flour, baking powder, and salt. Melt butter in a large saucepan then cook over medium heat until light brown. Take off the heat, add the brown sugar and stir to combine. Let butter-sugar mixture cool until barely warm.

Add the egg, egg yolk, honey, and vanilla to the saucepan and mix well. Add the flour mixture, chips, and nuts, and stir. Spread the batter in an even layer in the prepared pan. Sprinkle with sea salt, if desired. Bake 25-30 minutes (a toothpick will come out clean).

When completely cool, peel off the foil and cut into 16 squares.

## SAVORY:

### WILLOW'S PAO DE QUEIJO (Brazilian cheese breads)
*(24 breads)*

½ cup vegetable oil
½ cup milk
1 teaspoon salt
2 cups tapioca starch (tapioca flour)
2 eggs
1 ½ cups grated or shredded parmesan

Preheat oven to 375 degrees. Grease two cookie sheets (or line with parchment).

Bring oil, milk, salt, and 2 tablespoons of water to a boil in a medium saucepan. Take off the heat, add the tapioca starch, and transfer mixture to the bowl of food processor equipped with a steel blade. Run until a smooth and silky ball forms, occasionally scraping down the sides. Let sit 15 minutes. Add the eggs and parmesan to the food processor bowl and run to combine.

Using a tablespoon, shape the dough into 1½-inch balls placed 1½-inch apart on the cookie sheet. Bake for 20 minutes until light golden brown.

### CRAB COCKTAIL

1 cup fresh crab meat
2 tablespoons mayonnaise (preferably regular Hellman's)
1 ½ teaspoons fresh lemon juice
Pepper

Mix mayonnaise with lemon juice until smooth. Gently mix in crab meat and a bit of pepper. If desired, add more lemon juice and/or pepper to taste. Serve with crackers.

## JAKE'S FAST HOMEMADE CHICKEN SOUP

1 package (1-1.5 lbs.) boneless chicken thighs, cut into chunks
1 package boneless chicken breasts, cut into chunks
1-2 big carrots, thickly sliced
2 stalks celery, thickly sliced
1 onion, diced
2-3 tablespoons olive oil
1 (32 oz.) box chicken broth or stock
2 bay leaves
1 bag wide egg noodles
Salt and pepper

In a large pot or stockpot, sauté chicken and vegetables in the oil for 5 minutes or so. Add the stock and simmer until the vegetables are tender and chicken is cooked through, about 20 minutes. Add 4 cups of water to the pot and bring to a boil. Add noodles and cook per package directions. Add salt and pepper to taste.

## STEAMED SOFT-SHELL CLAMS
*(serves 4-6)*

4 lbs. live soft-shell ("steamer") clams
Kosher salt
Melted butter with a squeeze of lemon (for serving)

Soak the clams in plenty of salt water (dissolve 1 tablespoon of kosher salt per quart of water) in a cool spot for a few hours to help the clams spit out sand. Handle the clams gently—the shells are fragile—and throw away any with cracked shells. As they soak, their siphons will emerge.

After soaking, rinse the clams and throw away any that appear dead (siphons don't retract when touched, shells don't close when tapped, or a bad smell). Bring an inch of water to boil in a tall pot. Add a steamer basket (if you have one) and the clams. Put on the lid. Let steam for 5-10 minutes until the shells are wide open.

Remove the clams and pour the broth in a bowl. Toss any clams that didn't open.

To eat, grab the siphon to pull out the clam, swish in the broth to remove any last grit, then dip in the lemon butter. You can either bite off the chewy siphon (Jake) or let the siphon slip from its "skin" and eat the whole clam (Remy)!

## MUSHROOMY-REMY PASTA
*(serves 4-6)*

2 tablespoons olive oil
1 lb. mixed fresh mushrooms (shiitake, oyster, maitake, cremini)
2 shallots, thinly sliced
2 cloves garlic, minced
1 lb. spaghetti or linguini
1 cup heavy cream
Salt and pepper
½ cup grated parmesan, plus more for serving
Chopped parsley (optional)

In a large, deep skillet, sauté mushrooms in the olive oil until browned (about 10 minutes). Add shallots and garlic and cook until the shallots are soft. Add heavy cream and simmer until slightly thickened. Add salt and pepper to taste.

Boil pasta per directions and drain. Warm the mushroom sauce, and add the pasta and the parmesan to the pan, stir to coat. Serve with extra parmesan and a sprinkle of parsley if desired.

## TRUE LOVE BASIL-LEMON PASTA
*(serves 4-6)*

1 lemon (grated zest and juice)
3 garlic cloves, minced
2 tablespoons olive oil
2 tablespoons butter
1/4 teaspoon red pepper flakes
1 cup (loosely packed) fresh basil leaves, cut into very thin slices
1 lb. pasta (any shape)
1/2 cup grated parmesan (plus more for topping)
Salt and pepper


In a large deep skillet, sauté the garlic and red pepper flakes in the olive oil until the garlic just begins to brown. Turn off heat and set aside.

Boil the pasta per package instructions. When done, drain the pasta, reserving 1/2 cup of cooking water.

Add pasta to garlic-chili oil in the pan. Add the butter, lemon zest, lemon juice, parmesan, basil, and reserved cooking water and warm over low heat, stirring to coat pasta. Add salt and pepper to taste and top with additional parmesan.

# ACKNOWLEDGMENTS

An enormous thank you to everyone who has supported me as a writer—readers, friends, family, fellow authors, bloggers, booksellers—too many to list here! Particular thanks to my readers –Betsy, Lauri, Adrienne, Linda, Felicia, Mary, Aqsa, Barbara, Arlene, Rebecca, Elisabeth, Peggy, Jodi, Leslie, Alice, Joan, and Jessie—for their incredibly valuable suggestions, comments, edits, and insights. Thank you also, dear friends, family, and all who encouraged me to keep writing and contributed in ways large and small—Sherri, Bolla, Jackie, Laurel, Tory, Caroline, Julie, Meg, Olivia, Tilden, Avery, Ethan, Mat, Laura, Nicole, Julia, and Margaret—with special love and appreciation to my kids, my parents, and my sister. The kind words from readers of *Goats in Time of Love* provided a special boost, often when I needed it most. And endless love and gratitude to my husband, Chris, for his constant support and encouragement.

And thanks especially to the Island for inspiring me to share my love of Martha's Vineyard through words.

P.S. to my Readers: a huge, sincere thank you for reading *Chickens*, and I hope you enjoyed it—I'd love to hear from you! And I would be grateful if you would consider leaving an honest review on Amazon and/or Goodreads to help spread the word.

# ABOUT THE AUTHOR

T. ELIZABETH BELL is a lawyer and the author of two novels, *Counting Chickens* and *Goats in the Time of Love*. She has a husband, three children, and a very old dog—but no chickens (or goats!) and splits her time between Martha's Vineyard and Washington, D.C. Passionately in love with the Vineyard, she shares her photography and more about her life on @tb.dc.mv (Instagram), @telizabethbell (Facebook), and telizabethbell.com.